BIBLE

KIDVENTURES

NEW TESTAMENT STORIES

TYNDALE HOUSE PUBLISHERS, INC.
CAROL STREAM, ILLINOIS

Bible KidVentures: New Testament Stories
Copyright © 2014 Focus on the Family

A Focus on the Family book published by Tyndale House Publishers, Inc., Carol Stream, Illinois 60188

Focus on the Family and the accompanying logo and design are federally registered trademarks of Focus on the Family, 8605 Explorer Drive, Colorado Springs, CO 80920.

TYNDALE and Tyndale's quill logo are registered trademarks of Tyndale House Publishers, Inc.

The stories in this book were first published separately under their own names—*Crazy Jacob, The Worst Wish, Dangerous Dreams,* and *Escape Underground.*

Cover design by Jennifer Ghionzoli
Cover illustration © Andreas Schonberg

Cataloging-in-Publication Data for this book is available by contacting the Library of Congress at http://www.loc.gov/help/contact-general.html.

ISBN: 978-1-58997-729-7

Printed in the United States of America
1 2 3 4 5 6 7 8 9 / 19 18 17 16 15 14

For manufacturing information regarding this product, please call 1-800-323-9400.

CONTENTS

Crazy Jacob

by Jim Ware

To my wife, Joni.

And to my kids,
Alison, Megan, Bridget,
Ian, Brittany, and Callum.

Andrew lay on his back, gasping for air. Between gasps, he wondered if there could possibly be anyone he despised more than Demas. *Maybe Artemas,* he thought.

Artemas was Demas's uncle. He owned large herds of pigs that grazed on the plateau above Lake Kinneret in Galilee. Artemas was a successful, influential businessman. He was as powerful as he was mean-spirited. And Artemas had a bitter grudge against Andrew's father, Jacob.

Demas was nothing but an oversized hulk of a kid who thought being fifteen years old made him something special. Andrew would never understand why his father had taken Demas on as an apprentice in the boat-building trade. Supposedly it had something to do with a request from Demas's father, who had since died of some disease.

Demas was a big problem. He was big in *every* way—big and beefy and stupid. Artemas liked to say Demas was "large-boned." Demas was cowardly, superstitious, and thick-headed. Worst of all, Demas was, at that very moment, sitting on Andrew's chest, shoving Andrew's tousled brown head into the sand on the shore of Lake Kinneret.

"If my father were here . . ." gasped Andrew.

"Whatcha gonna do when he comes, *Jew boy*?" sneered the curly-headed, pudgy-cheeked bully. "Tattle?"

"No, but . . ."

"Guess you know what's good for you!" The larger boy released his victim and stood up. "Now go get me those smoothing blocks!"

Andrew jumped up, brushed the sand from his homespun tunic, and wiped an angry tear from his freckled cheek. Then he stumbled up the beach toward the shed where his father and a friend named Stephen kept their tools.

Working with Demas was no fun. They were supposed to be smoothing the hull of a new trading boat. So far at least half their morning had been taken up with bullying and fighting instead. Andrew's father wanted the new boat in the water by the next day. That would be early enough to allow time for the planking to swell before beginning to caulk, when they would fill the cracks with pitch. Now they were behind schedule. *We'd have been finished by now if it weren't for Demas,* grumped Andrew.

Stepping in under the shed's leather awning, he picked up two limestone smoothing blocks from the workbench. As he did so, his eye fell on a number of other tools that lay on the bench or hung on hooks along the walls. The big two-handled saws. The adze and the plane. The bow drill, the hammers, the wooden mallets. Andrew smiled. *One of these days,* he thought, *I'll use these tools to build my own boat. And when I do, I'll sail it as far away from Demas as I can, maybe even clear across the lake to Magdala or Capernaum!*

That was when he heard voices just outside the back wall of the shed. His father's and someone else's—a whiny, nasal voice. The voice of Artemas.

"As for the boy," the voice was saying, "I can put him to work herding my pigs. Why he was ever apprenticed to a boatbuilder, especially a *Jewish* boatbuilder, is beyond me. It was my brother's decision, not mine."

Andrew's heart leaped. Demas leaving to herd pigs? It was too good to be true! He bent beside the wall to listen more closely.

"I'm sorry, Artemas," he heard his father say. "I have no intention of closing up shop. And as long as Stephen and I are in business, we're going to *need* an apprentice. There's too much work for the two of us."

Closing up shop?

"But Jacob," intoned the voice, "wouldn't you be more comfortable back among your own kind?"

Not this again, thought Andrew. Artemas resented Jacob's Jewishness, as Andrew knew only too well. It was a subject that had caused him a great deal of personal suffering.

"I'm sure they can use a good boatwright over on the Jewish side of the lake," continued the pig man.

"What exactly are you trying to say, Artemas?" Andrew could hear the rising anger in his father's voice.

"Don't you see? A Jew conducting business on our side of the lake—it sends the wrong message. It tends to . . . well, attract other Jews. And once there's a sizable Jewish community, it puts a businessman like myself in a rather awkward position. No pigs, no pork, and so on and so forth, you understand. All because of that strange Jewish god and those picky Jewish codes and Jewish dietary laws."

I'd love to see you in an awkward position, thought Andrew. *Like on your back in the sand, with a big pig sitting on your head!*

"Artemas," said Jacob quietly, "I'm a craftsman. I didn't come here to teach anyone about the Jewish God. I fear *all* the gods—Jewish or otherwise! And I have no interest in enforcing Jewish dietary laws. That's *not* why I came to Gadara!"

There was a pause. Then Artemas cooed, "Perhaps a little gift will help you see things my way." Andrew heard the clink of coins in a bag. "I beg you to reconsider."

"Good day to you, Artemas!" Jacob answered.

There came a sound of coins scattering in the sand and then a muffled curse and heavy footsteps retreating up the beach. In the next moment Jacob poked his head inside the shed.

"Andrew!" he said, looking surprised. "Have you . . . been here long?"

"Um, no, not really, Father." Andrew blushed. "I only came in to pick up these smoothing blocks."

"Hey! Where are those—?" blurted Demas, jogging up at just that moment. He stopped short when he saw Jacob standing beside his son. "Oh. Good morning, Master Jacob," he finished. "I was just looking for young Andrew here. We have a lot of work to get done."

"You do indeed," said Jacob, rubbing his bearded chin and frowning thoughtfully. "The merchant expects that boat by the end of the week."

"Just what I was telling young Andrew!" said Demas. He grabbed the smoothing blocks and headed back toward the unfinished hull.

A knowing look passed between father and son as the older boy hurried away. "Don't worry," said Jacob, wrinkling his brow and placing a work-worn hand on Andrew's shoulder. "Everything's under control. We'll show them—all of them"—at this he touched a leather pouch that hung from his belt—"with the help of the gods and spirits."

CHAPTER 2

"Demas!" Andrew heard his father yell. "Strike that sail! *Now!*"

It was late the following afternoon. Andrew, Demas, Jacob, and Stephen were out on the lake in the freshly smoothed but uncaulked boat. A stiff wind had just begun to blow.

Crouching in the bow of the vessel, his nostrils filled with the scent of cedar planks, Andrew looked north to where a bank of dark clouds, edged with red, hung menacingly over the water. The wind gusted and flipped a strand of brown hair over his eyes. Two big raindrops slapped him on the cheek. He knew what it meant—another one of Lake Kinneret's unpredictable late-afternoon storms.

The iron ring at the top of the mast rattled as Demas hauled on the sheet rope to furl the sail and lower the yard to the deck.

Stephen, Jacob's smooth-shaven Greek partner, was already handing out oars. "Can you row?" he asked Andrew with a playful wink.

"Didn't I learn from the best?" retorted Andrew, grabbing an oar.

He could row, all right. He was proud of his growing abilities as a boatbuilder and sailor at only eleven years old. He'd been working with Demas and Stephen and his father for more than a year. And he was excited about having a chance to test his skills against the elements. *It'll be fun,* he thought.

"Scared?" prodded Demas as he sat down heavily beside Andrew on the rowing bench. "You can tell *me.*"

Andrew scowled at Demas.

"Get ready!" Stephen shouted into the rising wind. He pulled his linen tunic over his head. "By all the gods! Boreas must be angry. This came out of nowhere. Can you bring her about, Jacob?"

"I think so," answered Andrew's father, leaning hard on the steering oar. "As long as you three can get her moving!"

A feeling of pride swelled in Andrew's chest as he looked back and saw his father standing at the tiller. *What is there to be scared of?* he thought, carefully fitting his oar into the lock. *Father's at the helm.*

Jacob peered north from under eyebrows as dark as the sky itself. The wind ruffled his gray-streaked hair and beard. There was a look of concern on his sunburned face. But Andrew wasn't worried. *Father's the best navigator on the whole lake,* he thought.

"By the gods, Andrew!" said the helmsman, catching his son's stare. "This is a piece of bad luck! You'll have to row like a man if we're to get her beached before the whole sky breaks loose. There are only four of us, and we built her for a crew of twelve!"

"You heard him," said Demas, digging an elbow into Andrew's ribs and whispering into his ear. "Like a *man*, not a shrimp, Jew boy."

Andrew gritted his teeth. Why couldn't Demas just leave him alone? *Always* there was Demas, and *always* Demas was picking on him. What made it worse was that most of the kids in Gadara had started following his example. They all called him "Jew boy" now. It was so bad that Andrew had stopped going to town unless he absolutely had to.

Andrew sighed. Why didn't his father just let Demas go to work for his uncle herding pigs? He wished he could punch Demas's fat, mocking face. Instead, he pulled on his oar with all his might.

They all did. In response, the boat turned in the water and jumped lightly toward the shore. Andrew felt a thrill of delight as the hull rose and fell. He couldn't help thinking of the design they'd used in building her; she really *was* a *dancing ship.*

He remembered the care with which his father had laid her keel, how painstakingly he had smoothed and shaped her high-curving ends with the adze and plane. He recalled with satisfaction how precisely the cedar

planks of the shell—the *homoth*, or "walls"—had been fitted together
with mortise and tenon and dowel. And he smiled as he pictured the
stern patience in his father's face whenever he had to correct Andrew for
fudging on the spacing between the joints.

Andrew had refitted some of those joints four or five times. In the
end, not one of them was more than a finger's width distance from the
next. It was a lot of hard and very tedious work. But when the result was
an approving nod from his father, Andrew knew it was all worthwhile. Its
hull was as snug and tight as the finest cabinetry. No boat on the lake was
better made or more seaworthy.

A sudden downpour jarred him out of these pleasant thoughts. A
blast of wind shoved the boat sharply aside and threw him against his
rowing partner.

"Put your backs into it!" shouted Jacob. "And call upon the gods and
spirits of the winds!"

Andrew turned and searched his father's face, but he saw no clue as
to his father's feelings. Jacob might have been a stern-faced god himself,
standing there between sky and sea with his hand on the tiller. *No need to
worry. We'll be back on shore in no time at all.*

"Your father's an odd one, Andrew," laughed Stephen, leaning over
backward with the force of his rowing. "A Jew calling upon the gods and
spirits! Ha!"

"Sailors need all the help they can get," shouted the steersman, over-
hearing his partner's comment. "And they don't care where they get it!"

The waves were higher and wilder now. Andrew strained against his
oar. Sweat and rainwater dripped from his hair into his eyes. The wind
grew colder and beat him about the head until his ears began to hurt.

"Are we getting anywhere, Stephen?" he grunted between strokes. "I
can't see a thing!"

"Leave the seeing to your father!" shouted his dark-haired friend.
"You keep rowing!"

The sinews and tendons in Stephen's wiry arms stood out in bold relief as he plied his oar. He was a small man, not much bigger than Andrew himself, but he was very strong. Aside from his father, Stephen was the man Andrew admired most.

Already two or three inches of water had collected in the bottom of the boat. If this kept up, they'd have to stop rowing and start bailing. And the rain was increasing.

This is hard work! thought Andrew. He turned his face upward and stuck out his tongue, drinking in the rain to ease the dryness in his mouth and throat. A strange feeling was growing in the pit of his stomach. His heart pounded rapidly. This wasn't turning out to be as much fun as he'd expected.

He stole a sideways glance at Demas. The older boy's heavy face had grown pale, and his thick, red lower lip was beginning to tremble.

"Aeolus! Zeus! Baal Obh!" cried Demas, dropping his oar and thrusting his thick arms skyward. "Save us and I'll kill you a fat pig!"

A fat pig is right! thought Andrew. But he said nothing and went on rowing even harder than before.

"Yahweh!" shouted Jacob, turning his face up to the clouds. "May Yahweh, God of storms, and lucky Meonen help us now!"

He's calling on Yahweh. Andrew knew that for all his father's interest in spirits and the unseen world, he rarely prayed to the God of his own people. Andrew wondered why he was praying to Him now.

Suddenly the boat lurched and tilted. A sheet of spray flew over their heads as the high, pointed prow crashed through an oncoming wave. A loud cry came from the stern. Andrew turned to see his father lose his grip on the steering oar and fall heavily against the side of the boat. The boat tipped and shuddered.

"Quick!" shouted Stephen, grabbing Andrew by the shoulders and shoving him toward the rear of the boat. "Take the tiller and hold her steady, or we're going to end up with a man overboard! Row hard, Demas!"

Dazed, Andrew grabbed the steering oar and leaned on it. Stephen jumped into the stern, seized Jacob by the wrist, and pulled him to his feet. Andrew's father gave his friend a grateful look.

"It's all right," said Jacob, placing a hand on Andrew's shoulder and resuming his post. "Back to your rowing! We won't get a single drachma for this boat if she ends up at the bottom of the lake!"

At the bottom of the lake! Shaken, Andrew slid back into his place beside Demas and rowed feverishly. This time he dared not look the other boy in the face. But at odd moments, through the roar of the storm, he thought he heard muffled sobs coming from the other end of the bench.

Doggedly, they fought their way through the rising waves and shifting winds. Soon Andrew was conscious of nothing but the rhythm of his body—pull, lift, push, dip; pull, lift, push, dip—over and over again, minute after everlasting minute. He rowed until his mind was as numb as the muscles in his arms.

When at last the boat's keel rubbed against the pebbles on the shore, Andrew was almost too tired to care. He wanted to slump down into the sloshing water in the bottom of the boat and never get up again.

"Everyone out!" he heard his father shout. Stephen and Demas leaped ashore. Reluctantly Andrew followed, heaving himself over the side. Then they all laid hold of the boat and dragged it up the beach.

"Andrew!" came a woman's voice from across the sand. "Where's Andrew?"

"Here, Mother!" They dropped the boat on the sand, and Andrew ran to meet her. For a long moment, he stood hugging her silently.

Jacob joined them. "It's all right, Helena," he said.

"We made it!" said Andrew. "Didn't we, Father?"

"Yes," agreed Jacob, glancing back at the following darkness. "With the help of the powers."

For a moment Helena eyed her husband intently. Then she took his arm.

"Do you have any idea how you frightened me?" she asked as the little group hurried up the beach through the wind and rain. "I never *dreamed* you'd be on the water in such weather!"

"You worry too much," Jacob teased, pushing a dark ringlet aside and kissing her on the forehead. "We finished the planking this afternoon. I thought we had time to tighten the seams, that's all. It has to be done before caulking. You know how quickly these afternoon storms come up. At any rate, we made it back—thank the gods."

"'Thank the gods' is right!" chimed in Stephen, giving Andrew a hearty slap on the back. "We've seen a little bit of *their* power today, haven't we, boy?"

"I guess so," responded Andrew.

"You *guess* so!" snorted Demas. "Huh! I s'pose *you* believe in that phony Jew god! Right?"

"That's enough, Demas!" shouted Jacob, turning severely on his apprentice. "Now stow these oars and go on home!"

"Yes, sir," answered Demas, meekly lumbering off to the shed.

"I'm just glad you're all safe!" said Helena, releasing Jacob's arm. "I'd better hurry home and finish our supper. Your sister is there by herself."

"The boy and I will be along just as soon as everything's secured here," said her husband, eyeing the sky. "I don't think we've seen the worst of this yet."

Andrew saw his father take his mother's hand and squeeze it hard before letting her go.

"So . . . tomorrow," said Stephen as Andrew helped him lash down the last of the leather tarps. With the shed covered, their tools would be protected against the wind and weather.

"Early," said Jacob. "We've got at least a couple days' work left."

"Right," agreed Stephen, gathering his short cloak about him. "Good night, then!" he shouted as he hurried away. "And be careful up there. It's no place to get caught on an evening like this!"

Then Andrew followed his father to the grounded boat. Working quickly, they drove four long, wooden stakes into the sand and lashed the boat to them with strong ropes—a precaution against the wind. After that, they threw another tarp over the boat and tied it down securely.

"All right . . . let's go!" shouted Jacob. "We'll take the shortcut!"

The shortcut! Andrew shot his father an anxious glance. Then he followed him through the rain to a spot where a tan-colored dirt path snaked its way out from between gray rock walls. From here it was a short but steep climb to the top of the cliff. The natural palisade rose rapidly to a height of about two hundred feet above the shore of the lake.

Normally, Andrew knew, his father would have avoided this path. But today they were in a hurry. There were other roads home, but this was the quickest and most direct. On the negative side, it was difficult and narrow. And there was another point worth bearing in mind: It went past the Haunts of the Dead.

Andrew knew how his father felt about spirits. Like most sailors, Jacob was as cautious as he was resourceful. His interest in the supernatural world had always been strong, but recently it had grown into an obsession. For some reason, Andrew sensed, his father was more anxious than ever to keep the "powers" on his side. Failing that, he'd do everything he could to protect himself from them.

"Father," said Andrew, looking up at him with troubled eyes, "do you think it's . . . safe?"

In answer, Jacob stopped and untied a leather pouch that hung from his belt by a scarlet cord.

"An amulet," he explained. "It contains *baaras*—'burning root'—an herb my forefathers considered very powerful. They say that Solomon, the greatest of our kings, used it to ward off demons and evil spirits."

With that, Jacob turned and trudged up the slippery path. Andrew pulled his cloak over his head and hurried after his father.

"Was Solomon afraid of spirits?" he asked when they reached the trail's first sharp turn.

"I don't know," puffed his father. "What counts is that he knew how to *control* them. He feared Yahweh, the God of Israel, too. It's no wonder they called him the wisest of men."

It was growing dark. The wind gusted this way and that among the rocky clefts, pelting them with rain as they labored upward. Every so often the path took them past black, gaping holes in the rocks.

Andrew looked away as he hurried past one of these caves. Had he really seen something moving in its murky depths? Why did he have such a strong feeling that the darkness within was full of eyes? A choking lump was rising in his throat. He tried hard to think about the hot dinner waiting for them at home.

Suddenly there came a strong blast of wind. Andrew dropped to his hands and knees to avoid being swept off the face of the cliff. He saw his father pointing into the dark recesses of one of the caves. "In here!" Jacob shouted above the wind's roar. "It's becoming too dangerous to go on. We'll just have to take shelter and wait it out!"

In there? thought Andrew. *I don't believe this!* But it was either the cave with his father or the bare cliff with the wind and rain. He hesitated a moment and then followed Jacob into the hole in the rock.

Inside they crouched together in the dim light, looking out over the troubled face of Lake Kinneret, careful to keep their backs to the shadowy inner spaces of the cavern. Andrew shivered and drew his wet cloak closer.

Glancing up at the black ceiling and the dripping walls, he noticed that their rough surfaces bore the marks of iron cutting tools—marks that were yet another reminder of the very thing he was trying so hard to forget. He didn't want to remember that these weren't natural caves. They had been hewn out of the rock by human hands. Dug into the cliffside for a specific purpose.

To house the remains of the dead.

Andrew wished they could talk about something. He wanted to hear his father's voice filling the empty cavern. But Jacob was strangely silent. He sat hunched up, cradling the little leather bag in his hands.

Once again Andrew had a strong sense that the darkness behind him was filled with watching eyes—pale, dead eyes. And what was that odd smell? He turned his head ever so slightly. Were those really human shapes standing against the wall at the back of the cavern? Or were they something even worse: ossuaries and sarcophagi, stone boxes and jars filled with bones and rotting flesh?

"Mother's going to be worried," he blurted out at last. "Do you think we'll make it home in time for dinner?"

"Of course." His father's voice was flat and expressionless. As he spoke he never stopped fingering the leather bag.

Andrew shivered again. *Maybe it would be a good idea to change the subject.* "Father," he said, "I want to build a boat of my own."

Jacob looked vacantly at his son. "Do you?" he said. He seemed to be struggling to bring himself back from some distant place.

"Yes. A *dancing ship*," Andrew answered. "Like the big one we just finished. Sharp-keeled, wide at the top, with a high, pointed stem and stern."

"That's fine," said Jacob. A light was growing in his eyes. *Good*, thought Andrew. He knew how much his father loved to talk boats.

Jacob moved closer to his son and laid the leather pouch on the floor. He said, "You know, the merchants have promised me another load of good cedar the next time they come through. I'll let you have first pick of the lot." A hint of a smile flickered across his features. "It will be good to work together."

Yes, thought Andrew, suddenly glowing with love and admiration for his father. It was heartening just to hear Jacob talk about familiar things like cedar planks in this strange and terrible place. The man was his hero, his best friend. Not many Jews living in Gentile territory commanded such universal respect. The Gadarene Greeks knew Jacob as the best craftsman in the Ten Cities. And Andrew was Jacob's son. So what if Demas and the boys from the academy called him "Jew boy" and "half Jew"? He didn't care. He didn't need them. Not as long as he had his father. It *would* be good to build a boat together.

"And Father," Andrew added after a few more minutes of rain and silence, "do you think—when it's finished—I might be able to sail it on the lake *by myself*?"

A change came over Jacob's face. He picked up the bag of *baaras* and squeezed it hard. "Alone?" he said, the emptiness returning to his eyes. "No. Absolutely not. Not without Stephen or Demas or me."

"But Father," Andrew protested, "I've learned so much! I can raise and lower the yard by myself. I know how to tack into the wind and—"

"No!" shouted Jacob with sudden violence.

The cavern grew dim. There was movement in the stale air above their heads. Or so it seemed to Andrew.

"No!" his father yelled again. He jumped up, nervously fingering the leather pouch. "Haven't I told you no a *thousand* times?"

At that instant it was as if the darkness and violence of the storm outside had somehow forced its way into that dank, narrow space. Suddenly the world beyond the cave door vanished. Wind and rain were a distant memory. Watching eyes and rotting bones were forgotten. For Andrew, nothing existed but his father's face. A face distorted with pain and fear. The face of a stranger.

"Father, I—" he spluttered, climbing awkwardly to his feet. He was frightened and confused. Never before—not once—had he so much as mentioned the subject of sailing on the lake by himself.

"*Over* and *over* and *over!*" Jacob spat the words fiercely through clenched teeth. The fingers of his left hand twisted in his beard. His eyes roved over the rock walls of the cave.

"What's the matter, Father?" cried Andrew, stumbling backward as Jacob began to swing the little leather pouch in circles above his head.

"*Chashmagoz!*" Jacob chanted menacingly. "*Merigoz! Bar-Tema!* Haven't I told you *never?* Never *again! Chaliylah lecha meyasoth . . .!*"

Andrew continued backing away as his father's speech became a wild, nonsensical babbling. He stopped only when his shoulder touched the wall of the cave. Never in his life had he felt so afraid.

"Do not tempt me!" Jacob shouted, his face twisted in anguish. "It would be b-better—" he stuttered. "It would be better if—"

Andrew flattened himself against the wall as his father's left hand jerked upward. *He's going to hit me!* he thought. He raised an arm to shield his face. Then he slumped to the floor.

Nothing.

In a few moments the silence was broken by the sound of soft weeping. He opened his eyes. From over the hills a spark of the setting sun winked in through the door of the cave. The clouds had lifted. The wind and the rain had stopped. His father was kneeling on the floor, his head in his hands, whimpering like a little child.

"Father," said Andrew, getting up and laying a shaky hand on Jacob's shoulder. "Let's go home. Mother will have supper waiting."

CHAPTER 4

Early morning. The still time between darkness and dawn.

Ssshh-k! Ssshh-k! Sssh-k!

Andrew was planing boards at the workbench under the boat shed's leather awning, intent on his work, unaware of the sounds of the waking world.

Why doesn't Father come? he thought.

Oooooeeeeeoooooo . . .

"Andrew!" said Lyra. His younger sister came running up breathlessly. She dropped to her knees in front of him, spraying the workbench with sand. "What's that weird noise?"

Over their heads, pale, rosy fingers stretched across the Galilean sky, changing it gradually from empty gray to clear summer blue. But out on the lake there was mist—wispy, white, swirling mist. It hid the bright surface of the water and muffled the sounds of the fishermen coming in from a long night with their nets. And through the mist there came a cry—a single note, long, low, and mournful.

Ooooooooeeee . . .

"There! Didn't you hear it?" she demanded, sticking out her chin and pushing the dark hair out of her eyes.

"It's just a bird, Lyra," said Andrew, keeping his eyes glued to the workbench and the piece of cedar in the vise. "A bittern or a heron. Hunting for fish. You've seen them lots of times."

Lyra stood up, leaned her elbows on the workbench, and rested her chin in her hands. "Whatcha doin'?" she asked, looking up at him out of her big brown eyes.

"Working on my boat," he answered, trying to sound as annoyed as possible. "Father said he'd come and help me if I got here early enough. Can't you see I'm trying to concentrate?"

The strokes of the plane had to be kept smooth, straight, and even. Otherwise he'd end up with bumps and dips in the edges of his planks—gaps to fill when it came time to piece them together into a shell.

"Well, anyway, I think that bird noise is weird," said Lyra carelessly, jumping up and brushing the sand from her linen shift. "It makes me think of scary creatures . . . monsters in the mist . . . like the ghosts in Father's stories. Don't you think so?"

"No, I don't." Andrew winced at the thought of his father's stories. He didn't like them. Neither did his mother. And Father had been telling them more often lately. Ever since that evening in the cave . . .

"Where is Father, anyway?" he added, glancing up. The sun had risen, touching the tops of the palms with gold and sending the mist scattering. "Stephen and Demas will be here soon. Then we'll have to start the regular work."

"Father?" chirped Lyra, skipping to the corner of the shed. "Oh, I don't know! He doesn't like to work anymore. He likes to tell stories. Andrew, when do we eat?"

"Eat! How can a skinny five-year-old girl eat so much?" he scolded. "We just had breakfast!"

"But I'm bored!" she whined.

"Well, go hunt for rocks or something," he urged. "I'm busy."

How am I supposed to build a boat and babysit at the same time? he wondered. Immediately he felt sorry for even thinking it. Andrew understood the situation all too well. He had to keep an eye on Lyra because Mother had to go to Gadara to sell her skeins of yarn and bolts of cloth. And mother had to sell her yarn and cloth because things had been "tight" lately—ever since Father began behaving so strangely.

Where is Father? I wish he'd come! Andrew remembered the way he had pictured this project in his daydreams. Just the two of them working together early in the morning, before Lyra or the sun or anyone else got up. It was going to be so great! And it would have been great, if only . . .

But no! He wasn't giving up yet! Yes, his father had been acting strangely. But this project was just the thing to cure him of it. Andrew tried hard to pump up a sense of confidence. His father would come. Everything would be the way it used to be. They'd work and talk and talk and work, and then—

"*Chaire*! Good morning!" came a voice like a silver trumpet. "A true craftsman at his work!"

"Oh, hi, Stephen." Andrew grinned as the dark-eyed Greek ducked in under the awning.

"Looking very good!" Stephen commented, thoughtfully inspecting the wood in the vise. "You have a fine feeling for this sort of thing—like your father. It's going to be an excellent boat when it's finished."

"I hope you're right," Andrew answered doubtfully. "Father promised to help me, but—"

"I know," Stephen interrupted with a frown.

"I guess everybody knows," sighed Andrew, turning back to his work. *Ssshh-k!* A fragrant curl of cedar dropped to the ground as he drew the plane swiftly down the length of the board.

"Don't worry," said Stephen, touching his shoulder. "Perhaps I can help you myself . . . in a few days . . . once we get on top of things."

"Stephen, what's going to happen? To the business, I mean. Mother says the customers aren't happy."

"Nor the creditors!" agreed Stephen, laying his bread bag on the bench and picking up a brush and bucket of pitch. "Would you be happy with a man who doesn't finish his work or pay his bills on time?"

"But it's so unlike Father!" Andrew said. "What are we going to do?"

Stephen frowned. "I'm not sure. Demas is learning, but he has a long way to go. His attitude leaves a lot to be desired. You show great promise, but you're just a beginner. If Jacob doesn't snap out of it soon—"

"Andrew!" came a small voice from down the beach. "Look at me! Look at me! I'm a heron! Ooooeeeeoooooo!"

He looked up. Through the dissolving mist, he saw Lyra dancing up and down on one leg atop a big rock that stuck out of the water about ten cubits from the shore. She was dripping wet from head to toe. Her hands were tucked up under her armpits, and her elbows were out at the sides of her body, flapping like the wings of a bird.

Stephen burst out laughing.

"I'd better go and get her," said Andrew wearily. "She swims like a catfish, but I don't think I should leave her out there all by herself."

He dropped the plane and ran down toward the water.

"Stay put, Lyra!" he shouted. "I don't want you to—*unnhh*!"

Before he knew what had hit him, Andrew was lying on his side with a mouthful of sand. Another runner—someone much bigger and heavier—had slammed into him from the side and sent him sprawling. It was his father.

"Aaiiiieeeee!" screamed Jacob, tearing off his outer cloak. His arms flailed this way and that. His hair and beard stuck out wildly around his head. Andrew sat up and gaped. A group of fishermen on the shore dropped their nets and stared.

Now what? thought Andrew. He watched helplessly as his father thrashed his way to the frightened Lyra, yanked her down from her rock, and waded with her back to shore. "Away! Away!" Andrew heard him yelling. "Away from here!"

Andrew got to his feet and rushed to meet them. He reached the water's edge just as Jacob, with a frenzied look in his eyes, set Lyra down upon the sand. Wordlessly, the little girl looked up at her brother, brown eyes wide with terror.

Not again! thought Andrew, inwardly groaning. It was the cave all over again! Not that there hadn't been some strange and scary incidents since that night. Andrew and his mother had been disturbed by Jacob's prolonged silences, vacant stares, and unpredictable wanderings. But in all those weeks, there had been nothing quite like this.

Stephen ran up and joined them. He and Andrew exchanged looks.

"It's all right, Father," Andrew began. "I was just—"

Jacob grabbed him by the tunic. "You should have been watching!" he breathed heavily. "Watching!" His eyes burned strangely. Andrew felt as if they were staring right through his body, boring a hole into the cliffs beyond the beach. "I told them—I told you!—" he shouted, gazing up at the sky. "Leave her alone!"

Andrew shot a glance at Lyra. Tears trembled on her dark lashes.

Then, just as suddenly as Jacob had seized him, he released his son. He sighed, closed his eyes, and dropped heavily on the sand. Taking Lyra by the hand, Andrew backed away slowly.

"Well, then," Stephen ventured after a tense pause. "It's . . . ah . . . good to see you, Jacob."

When Jacob responded, it was in his normal voice. He appeared quiet and calm, though completely exhausted. "Stephen," he said, "have we paid the merchant Hadad-Ezer for that load of cedar and oak?"

Andrew saw Stephen's eyebrows arch upward. "No," the Greek answered. "We can't pay until we're paid. And we won't be paid until we finish Alexander's boat. Are you planning on coming to work today?"

Encouraged by Stephen's straightforwardness and the sudden change in his father's behavior, Andrew spoke up. "We need you, Father," he said eagerly. "I'll help too. We can do it together! And when we're finished, there's the shell of my own boat to get started on. I've begun the planing, but without you, I—"

Jacob's eyes stopped him in midsentence. They had suddenly become dreadful again—distant and burning.

"W-what is it, Father?" stuttered Andrew. Lyra ran and crouched behind her brother, burying her face in his cloak.

Jacob got unsteadily to his feet and began combing his fingers through his hair. "To work," he mumbled. "Coming to work . . . Hmm . . ." He sounded like a man trying desperately to remember something. "No. Not there . . ." He began stumbling up the beach in the direction of the cliffs.

"But Jacob," said Stephen, following his partner and laying a hand on his shoulder, "what shall I tell Hadad-Ezer and Alexander?"

"To the tombs," muttered Jacob, turning and leaning into his friend's face. "Tell them I'm going to the tombs."

As Andrew watched, the confusion in his father's eyes gave way once more to angry fire. Suddenly Jacob wrenched Stephen's hand from his shoulder. "Yes!" he shouted. "Tell them I've gone to the Haunts of the Dead! I'm wanted there!" With that he ran off.

Just then Demas arrived for work. "Family problems?" said Demas with a significant sneer. "I understand. Uncle Artemas has told me all about it."

"You're late, Demas," said Stephen, shrugging his shoulders and walking back toward the boat shed.

Lyra whimpered softly. Andrew sat down on the sand and put his head between his knees.

CHAPTER 5

The clay weights that hung from the bottom of the loom clacked noisily. Even out in the road Andrew could hear them. He stopped to listen as he approached the courtyard. It was a sound he had known all his life, and it never failed to bring him a measure of comfort. And comfort was something he needed badly right now. Shoving old Baal, the stubborn gray goat, out of his path, he pushed the gate open and stepped wearily into the enclosure.

"I'm home, Mother," he called, mopping his forehead with his old felt cap and sitting down on a wicker crate.

Helena wiped her eyes with the corner of her robe as she turned from her weaving to greet him. "The sun . . ." she explained.

"I know, Mother," he agreed, doubtful that any amount of glare could cause so much redness in her eyes.

Andrew had always loved this part of a summer day. Many, many times in the past—when Jacob was still himself and still living with them—he had savored these peaceful moments in the late afternoon. After long hours of labor at the boat shed, Andrew and his father would make the long walk home together. In the coolness of the approaching evening, they would return to the cluster of white houses to rejoin the busy little world within the courtyard.

Things always seemed to come to life again once the midday heat was past. Pigeons would flutter and coo in the dovecote. Welcome breezes would stir the striped awnings that hung over the doorways of the houses. Children would run this way and that, laughing, playing, chasing the goats and chickens, kicking up the dust. It was like that now, and it made him miss his father even more.

"Hi, Andrew!" bubbled Lyra as she burst from the door of their house. She darted past him and ran straight to the old gray goat, whose neck she patted and hugged with obvious affection. "I'm going to teach old Baal to pull a cart. What do you think?"

"Whatever," said Andrew, stuffing his cap into his belt.

It was nearly a month now since his father had gone away. No one in the village had seen him during that time, though everyone pretended to have the latest information on his whereabouts.

Once two travelers, beaten and bloody, had passed through on their way to Gadara. They claimed that a wild man had attacked them on the steep path at the south end of the lake. A naked savage who was incredibly strong. Some of the villagers had laughed at them. A few had warned them severely never to go near the Haunts of the Dead again. But most had simply nodded and exchanged knowing glances. "Crazy Jacob," they said.

There were all kinds of rumors, of course. Some said Jacob had lost his mind because he was a Jew who denied the power of the *real* gods. Others were certain that he had sold his soul to Chemosh and Temaz or that the spirits of the dead had taken possession of his body. Still others claimed that he was a conjurer whose spells had backfired.

Whatever the reason, Jacob bar Hosep, master boatwright, originally of Magdala across Kinneret, had lost his mind and was living like a beast among the cave tombs on the side of the cliff. And everyone knew it.

Andrew was sitting there on the crate wondering what it all meant, when his mother, laying aside her shuttle, came over and touched his hand. "Did you stop on the way home?"

"Yes," he answered. "I took the basket of bread and fish too. Left it in the cave—the same one we sat in together during that storm."

"Did you see him?" she asked.

"No. But I . . . heard things." Andrew looked at the ground.

Helena sighed. She removed her head covering and pushed a few curls of dark hair away from her face. Then she untied a soft leather purse that hung from her girdle and handed it to Andrew.

"This is all we have left," she said. "I'll have more cloth to sell in Gadara by the end of the week. But we're out of grain and oil, and I need them to bake our bread. There are still a few hours of daylight left. Can you go into the town and buy some for me?"

"Won't the merchants be closed?"

"Not until sunset. You'll have time if you go quickly."

"I'll run!" said Andrew, getting to his feet and taking the purse from her hand. He was pleased to have some way of helping her.

"Can I go too?" begged Lyra. "Me and old Baal?"

"Not this time, Lyra," said Helena. "Andrew is in a hurry."

She bent to kiss his cheek. "Be swift, my son." After a pause, she quickly added, "And may the gods go with you."

Andrew stopped halfway to the gate. "Mother," he said, "is it the gods and spirits who have made Father this way?"

She shook her head. "I don't know, Andrew."

"Well, if it is, do you think there might be a way to get them to make him better again?"

"I know very little about the gods and spirits," she answered. "To tell you the truth, I'm sick of the whole subject. As far as I can see, no good has ever come of it. I don't know what it would take to make him well," she added wearily. "Some kind of a miracle, I suppose."

A miracle, Andrew thought. *I wonder if Stephen would know . . .*

"Good-bye, Mother!" he called, replacing his cap on the top of his head. "I'll be back as soon as I can!"

Then he ran out at the gate, leaving a flurry of squawking chickens and flying feathers behind him.

Gadara. Its roofs and columns glowed pink in the light of the setting sun as Andrew trotted down the dusty road toward the city's northwest gate. The sun had not yet dipped below the silhouetted summit of Mount

Moreh in the west. He should be able to make it in plenty of time. *And when I'm done,* he thought, *I'll find Stephen. Stephen seems to know something about the power of the gods and spirits.*

There was nothing else in Andrew's experience that could even compare with Gadara. The *agora,* or marketplace. The temples, the gymnasium, and the stadium. The wide, paved streets crowded with people and horses and carts and chariots. The scholars and statesmen and dignitaries in their flowing white togas. Andrew loved it all. The trip to Gadara, which he had made many times with his father, never failed to stir his imagination.

It was about three miles from Andrew's village to the city—a distance he could cover in a surprisingly short time by walking and running in turns. He was used to it. Like most people of the trades and laboring classes, Andrew went everywhere on foot.

Heavy traffic caused him to slacken his pace as he approached the gate. The people on the road slowed to a stop as from somewhere behind them there came a trumpet blast. The crowd divided. A red-bearded seller of purple fabric pulled Andrew out of the road. "Legionnaires coming through!" he said.

Andrew stood gaping as a troop of one hundred Roman soldiers marched into the town. He recognized them as members of the Fourteenth Legion. It was an awe-inspiring sight. Everything about the Romans was terrible and impressive. Their brassy armor, their bright-red tunics, their flashing spear points, their square jaws set tightly within the leather cheek guards of their helmets. *What must it be like to see an entire legion marching together? Six thousand men and their weapons!* It was no wonder, Andrew reflected, that Rome had mastered the world.

When the soldiers had passed and the people were moving again, Andrew stepped within the shadow of the gate. Once under the archway, he paused to glance up at the familiar images carved there. The golden eagle, the symbol of imperial Rome, flashed red in the dying light. Below that, Olympian Zeus (or Baal, as some of the local people said) was riding on a rain cloud and gripping thunderbolts in his fist. Last of all, he gazed at a nameless, grinning demon his father had always called lucky Meonen. *Maybe not so lucky after all,* Andrew thought.

Skillfully picking his way through the jostling donkeys, carts, merchants, and farmers, Andrew emerged inside the city walls. Ahead of him stretched a canyonlike street of close-clustered two-story buildings. At its end he glimpsed the bright awnings of the booths in the *agora*. Avoiding the muddy gutter that trickled down the middle of the pavement, he took off at a run in the direction of the marketplace.

He was only two houses away when a bulky figure emerged from a narrow side lane and stopped him cold.

"Well, now! If it isn't the Jew boy!" jeered a painfully familiar voice. A chorus of laughter followed.

Demas.

Behind the apprentice lurked seven or eight other boys. Andrew recognized a couple of them from his days at the academy. He guessed the others were swineherds from the pasturelands that lay between Gadara and Lake Kinneret. All of them were dirty, scruffy, and mean-looking.

"*Bar Meshugga!*" taunted a tall, hollow-cheeked boy dressed only in a soiled linen tunic.

"That's Jew talk, in case you didn't know," teased a stocky little fellow with thick black hair. "It means 'son of a crazy man.' "

More laughs.

"What are you doing here, Demas?" said Andrew.

"Me? Just working out the details with Uncle Artemas," the big boy replied. "About my new job."

"New job?" Andrew asked.

"You heard me," Demas said. "Herding pigs on the plateau above the cliff."

"But Stephen needs your help!" Andrew shouted. "You can't do that!"

"*Can,*" Demas retorted, smirking. "And *will.* Uncle Artemas says your old boat business is finished anyhow. And good riddance!"

"Oh yeah?" Andrew's throat tightened with anger.

"Yeah!" laughed one of the pig boys. "Crazy Jacob's Boat Brigade."

"Shut up!" said Andrew, making a fist with his right hand.

"Crazy Jacob! Crazy Jacob!" a few of the boys began to chant.

"Stop it!"

"He *is* crazy!" said the black-haired boy. "I know 'cause I seen him with *no clothes on!*"

Everyone laughed again. Then they all took up the refrain:

Crazy Jacob! Crazy man!
Lost his robe and away he ran!
Danced in the sun till he got a tan!
Dance, crazy Jacob!

Before he knew what he was doing, Andrew was on top of Demas. His fist was in the air, poised to slam itself into the quivering pink flesh of the round, pudgy face. But before he could strike, two or three of the other boys pulled him off and threw him to the ground. There they pinned him while Demas lumbered to his feet.

"Well, now. *That* was a mistake," said Demas, feigning coolness but trembling violently. "When I get through with you, you're gonna—"

He stopped, catching sight of Andrew's purse. "Oho! What's *this?*"

"Leave it alone!" yelled Andrew, struggling to free himself. Demas bent down and yanked the purse from its cord.

"Jingle, jingle, jingle!" sang Demas, shaking the little bag of silver coins. "Looks like lucky Meonen's on *my* side now!"

Andrew twisted and turned. "You give that back!"

"Demas!" came a man's voice from the other side of the street. "Drop that and let him go! *Now!*"

The purse fell. The boys all jumped up and ran. Andrew sat up and looked.

It was Stephen.

CHAPTER 6

"Stephen!" At that moment Andrew felt as if he'd never been so glad to see anybody in his whole life.

"Demas trouble?" asked Stephen, helping the boy to his feet and brushing the dust from his cloak and tunic.

"'Crazy Jacob' trouble," Andrew responded, fumbling to reattach the leather purse to his belt.

"I see," Stephen said. "And what brings you to town so late in the day?"

"Mother needs grain and oil tonight, or we won't have any bread tomorrow. This is the last of our money," he added, patting the leather purse.

"The last!" said Stephen, raising his bushy eyebrows. "That won't do! Here, I have a few coins of my own left. That should be enough to buy her an extra measure of barley, I think. But we'd better do it quickly. The merchants are packing up to go home."

The grain merchant grumbled about having to reopen a sack of wheat that he had already loaded on his donkey for the trip home. Yet he showed no lack of eagerness when it came to taking Andrew's money.

The shadows were lengthening over the *agora*, and a dry wind was sporting in the shop awnings when Andrew and Stephen set out for home. It would be dark by the time they reached the village. But then a walk under the stars on a summer evening would be pleasant, especially with the black-eyed Greek as a traveling companion. *This will be my chance to ask him,* Andrew thought.

"Thanks, Stephen," he said as they came out of the gate and set foot upon the road. "Again."

"Well," laughed his friend, "it's just lucky I happened to be there!"

"Lucky," mused Andrew, glancing up at the leering gargoyle above the gate. "Like old Meonen. Maybe he *was* watching out for me, after all."

"You mean you'd begun to doubt it?" asked Stephen.

"Haven't *you?*" returned Andrew, staring back at him. "I mean, Meonen was always sort of a favorite of my father's."

"Ah yes. I see."

Far to the west, out where Andrew knew the Great Sea stretched away to the end of the earth, the sky was aflame with orange, copper, and violet. Above the craggy ridges to the east, the horned moon sailed like a dancing ship. Andrew and Stephen quickened their pace as they felt the darkness gathering.

"Stephen," said Andrew in a little while, "you believe in the gods and spirits, don't you? As my father does . . . I mean, *did?*"

"Perhaps. Perhaps not quite in the same way."

"In what way, then?" Andrew asked.

"That's difficult to say," Stephen replied after a thoughtful pause. "I suppose I'm a little bit like Plato."

"Plato?" Andrew asked.

"One of our greatest thinkers—the Greeks', I mean. You would have heard about him if you'd stayed on at the academy."

"Really? Could you introduce me to him?"

"No, no, no!" laughed Stephen. "He died about four hundred years ago! But he wrote things about our Greek gods that would make you think he both *believed* and *didn't* believe in them."

"How could he do that?" Andrew said.

Stephen answered. "I'm not sure. I think he believed in them as pictures or shadows of . . . well, I don't know . . . some greater God, maybe. The one true God. Sort of like the God of your father's people."

Something inside Andrew perked up at this. "Do you believe in Yah-weh, then? The God of the Jews?"

"I've often wondered," Stephen replied.

They walked on into the hazy distance. Ishtar and K'siyl—Venus and Orion to the Greeks and Romans—began to twinkle in the blue dome above their heads.

After a while, Andrew said, "What about miracles?"

"Hmm?"

"Miracles. Do you think that the gods cause things to happen? Like making sick people get well? Or does the one true God, whoever He is?"

Stephen stroked his smooth chin and was silent a moment. Then he answered, "A few weeks ago I think I'd have said no. And yet . . ." Here he paused, putting his face very close to Andrew's and lowering his voice. "I've been hearing stories about happenings of that very sort. On the other side of the lake."

Andrew's mouth dropped open. "Who told you?" he said, surprised at the eagerness in his own voice.

"Fishermen. From Capernaum," Stephen replied. "One of them said that his wife's mother had been cured of a fever—just like that!—by a man named Jesus."

They walked on in silence while Andrew's imagination burned with the things Stephen had told him. At last the lights of the village appeared at the end of their road. They flickered strangely, it seemed. Andrew said, "Stephen, do you think there might be anyone like this Jesus on *our* side of the lake?"

"I couldn't say for certain," Stephen answered. "I'm not sure what kind of man he is. There are the conjurers, of course—"

"Conjurers?" Andrew was curious.

"Magicians. Wizards. All the old women swear by them."

"Do you know where I can find any of them?" Andrew was excited at the idea.

Stephen eyed him oddly in the light of the moon and stars. "At the

Place of the Stone," he said. "Near Philoteria, where the Jordan River leaves Kinneret. The place the ancients called Beth Yerah, the House of the Moon." He paused. "Are you going to tell your mother?"

"Tell my mother—?" Andrew began. But then he stopped in midsentence and pointed. "Stephen, look!"

They were now close enough to see the cause of the odd flickering of the light from the village. Fire!

They ran the rest of the way to the cluster of houses, dashing into the courtyard just in time to see several men beating out the last of the flames with leather tarps. It was a scene of complete confusion. Men coughed and hacked and waved their arms and cloaks at the thick smoke. Children, goats, and chickens ran this way and that, crying, bleating, and clucking. Women came and went between the ring of houses and the well, pouring water on the smoldering heap and then hurrying away to refill their jars. The donkey stamped and brayed.

It seemed the fire had begun in the straw around the donkey's manger and spread along the wall of one of the houses. That wall was badly blackened but still standing. The awning seemed to have had the worst of it. It was now nothing more than a flutter of smoking black ribbons. Andrew breathed a sigh of relief. It could have been so much worse.

Through the smoke he caught sight of his mother standing by the door of their house with Lyra in her arms. He ran to her at once.

"Your father," said Helena, looking not at Andrew but at the blackened wall. "He was here."

"Father did this?" exclaimed Andrew.

"What happened?" asked Stephen, stepping up and laying a hand on Helena's arm.

"Something I wouldn't have believed unless I had seen it with my own eyes," she answered. "I was working at the loom when I saw him run into the courtyard. Naked, filthy—like a . . . a *beast*! I picked up Lyra and ran with her into the house. I didn't want him to frighten her again. When I returned, he was standing at the open door of the big brick oven. I saw him reach inside. He took out a coal—a coal as hot and glowing as the fire in his eyes—and just stood there with it, holding it in the palm of his hand! He didn't even seem to feel it. I screamed. He looked up at me—I think I startled him—and dropped the coal. It rolled into a pile of straw. Then he ran away. That's all." She bent her head and laid her cheek against the hair of her little girl, who lay sobbing on her shoulder.

"I'm afraid that *isn't* all," said a high-pitched, nasal voice. Andrew turned to see the short, round shape of Artemas. The wispy black whiskers around his thick lips waved in the air as he nodded in greeting.

"As a matter of fact," Artemas went on, "this is probably just the beginning. There is sure to be more of the same . . . unless measures are taken." He smiled unpleasantly.

Andrew felt the muscles of his jaw tensing.

"What kind of measures?" asked Stephen.

"I wouldn't like to guess," the herdsman responded. "*Extreme* measures, no doubt. I mean to speak with the authorities in the morning. The man is out of his mind. Dangerous. A menace to the community. Something *has* to be done."

"But he's my father!" said Andrew.

"Unfortunately, yes," agreed Artemas, pulling his tasseled cloak over his head. "A good evening to you all." He smiled, nodded, and walked out of the courtyard.

Helena sat down on a stone with Lyra on her lap. "What do you think he means, Stephen?"

Stephen brooded silently, staring at the remains of the fire.

"He's right about one thing, the old pork face!" said Andrew. "Something *has* to be done! And it *will* be done—*tonight*!" Catching up a walking staff that was leaning against the doorpost, he wrapped his cloak around himself and turned to follow Artemas out the gate.

"Andrew!" his mother called after him. "There's nothing you can do, especially not tonight! Where do you think you're going?"

"The House of the Moon" was his only answer.

CHAPTER 7

Beth Yerah, or the House of the Moon, lay at the extreme southwest tip of the lake, near a marshy place where the waters of Galilee flowed into the river Jordan. Andrew had heard his father speak of it more than once. In those early days, Jacob had said, long before Joshua and Israel had entered the land, Beth Yerah had been a shrine dedicated to the worship of the moon god, Sin. Andrew wondered what kind of god Sin might be. He imagined that Sin trekked over the dark, rocky landscape, staff in hand, with the light of the thumbnail moon glinting on the darkened face of the lake. *Maybe Sin can help my father,* Andrew thought.

The night was deep and far spent by the time he reached a ridge from which he could see the town of Philoteria lying in the distance across the river. Much closer, down in a reedy hollow at his feet, stood the black shape of a huge boulder. Andrew stopped and leaned on his walking staff, staring down at the dark mass, wondering what he should do next. Suddenly a hand touched his shoulder. He jumped.

"You found it!" whispered a voice at his ear.

"Stephen!" gasped Andrew, falling against his friend and grabbing his arm. "You nearly scared me to death!"

Stephen laughed. "Sorry. I followed you. Couldn't let you come alone." He shrugged. "Not while your mother was watching, anyhow. I promised her that if I couldn't stop you, I'd at least keep an eye on you." He grinned in the moony darkness.

Andrew pointed to the dark shape in the hollow. "The Place of the Stone?"

Stephen nodded. "The one and only. They *live* there, from what I'm told. Around on the other side of the rock."

"*Live* there?" Andrew gasped.

"Yes." With a sweep of his arm, Stephen indicated the downward path. "Shall we?"

"Why not?" gulped Andrew. He shook himself, gripped his staff tightly, and stepped down the slope, determined to do whatever was needed to find help for his father.

It was slow going. Together they slogged and squelched their way through the muck, pushing tall reeds aside and slipping on slimy stones. Once Andrew had to stop to retrieve a sandal that got stuck in the mud. But before long they had rounded the shoulder of the huge rock and stood facing a large hole that gaped like an open mouth in its western face. *Great,* thought Andrew. *Just what I need. Another cave.*

He stood hesitating in the wet gravel outside the cave's entrance. He could feel his heart pounding in his chest as he looked down into the hole. Everything about it was black. The smoke stains around its edges, the empty spaces inside, even the feelings it stirred inside him as he stood in front of it were black. *What now?* Andrew didn't know how to speak to a conjurer. Should he cry out or strike the rocky doorway with his walking stick or repeat some kind of spell? Or turn and flee?

Then he heard voices. "Somebody's in there!" he whispered.

"Of course somebody's in there!" said Stephen. "Isn't that why we came?" Raising his voice, the Greek called out, "Hello? Anybody home?"

Andrew gaped at his greeting. Stephen shrugged.

More sounds. Someone was coming. A dark shape appeared in the doorway.

"Who is it? Who, who indeed?" croaked a thin, dry voice. The voice was as dry and crackling as the dead reeds surrounding the entrance to the cave.

Stephen gave Andrew a nudge. "Speak up!" he said.

Andrew cleared his throat and stepped forward. "I've . . . uh . . . come to see the conjurers. Are you one of them?"

"One of two! One of three! One of four! One of many!" crackled the dry voice. "Who wants to know? Who wants to know?"

"Andrew. Son of Jacob the boatwright."

A light flickered and flared. In the glow of a handheld clay lamp, a face appeared—an old woman's face, yellow, long, furrowed, and skull-like, with a narrow, pointed chin and barely any nose at all. It was surrounded by stray tufts of gray hair and set deep within the shadowy folds of a woolen cloak.

"Step in," said the woman, ushering them into a dank chamber that looked as if it had been hewn out of the rock. *Like the Haunts of the Dead,* thought Andrew, shivering. The place was strewn with bleached bones, broken pottery, cold ashes, and row upon row of sealed stone jars. Andrew wondered how the bones had gotten there. Were they animal bones? Human? A chill crawled up his back, and he quickly looked away.

"Who is it, Anath?" said another voice—this one sleepy and deep-toned—from the inner recesses of the cave.

"A boy. A man. A man and a boy," answered Anath, squinting at Andrew and Stephen through the smoke. She set her lamp on a ledge of rock and unceremoniously seated herself on the floor. "Company! Customers! Come out, Enkidu! Come out!"

A man, elderly but straight and tall, stepped into the light. He, too, was cloaked in gray. His hair was thick and white. Around his neck hung a long gold chain from which dangled countless silver pendants and amulets—star shapes, crescent moons, spearlike sunbeams, serpents, grinning demons. Unlike the old crone, the man had a full, round face. He almost looked kindly. He yawned, glanced absently from Andrew to Stephen, and then from Stephen to Anath.

"What is it?" he said. "A man needs his sleep."

"No time for sleep!" scoffed the old woman, picking up a small bone and twirling it between her fingers. "They are wanting something from old Anath and Enkidu, I think. Yes?"

Andrew gulped and nodded. He tried to speak, but his tongue felt like a wad of wool. His knees began to buckle. Supporting himself on his staff, he leaned forward and opened his mouth. "My father . . . he's gone crazy," he heard himself say in a voice nearly as thin and dry as Anath's own. "It's because of the spirits or the gods or something. He's living in the tombs, the Haunts of the Dead."

"The Haunts of the Dead!" whispered Enkidu. His forehead lifted into a series of wrinkles. He stuck out his lips and whistled. Anath grinned and nodded.

"Yes," said Andrew, taking courage. "The Haunts of the Dead. He runs around naked and beats people up. He started a fire in our village. He held a hot coal in his bare hand!"

The two conjurers turned and stared at one another. Then in unison they pronounced a single name: *"Chashmagoz!"*

"Can you help him?" pleaded Andrew. "Can you make him better? Can Sin, the god of the moon, do anything for him?"

Anath and Enkidu smiled. "It all depends," said the hag. "Have you brought *keseph*?"

"Keseph?" Andrew darted a confused glance at Stephen. "Money? But I don't have—"

By way of response, Stephen reached inside his cloak, pulled a small bag of coins from his belt, and tossed it to the floor. It landed with a chink in front of the two magicians. "I had a feeling we'd need it," he said.

Old Enkidu beamed. His baubles jangled, and his rich white hair gleamed in the lamplight as he leaned forward, picked up the purse, and tucked it safely inside his robe. Then, with a sudden change of expression, he folded his hands, closed his heavy-lidded eyes, and frowned gravely. "Plainly a case of fire demons," he said.

"Fire demons?" echoed Andrew.

"Plainly?" said Stephen dryly.

"Most certainly," said Anath, bobbing her head up and down so vigorously that the whole of her bony frame shook with it.

"Chashmagoz, chief of the demons, demands appeasement," continued the old man.

"Yes, indeed," agreed the hag. "Sacrifice."

Sacrifice? Andrew squirmed uneasily.

"But we will subdue him by the power of Sin, god of the moon," the man added.

"Subdue him, yes! But only at great cost!" The hag's face shone with greed.

"*That* part I can believe," muttered Stephen.

"Then you can help us?" Andrew asked hopefully.

"Can—and will—yes, indeed," croaked Anath.

"Tomorrow," affirmed Enkidu, opening his eyes. "We will meet you tomorrow at the Haunts of the Dead. At moonrise."

"Moonrise," repeated the old crone. She smacked her lips and wagged her narrow chin from side to side within the folds of her robe. Then her toothless grin faded, and she scowled. "Now go!" she said, pointing a bony finger at the door.

With that, Stephen grabbed Andrew by the arm and almost dragged him from the cave. In a moment the two of them were standing once again on the mushy gravel outside the entrance. The sliver of moon had passed the peak and was bending its course toward the west. The darkness of the marsh and the heights above lay before them. Andrew leaned on Stephen and breathed a sigh of relief.

"My feelings exactly," said the Greek.

"Tomorrow night, then?" said Andrew, giving his friend a tentative look.

"Yes," said Stephen. "Tomorrow at moonrise we shall see just how much power Sin really has."

CHAPTER

8

The following day was one long agony of waiting. From sunup till sundown, Andrew and Stephen labored beside Lake Kinneret's sparkling waters, just as they did every day.

Without Demas's help, it had been necessary to put in long hours and exert extra effort just to complete the boats Jacob had promised to his customers. It was no longer a question of finishing on time but of finishing at all. Yet even with so many other tasks to be done, Andrew still somehow found time to continue working on his own boat. That, he felt, was something he simply couldn't give up.

And he had made good progress too. By this time the hull was finished. Edge to edge, Andrew had joined the cedar planks, fitting every tenon snugly into its mortise, just as his father had taught him. Every seam was as smooth and as tight as he could possibly make it. Now it was simply a matter of inserting the oak frame and securing it to the sides with more wooden pegs and brass nails. Then he would install a bench or two and brush on a couple of stiff, heavy coats of pitch.

Andrew took great pleasure in the work. He saw it as his last link with the man who now wandered wild and naked somewhere among the tombs on the side of the cliff.

When it was dark enough for the first stars to appear, Andrew turned toward the rugged eastern horizon and saw the sickle moon poke the tip of one bright point up into the darkness. From the surface of the lake, an evening mist arose. He and Stephen exchanged looks. It was time.

They took the narrow trail up the side of the cliff and wound their way higher and higher. Andrew had a curious feeling that the darkness and dampness were following close behind, clinging to the hem of his cloak and tickling his heels.

Looking over his shoulder, he saw that the fog was indeed making its way up the cliff, quickly covering that part of the path they had already traveled. He felt his chest tighten as they approached the curve in the trail where the first of the cave tombs gaped among the rocks. He tried to put out of his mind the deep, black holes that contained the rotting bones. He tried to ignore his certainty that they were full of watching eyes. But he couldn't fool his stomach, which churned within him.

"Stay close, now," Stephen called back to him. "I don't want to lose you in the fog."

"I wish we knew exactly where they were planning to meet us," said Andrew, shivering involuntarily. "They never even—"

He was cut off by a shriek like the cry of a frightened or wounded beast. He and Stephen covered their heads as a small shower of rocks and gravel poured down over them from above.

"What was that?" whispered Andrew after a tense pause.

"Shhhh!" warned Stephen. "Keep still! Might be a jackal or—"

Suddenly a bony hand touched Andrew's shoulder. He gasped and whirled around.

"Moonrise—yes, indeed," croaked a thin, dry voice at his ear.

"And the patient is nearby, I assume?" added a second voice, calm, complacent, and vaguely sleepy.

"He *must* be close!" breathed Andrew to Anath and Enkidu once he had regained control of his voice. His heart pounded as if it would burst. "We know he's living here among the tombs. Do you think you can find him?"

"He won't be easy to catch," offered Stephen, peering at the two con-jurers through the thickening mist and darkness.

"Catch? Don't have to catch—no, indeed," cackled the old woman, bouncing up and down on her toes.

"Certainly not," agreed Enkidu with a warm, assuring chuckle. "No need to get any closer than this. Why take unnecessary risks?" A pleasant smile spread over his broad, kindly face.

"Seriously?" asked Stephen. "You mean you don't need to see him or touch him or—?"

"No! No touching! Too dangerous!" said Anath, squinting and shaking her head. "Just *spells*. Watch."

From under the folds of her cloak, she drew a piece of flint and a long, knobby stick of wood covered with thick, black tar at one end. Striking the flint against the rocky face of the cliff, she lit the torch. In a few moments it was flaring out brazenly against the surrounding darkness. Immediately there came another animal-like cry from above.

"Hmm," said Enkidu, raising his sparse eyebrows. "Perhaps we had better proceed quickly."

"Indeed!" agreed his partner, cocking an ear toward the cliff.

With his right hand, the old man fumbled in the folds of his gown and produced an amber-colored glass vial. From this he poured a small amount of white powder.

"What's that?" asked Andrew.

In answer, Enkidu tossed the powder into the flame of Anath's torch. Andrew flinched as the fire flashed bright red and then green and then blue. Through the thick white smoke that followed, he gazed upward, searching for any sign of movement among the rocks.

"Incense! Good, good, good!" cackled the hag. "And now the *sacrifice*!" From a sack that hung within her outer garment, she pulled out something stiff and fuzzy and strangely odorous.

"A dead cat!" gasped Andrew.

"*That's* a sacrifice?" mumbled Stephen.

"In the name of Sin!" shrieked the crone, hurling the carcass up the side of the cliff.

Enkidu smiled and patted Andrew's shoulder.

Then, as Andrew watched, the old woman started bobbing from side to side. She lifted her hands above her head, splayed her fingers wide, and padded her feet upon the pathway in an odd, rhythmic dance. Enkidu joined in, shaking his pendants and amulets and humming a single low note. Then he produced a small tambourine and began beating on it slowly. Together, the two conjurers chanted:

Agrath, Azelath, Asiya,
Amarlai, Sharlai, Belusiya!
Burst and curse! Dash and ban
Chashmagoz, Merigoz from this man!

Andrew stood entranced. Never in his life had he seen such a display. The fire, the smoke, the mysterious words—all of it made a deep impression upon him. *This will do the trick!* he thought, a surge of hope rising within him. *This will save Father! If this won't do it, then nothing—*

Crash!

A small avalanche of dirt and rock rained down on the little group. A horrendous howl pierced the night. Something as fierce and powerful as a lion from the Jordan thickets exploded off the ledge above them and threw itself on top of old Enkidu.

"Aagghhh! Off! Off!" the old man cried as he fell. The tambourine bounced on the path and jangled away into the mist.

"Not *me!*" shrieked Anath, flinging her arms skyward and casting the torch aside. It plummeted down the cliff, briefly illuminating the bleak rocks below before snuffing itself in the swirling fog. "Help, O Sin!" she screamed, frantically wedging her skinny body into a narrow space between two large stones. "Murder! Death! Betrayal!"

Trembling, Andrew edged his way along the path away from all the confusion, darkness, cries, and thrashing of arms and legs. The mist around his head filled with screams and snarls and dull, thudding sounds. Where was Stephen? Had he been able to escape? Andrew couldn't wait around to find out. He crept along until he felt an empty space open up in the side of the cliff. One of the caves. Gasping for breath, he backed into the hole and fell to his hands and knees just inside the entrance. Then he waited to see what would happen next.

As he listened, the scuffle reached a climax and then suddenly ended with a chilling screech. This was followed by the sounds of feet scrabbling hurriedly down the gravel path, and the howls of the two conjurers fading into the murky distance below.

When everything was still, Andrew called, "Stephen!" Cautiously he stuck his head out of the cavern to listen. "*Stephen!* Are you there?" A moment later he heard footsteps, followed by a cough and a groan.

"Andrew?" Stephen replied in a weak voice.

"Here! I'm here!" Andrew called.

Stephen approached slowly and as if he were in pain. His cloak was gone. His tunic was half torn from his upper body. The right side of his face was covered with blood that streamed from a gash above his eyebrow. He stumbled to the opening of the cavern and leaned against it.

"Was it a lion?" Andrew asked, afraid of the truth.

"It was your father," Stephen said.

*J*esus.

Andrew couldn't get that name out of his mind. Over and over it pushed its way to the top of his brain as he prepared to launch his newly finished boat on the waters of Kinneret. Again and again Stephen's words replayed in his memory: "stories about happenings of that very sort" . . . "on the other side of the lake" . . . "cured of a fever" . . . "a man named Jesus" . . .

Nearby stood little Lyra with old Baal and his cart. She had two fingers in her mouth and a strand of brown hair across her nose. Her brown eyes were wide with wonder at the spectacle unfolding on the shore.

"They're just pigs," Andrew said with disgust, grunting as he untied the ropes and prepared to push the boat into the water.

Over the lake, small birds wheeled and chirped, their peaceful existence shattered for the moment by the squeals of the animals on the beach. Dogs barked. Boys shouted and waved sticks in an attempt to herd the pigs through the shallow water, up a plank, and onto a large boat anchored just offshore.

"Swine for Susita and Gergesa," Andrew heard a high-pitched, nasal voice say. Glancing up, he saw Artemas standing a few feet away, broad and impressive in a black robe and white turban. He handed a papyrus scroll to the boat's grizzled captain.

"Mmmph." The captain unrolled the scroll and studied it. "Lucky for you that's where I'm goin'."

"I expect they'll fetch a handsome price," the pig farmer went on smilingly. "You'll have your share, of course, when we settle accounts."

"Nobody gets nothin' unless those pigs get on the boat," said the captain, spitting in the sand and eyeing the boys at their work.

"We *will* be needing a reliable agent on the northeast shore," Artemas added with a wink. "There are lots more where these came from—all growing fat up on the plateau." He jerked a thumb at the cliffs.

"Fat," said the captain. "I can believe that."

Suddenly Andrew felt himself being shoved from behind. He pitched forward and fell into the boat. Lyra squealed. The herding boys laughed.

"Nice boat, *Bar Meshugga*. Is it for your little sister?" Demas taunted.

Andrew scrambled to his feet. "Shut up, Demas!" he said.

Demas ignored him and said, "Too bad it's not big enough to carry any of Uncle Artemas's pigs up to the northeast shore. That's where the *real* money is. But you poor people wouldn't know anything about that, would you?"

Andrew climbed out of the boat and turned away.

"How's your old man these days?" Demas persisted with mock concern. "Finding his chains comfortable? Hmm?"

"Demas!" shouted Artemas. "Get back to work!"

"Yes, Uncle! See you later, *Bar Meshugga*—in a cave somewhere, probably, with crazy Jacob!" Demas and his companions moved off.

"Come on, Lyra," said Andrew. "Let's go help Mother."

He took her by the hand and trudged up the beach to meet his mother and Stephen. They were headed down to the boat with armloads of yarn and cloth to sell on the other side of the lake. Andrew's jaw tensed at the thought of Demas's taunts. It was too much! His father—with iron shackles on his wrists, fetters on his ankles, chained to the bare rock. *And all because of Artemas,* he thought bitterly.

It was true. After Enkidu and Anath had run screaming into the village, babbling about the "madman on the cliff," Artemas had lost no time bringing in the city authorities. Soldiers from Gadara had hunted Jacob down, bound him hand and foot, chained him to the cliffside, and left him to die.

"What was that all about?" asked Helena as she approached.

"Oh, just Demas," said Andrew. "He thinks he's so tough and smart! What he doesn't know is that Father *broke* those stupid chains last night. And I sure won't tell him."

Stephen whistled. "Broke them *again?*"

Helena shook her head. Then she turned to Lyra. "Now you mind Stephen while Andrew and I are gone," she said, laying her fabrics inside the boat and stooping to kiss the little girl's head. "We'll be spending the night with Aunt Hadassah and Uncle Yohanan in Capernaum."

"Yes, Mother," said Lyra. "I'll make sure old Baal minds too."

Stephen laughed. "You two had better be on your way," he said.

Together Andrew and Stephen pushed the little boat into the shallows. Andrew watched as Stephen took his mother by the arm and helped her in. Then he, too, jumped aboard, grabbed the oars, and took his place on the rowing bench.

"I hope you sell every last bit of it," said Stephen, touching Helena's hand. Andrew didn't like that. "May the gods—" The Greek hesitated and then winced, gingerly putting a finger to the scar above his eye. "May *good luck* go with you."

"We could use it," said Helena with a sigh. "There's not much hope of selling anything on *this* side of the lake anymore."

Stephen shoved them out into the deeper water. "Good-bye," he called. "And Helena, think about what I've said."

"I will," answered Andrew's mother.

Andrew stared back at Stephen, puzzling over the meaning of his words. Then he bent to the oars as Lyra waved from the beach.

The little craft bounced over the waves like a cork. Suddenly, in spite of everything—his father's madness, his mother's fears, the family's growing burden of poverty—it was a glorious day. The sun shone like gold. The blue water sparkled. It was his boat's maiden voyage! *A dancing ship,* he thought excitedly. *She really does dance! And I built her myself! Father would be proud.* But as he remembered the night in the cave, Andrew wasn't sure what his father would have said about this trip. *I'm not exactly alone,* he thought. *Mother is with me.*

"Mother," he wondered aloud as his oars beat the water and the waves slapped the sides of the boat, "why didn't Father want me to go out alone in my boat?"

She regarded him gravely. "Did he tell you that?"

A dark cloud crossed Andrew's face. "Yes. I never told you, but the first time I mentioned it . . . well, *that* was when he started to go crazy. So I've always kind of felt like this whole thing was *my* fault."

Helena frowned. Her dark eyes grew a shade darker. She reached over and put a hand on his shoulder. "It's not your fault," she said.

"When your father was a boy in Magdala," she continued in a moment, "he had a younger brother. Benjamin. They learned the craft of boatbuilding from *their* father. They were always together, working in the shop, fishing, sailing on the water. Jacob loved his brother. One day there came a storm. Benjamin was out on the lake alone in a small boat, like this one. He never came back."

Andrew stared. Not once had he heard a word about this part of his father's history.

"Your father cried out to his people's God, to Yahweh," his mother said. "He prayed that *his* life might be taken in exchange for Benjamin's. But his brother didn't return. So Jacob grew angry. And afraid. In time his fear and anger grew into bitterness. When he was old enough, he left his people and came to live on our side of the lake. When I met him, I grew to love him. He was quiet and gentle but strong, and he seemed to feel things very deeply. In time we were married. But I never understood why he felt so strongly about the gods and spirits. Or why he feared them so much and tried so hard to avoid angering them, until he told me about Benjamin."

Jesus. The name whispered itself to Andrew once again. Was the God

of Jesus the same as the God of the Jews? Stephen had heard such marvel-
ous things about this man Jesus. And yet the God of the Jews had failed
to answer his father's prayers.

"Mother, what did Stephen say?" Andrew said again after he had been
rowing in silence for what seemed a very long time.

"Stephen?" she said, looking up abruptly. Andrew thought he saw a
hint of color in her cheeks.

"He asked you to think about something," he reminded her.

She cast her eyes down. She seemed embarrassed to tell him. "Andrew," she said, "Stephen is concerned about us. A woman alone with two
children. He sees how we're struggling."

"So?"

"He has offered to marry me."

"Marry you!"

"Yes."

"But he *can't* marry you!"

"Why not? You like Stephen, don't you?"

"Of course I like Stephen! But he's not my father! He *can't* be!"

"Andrew . . ." she faltered. "It's hard to live with so much shame. And
what about the money? What about the bread? What about Lyra?"

Andrew scowled at her. "If you marry Stephen, what happens when
Father gets well?"

She tried to smile but couldn't. Tears welled up in her eyes. "Your
father—" she began and then broke off. "I just don't think—"

"But he *will!*" Andrew shouted. "He will get well!" It was the last
word either of them spoke until they reached the other side of the lake.

Aunt Hadassah and Uncle Yohanan were waiting for them when they
came to shore in Capernaum. Uncle Yohanan helped them unload the
bolts of fabric and hanks of yarn and bring them to the marketplace. Aunt
Hadassah arranged for Helena to spend the day selling her wares at the
cloth merchants' booth.

For an hour or two, Andrew worked with them, carrying the fabrics to the stand and spreading them out on the display racks. Then, when it seemed that his help was no longer needed, he quietly slipped away.

Stephen marry Mother? he thought as he ran through the marketplace. He couldn't imagine such a thing. Andrew might as well let Lyra sail his boat!

He knew now what had to be done. He dashed past the covered merchants' booths, dodging carts and donkeys, hopping over baskets of fruit and vegetables, avoiding collisions with buyers and sellers. He searched the face of every man, woman, and child he passed, looking for someone who might be able to answer the question that was burning in his heart and mind. At last he saw a group of fishermen coming up from the beach. *Fishermen. From Capernaum.* With a sudden burst of determination, he ran straight up to them.

"Please," he said, grasping the sleeve of the first one, "do you know where I can find the man called Jesus?"

The big fisherman turned and looked down at Andrew. "Follow me," he said and then strode off.

Andrew's heart sank. "In *there?*" he said. "How am I ever going to get in *there?*"

The little white house was bursting with people—people standing, people sitting, people jammed into the doorway, people clinging to the latticework shutters of the two small windows. Never had Andrew seen such a big crowd in such a small place.

"Who said anything about getting in?" said the big fisherman at his elbow. "I only promised to take you to where you could find him."

"His own mother and brothers couldn't get in!" said a ragged young woman cradling a feverish baby in her arms. "They gave up and went home two hours ago!"

His own mother and brothers? Andrew was confused. Was *this* the man he expected to help his father?

"That *was* strange," commented a white-whiskered man in a blue-and-white robe. "He just said, 'Who are my mother and my brothers?' Then he pointed to the people sitting around him and said, 'Look! *Here* are my mother and my brothers. For whoever does the will of my Father in heaven, this one is my brother and sister and mother.' "

Father in heaven?

A ripple of wonder ran through the crowd. Something was happening inside the house. Andrew just *had* to see what it was. He pushed and shoved his way through the press of onlookers at the door, getting kicked and elbowed several times in the process. After two or three attempts, he finally succeeded in sticking his head into a narrow space between the doorpost and an elderly woman's bony shoulder.

It took a few moments for his eyes to adjust to the dim light. At first he saw nothing but lamp smoke and clouds of dust swirling in the shafts of sunlight that slanted in through the two tiny windows. Then the heads of people came into view. Next he saw a man in a peasant's cloak and tunic, seated in their midst, raising an arm to shield himself from a shower of debris that fell from somewhere above. Then a third beam of light opened into the room. In its brightness Andrew saw a woven reed mat coming down through the ceiling. On the mat lay a man.

Suddenly a round-bellied tax collector in a Roman toga pushed in front of him, blocking his view. *Not now!* thought Andrew.

"What's happening?" shouted an old man on the left.

"He just said, 'Your sins are forgiven!'" replied a rather large woman down in front. "Imagine that!"

"*Fpphh!*" spluttered the man in the blue-and-white robe, waving a hand in the air. "Who can forgive sins but God alone?"

But inside the house the surge of murmurs and whispers had grown to a chorus of astonished shouts. *What is it?* wondered Andrew. *I can't see a thing! If only—*

"Make way!" came a voice from within. "Let him out!"

Andrew gasped for breath. From where he stood, trapped between the tax collector, the bony woman, and the doorjamb, he could just see someone go prancing out the door. In astonishment he realized who it was—the man who had been lowered into the room on the reed mat just moments before! He had his bedroll tucked up under his arm, and he was leaping and dancing and singing.

"Praise to Yahweh!" sighed the young mother. "Jesus has healed him!"

Jesus!

"The lame walk and the blind see!" shouted someone else.

"It's the coming of the kingdom!" cried another.

The bony old woman fainted.

Then it was as if Andrew's entire world had been turned upside down. Faces, arms, and hands crossed his field of vision in a confusing blur. He was pushed and pulled from all sides at once. The crowd flowed out the door after the dancing paralytic, and Andrew was carried along in a river of oiled, perfumed, and sweating bodies.

Through the flagstone courtyard the crowd swept him, toward a jumble of stone water jars that stood beside the gate. Someone's foot caught between his legs. A large hand jammed itself against his throat and shoved him aside. He choked and then fell, striking his head against one of the jars.

When he awoke, he was lying beside the lake. It was late afternoon. Waterbirds circled and screamed overhead. Mending their nets nearby sat the fishermen who had led him to the little house. As his head cleared, Andrew heard a voice, strong and vibrant, speaking above the murmur of waves, wind, and muffled crowd noises. He couldn't understand the words, but the very tone of that voice stirred something within him. He sat up and looked around.

"Ah!" said one of the fishermen. "Our young adventurer has come to his senses!"

"Lucky for him!" said another, snapping a piece of cord between his teeth.

Andrew rubbed the back of his head. There was a big lump just behind his left ear. "Ooh!" He sucked the air in between his teeth. "Where am I?"

"Lakeside," said the first fisherman. "Didn't know where else to take you. Thought you could rest here awhile. Where are your mother and father?"

Ignoring the question, Andrew turned and gazed out toward the water. There in the prow of a fishing boat anchored just offshore sat the man in the peasant tunic and cloak—Jesus. He was speaking to a crowd of people on the beach.

"What's he saying?" Andrew asked eagerly, getting to his knees and rubbing the back of his head.

"Take it easy, young master," said the fisherman, laying a callused hand on his shoulder. "You've had a nasty fall. You ought to go home."

"But I want to hear it!" Andrew insisted.

"It's just a story. I've heard it before—about a father and a son," the fisherman replied.

"A father and a son? What about them?" Andrew was curious.

"Well, the son leaves home, you see," the big man began slowly, turning back to his nets. "Then, when he comes back, the father runs up to him and gives him a big hug. After that there's a family reunion, and they all live happily ever after. You know, that sort of thing."

Andrew jumped to his feet. "I've got to hear this," he said. "I need to talk to Jesus!"

"Wait!" called the fisherman. But Andrew was already running as hard as he could in the direction of the crowd.

He wasn't halfway there before the gathering began to break up. People were getting to their feet, picking up their things, and going home. Andrew slowed, stopped, and stood there rubbing the bump behind his ear, a dizzy feeling in his head. The story was over! He was too late!

To make things worse, Jesus and the other men in the boat were casting off and putting out into the lake. *Leaving!* Already they were rowing away and raising their sail.

The sun was sliding into the far west.

Andrew stared at the boat as it moved away from him. He *had* to get to Jesus. He hesitated. His mother and Aunt Hadassah would be looking for him everywhere, he knew. They would be terribly worried. They would probably get very angry. But there were worse things than that.

Down by the water's edge lay his boat—his own tight-seamed, little *dancing ship*. He cast a backward glance up the beach to the town of Capernaum, its whitewashed walls and buildings turning bronze in the fading light. He pictured the crowded house, the shouting people, the paralyzed man as he went leaping out the door.

Then, without another thought, he ran down to his boat, pushed it out into the water, leaped aboard, and began rowing for all he was worth.

CHAPTER

11

Alone on the lake in his *dancing ship*, Andrew pursued the man called Jesus. Stroke after stroke, labored breath by labored breath, he poured his heart and soul into the chase. *I've got to catch him,* he thought. *For Father. It's his only chance!*

Soon a stiff breeze began to blow. Andrew paid no attention but bent to the oars with even greater determination. Pull, lift, push, dip; pull . . . Glancing over his shoulder, he saw Jesus' boat about a hundred steps ahead, running swiftly before the wind, its triangular sail bellied out beyond the curve of its pointed prow.

I'll never make it at this rate, Andrew thought. *I've got to go faster somehow!* Even as he watched, the distance between the big fishing boat and his own small craft widened.

Andrew stowed one of his oars. Then, using the other oar to hold the boat steady, he slipped the sheet rope from its cleat, hauled the slanting yardarm to the masthead, and unfurled the small sail. With a snap, the triangle of canvas caught the wind. The little boat bounced forward.

No sooner had he raised the sail than the wind increased in strength, whipping Andrew's brown hair, gray cloak, and white tunic around his face and head. *Good,* he thought, steering straight for the fishing boat. He could almost see the faces of the men as their vessel rose and fell over the watery ridges and dipped into the troughs between the choppy waves.

Suddenly something plopped on the back of his head. It was a raindrop.

He turned. Another struck him on the cheek. Then another. To the northeast, all was dark as night. Black clouds, seamed with gray-green threads, were bunching up straight over his head, rapidly blocking out the fading light of the summer evening sky. *A storm!* Andrew felt his stomach tighten. *Strike the sail!* he thought, reaching for the sheet rope. But before he could get a firm grip on it, the wind gusted violently, throwing him into the bottom of the boat. There was a loud *crack!* and a *snap!* as the mast splintered and the little sail burst.

Frantically, his heart pounding, Andrew refitted his oars into the oarlocks and took two strokes. All at once, the nose of the boat plunged under an oncoming wave. The stern flipped up, thrusting Andrew forward and slamming him against the curved prow. Lightning flashed. Thunder ripped through the air. A driving, pelting rain lashed the tiny boat. Breathing hard, fighting dizziness, Andrew desperately scrambled back to the bench and seized the oars again.

For a moment he sat without moving. His head spun. His arms felt wooden. Caught in one of Kinneret's unpredictable storms! The scene in the cave and the words of his father came back to him: "Alone? . . . No. Absolutely not. Not without Stephen or Demas or me."

Something—a flash of anger as bright as the lightning—exploded within him. He shouted and screamed and lashed the raging foam with his oars. The boat tipped to one side and then the other. Andrew leaned back and peered over the tops of the seething waves. Jesus and his boat were nowhere in sight.

"One day there came a storm," he heard his mother saying. "Benjamin was out on the lake alone in a small boat, like this one. He never came back."

Pictures filled his mind. His mother's face. His father taking her in his arms, kissing her on the forehead, stroking her long brown hair. Lyra and old Baal coming in at the courtyard gate. All four of them sitting down to a dinner of flat bread and steaming broth.

"Mother!" cried Andrew, turning his face up into the pouring rain. "Father! Baal! Zeus! Meonen! Somebody! Anybody! Help me!"

At that instant a wave that seemed the size of a small mountain rammed the boat from the left side. There was a splintering sound. In a rush and tumble of foam and spray and water, Andrew and his *dancing ship* were overturned and thrust beneath the surface of the water.

And then there was darkness—darkness and bubbles and a ceaseless churning motion, up and down, side to side, as Andrew held his breath for what seemed like an eternity. He wondered what it would be like to drown. He would feel the cold water gushing into his lungs, filling him like a stone jar, cutting off his life and breath, driving him to the bottom of the lake.

Then, just as he felt that his lungs would burst, his head broke the surface. Coughing, spluttering, and sobbing, he flailed around with his arms until his right hand touched something solid. It was one of the cedar planks from the shell of his boat. He seized it and held it tightly to his chest, clinging to it for his very life. It was smooth, finely shaped, expertly crafted.

Jesus. Even in the midst of the wind and rain and surging blackness, that name forced its way to the top of his consciousness. He opened his mouth, shouting at the sky, "Jesus!" At that moment, another wave crashed over him, filling his mouth with water and pushing him below the surface again.

Spinning and turning in a dark and watery abyss, Andrew fought the urge to gasp for air. Images of sea monsters flashed before his eyes. Leviathan. Rahab. Gigantic, scaly serpentine bodies, backs ribbed with razor-sharp spines. *I'm going to die,* he thought. Within his own mind, he offered up one last desperate prayer: *Jesus! Help me!*

A surge of water pushed him upward, combined with a rush of sound. Then silence. And, oddly enough, moonlight. He looked around. His head was above the surface. He was breathing freely, gripping his plank, floating on water as smooth as glass. Overhead, the clouds were parting, revealing a spattering of stars and a pale white moon. *Is this the land of the dead?* he wondered. *Sheol? Or Hades?*

But it wasn't. It was Galilee under a clearing sky on a summer evening. It was Lake Kinneret, as calm and serene as he had ever seen it. It was almost as if the violent storm had been a dream. *Where did it go?* he wondered.

He turned around. There, gleaming silver in the light of the moon, its image reflected in the surface of the water as in a mirror, loomed the rocky bulk of the cliffs on the lake's southern shore. The Haunts of the Dead. The place of his father's mad wanderings. The road home.

With his last ounce of strength, Andrew paddled to shore and dragged himself onto the pebbly beach. There he sat down and put his head in his hands, feeling as if he were in a dream. He had been sitting there for what seemed a very long time, gratefully gulping down the sweet night air. Suddenly he was startled by a familiar sound—the sound of calm waters slapping the smooth sides of a wooden vessel.

He lifted his eyes. There, just offshore, stood the big fishing boat, its polished prow and white sail shining in the moonlight. And from the boat, first through the shallow water and then over the pebbles and sand of the narrow beach, strode a man.

Jesus.

This must *be a dream!* thought Andrew. Jesus was coming! And with him were several other men—fishermen, like the ones who had befriended Andrew in Capernaum. It was too good to be true.

Jesus the healer had come! Jesus would cure his father. At last Jacob would be himself again. Their troubles would be over. Everything would be the way it used to be!

Shakily, Andrew got to his feet. He opened his mouth to shout to the man on the shore. And then—

"Aaaaiiiieeeeeeee!"

His call was cut short by a bloodcurdling cry. He turned to see a fearsome shape—half animal, half human—come hurtling down the path from the cliff and onto the beach. His father.

Once on level ground, the shape picked up speed. There could be no mistake about where he was headed. Like an arrow shot from a sturdy bow, he flew over the sand straight toward Jesus, screaming and gesturing wildly all the way.

The scene among the tombs thrust itself into Andrew's mind. He remembered the frantic cries and wails of old Anath and Enkidu. He thought of the two poor travelers, beaten and bloodied on their way to Gadara. In despair he dropped to his knees and covered his face.

He'll kill him! he thought. *Father will kill Jesus!*

CHAPTER 12

Andrew knelt there with his face in his hands as morning dawned. But his soul was still dark. He found himself wishing he'd been drowned in the storm. *Now I'll never get my father back,* he thought. *He'll kill Jesus! And then Artemas will have Father put to death!* Jesus had been his last hope, and now hope was gone. In silence he waited for the inevitable.

Then he heard a voice. "What do you want with us, Son of God! Have you come here to torture us before the appointed time?"

Such a strange voice! Rasping, ragged, utterly foreign and inhuman— a voice, it seemed, made up of many voices, all of them tortured and strained. Andrew raised his head at the dreadful sound.

He wasn't prepared for the sight that greeted his eyes. The men who had followed Jesus up the beach were running back to their boat. But their leader stood straight and still upon the sand, his face calm, his hands at his sides, his dark hair ruffled in the early morning breeze. His gaze was directed downward at a figure on the ground.

Father?

Was it possible? *Could that horrible voice be coming from my father?* wondered Andrew.

There was no mistaking Jacob's physical appearance. He was naked, bruised, and bleeding. His wrists and ankles bore the marks of the iron fetters. Writhing and foaming at the mouth, he lay on his face in the sand at Jesus' feet, like a tormented but submissive dog. It was a picture that filled Andrew with feelings of fear, awe, and pity.

When they were ankle-deep in the water, the fishermen stopped and turned. Some of them stood fingering the knives and swords that hung from their belts. Again Andrew found himself holding his breath.

Then Jesus spoke. "What is your name?"

"Legion!" screamed the voices that burst from Jacob's mouth. "Legion is my name! For we are many!"

Andrew froze. *Legion!* Another picture flashed before his mind's eye—thousands of Roman soldiers, terrible with their flashing shields and spears, marching through Gadara's northwest gate.

Now he'll kill Jesus for sure! Andrew thought. *And me too!*

Andrew jumped up and looked around for a way of escape. The sun's glow, full of the promise of day, pulsed in the east. To the south, at the top of the cliff, a small clump of observers stood gaping down at the scene on the shore. Even at this distance, Andrew knew who they were—Demas and the other pig boys.

Even here, even now, he thought absently. *Even when I'm about to die, Demas can't leave me alone.*

"The swine! The pigs!" Jacob was on his knees, trembling from head to toe, gripping Jesus' ankle with one hand and pointing up at the cliffs with the other. "Up there! Let us go into the swine!" screamed the voices. "Don't send us away into the Abyss! The pigs, not the pit!"

For a moment Jesus stood gazing up at the plateau. Andrew saw his brow wrinkle and the edges of his bearded lips curve downward in the hint of a frown. But in the next moment his eyes dropped decisively to the man who lay groveling at his feet. Instantly the clouded expression cleared like mist before the rising sun.

"Very well, then," he said. "Go!" Then Andrew saw the hand of Jesus—a strong, work-hardened hand like his father's—reach down and touch a lock of Jacob's dirt-encrusted, twig-matted hair.

A pause. Then Jacob convulsed violently, cried out, and fell to the ground. Silence.

What now? Andrew took one hesitant step toward Jesus and his father. He was about to take another when—

Rrrmmrrbbbbllmbl!

Thunder! Another storm! But from the south? Storms on Lake Kinneret almost always came down out of the north. Pivoting on his heel, Andrew looked up at the cliffs.

What he saw nearly took his breath away. There, amid clouds of rising dust or smoke (he didn't know which), a dark torrent suddenly poured over the edge of the plateau. The storm obscured the rocks and cave tombs. Was it a flood? Andrew stared hard. He couldn't tell.

The ground beneath his feet trembled as the torrent fell farther and drew nearer. Now he could see that it wasn't made up of water at all but of solid shapes—stones or boulders, perhaps.

An avalanche! He turned to run. But then a new sound reached his ears—a sound made up of squeals, grunts, screams, and the shouts of angry herdsmen. He squinted up at the cliff again. All at once he realized what he was seeing.

Pigs. Hundreds of them. Rushing headlong down the crags and onto the sandy beach. On and on they thundered, past the boat shed, past Andrew and Jacob and Jesus, past the astonished fishermen, straight into the lake—splashing, floundering, drowning. In a matter of moments there was nothing left of them but bubbles and foam on the surface of the waves. Andrew could do nothing but stare.

He was shaken out of his reverie by the sound of a comfortingly familiar voice calling to him from the lake. "Andrew!"

Looking out beyond the spot where the pigs had plunged into the water, he saw a boat approaching. And in the boat two familiar faces—his mother and Uncle Yohanan!

"Thank heaven you're safe!" called Helena.

Uncle Yohanan leaned on his oars and wiped his brow.

Then came another well-known voice, behind him this time. "Well! A man never knows *what* he'll find when he comes to work!"

"Stephen!" shouted Andrew in surprise. "Lyra!"

"And old Baal too!" piped up Lyra. As always, the gray goat was pulling a small cart with a worn rag doll aboard.

Together, Stephen and Andrew ran down to the water's edge to help Helena out of the boat.

"Helena," said Stephen. "I didn't expect you back until—"

Andrew interrupted him. "Mother, I—"

Helena hugged her son and then held him at arm's length. She looked at him severely. "What were you thinking, Andrew? When we saw that your boat was gone, we realized what must have happened. We followed you as soon as the storm ended . . . so suddenly and strangely."

"A miracle—that's what it was," said old Uncle Yohanan, climbing ashore and tossing his oars into the boat. Then he sat down and mopped his forehead again.

Suddenly Andrew's mother raised her hand in a silencing gesture. "Look!" she said, her eyes as round as two silver coins.

They followed her gaze up the beach. There, at the feet of Jesus, in the middle of a circle of ten or twelve men, sat Jacob. He was wrapped snugly in a brown fisherman's cloak. Gratitude, relief, and intelligence shone from his weary face.

"Jacob!" screamed Helena. Her hand shot to her mouth. Her face went white. Then she picked up her skirts and rushed toward her husband, who was already on his feet and running to meet her.

Andrew glanced over at Stephen. Stephen grinned back. "Well," he said with a shrug, "I guess that's that!"

Andrew was about to give Stephen a good-natured punch in the arm when out of the corner of his eye he saw his father coming toward him. He was running, just like the father in the story the fishermen had heard Jesus tell.

What now? He backed away, trembling. Should he run? Would his father attack him, attempt to strike him as he had done in the cave? Was this only a dream after all? Or was Father really cured, really himself again?

Andrew's face burned. He started to shake. He felt cold perspiration break out on his forehead.

And then, before he had time to think another thought, he found himself enfolded in his father's strong arms. His face was pressed against his father's chest, weeping hot tears into the brown folds of the fisherman's cloak.

CHAPTER
13

It was about the third hour of the day. All of them—Father, Mother, Andrew, Lyra, Uncle Yohanan, Stephen, and Jesus and his men—were sitting together. A breakfast of carp and catfish was roasting over the glowing coals of a wood fire.

Andrew sat looking out over the sun-flecked waters of the lake. Distantly he recalled the cold, the darkness, and the hopelessness he had known while struggling beneath their surface the night before. A feeling of unreality flooded over him. His father restored! Normal! Somehow or other, he couldn't believe it, didn't trust it. Somehow he felt he must stay on his guard.

"See! Old Baal likes it too," said Lyra, letting the goat gobble a piece of fish out of her open palm.

"Is there anything old Baal doesn't like?" scoffed Andrew.

Lyra ignored him. "And look what else he can do," she added, jumping up. Without introduction or explanation, she led the goat, cart and all, straight up to Jesus.

Oh no! thought Andrew. *She's going to embarrass us all! She's going to ruin everything!* He got to his feet, feeling that Lyra had to be stopped before she did something to shatter this fragile, beautiful dream. Old Baal? A goat named after a pagan god? What would Jesus think? He wouldn't understand. He might even get angry. He might change his mind about Father.

But the silent man in the peasant cloak and tunic showed no sign of anger. Instead, he looked down at the little girl and her goat, smiling as she drew near. Lyra smiled back. Then, as Andrew stood rooted to the ground, wondering whether to grab her arm and yank her back, she took the rag doll from the little wooden cart and held it out to Jesus with both hands.

"For you," she said. "From old Baal—and from me too. For helping my daddy. Her name is Iphigenia."

Andrew's jaw tensed as he waited for Jesus' response. But Jesus said nothing. Instead, his smile broadened and he bent to brush a strand of stray hair away from Lyra's nose. Then he took the little rag baby from her hands and gently tucked it into his belt.

Andrew breathed a sigh of relief. But in the next moment, he heard the sound of approaching voices and footsteps. He spun around and saw twenty or thirty men and boys heading straight toward the little group gathered around the fire. Some were carrying sticks and clubs. At the head of the group strode Demas, jabbering and pointing a stubby finger at Jesus. Beside him stumped his portly uncle, his face as round and red as a juicy ham.

Demas! If Lyra can't spoil everything, Demas will!

"A word with you, sir," called Artemas. "With *all* of you." The rotund figure waddled into the circle and stepped straight up to Jesus. A few of the fishermen scrambled to their feet and drew their weapons.

"There is the little matter of my herd!" whined the pig farmer. With every word, his voice rose in pitch. "Extremely valuable animals, I assure you. Destroyed this very morning!"

"Yeah! And *he* did it!" volunteered Demas, pointing at Jesus. "With some kind of *Jew* magic! I saw it myself! From up on the cliffs!"

"Payment of some kind is in order!" demanded Artemas. "What do you plan to give me in exchange for my property?"

There was a pause. Andrew's fists tightened involuntarily.

"What about a man's life?" said Stephen quietly.

Artemas stared. "What man's life? What are you talking about?"

"*My* life, Artemas," said Jacob. In silent amazement Andrew watched his father rise slowly to his feet. There was a light in Jacob's eyes. Andrew realized in a moment that he was a different man than he had been. It was a realization that frightened him even more than the insane things his father had done while possessed by demons.

As for Artemas, he was dumbfounded. It was the first time Andrew had ever seen the man speechless. His mouth dropped open. His face looked like a slab of bacon—half red, half white. Anyone would have thought that his eyes were about to pop out of their sockets.

"You!" he squealed at last. "I might have known *you* had something to do with this! But . . . how? How is it possible?"

"I can tell you that," said Andrew, stepping to the center of the circle. "Demas is right. This man," he said, pointing to Jesus, "*healed* my father! I watched him do it!"

There was a murmur from the crowd.

"But it wasn't magic!" Andrew went on. "It was . . . well, something else. It was"—he flushed, faltered, and groped for words—"it was the work of the one true God! Jesus saved my father when nobody else could! And that's worth all the pigs in the world, if you ask me!"

An odd silence fell upon the gathering. Artemas stood shifting his gaze from Jesus to Jacob and back to Jesus again.

"So," he said at last, "the game is clear to me now. My nephew was right! It's a case of Jews, Jews, and more Jews! Jews with their tricks! Jews with their infernal rules against eating pig flesh! Jews bent on destroying my business, determined to undermine my trade! Am I right? Am I right?"

"No, Artemas!" Andrew heard his father say.

"What next?" continued Artemas. "Does every single Jew in Galilee intend to relocate to our side of the lake?"

Andrew glanced over at Jesus, wishing, hoping, and praying that he might do something to silence the pig man. But Jesus said nothing. He sat perfectly still, his sad eyes fixed on Artemas's face.

"Go on! Get out of here!" The pig farmer had worked himself into a frenzy. "Get back on your boat! Go back to your Jew towns! We don't want you around here!"

By this time the crowd was shouting with him. Jesus' friends raised their blades, ready to strike in defense of their master. But Jesus simply stood up, turned without a word, and walked down to the big fishing boat. The fishermen hesitated a moment and then followed him.

"You sure told them, Uncle!" said Demas, grinning stupidly.

Artemas smirked and mopped his dripping brow with a silk handkerchief.

"Too bad, *Bar Meshugga!*" added Demas with a sneer as the crowd broke up and moved off. "Looks like you lose again!"

Andrew was too tired to respond. Exhausted and shaken, he sank down beside Lyra and his mother. *I guess that's that,* he thought.

That was when he caught sight of his father.

Jacob stood unmoving, eyes fixed, jaw set, watching Jesus and his friends climb aboard their high-prowed fishing boat. Suddenly he stooped and kissed his wife's forehead. "Helena," Andrew heard him say as he took her by the hand, "I'm sorry. I don't know how to tell you this, but . . ."

The blood was pounding in Andrew's temples. He didn't know what his father was about to say, but he felt certain it was something he would rather not hear.

"Everything is different now," Jacob went on. "*I'm* different. And somehow . . . well, I can't help feeling that my place is with *him.*"

Tears stood in his mother's eyes. Andrew saw them glinting in the morning light. She nodded as if she understood, but she said nothing. Andrew wanted to scream, but he was powerless to utter a sound. Instead, he stood paralyzed, rooted to the ground. Helpless, he watched as his mother released her husband's hand.

With that, Jacob turned and followed Jesus down to the water's edge.

CHAPTER 14

So. It was just as he had suspected. His father—taken away from him *again*. As quickly and as unexpectedly as he had been restored. And by the very man who had healed him!

Jesus, he thought, *how can you do this to me?*

Andrew couldn't stand to watch his father climb aboard that boat. To see him sail away, across the lake, out of his life and his mother's and sister's lives—for good. Tears clouded his vision. *It's the way things always go,* he thought. *Benjamin was taken away from my father. Now my father's being taken away from me!*

Anger as hot as the rising summer sun steamed inside him. All his thoughts were fogged and blurred. He bit his lower lip and clenched his fists. Then he turned and ran to the path at the base of the cliff, to the trail that wound among the rocks and tombs.

To the Haunts of the Dead.

"Why?" shouted Andrew to the echoing caverns. "Why did you give him back only to take him away again?"

Finding the open tomb that had once sheltered him and his father from the storm, he fell inside and pressed his cheek against the cold stone floor. *The one true God!* he thought bitterly.

True God, false gods—what was the difference? Either way, an eleven-year-old boy didn't stand a chance. He sat up, seized a rock, and hurled it with all his might toward the lake. It fell with a harmless rustle in a hyssop bush about fifty feet down the cliff.

Yes, the gods were angry with him. Hadn't the villagers known it all along? Wasn't this why Artemas wanted to keep the Jews from coming to Gadara? The Jews wouldn't acknowledge the power of Zeus, Sin, Baal, and lucky Meonen. The Jews had funny customs and strange beliefs of their own. And he, Andrew, had delivered his own father into the hands of a Jew! He pounded his fist against the rock until it bled.

At last his supply of hot tears was spent. He could cry no more. Drained, empty, and oddly quiet inside, Andrew sat up and looked out the door of the cave. Far out on the lake he could see the big fishing boat moving off toward the north—to Capernaum.

Capernaum.

Unbidden, pictures of the day he had spent in the town on the north shore flooded back into his mind. The small white house, bursting with people. The glittering motes of dust in the beam of light that broke through the hole in the ceiling. The paralyzed man, his mat rolled up under his arm, dancing out the courtyard gate. The smile on the face of Jesus as he brushed twigs and bits of clay from his hair and beard.

Jesus. For weeks that name had possessed his imagination. He had called upon that name in the midst of the churning waves. At that name the waves and wind had become calm, suddenly and strangely calm.

And now Andrew could hear the voice of Jesus again—calming, soothing, stirring, challenging. He saw the face of Jesus—frowning up at the cliffs, smiling down at his little sister and her pet goat. And the hands of Jesus—touching his father's matted hair, sending the evil spirits into the herd of pigs, tucking the rag doll into his belt.

Could the hands of any god heal more powerfully than those hands? *No,* he thought. And wouldn't a god's face—if there were any god worth fearing or loving in heaven above or the earth below—look like that face? Wouldn't any god worthy of the name have a voice like the voice of Jesus? Wouldn't he say the kinds of things Jesus said? *Yes,* thought Andrew. It would have to be so.

In that moment the words of Jesus came back to him: "Who are my mother and my brothers? . . . Whoever does the will of my Father in heaven, this one is my brother and sister and mother."

Gazing out at the boat as it raised its sail and faded into the blue of the lake, Andrew thought hard about those words. The picture that had loomed before him in the face of death leaped before his mind's eye again. A leather mat spread on the paving stones of the courtyard. Great round disks of hot bread and wooden bowls filled with steaming broth. Lyra sneaking her vegetables to old Baal when Mother wasn't looking. Father urging Andrew to have more broth.

Father. "The will of my Father in heaven." Never before had Andrew heard of any god called "Father"—Abba, Daddy. What if it were true? And what if that Father-God really wanted Andrew's father to follow Jesus? What if that were His will, after all? Could any father be more powerful, more loving than that Father? Did any family matter more than His family? Perhaps, thought Andrew, just perhaps, Jesus needed Jacob more than Andrew and his mother and Lyra did. And what could be better than knowing that his father was working for Jesus?

Andrew jumped up. "What have I been thinking?" he shouted, fixing his eyes on the distant speck that he knew to be the fishing boat. "Who am I to keep my father from doing the will of his Father?"

He fell to the floor once again and squeezed his eyes shut. "Jesus," he whispered into the darkness of the cave, "if you really want my father, you can have him! He belongs to you now. After all, you made him well!"

He heard footsteps on the path outside. A hand touched him on the shoulder. He looked up to see his mother's face.

"Your father thought we might find you here," she said softly.

"H-he did?" stammered Andrew.

It was true. There at her side stood Jacob. And bunched up behind him were the beaming faces of Lyra, Stephen, and the scraggly-bearded goat.

The sun was high in the sky now. Its light streamed in at the cavern door. Jacob reached down, took Andrew by the hand, and drew him to his feet.

"Come on, Son," he said. "Let's go home."

It was late in the afternoon. Coppery sunlight was slanting across the waves and splashing up against the smooth trunks of the palms around the lake.

Ssshh-k! Ssshh-k! Ssshh-k!

Andrew stopped planing, wiped his dripping forehead, and looked up at his father, who stood just outside the shed, deep in conversation with the grizzled old merchant captain. "It was what he wanted," Jacob was saying. "I would have followed that man anywhere. Anywhere! But he wouldn't let me. Ordered me to go back home, back to my family—to the people of Gadara—to tell everyone what he'd done for me. As if I could keep my mouth shut!"

"Good for him," drawled the captain. "We need you here, Jacob. Anybody with the power to give you back to us, whether god or man . . . well, I'm on his side, that's all." He paused to spit in the sand.

"As for those pigs," he added, raising an eyebrow and lowering his voice, "good riddance to 'em! You should've had a whiff of my hold after I hauled that one load up to Gergesa. Phew-eee!" The two men broke into loud guffaws. Andrew leaned against the workbench and grinned. It was good to hear his father laugh again.

"Whatcha doin'?" said Lyra, running up, jumping through the air, and landing on her knees in the sand. The old gray goat trudged along after her, stopping every so often to chew stray tufts of beach grass. In the little cart behind him rode a brand-new doll—a wooden doll. Andrew smiled, remembering what fun it had been to watch his father carve it.

He had sat with his father under the billowing awning outside the door to their house on a warm summer evening.

"I'm building a new boat," proclaimed Andrew in answer to his sister's question. "Father's helping me this time, so it's going to be even better than the first one. I've learned from my mistakes."

"That's good!" said Lyra. Then, as if remembering something far more important than Andrew and his boat, she jumped up. She tossed her hair over her shoulder, and trotted off to join a group of children who were playing along the shore.

"Off to a great start," said Stephen, ducking in under the awning and giving Andrew a wink. "Think you'll be doing any solo trips in this one?"

Andrew grinned. "No. I don't think I'll ever do anything alone again!"

"Everything's ready!" It was his mother calling. She stood a short distance up the beach, between the boat shed and the shining cliffs. She had spread a leather tarp on the sand beside a small wood fire and set out reed baskets of bread and fish. "Supper on the beach tonight!"

"Hurray!" shouted Andrew, dropping his tools on the workbench and running to help his mother with the picnic. "Come on, Lyra! Supper on the beach!"

But Lyra couldn't hear him. She was too busy dancing and singing with the other boys and girls on the shore. Andrew could hear their song drifting up from the water's edge, mingling with the evening cries of the birds and the music of the lapping waves:

Jacob and Jesus down by the shore,
Jacob's not crazy anymore!

"Andrew," said Helena, filling a wooden bowl with grapes and pomegranates and glancing up at the men, "your father seems a little . . . preoccupied. Do you think you could convince him to join us for supper?"

Andrew picked up a loaf of the hot bread, sniffed it, and smiled. "*That* shouldn't take a miracle!" he said.

LETTERS FROM OUR READERS

I know I've seen this story in the Bible before. But I can't find it. (Callum M., Dallas, Texas)

The basis for this story is found in the New Testament of the Bible: Mark 4:35–5:20 and Luke 8:22-39. In both the calming of the storm and the casting out of the man's demons, the power God gave Jesus is evident.

You won't find any mention of Andrew in the biblical accounts. We have imagined what it must have been like for the family of this man possessed by demons. Surely he had people who loved him and were concerned about him. Imagine their joy when he was healed. There must have been lots of hugs and laughter that day.

Notice that the events in this tale take place right before *The Worst Wish*, the story about Jairus's daughter that we tell in this very book.

Did Jesus really have a doll that a little girl gave Him? (Brittany N., Las Vegas, Nevada)

That isn't in the Bible. But we presume many people gave Jesus gifts from their hearts that the Bible doesn't record. We feel that if Jesus did get a doll, He would have thanked the giver and valued that doll because He loved the one who gave it to Him. We also know Jesus loved children.

Why isn't the lake called the Sea of Galilee? (Angie I., Fresno, Ohio)

The Sea of Galilee (which isn't really a sea at all but a freshwater lake) was known by several different names in Jesus' time. Galilee was one of them.

The others were Kinneret or Chinneroth (which comes from a Hebrew word meaning "harp"—after the shape of the lake), Gennesaret, and Tiberias. We chose Kinneret because it's the oldest name of the lake (going back to Old Testament times) and for that reason was probably the most common with the Jewish people in those days.

Why is this book so scary? (Bridget E., Boise, Idaho)

Anytime someone becomes involved with demons, things get very scary, because the power of evil is frightening. Demons aren't harmless as some television shows and movies might tell us. Although demons and spirits can seem to be friendly and to possess knowledge and power we want to have, getting involved with them is always disastrous.

However, there is good news! If you belong to Jesus, there is no need to be afraid. For if you belong to Jesus, you cannot belong to anyone else. Not only that, but it's also good to know that God is bigger, stronger, and more powerful than evil. There is a verse that says, "The one who is in you is greater than the one who is in the world" (1 John 4:4). God has more power than any demon or so-called god. With your hand in His, you never need to be afraid. Try reading Psalm 91. It reminds you that no matter what happens, God is always with you.

What was happening to Crazy Jacob? Why was he going crazy? (Megan W., Bangor, Maine)

Since Jacob believed in whatever "god" might help him, he opened up his heart to some evil spirits. He didn't put his trust in God, but in many other things. He wasn't really "crazy" but was controlled by demons. The more the demons took over, the more strange and destructive his behavior became. Only God was more powerful than the demons. And since Jesus is God, He could send the demons away.

Are all "crazy" people just demon-possessed? (Megan J., Venice, Florida)

No. There are many illnesses that affect the normal functions of our brains. Our brains are very fragile. It doesn't take much to keep them from working the way they're meant to. That's why we try hard to protect them by wearing helmets when we ride bikes or being careful what foods we eat or medicines we take. Our brains are a great gift from God! We need to take good care of them.

ABOUT THE AUTHOR

JIM WARE is a graduate of Fuller Theological Seminary and the author of *God of the Fairy Tale* and *The Stone of Destiny*. He and his wife, Joni, have six kids—Alison, Megan, Bridget, Ian, Brittany, and Callum. Just for fun, Jim plays the guitar and the hammered dulcimer.

The Worst Wish

by Lissa Halls Johnson

For my siblings:
Tim, Mindy, and Shelly
I'm sure you wished to be rid of me
when I was a pesky kid,
but I'm glad we're friends now.

As Seth leaned against the gnarled olive tree, he could think of only two things he hated.

His pesky older sister, Talitha.

And waiting.

Right now he was waiting—for his best friends. The only good thing was that Talitha was nowhere in sight.

Yet.

Where are they? he wondered. He picked at the bark on the tree and waited some more. He wished it would cool down. As long as it was so hot, he knew he and David and Joshua would barely be able to plod through their homework assignment, leaving no time for anything fun.

A small cloud of dust caught his attention. He could see David approaching, trying to walk like his father always did—slow, dignified, his chin tilted up just a bit. David didn't look dignified, though. He just looked dumb.

"David," Seth called, "hurry up! Where's Joshua?"

David looked around, maybe to see if anyone would notice if he changed his stride. He broke into a trot, not looking any less dumb than before. "Joshua said to come meet him by the almond orchard," he called. "He's got something to show us."

"Do you know what it is?" Seth asked.

David slowed when he reached Seth, then shrugged. "If it's Joshua, it could be anything. But it's probably gross."

Seth laughed. Joshua, a fisherman's son, seemed to like gross things.

He could gut a fish before Seth could even figure out where to puncture it with his knife. After gutting the fish, Joshua would be fascinated with how the fish was put together, while Seth just wanted to throw the stinky, slimy inside stuff away.

Heading toward the orchard with David, Seth glanced over at his friend. David walked like any other ten-year-old kid when he didn't think people were watching. Since he and Seth were almost the same size, they kept in step easily. They looked so much alike, with their brown, curly hair, that people often thought they were brothers. The only difference was that David's face was speckled with freckles, and Seth just had two— one on the end of his nose and one underneath his right eye.

It was good to have friends like David and Joshua, Seth thought. He couldn't imagine what he'd do without them. He hoped he'd never have to find out.

It took them a few minutes to find Joshua. Finally they saw him, looking tall and strong as ever, standing on the edge of a grove of trees. He was motioning them over so excitedly he couldn't stand still. Either that or he needed to go to the bathroom real bad, Seth thought.

"Don't come any closer," Joshua said, holding out his thick hands to warn them away. He looked behind himself as if whatever was there might disappear at any moment. His straight, dark hair stuck out every which way from his head. He'd probably been running his hands through it like he always did when he was impatient or getting really excited about something.

David stopped, glaring at Joshua. "So what is it?" he demanded.

Joshua smiled. "You have to guess." He dug his finger deep into his ear. When he brought it out, he studied it and then wiped it on his short summer tunic.

"I don't want to guess. I want to study," David said.

Joshua frowned. "That's all you ever do." He dug a finger into his other ear.

"I like learning," David said for the thousandth time.

I don't want to study, and I don't want to guess, Seth thought. "You've found . . . a broken pot," he said, knowing and not caring that his answer was lame.

Joshua threw out his arms, the smile leaving his face. "You've got to be kidding! I wouldn't bring you all the way out here for a broken pot."

David's eyebrows pulled together. He scrunched his eyes closed like he always did when he was thinking. Suddenly his eyes flew open as he raised his hand in the air. "It's a scroll. You found an ancient scroll!"

Joshua shook his head, offended. "No."

"It's something horrible and disgusting," Seth suggested.

"You're close!" Joshua said, brightening.

"It's your scab collection," David muttered, his voice flat.

"No," Joshua said. "But I can show that to you later if you want."

"I'll skip it," David mumbled.

"Guess again!" Joshua shouted, flapping his arms around and turning in circles.

"If we don't hurry up and guess, I think he's going to fly apart," David warned.

"Yes! Yes!" Joshua screamed. "Hurry. I want to show you." He looked like he might explode at any moment.

"Well, show us then!" Seth ordered. "We can't guess, and I want to get through our homework assignment as soon as possible."

"Okay, okay," Joshua said, moving aside and pointing at an object on the ground. Seth and David came closer.

"Wow," David said, looking at the dead bird. "How do you think it died?"

Poor thing. Seth tilted his head, studying the broken carcass. *Dead things are so sad.*

"Isn't it great?" Joshua asked. He picked up a stick and began to poke and prod the dirty feathered creature. As he moved it, white worms that looked like moving rice started to come out of it. "Ewww! Look at that. Must be hundreds of the little critters."

Seth grinned. Joshua's joy over gross things was funny. David didn't look joyful, though. He was studying the whole situation as if he was trying to learn something.

Seth squatted down to get a better look. *Why do maggots eat dead things? Did God make maggots too? Does God care about dead things? Or is He done with them once they're dead?* He picked up a stick and poked gently at the bird. The beak was open, and a thin red tongue dangled toward the ground.

"Speaking of maggots," David said, "where's your sister today?"

Seth stared at the busy worms while Joshua moved the bird around. "I don't know. She won't bother us."

Joshua snickered. "She *always* bothers us."

Seth looked down. A smile crossed his face. "If she does, I know exactly what we can do." He looked up at his friends. "She hates maggots."

Nodding, Joshua smiled too.

"I'm not touching those disgusting things," David said. "You guys are unclean as it is, touching that bird."

"Who's going to know?" Joshua asked. "You don't tell, and I won't."

"I *have* to tell," David said, acting like a smaller version of his father, a strict, religious man called a Pharisee. "If anyone breaks God's law, they must pay the price."

"Don't listen to David," Seth argued. "We're not unclean."

"You've touched a dead animal," David insisted. "God's law says that your family will have to sacrifice because you're unclean."

Joshua looked worried. "My dad will kill me."

Seth shook his head. "No, we only touched it with a stick. You aren't unclean if you just touch it with a stick. You have to touch it with your hands."

Joshua held up his hands, the stick dangling from his fingers. "I haven't touched it with my hands."

David shook his head. "Well, I still think you're unclean."

"Quit arguing," Seth said. "Let's get our assignment done so we can go down to the lake."

"We can do it here, can't we?" Joshua asked. "I don't want to leave this bird."

"It *is* a little cooler here," Seth agreed.

David sat on a rock and gathered some pebbles and small, jagged stones from the ground around it. He turned to face a larger rock and pitched a small one at it. The smaller rock shattered. "Have Joshua recite first."

"You always make me go first!" Joshua complained.

"That's because you're always the worst," David said. "I wouldn't want you to feel bad if I went first and did better than you."

Joshua glared at David. Then he looked at Seth and shrugged. "I think my brain has stopped working," he announced.

"I don't think it ever started," David mumbled.

"Funny." Joshua kept looking at Seth. "Do you think your dad would let us skip a day of schoolwork?"

"No way. We'd be behind everyone else," Seth said. "He doesn't stop teaching even when he's at home."

"I'd hate being the synagogue ruler's son," Joshua said, using the stick to make the bird's wing go up and down. "All that teaching all the time. And you have to act nice and proper everywhere you go. Ugh!"

"I'd love it," David replied. "You get to meet all the travelers who stay in the synagogue. You get to have dinner with most of the rabbis. Your father is the one who chooses which rabbi gets to read Torah and explain it. What an honor!"

"Yeah, but then you have to listen to them all too," Joshua added. "Boring ones like Rabbi Kohath."

The boys groaned in unison at the memory of the stuffy rabbi's long-winded talks.

"He came to our house for dinner," Seth told them. "Even Mother almost fell asleep."

They all laughed.

"Well, there are good rabbis too," Seth said. "Ones that are really interesting but don't get a chance to read or speak. It's fun to listen to Father talk with them after dinner."

"I liked Rabbi Jesus," Joshua said, his eyes lighting up. "He likes fishermen."

David grunted. "My father says he talks like a know-it-all. He read Torah—*God's* holy Word to Moses—like it was his *own* words." He paused and then looked around as if making sure no one was listening. "But I liked his stories."

Seth sighed. He'd had a sore throat the day Rabbi Jesus read and spoke in synagogue. He was sorry he missed the stories.

"If my father were synagogue ruler, I would be very proud," David said. "But I don't think I'd want him as my teacher at school *and* home."

"I'm sure glad my dad's not *my* teacher," Joshua said. "Except about fishing, of course." He flipped the bird over and began poking it in the back.

Seth wiped the sweat from his face with a corner of the linen cloak that hung to his knees. "Listen. The sooner we get this memorized, the sooner we can go do something else." He looked longingly across the dried grass on the hill toward the lake below.

Joshua followed his gaze. "Why don't we just go to the lake and stick our feet in?" he suggested. "We can throw rocks in the water, and maybe we'll learn better."

Seth looked at him. "We tried that once, remember? We got in a water fight, and that was the end of memorizing."

"My dad almost killed me for not knowing the verses better." David frowned.

"Okay, okay," Joshua said. "Then let's hurry up."

Seth looked at the lake again, wishing he could lie in the cool water with only his face showing. He'd stare up at the brilliant blue sky. He figured Joshua was thinking only about catching the next fish. David was probably the only one with his mind on Torah.

"I think I've got it memorized," David said.

"Well, spit it out then," Joshua said. "Maybe it'll rub off on me."

Seth turned away from the lake, forcing himself to pay attention.

David stood, dusting off his backside. His brown eyes took on a vacant look, seeming to scan the trees for the words. He cleared his throat. "This is from the prophet Isaiah. 'Forget the former things; do not dwell on the past.'"

"Good goin'," Seth said, smiling. "Keep it up."

"I will if you be quiet," David said. "I can't think if you interrupt." He looked at the trees again and swallowed. "See, I am doing . . . uh . . . I will do a something . . . and it springs . . . no, that's not right . . ."

Suddenly a confident voice came from the grove behind Joshua. "'Forget the former things; do not dwell on the past. See, I am doing a new thing! Now it springs up; do you not perceive it? I am making a way in the desert and streams in the wasteland.'"

Seth dropped his head into his hands and groaned.

It can't be! he thought. *Not now!*

"Seth!" David shouted. "You promised she wouldn't come! Why is she here?"

"I don't know," Seth mumbled, feeling as hopeless as a certain pile of feathers on the ground.

CHAPTER 2

S eth looked up at the same moment his older sister saw the bird.

"Ugh! Maggots!" Talitha shrieked. She backed up so fast, she ran into a tree.

"Want some?" Joshua said, catching a few on the end of the stick and flinging them toward her.

Talitha shrieked again and jumped out of the way.

"Why don't you go fall in the well, Talitha?" Seth said.

"No!" she said, crossing her arms.

Joshua flicked more maggots toward her.

She flinched. "I'm not moving," she said.

"Make her leave," David said.

"I don't have to leave if I don't want to!" Talitha replied. "I can go anywhere I want." She kept her arms crossed. Her long brown hair hung loosely about her shoulders. Her dark brown eyes glared at them, daring them to force her to do anything.

Everyone looked at Seth. He stared at the ground but could feel their eyes on him. He could also feel his cheeks flushing. The thought of his friends seeing him embarrassed made him even *more* embarrassed.

You're the man here, Seth, he told himself. *You're the firstborn male. She may be a lot taller, but you have a right to tell her what to do.* Seth lifted his chin and pretended to have the authority he didn't feel. "We are reciting Torah, so you must leave," he said.

"And not doing a very good job of it," Talitha added.

David and Joshua muttered something Seth couldn't hear. He

clenched his teeth and his fist. He wanted to hurt her, but he couldn't.

He took a few deep breaths and then spoke. "We're still learning. And because we're trying to do lessons our *father* assigned us in school, I really think you should go."

"Come on, Seth," Talitha said, exasperated. "Just let me stay and listen. I'll keep quiet, honest."

"No." Seth kicked at the dirt, sending up a cloud of dust. "Just go away!"

Talitha turned up her nose. "I like it here." She dropped to the ground, then re-crossed her arms.

"*We* don't like you here," Seth said. "*Father* wouldn't like you here."

"The *maggots* don't like you here either," Joshua said.

David nodded in agreement.

Seth took a step in her direction, and his nose twitched. It tickled. He took in a deep breath and choked. "Besides, you stink."

"I don't stink," Talitha protested. "I smell pretty."

"I'm with you, Seth," Joshua said. "I think she stinks."

Talitha stuck her tongue out at Joshua. "What do you know? You're only ten. And you stink like fish."

"I know more of Torah than you," Joshua replied.

"Prove it," Talitha said.

"Why are you wearing perfume?" Seth interrupted. "Does Mom know?"

"I'm almost thirteen," Talitha said, tipping her head back. "It's time I started to look and act my age."

David rolled his eyes. "As if anyone but you cares."

"Eli cares," Talitha said, her cheeks turning red.

"That old goat? He must be at least twenty-four years old," David said. "He's so blind, he'd fall in love with a donkey if it smelled right."

Seth and Joshua howled.

"At least Eli can recite Torah properly," Talitha countered, her eyes flashing fire. "I'd rather marry an old goat like him than a little boy like you."

"He's studied Torah for years," David argued. "If he *didn't* know it better, he'd be the laughingstock of Capernaum."

"And all Galilee *and* Judea," Joshua added.

"Which is what our family will be if you keep trying to be a boy," Seth said bravely. He hated the thought of everyone laughing at his family behind their backs. His father would be especially embarrassed. It would be horrible to have his daughter bring him shame.

"I am not trying to be a boy," Talitha said, her eyes welling with angry tears. "I just want to go to school. I want to learn."

"And you think old Eli would like it if you did?" Seth asked.

"I don't care what he thinks," she snapped.

"I thought you did," David said.

For a moment she looked flustered and then she frowned. "I mean I don't care what people think when it comes to me learning things. At least Mom understands. She teaches me what Father has taught her."

At the same instant, all three boys' mouths dropped open.

"Can women learn?" Joshua asked, letting go of his stick and apparently forgetting the bird.

"Do they even *want* to?" David asked, his words barely audible. "My mom only knows the basic stuff. She leaves the room when my father and I discuss my lessons."

Seth couldn't speak. He'd heard whisperings coming from his parents' room long into the night. But he'd had no idea his father was teaching his mother.

It wasn't that women weren't supposed to learn things, he thought. It was just sort of presumed that most women didn't care. And once they became wives and mothers, teaching them about Torah seemed pointless—except for the things most important for daily living and passing on to the children.

Seth's obvious shock seemed to make Talitha stand taller. "It's not against the law, you know," she said. "Mom told me I could come listen to you."

"I don't believe you," Seth said, hoping his words covered how unsure he felt. "I don't think you belong here, and neither do David and Joshua."

Talitha let a slow smile cross her face as she stood up. "I'll be around," she said. "Do you really think you *little* boys can scare me away?" She winked at them. "Remember. I know you are unclean. Don't you think your parents would want to know?"

"I am *not* unclean!" David announced, indignant.

"We aren't either!" Joshua said.

"We didn't touch the bird," Seth added. "Not with our hands." *Why is it that when I say it to Talitha, I feel unclean?*

"I don't think that matters," Talitha said. "Dead is dead. Unclean is unclean."

Seth glared at her and shook his head. He knew what she was doing. David wouldn't tattle on his friends, but Talitha would force the issue.

"So can I stay?" She stood with her arms crossed, her right foot planted off to one side.

"Okay," Seth grumbled, hoping that would keep her from talking to any parents.

"No!" David said firmly. "I will *not* recite Torah around a girl."

"You can't make me do what I don't want to do," Talitha announced.

The boys glared at her. She was right, of course. Joshua dug the stick into the squirming maggots. Seth could tell he was considering tossing more at her. Making her unclean. But then he would be guilty too.

"That's okay," she said with a smirk. "I have to go anyway. I'm sure Eli would like some help in the field."

Seth hated that smirk. He hated the way she stood. She knew exactly what she was doing—ruining his life. And worse, she *enjoyed* it.

She turned on her toe, so slowly that Seth wondered if she would really leave. She moved away gradually, glancing back over her shoulder and looking at each boy. "See you soon."

When she was finally out of earshot, David looked squarely at Seth. "Are you sure you want friends?"

Seth looked at David, his stomach getting fluttery inside. "What do you mean?"

"You heard me," David said, lifting his chin slightly.

Seth could feel his heart starting to beat faster. "We've been friends almost since the day we were born. Why wouldn't I want to be your friend?"

"I just wondered," David said, "because you don't seem to need any."

"I don't understand." Seth swallowed hard. The truth was he *hoped* he didn't understand.

"It's your sister, locust face," Joshua added. He picked up a beetle, letting it crawl over his finger. "Seems to us like you would rather be with her." He set the beetle on a rock and quickly smashed it with another.

The blood drained from Seth's face. "No, of course not."

"I don't want anyone as my friend who likes to stick around girls," David said. He stood in front of Seth, his chest puffed out.

"Come on. You have pesky brothers and sisters too," Seth argued. "What's the difference?"

"Wherever you go, there *she* is." Joshua jerked his head in the direction of the small dust clouds Talitha's sandals kicked up. He stepped next to David, adopting the same stance. "At least *our* brothers and sisters stay out of the way."

Seth's stomach bounced and flipped and turned over and over. "You'll give me another chance, won't you?" he said, his voice barely coming out in a whisper.

David and Joshua looked at each other, seeming to trade thoughts without trading words. David turned to Seth. "We've been talking."

Seth didn't know if he wanted to hear what was coming next. His heart picked up its pace.

Joshua dug his finger into his ear again. He looked at his finger and then wiped it on his clothes. "If this keeps up, we don't know if we want to be around you anymore."

Seth gulped. *No friends?* The days would be torture—not just long and hot, but boring too. *They won't. They can't.* But when he saw their angry faces, his heart skipped a beat.

Joshua squinted up at the sky. "It's not like we haven't given you a lot of chances."

"She listens in on everything we say," David said.

"She follows us around and says stupid things," Joshua added.

"She gets in the middle and just stands there so we can't shoot our slingshots," David pointed out.

"When we play Hide and Find, she tells where everyone is." Joshua rolled his eyes.

"When we're counting, she off-counts so we'll get confused and have to start over," David declared. "And that's not all. We'd be here until Rosh Hashanah if we said everything she's done."

Seth nodded grimly. Everything they said was true. In the old days his sister had only bothered them every few weeks or so. But lately she'd been coming around almost every day. Sometimes she acted like she was their mother. Sometimes she acted like a little girl. She was a grown-up one minute and a little kid the next.

Why couldn't she be like his friends' sisters? They might run up to ask something, deliver a message, or bring a jar of water. But they never hung around. One look from their brothers and they would be off, sometimes giggling behind their hands. *Their* sisters didn't try to teach them Torah or show them up. *Their* sisters acted like girls were supposed to. *His* sister was an embarrassment, a bother, a pain the size of Mount Hermon.

Seth scooped up a sharp rock from the ground. He rolled the rock around in his hand, feeling the jagged edges. He willed himself not to throw it at his sister, who had stopped just out of earshot. He clenched his jaw so tight his teeth hurt. He spun on his heels and heaved the stone so hard, it shattered on the target rock.

"Good one," David said.

"I wish it had shattered on her head," Seth said.

The other boys nodded their agreement.

CHAPTER 3

Seth dragged himself home. He hated every rock, every stone, every tree he saw. He hated them all, and he didn't know why.

Prove it, David and Joshua had said—more or less. *Prove you don't like your sister more than you like us. Prove you're a guy like one of us.*

What did he need to prove? Did he like his sister more than his friends? *No! I have much more fun with my friends than with Talitha! She's boring. She likes stupid things. She's a girl. She'll never know Torah.*

Seth picked up a rock, threw it at a tree, and missed. *Well, she may know Torah, but she shouldn't.* Girls were only supposed to know enough Torah to help them behave and teach their children well. Maybe there was no law that said that, but . . .

He kicked a rock. It bounced down the path. *I wish Talitha could get in trouble for knowing too much. That would be nice.*

But he knew it wouldn't happen. He kicked the rock again. Instead of flying out in front of him, it stuck itself deeper into the dirt. *Just like me. Stuck. How am I going to prove to my friends how important they are to me?*

They had given him one week to come up with something—and do it.

Seth shuffled into the courtyard of his family's home. His mother, slender and brown-haired, sat cross-legged on a mat, pouring grain into the center of two round, flat stones. She grabbed hold of a stick that was stuck in a hole in the top stone and began turning the mill.

The shade of an old olive tree draped a cool blanket over her. Even so, sweat stood out on her upper lip and forehead. She wore her simple work dress. The only time she wore her purple tunic with an embroidered sash was on the Sabbath, when they went to synagogue. Seth thought she looked pretty when she wore her purple tunic and wished she could wear it every day.

Without even a greeting, Seth blurted, "Talitha's already talked to you, hasn't she? What did she say this time?"

He hoped Talitha hadn't told his mother about the bird. His sister was always telling their mother stories about him and his friends. *I wish she'd tell the good things too. Like when we helped the old, crippled woman when she fell. Or when we gathered the quail that escaped from Sarai's basket.* No, Talitha only told the bad stories, the stupid things.

"What she said isn't important," his mother said, brushing a stray strand of hair out of her eyes.

"It is to me," Seth insisted. "She's always lying about me."

"Is everything she's ever told me about you a lie?" she asked.

Seth stared at the ground. "No."

"Then she doesn't always lie, does she?" His mother's voice was soft. She hardly ever raised her voice to anyone for any reason. It was just one of the things he liked about his mother. She might not be the loudest in the village, but she was the best.

"No," he said, his voice soft, matching hers. "Talitha doesn't always lie."

His mother nodded. She added more grain and turned the flat stone wheels that crushed the grain between them.

Seth watched, remembering his sister's taunts, her refusal to leave him and his friends alone, and his anger flashed. "I hate her," he announced.

"Seth," his mother said, looking up briefly. "You don't hate her."

He remembered that David and Joshua didn't want to be his friends anymore. "I do hate her."

"What does she do that's bad enough to hate?" she asked.

"She spies on us and then makes fun of us later." Seth plopped down in front of her. He dug his toes into the soft dirt.

"If you don't talk about foolish things, she will have nothing to tease you about," his mother said.

"She finds a way to tease us about Torah," Seth said.

His mother's worn, sun-darkened hands continued to turn the stones. Flour began to spill out from between them. She looked at the powder as she spoke. "I've talked to her about that. She won't do it again."

"But, Mother! What about her coming and trying to do things only boys should do?"

A wistful smile crossed her face. It was the same one that appeared whenever she was about to tell him something from her own childhood. This time, though, she didn't tell a story. She stopped her grinding and looked at him, still smiling. "If you let her join you, she might become bored and leave."

"No, she wouldn't." Seth didn't like the churning in his stomach. He didn't like the bad taste in his mouth. He didn't like his sister.

"She's your only sister."

"A good thing," Seth mumbled.

"What was that, Seth? I didn't hear you."

"Nothing, Mother."

"Where is your gratitude to God that you have a sister?" She poured more grain into the stones.

"Does God want us to be grateful for things that are bad?"

His mother stopped her grinding and looked into his eyes. "You know the answer to that, Seth."

Seth sighed. *I know the answer, all right. I hate the answer as much as I hate Talitha.* He wanted to spit in the dirt but couldn't. He knew he was supposed to be grateful for all God gave. Grateful to the God who gave good things. And the God who allowed bad things. They were to always be grateful.

But Seth couldn't stop there. "Should we be grateful even for sisters who make us lose our friends?"

The grinding stopped. Seth's mother looked at him with such love, he had to look away. "It would hurt to lose friends, but it would hurt worse to lose a sister," she said.

Seth stared at the ground. He thought about that, but it didn't seem right. It would hurt more to lose his friends; he knew it.

His mother cupped her hand underneath his chin and raised his face toward hers. "If your friends would ask you to choose between them and your sister, they aren't good friends at all. And if you would lose them simply because your sister can be a pest sometimes, they can't be very good friends."

She let go of his chin and went back to her work. "Here, gather the flour, and I'll make your favorite bread."

Seth's eyebrows rose. She called Talitha a pest? He took a clay bowl and began to scoop up the flour from the tray around the millstones.

"Your sister won't always be in this house," said his mother. "She'll be betrothed soon, and then she'll be married. You'll miss her when she's gone."

Seth couldn't imagine that. She couldn't leave soon enough. And miss her? He planned to throw a party when she left! But he said nothing.

He watched the expression on his mother's face change as she continued grinding. There was a frown and then a slight smile. She didn't look up as she spoke. "If you don't like how things are going with your sister, you can change them."

"How?" Seth stopped scooping flour. "I've tried to change her. I've asked her to stop. I've asked her to go away. Nothing works."

"I didn't say to change *her*. I said you need to change something in the way you get along."

Seth sat down and hugged his knees. "What am I supposed to do?"

His mother looked at him carefully and then back at her work. "What have you wanted to do?"

Seth didn't hesitate. "I'd like to make a wall in our room so I don't have to see her."

His mother's knuckles turned white as she grasped the wood handle and turned it. "Do you think this is the way to change things?"

Yes! he wanted to shout. *Then I can pretend she doesn't exist!* Seth swallowed the words, knowing his mother wouldn't like that answer. "I think it might help," he said quietly.

His mother stopped grinding. She didn't look at Seth but at the stones. Her small smile spread across her face. "Yes. You may make a wall in your room so you don't have to see her."

Seth stared at her. He hadn't expected his mother to agree. He'd thought for months about building a wall, but he never thought he'd get to do it. He smiled to himself. His dream was about to come true!

Best of all, it'll prove to my friends that they're important, and Talitha isn't!

"Tomorrow," his mother said, smiling as if she had some kind of secret. "You may start building tomorrow, after your studies."

CHAPTER 4

That night, as they usually did during the six hot and dry months of the year, Seth and his family ate their evening meal in the courtyard. It was cooler and brighter outside. Seth liked it; he could stretch out a bit more. He didn't even mind helping his mother lay out the round reed mat upon which they put the dishes of food.

Tonight there was baked fish and fresh bread. To Seth, the smell was better than any perfume. It would only fill his nostrils, though. The food itself, cooked with dill and garlic and onion, would also fill his stomach.

After the hot food, there were split, juicy melons to share. The sticky juice would run down his face and arms, and he would sprint down to the cool lake to wash it off. When he was younger, he liked playing in the dirt after eating a good melon. The dirt would stick to him in patterns and streaks. Then he and David and Joshua would chase after the smaller children until they screamed.

Seth looked at the spread and smiled. This was his favorite meal. *I wonder if Mother made this on purpose for me?*

When everything was ready, they all lay on their left sides. As required, Seth fingered the fringe at the bottom of his tunic to help him remember God's commandments while his father prayed: "Thanks be to Him, the Lord our God, who has given us bread from the earth."

"Amen," the family said together.

Many times Seth didn't feel close to this God. Yet when he prayed and let the knotted tassel that stood for the commandments of the Lord run through his fingers, he was again amazed that this powerful, almighty

God had chosen the Israelites to be His people. Why would God choose *them* to give His law to? Why would He choose *them* to show His mighty power in battle after battle? It made Seth feel special and important. At these moments, nothing else mattered but God.

Tonight the moment of closeness flew as soon as he opened his eyes. Since his parents weren't looking, Talitha threw him a smirk. He knew exactly what it meant. She thought he was going to get into trouble for whatever she'd told their mother earlier.

But this time her sassy look didn't make him want to jump up and put his hands around her throat and shake some sense into her. This time when she smirked, he didn't feel like his fist might smack her a good one. This time he had a secret of his own. He hoped his return smile was more of a sneer. *I'm going to build a wall. So how do you like that one, my pesky sister?*

His sister tried her aggravating look several more times, but his return smiles confused her. Soon she looked uncomfortable.

Good, thought Seth.

Next came evening prayers and discussion, which Seth usually loved. It was a time when he had his father practically to himself. He could ask stupid questions, and his friends wouldn't laugh—only Talitha would. He could ask smart questions, and his friends wouldn't think he was showing off. He could listen to the wisdom of the proverbs of King Solomon. He could give his ideas about the Messiah—who he might be and when he might come.

At those times Seth would try to imitate the gentle way his father moved his smooth, clean hands. Seth was proud of his father's hands. Because they weren't singed brown by the sun or hardened by manual labor, it meant his father was someone special, a respected elder in the community. Whenever he and his father walked through the village, and especially when they journeyed to towns farther away, Seth wanted to bring attention to his father's hands so everyone would know how special he was.

But even though Seth looked forward to conversations with his father, he couldn't seem to concentrate tonight.

"Esau gave up what?" Seth's father asked him.

"His birthright," Seth answered flatly.

"What was more important?" His father stroked his beard many times with his fine hands. Seth knew this meant he was getting frustrated.

"Food," Seth said.

"Seth," his father asked, "where are your questions? Where are your well-thought-out answers? The story of Jacob and Esau reminds us that God's laws are higher than our ways. We must learn how placing the wrong things above the right things—even for a few moments—can hurt us for the rest of our lives."

Seth nodded. But he wasn't really paying attention.

His father ran his fingers through his curls, which were as thick as Seth's. Seth knew this meant he was about to be dismissed.

"Seth," his father said in his quiet tone, "if you cannot participate, perhaps it would be best for you to get along to bed."

It was intended as punishment, but Seth was glad for it. He could lie on his bed and dream of the wall he would build. "Yes, Father," he said.

He jumped up and moved from the courtyard toward the bedroom—a room just large enough for him and his sister to sleep in. *With a thin wall in between*, he thought. Passing Talitha on the way, he couldn't miss the twist of her mouth and the light of pleasure in her eyes—as if she'd won some unspoken game.

Glancing back, he watched as his sister sat on the mat he'd just vacated. "Father," she said, her voice filled with eagerness and wonder. "What do you think really happened at the Tower of Babel? Did families get to stay together?"

Talitha was thrilled to have Father all to herself. Tonight Seth didn't care.

Entering the bedroom, he dropped to his lightly padded mat and lay on his back. He put his hands behind his neck and stared at the ceiling, not even trying to sleep. It was time to plan his wall.

He rolled over and lifted a few flagstones from the floor. He drew the outline of the wall in the dirt. He could see in his mind the digging he and his friends would do: They would laugh, and Joshua would get messy mixing the clay and water, and they would probably end up in a clay fight. David would drip with sweat, lifting heavy stones. They would work hard like real men.

It would be the best day.

Later, when Talitha tiptoed into the room, he pretended to be asleep. He was still awake when she fell asleep. Listening to his sister's slow, easy breathing reminded him that soon he wouldn't hear that anymore. He wouldn't have to remember that his sister was in the room. He could stare at the wall and pretend.

Life was going to be sweet.

The next day in school, Seth kept yawning. His hands kept smacking together as if they had a life of their own. He'd get frustrated with them and sit on them. But that didn't seem to help. Soon they'd be doing something else they shouldn't.

His father, a very patient man, glanced at him occasionally, his eyes willing Seth to sit still and pay attention. But it seemed impossible. When Seth's arms weren't twining around each other, his toe drew invisible designs on the cobblestone floor.

Seth looked around at the class, twenty-three boys of all ages, as his father asked a question. "What was Joseph accused of doing?"

Several hands shot up. Seth bit his lip and watched his toe. He knew the answer. He'd answered this one before. But his mind was filled with walls. Walls of Jericho. Walls for the Egyptians. Walls of water. *Now if Joseph had built a wall instead of . . . instead of . . . Why can't I think of what it was he did?*

"What was the result of his actions?" his father asked.

Seth stared at the raised hands around him. Who had answered the last question? What was the answer? He licked his dry lips. *We need a water break, Father,* he thought. That made him think about how much water they'd need to make the clay and dirt just right for building . . .

He looked over at David and Joshua, who also squirmed in their seats. He'd already told them about the wall. He looked at his father, who stroked his beard, and wondered whether the man would soon run his fingers through his hair and throw Seth and his friends out of synagogue school for the day.

That might not be such a bad thing, Seth thought. Then he sighed. If they left, the schoolwork would be difficult to make up.

Seth put on his best serious look. He drew his eyebrows together. He cupped his chin in his hand. He nodded when his father said something really important. But soon he discovered he was thinking about the height of the wall. Should they make it all in one day? Or would they have to let some of it dry before they began again? In the dark room, it would take longer to dry . . .

Hands went up and down around him. Voices spoke, brief moments of noise altering his thoughts.

"Joseph could have been stoned if the Law had already been in place," one student offered. *Stones. The best stones are along the shore just beyond where the boats rest.*

"Joseph never got a chance to prove he didn't do it," someone said behind him. *We all need a chance. A chance to dig. Joshua will want to dig the most. David will just get mad if he doesn't get a chance.*

His father's voice ran smoothly, like a stream without rocks. Seth let it wash over him without penetrating his thoughts. The only thing that pulled him back was hearing his name.

"Seth? How long was Joseph in prison?"

Seth's mouth went dry. He'd been caught.

Thinking fast, he decided that if he said some number confidently, it would at least look as though he'd been listening. "Six and one-half years."

Seth's father shook his head while the other boys snickered. "Please pay attention," his father said.

Seth sighed. He had to obey. He was the only boy in class who'd have to deal with the results late into the night if he didn't.

His father moved toward him and then stood right in front of Seth. He peered at Seth again, his eyes boring right into his son's. The man stroked his beard, looking like a giant even though he wasn't very tall. Seth gulped, waiting for the fingers to go through the curls. Nervously he ran his fingers through his own hair.

Finally his father broke into a smile. He bent down and said softly, "Pay attention."

Seth nodded. He squirmed in his seat. *It won't be long now.*

5

"I'll get the water" was the first thing Joshua said when the boys gathered in Seth's room.

"That's a girl's job," David said.

"But I need it for a man's work," Joshua reminded him. "I'm going to build a wall."

They all grinned and slugged each other on the arm. They stared at the ground for a few moments, basking in the fun they were about to have.

"What are we going to do first?" David asked.

"Dig, you goat," Joshua said.

Seth spoke up. "First we have to gather what we need. David and I will find rocks while you get the water."

The boys split up and then returned a short time later with their supplies.

Seth got to dig first, since it was his wall. As he plunged the shovel into the packed ground, a shiver of delight went through him. *This,* he thought, *will be all the proof they need.*

"Did you see all those people out there on the hill by the lake?" Joshua asked.

"How could anyone miss them?" David said.

"What do you think was going on?" Joshua said.

The boys looked at Seth for the answer. Since his father was the synagogue ruler, no community event happened without his father's knowledge—and usually not without his invitation and plan. Seth shrugged. "I don't know. Maybe it's just a traveling storyteller."

"Are you tired yet?" Joshua interrupted.

"No!" Seth said. "I'll let you have a turn in just a minute. Let me at least dig the outline."

"I hope it isn't that rabbi Jesus," David said. He started putting some of the discarded dirt into a bucket. "I mean, some think he's a good teacher and all, but . . ."

Joshua didn't hesitate to speak what he thought. "If he's telling his stories, all the people in town will block the streets. It'll be harder to get more water if we need it."

Seth frowned. He hadn't thought of that. Ever since Rabbi Jesus had chosen Capernaum as his temporary home, no one ever knew what would happen next. No one knew when he was going to be in town and when he wasn't. He was kind of like the wind, some people said. You couldn't know when it might show up and make a mess of things. All three boys sighed and looked at each other.

Seth drew a line across the middle of the ditch he'd started. "Here. Your turn. Dig this half." Seth handed Joshua the shovel.

Joshua dug quickly, his portion done in no time. He handed David the shovel.

David kept talking. "I was going to say that too many people are believing what he says."

Seth added water to the bucket of dirt. "We really shouldn't say anything bad about a rabbi," he said.

"We weren't really," Joshua said quickly. "I just meant that today it would kinda hamper our work if he was teaching. He really is a good teacher, though," he added. He paused. "Have you seen Peter the fisherman lately? My dad says he's gone most of the time following this rabbi. And when he does come back to fish, all he can talk about are all the things Jesus has done."

David leaned on the shovel and looked at Joshua skeptically. "Does anyone believe Peter? He's always saying or doing something stupid. I sure wouldn't believe anything he says." He scooped out the last two shovelfuls of dirt.

Joshua shrugged. "I don't know. The stories are pretty amazing. My dad seems to think Peter must be telling the truth." He scooped out some mud and plopped it in the hole.

"My father respects Rabbi Jesus," Seth told them as he laid the first stone in the ditch on top of the layer of mud. "He doesn't understand why so many of the others fight about Jesus all the time."

"I've heard he's healed people," Joshua said, packing mud around the stones Seth was placing in the shallow ditch.

"Really?" Seth asked. "I'd like to see that. But I've never even been in the right place to hear him tell a story."

David frowned. He put his hands behind his back and paced the small room. Five steps over. Five steps back. "My father says Jesus is nothing but trouble. He teaches things that aren't right."

"Aren't rabbis supposed to make us think?" Joshua asked, standing up to face David. "Aren't they supposed to get us to look at things differently?"

David lifted his chin. His eyes narrowed. "But when their words are blasphemy . . ."

Joshua tipped his head back and laughed. "He hasn't said anything that would make God less. He doesn't curse God or deny Him. He speaks of Him as though he knows Him very well. Just because he speaks the truth about Pharisees like your father . . ."

In a blur of flesh, fabric, and fist, Joshua was on the ground, rubbing his chin. David stood over him.

"Never talk about my father like that!" David yelled.

Seth yanked David away. "Quit it! Let's finish building our wall. If talking about Jesus is going to cause fights, then let's find something else to talk about." He glared at each of his friends. "Got it?"

Both nodded.

"Let's work," Seth added.

Joshua bent over to slap some mud between the rocks. David and Seth exchanged a look. Seth picked up a wad of mud. He flung it at Joshua's backside. Thwack!

Without seeming to pay any attention to the wad of mud that hit him, Joshua flicked his wrist. Mud flew and smacked Seth's cheek. David dropped a rock on top of the other rocks, just a bit too hard, and mud pellets sprayed them all. "War!" Seth shouted, and soon they were all covered with mud.

After the war, it took them another two hours of singing loudly and badly, punching each other, and casually throwing a few more rounds of mud wads at each other before they had a nice wall about chest high. Seth figured that was enough, especially since the work was so slow. The mud in the wall began to dry quickly in the heat of the day, but they all knew it wasn't ready for the final coat. That would have to wait till tomorrow, after the inside of the wall had dried.

As they stood admiring their work and wondering what exactly to do next, they heard a gasp from the doorway. "What are you doing in my room?" Talitha cried, her hands on her hips.

David and Joshua looked at Seth. Seth shook his head.

"Well?" she demanded.

"It's my room too," Seth said.

She jerked her head at David and Joshua. "It's not *theirs*."

"I'm building a wall," Seth said, folding his arms across his chest.

"Why?" she asked.

David and Joshua started to snicker.

"So I don't have to look at you or listen to you every night," Seth said. "It will be a constant reminder to you that I don't want you being a pest. That I don't want you around. That I don't even *like* you."

Seth looked at David and Joshua to see if his words were harsh enough for them. Surely this would be enough of a test of his friendship. *They'll see I'm their friend first, and a brother second.*

He was glad to see them smiling, with a sort of hardness around their eyes. It was as if they were ready for a battle—one they knew they would win.

Talitha didn't move. Seth expected tears to form little pools in her eyes, like they always did when she wanted Seth to get in trouble. Then she would burst into full-blown crying and run to tattle on him. He waited.

Instead, her eyes narrowed. Her crossed arms tightened. She leaned forward. Seth and his friends leaned forward too.

"You're all stupid!" she hissed, spittle spraying all three boys. "Do you think I care about what little smelly boys think?"

They jerked back, wiping their faces. As Seth's arm moved away from his eyes, he saw Talitha's foot swing forward.

"No!" he shouted.

Seth reached his arm out to stop her, but it was too late. He and Joshua and David stood staring in horror as the wall tumbled into pieces at their feet. Clumps of mud flew about, sticking in globs on their arms, their legs, their clothes.

Talitha stomped out into the sunshine.

The boys stared at the remains of their masterpiece. Kneeling beside the ruins, Seth picked up a rock and examined it. The mud had been wet enough to crumble but dry enough that the rocks wouldn't stick together again. The only way to rebuild the wall would be to haul the rocks to the river, wash off the hardening mud, and start all over again.

"All our hard work," Seth said, his voice quavering a lot more than he wanted it to. *Don't cry,* he told himself. *Then they'll* really *think you're a weakling.*

"Stupid!" David said, kicking at the one rock that remained on top of another. "If I was her father—"

Joshua interrupted. "What do you mean, if you were her father? If I were her *brother* . . ." He let his voice trail off as he glared at Seth. His right fist slammed into his left palm, over and over.

"What?" Seth said, his mouth going dry.

"If I were her brother," Joshua said, "I would have at least planted my fist in the middle of her face. I can't believe you let her get away with that."

Seth opened his mouth, but no words came out.

"You haven't done it yet, you know," David said.

"Done what?" Seth mumbled, his hope as crumpled as the wall.

"Proven to us that you can stand up to your sister," David replied.

Seth stood, pointing to the pile of rocks. "That was going to be it."

Joshua and David traded looks and began to laugh. "You're kidding, right?" Joshua asked. "That lousy wall wasn't what we had in mind."

"It has to be something public," David said.

"And humiliating," Joshua added.

David gave Seth a fake smile. "You have five more days."

The boys stepped over the mess and walked out of the house.

It took Seth half an hour to get the rubble out of his room and haul it behind the house. When he was done, he went to the courtyard and sat in front of his mother.

He wanted to scream but knew his mother wouldn't appreciate it. He put his head down so she wouldn't see the fire in his eyes.

She'd been working at the loom, watching him while he hauled the rocks. She'd said nothing. But he could tell she knew what had happened.

After a minute or so of silence had passed, Seth's mother spoke. "So what do you think this means?" she asked.

"If I knew, I wouldn't be here," he said, angry.

"What did you expect would happen?" she asked.

Seth picked up a stick and drew designs in the dirt. He shrugged his shoulders.

His mother said nothing. She sat still, her hands in her lap.

After a few moments, Seth said, "I thought she would leave me alone."

"What did I tell you that you needed to do?"

"Nothing."

"I told you that you needed to change something in the way you get along with her. I knew the wall wouldn't give you what you wanted."

"Then why did you let me build it?" Seth grumbled.

She smiled. "I knew you would learn something important."

"And what should I have learned?"

Again his mother sat silent, her hands still, her mouth restraining a smile.

Seth jabbed at the ground with his stick. Then he swirled it around quickly, destroying his dirt drawing. "Aren't you going to tell me?"

"No," she said.

He got up and began to walk toward the courtyard entrance.

"Come back and sit," she told him.

Seth stomped back and sat down hard, hoping his mother would see the unfairness of it all.

"Sit until you can understand what it is you've learned."

"I've learned not to listen to my mother," he blurted.

"Was it my idea to build the wall?"

"No."

"Think, Seth. Stay here until you know."

Seth swatted a gnat that kept trying to get close to his mouth. He knew his mother would make him stay until he figured it out.

Think. Think back. He forced himself to remember the conversation he'd had with her about building the wall. Well, it wasn't really about the wall. It was about doing something to make things better between Talitha and him.

He sighed. "Building the wall didn't do anything to make things better. It only made things worse." He thought about what she would like to hear. "If I build a wall, it keeps Talitha away from me. But it only makes her madder. It doesn't make her nicer."

His mother clapped her hands once, her face breaking into a full grin. "Yes. Go and play. But think about what you can do to change what you say or do with your sister that doesn't keep her away but honors her as your sister."

Seth walked into the street, letting his stick drag on the ground. He didn't want to think about what would honor his sister. He had to think of what he could do to humiliate her.

If he didn't, he would lose his friends.

Nothing could be worse than that.

*P*rove it.

"How?" Seth said aloud as he hiked up the dirt path worn into the side of the hill. "How can I prove that I agree Talitha is a pest? How can I prove my friends are most important?"

Usually he asked his friends for help on things like this. But this time he had to come up with something all by himself.

Talitha hates to wear wet or dirty clothes. Seth bit his lip as he thought and then talked to himself. "If I got her soaking wet and then pushed her in the mud, she'd have to walk through town all filthy." He frowned. "No, she'd just rinse off in the lake. She'd be wet, but it wouldn't be enough."

He could dye her clothes blue or purple. But she might like that.

He could dye Eli's sheep—put different colored spots all over them. No, that would make Eli mad, but it wouldn't really affect Talitha.

His mind went blank. He couldn't think of anything else.

Looking over his shoulder, he saw the lake sparkling in the sun. He turned around and kept walking up the hill—backward. He could see boats here and there. It looked so perfect from his place on the hill. Yet at any minute a storm could blow in and chew up the water something fierce.

Just like Talitha, he thought. Things were perfect without her. Then she would come in and mess everything up.

How can I mess everything up for her? he wondered.

Turning, he continued up the hill to the very top. A breeze blew through the grass, making a shushing sound that almost sounded like the tiny waves that lapped the shore of the lake.

He found his favorite rock and sat on it, but soon he was fidgeting. He hated being alone. It was too quiet. Mostly it was boring.

His mind seemed sluggish as he kept trying to think of things to do to Talitha. Suddenly he realized he didn't *want* to do anything to her. He wanted her to leave him and his friends alone, but he didn't really want to do anything mean to her. He just longed to play with his friends—with nobody disturbing them.

I could tell David and Joshua to forget it, he thought. But then every day would be like today. Alone. Sitting on a rock. No one to test his skills against. No one to compete with. No one to recite with. No one to wrestle with.

I've got to think of something good.

He could remember something "good" that had happened to Talitha once. They hadn't even planned it, but it was perfect.

He, David, and Joshua had been having a pomegranate-seed-spitting contest, splattering a nearby rock with blood-red juice and white seeds. Talitha had appeared after dark, bringing the message that the boys' mothers were looking for them. The boys convinced her to tell a scary story first, so she sat on a rock and told a tale that made them all shiver. Then, following her into town, they were astonished to see that red spots from hundreds of pomegranate seeds were speckling the back side of her robe, all the way down to the hem. She'd chosen the worst rock to sit on!

"She'll think we did it on purpose," David had whispered as they followed her. They'd all started snickering.

Talitha had been embarrassed at first, and furious later. Seth had managed to convince his mother and father that he and his friends hadn't done anything wrong.

Now, sitting on the hilltop and staring at the water below, Seth wondered what his friends might want him to do. Would they be satisfied if Talitha was just embarrassed? No. They wanted him to do something harsh. Something that would prove to her what a girl she was and how she didn't belong.

At that moment he knew what he would do.

He climbed on top of the rock and jumped off. Then he ran down the mountain to find his friends.

The next day the boys pooled their lunches. Joshua brought fish broth. David brought lamb stew. Seth had told his mother he was extra hungry, and so he brought a double portion of a lentil soup she'd made.

"Pour it in here," Seth said, holding out a clay pot. He picked up a stick from the ground and stirred the three together. "Anyone want to taste?" Seth asked.

David shook his head.

"Sure!" Joshua said. He took a drink. "Delicious."

"It's not supposed to be delicious," David complained. "It's supposed to be gross."

"But it should taste okay at first," Seth said. "We want her to eat it all until she gets to the special prize."

The boys all looked at each other and grinned.

Kneeling, Seth picked up a small handful of dirt. He dumped it into the pot and stirred, his heart starting to thump.

He removed a pouch from the cloth tied around his waist and crushed it against a rock. When he opened it, he saw the remains of several beetles and bugs mixed together. He put that into the pot too, and stirred.

He looked up at David and Joshua. "Should we really do this?"

David nodded. "It's this—or you're on your own."

Seth swallowed. He forced a fake smile.

"It's your choice," David said. "Friends or not?"

Seth sighed and took another pouch from his waist. "I was going to save this for something else, but I guess it would go okay here." He opened the pouch and slipped in the special surprise, shaking it from the piece of goat hide it was wrapped in. He was careful not to touch the surprise itself.

Joshua's eyes grew especially bright. "This is going to be *real* good."

Moments later the boys were searching the town for Talitha. They found her and some of her friends by the lake. *Perfect,* Seth thought. *This will please Joshua and David even more—an audience.*

"Hi," the boys said, greeting Talitha and the other girls.

"We wanted to apologize," Seth said, trying to keep the apprehension out of his voice. "So we brought you a peace offering. It's soup." At that moment he felt sick inside and happy, all rolled into one.

Talitha looked at them skeptically.

"It's good," Joshua said. "I tried it."

Talitha took the pot. She smelled the soup. It had lost some of its warmth, but the aroma was still enticing. "Who made it?" she asked.

"My mother," David told her.

"Your mother is the best cook in town," Talitha said, still looking at the soup warily.

David beamed. "It's lamb."

Talitha brightened. "I *love* lamb." Then she frowned. "It smells like fish too."

"It's a new type of soup she's trying," David said. "Fish and lamb together. Soon all the women in Capernaum will be making it."

Seth bit his lip. He didn't want to say anything and mess everything up. He was afraid he'd shout, "Don't, Talitha!" or that he would grab the pot and yank her head back by her hair and force it down her throat. He wanted her to dump it. He wanted her to drink it. Mostly he wanted Joshua and David to always be his friends.

Talitha looked at each of them. Then she took a tiny sip. She took another. Then she drank a lot more. "Thank you," she said. "I was famished, and this is good. And I don't have to go home to eat."

Talitha passed her lunch around and the other girls each had a swallow.

Seth thought he was going to burst if she didn't get to the bottom soon.

"What are these dark things in it?" Talitha asked.

"Special spices!" David said. Seth thought he sounded a bit too eager.

Talitha continued to drink. When she neared the bottom, Joshua couldn't keep quiet any longer. "There's also dirt, a few mashed bugs, and . . ."

Joshua never got to the last ingredient. Talitha screamed and dropped the pot. As it broke, a dead lizard rolled out, its soft, white belly shining in the sun.

Talitha and her friends stared at the lizard. Talitha clutched her stomach. Her eyes grew wide. She put her hand to her mouth, and her words could barely be heard. "There was a *lizard* in my soup."

Joshua and David laughed.

Seth winced. His sister's whimpering struck him deep inside. *You betrayed me,* she seemed to be saying.

"A *dead* lizard," Talitha said faintly. "I'm . . . unclean." Her friends gasped and looked in horror at each other.

Joshua nodded. "You'll get over it." He poked at the belly of the lizard. A little bit of soup squirted from its mouth.

Talitha bent over and then emptied her stomach on the ground next to the creature. Her friends turned away, looking as if they were about to do the same.

David and Joshua set off at a run, and Seth followed. "You did it!" David declared over his shoulder.

Seth let relief take over, washing away all doubts over whether he had done the right thing. He joined in as the other boys laughed, and accepted their congratulatory slaps on his back.

That night at dinner Seth had his parents all to himself. At first he was nervous, certain Talitha had told on him.

"Talitha's not feeling well," his mother said.

"What's wrong with her?" Seth asked.

"Her stomach is unsettled," his mother answered. "It's probably something she ate."

"What did she eat?" Seth asked, his heart pounding.

"Something some of her friends gave her."

His mother said nothing more about it. Seth wondered why Talitha hadn't told. Then he smiled. *I guess we really did silence her. Success!* He couldn't stop smiling as he ate a double portion of fish and fruit that evening.

The next morning on the way to school, Seth could hardly contain his excitement. *It worked,* he thought, grinning. He felt so giddy. He kept punching David and Joshua until David said, "Quit it!"

Seth stuck out his foot and tripped Joshua, who fell into the tall grass. Joshua reached up and pulled Seth to the ground with him. They rolled around, wrestling until Seth pinned Joshua.

I can't believe it, Seth thought. *Everything worked perfectly.* Talitha would know better than to mess with *him* anymore. He put a swagger to his walk, his chin in the air, and marched ahead of the other two. "Hello, *boys*," he said to a group of younger classmates.

The boys turned to look at him. Instead of looking at Seth as though he were a smarter, more important elder classmate, they looked at each other and burst into laughter.

Seth turned to Joshua and David and shrugged.

Joshua popped a piece of dried fish into his mouth. He spoke as he chewed. "I think I'm going on the fishing boat again the day after Sabbath."

"How can you miss synagogue school?" David asked, shocked.

"Father thinks learning my trade is more important," Joshua replied.

"There is nothing more important than God's Word," David said in a lofty tone.

"Ah, but one must learn to be a man," Seth added, feeling wise and important.

Joshua dug his finger into his ear as they waited for David's approval. David shook his head. "The Law's the Law."

"Look," Joshua said, pointing at the younger boys, using the finger he had withdrawn from his ear. "Are they laughing at us?"

Seth shook his head. "Of course not. Why would they be laughing at us?" His happy feeling grew and grew. He wished he could make something that could float into the sky. He'd hold on to it and go up and up—just like his insides were doing right now.

"Then what's going on?" Joshua said, popping another piece of fish into his mouth.

"Probably laughing over something dumb," Seth said. "Little boys always laugh over dumb things."

As they got closer and closer to the synagogue, it seemed that *all* the boys around them were laughing about something.

"What are we missing?" Joshua finally said to one group of young boys. They didn't answer but laughed even harder and ran.

"Baby," said a voice behind them. They turned to see a group of older boys snickering.

"I didn't know you wet your bed, David," one of them said. "A big holy boy like you?"

David's face grew dark.

"Is that why your father is always offering sacrifices?" the older boy asked. "Because of his unclean son?"

"That's not true," Joshua defended his friend.

"Yeah, nose picker?" taunted another boy. "We heard you have such a problem that your mother puts cloths over your hands at night."

Joshua's mouth flapped open and closed like a fish's.

"What's wrong with you guys?" Seth said. "Why are you making up these things?"

"No one's making up anything," the largest boy said. "Thanks to your sister, Talitha, we know all the interesting things about you."

"Like you suck your thumb sometimes when you sleep," the boy next to him said.

Seth's head swam. Everything felt jumbled in his head. He wanted to deny it—but he couldn't. He *had* sucked his thumb in the middle of the night when he'd awakened, scared. But not recently. Not *really* recently.

He tried changing the subject. "What makes you think you know anything? You don't know if anything Talitha said is true."

The big boy laughed. "You forget she's a woman. And all women talk. They talk while they wash clothes. They talk while they cook together, while they weave together. And I guess Talitha just listens well."

"She's making sure all the kids in the synagogue know all your secrets," a small but older boy said.

With a final round of laughter, the boys moved past Seth, David, and Joshua.

David and Joshua moved in front of Seth and stopped. Joshua's arms looked larger, his legs longer and stronger as he stood like a soldier defending something. David crossed his arms, and his eyebrows drew together.

"No more!" Joshua said. "I'm not going to hang around with some kid whose sister tells things about *me*. Don't even *think* about being my friend anymore."

David glared. "Enough! I've had enough!" Without another word they turned toward the synagogue and quickly walked away.

Seth stared after them. The farther they got from him, the emptier he felt. He wanted to run after them, but he knew it was over.

Other boys on their way to the synagogue passed him, laughing as they went. Did they believe what Talitha had said about him?

He barely made it through synagogue school. He was glad they had a visiting rabbi who taught them his own interpretation of Scripture. Visiting rabbis usually didn't pay as much attention to the boys. Seth had the chance to sit and think.

What am I going to do without my friends? Seth pictured long afternoons trying to remember and recite Scripture alone. He pictured hot days without anyone to pitch rocks with him. He thought about rainy days alone in his house. Alone with *women*.

Talitha did it. Talitha has ruined me. Anger began to seep in. It grew stronger and warmer with each thought.

Seth couldn't wait until school was over.

Talitha sat outside the courtyard of their home. She was embroidering some piece of linen, but Seth didn't care what she was doing. He stomped over to her and stood with his arms crossed. "You've ruined my life!" he told her.

Talitha looked up at him, smiling sweetly. "You know I like games, Seth. And it seems you wanted to play the revenge game."

Seth was so angry he could feel his crossed arms start to shake. Everything seemed to go white. Through a pinhole of sight he could see Talitha's grin as she began to laugh.

Knowing—but not caring—that he was about to get into big trouble, Seth drew back his arm. With all the force he could muster, he slammed his fist into his sister's arm and followed with a kick to her shin.

Talitha's laugh turned into a howl of pain.

Instead of running away to postpone getting in trouble as he usually did, Seth stood still. He wanted to see her hurting. *She deserves it,* he thought.

"Mother!" Talitha screamed.

A moment later Seth's mother appeared, her hand holding up her robe so she didn't trip as she ran. Her face showed a mother's fear. "What happened, Talitha? Are you all right?" She examined her daughter, apparently checking for blood.

Seth straightened himself as tall as he could manage. "I hit her."

Mother slowly turned and looked at him, her fear turning to anger. "You what?"

"She deserved it. She's ruined my life!" The rage continued to pulse through him. His breath came in rapid, short bursts as if he'd been running a long distance.

"Has God given up His throne to you?" his mother asked.

Seth's eyebrows pulled together, confused as he was by the question. "Of course not."

"Yet you take revenge into your own hands? It is only for God to decide whether or not there should be revenge. He also is the only One who decides what kind of revenge there should be. Anyone who takes revenge into his own hands has decided to become a god."

Not this time, Seth thought. God hadn't acted soon enough. God hadn't done His job. Besides, Talitha was playing the revenge game too.

"Go to your father and tell him what you've done," his mother said.

Talitha's tears had stopped. She rubbed her arm.

Seth could tell she held back a smile. He glared at her, turned, and started toward the synagogue.

CHAPTER 7

Powered by an energy that churned inside him, Seth marched past Capernaum's houses and groups of houses called *insulae*. It was as though one of the violent storms that gathered over Galilee had swirled around and gotten sucked inside him. Lightning bolts of thought lit up his mind. He could see Talitha's smirking face with each bolt.

Thunderous anger rumbled through him. He wished it could come out in a way that would make her hurt as much as he did.

So Mother wanted him to be more understanding toward his sister, did she? He'd been understanding long enough. He'd endured her bossy ways for as long as he could remember. He'd listened to her tattle on him about stupid things, as well as things he really shouldn't have done.

A soft rain started to fall. He marched on, getting as mad at the rain as he was at his sister. Why did it have to rain now? The drops felt hot and sticky, not cool and cleansing like a winter rain. Each drop watered his anger, making it grow like a weed.

Pictures flashed through his mind, pictures of everything his sister had done to irritate him, pick at him—torture him. *That's what it is,* he thought. *Torture.*

If she'd ever been even a little bit sorry, he probably could have let some of his anger go. But she never was. The thing was, she *enjoyed* pestering him.

Pictures of Talitha's smirking face taunted him over and over. He clenched his fists. His breath came in shorter and shorter bursts. *How dare she? How dare she ruin my life?*

He kicked over a water pot, wishing it would shatter on the ground. He walked by a tail of onions hanging out to dry. He punched it so hard, the strand flew apart and the onions scattered, rolling across the rain-spotted dirt.

He started to trot and then broke into a run. He could see the synagogue on the hill, growing closer with each step. He didn't want to get there. He didn't want to see his father and be put to work. He didn't want to have to come before his father and see the disappointment on his face.

He also didn't want to spew anger on his father. That wouldn't be accepted, not for one minute. His father controlled anger, letting his jaw muscles work on the problem until he could speak of it without letting the wrong words fly from his mouth. Any outburst from Seth would be reprimanded.

He made a sharp turn and ran up the hill, leaving the town behind. *I hate her,* he thought. *I hate her more than . . .*

The truth was that at the moment, he couldn't think of anything else he hated more.

He ran to the top of the hill, anger driving him, forcing him. He didn't care that his lungs hurt. He didn't care that his muscles screamed at him to take it easy. None of the pain compared to the hurt of losing his friends, of being made to look like a fool in front of all the other boys. *I hate her,* he repeated.

When he reached the top, he stood in the rain, arms swinging, as if he could punch the raindrops. He slapped at them. He kicked the rocks. He didn't care that his sandals might be ruined. "I hate her!" he said aloud, the rain dripping down his face. Then he shouted at the top of his lungs, "I hate her, God! I hate her! I . . . I wish she was *dead*!"

For a moment it felt like the truest thing he had ever said in his life. He tipped his face toward the gray sky and said it again: "I wish Talitha was as dead as that bird! No, I wish she was *more* dead!"

As he said the words, an eerie sort of peace came over him. The anger was still there, but something about voicing the words felt very good.

He moved down the hill slowly, cherishing the words. *I hate her.* He planted his feet carefully, one word for every step. *I wish she was dead.* He smiled to himself.

By the time he reached the synagogue, the rain had made mud in the streets. He took off his sandals underneath the portico of the synagogue. The roof stuck out over stones carefully set into the ground. Unless the wind blew the rain, it stayed dry there.

Seth found his father in the largest room of the synagogue, the room where they held the Sabbath services. "Hello, Father," he said.

"Seth!" his father exclaimed. "You've finally come to help the old man, huh? Come to keep me company in my work?"

Seth wished he felt sorry, but he didn't. He hung his head anyway. It wouldn't hurt to at least *fake* being sorry. "Mother sent me," he said, as if talking to the ground. "I'm in trouble."

Seth looked up in time to see his father's look of joy turn to one of disappointment. Usually seeing that look on his father's face would be enough to dispel his anger and bring about a true sense of sorrow, but not this time. Talitha deserved more than what he had given her. She probably didn't deserve to die, but he wished she would.

Without a sound, his father gave Seth the broom and left the large room. *I hate sweeping, and Father knows it. This is Talitha's fault too.*

Seth began to swipe at the walls, knocking down spiders and webs and dirt. With each swipe he thought of all the bad things that had happened to him because of his sister. With each sneeze from the dust, he wiped his drippy nose with a sleeve and thought, *I hate you, Talitha.*

After what seemed like hours, he turned to see his father looking at him. "I've just had a visit from the widow Shiphrah," Father said. "It seems you have knocked over her water pot and scattered her onions. Do you deny it?"

"No," he mumbled, his nose still dripping.

"Tomorrow you will go help her after synagogue," his father said. "And you won't damage another's property again."

Without waiting for Seth to answer, his father walked away. Seth's anger, already burning like coals in his chest, flared hotter than ever.

At supper Seth was told to sit away from the family, alone. He couldn't hear the others' subdued conversation. He drank his water and ate his dinner of fresh-baked bread and fruit faster than usual. Talitha's loud laughter didn't even make him jealous. He'd lost everything because of her; he certainly didn't want to *eat* with her.

After dinner he slept with his back to her. When he woke in the morning, he didn't even look at her as he left the room.

School was even worse than the day before. Joshua and David acted as if they didn't know him. The other boys laughed and teased him. *"Girl,"* he could hear them say. It was as if he had leprosy. No one wanted to be with him. They might catch the disease called "Talitha."

That night before supper, Seth's mother sat him down underneath the olive tree. "You must speak to your sister and apologize."

Seth dug into the dirt with his toes. He ran his hand through his curly hair. He didn't want to apologize. He wasn't sorry; he wanted to do *more* to her!

Still, he nodded. He stood and went to his sister, who was weaving at the opposite end of the courtyard. He sat in front of her and glared at her. She gave him one of her smiles—the kind that reminded him she was glad for what she had done.

"What did you and your friends do for fun today?" Talitha asked.

"I don't have any friends," Seth hissed.

She wove the yarn deftly in and out of the stretched threads. "*I* have *lots* of friends."

Seth bit his tongue. Then he took a deep breath and spoke. "I'm sorry I hit you!" he said loudly so his mother would hear.

Talitha looked at him. Both of them knew he wasn't sorry at all—and neither was she.

The next day at synagogue school was no better. He volunteered to stay after and sweep, just to give himself something to do.

When he got home, his mother looked worried. "Talitha isn't well," she said. "I need your help. Could you please fetch the evening water from the well?"

Seth stared at her. *Girls'* work? "That's Talitha's job," he said flatly.

"I told you, she's sick."

"Sure," Seth said sarcastically. *This is part of her plan to ruin my life,* he thought. *She can't wait to have the boys see me hauling water.*

His mother put her hands on her hips and tilted her head. "Whether you believe she's sick or not doesn't matter. She isn't well enough to fetch the water. I can't leave my supper. So you must go get it."

Seth picked up the large water pot from the kitchen area. He marched out the gate and through the town. He didn't look at anyone. He knew everyone had to be pointing and laughing. A grown boy fetching water? That was ridiculous!

He stood in line at the well, waiting his turn to get water. He was the only male in the group.

"How is your mother?" a woman named Rebekah asked.

"She's well," Seth muttered.

"And Talitha?" the woman persisted.

"She claims to be ill," Seth said.

Rebekah raised one eyebrow but said nothing more.

Seth filled his pot with water and tried to heft it onto his shoulder. It was heavy and awkward. He realized he'd never done anything with a water pot except tip it to pour water out. Struggling, he still couldn't lift it high enough.

"Let me help," Rebekah said kindly.

Seth let her, but his face burned with embarrassment.

He walked home slowly, trying not to drop the pot or let too much water slosh out of it. By the time he reached home, his hair was completely wet, and his tunic was quite damp.

"Take this soup to Talitha," his mother told him as he set the water pot down. She handed him a small bowl of warm broth.

Seth walked toward their room but changed course when his mother wasn't looking. Behind the house he dumped the contents of the bowl into the dirt.

He went into the room. Talitha lay there, asleep. He waited a few minutes and then returned the empty bowl to his mother. *If Talitha wants supper, she can come out and eat with the rest of us and not be so lazy.*

Three days passed. Seth fumed at his new tasks that only girls did. He fumed at Talitha and her supposed illness. *She looks fine to me,* he thought. So she had a cough. So what? Didn't everyone have a cough at least once each winter? Why not in summer too? She coughed at night and kept him awake, so he slept in the courtyard.

On the two occasions when his mother asked him to take broth to his sister, he dumped it on the ground behind the house. He overheard his parents speaking in worried tones about her. He was sick of seeing Eli every day with his eyebrows pulled together, asking how Talitha was doing. *Don't worry,* he wanted to say. *She's faking it to get attention.*

On the Sabbath, after Seth and Father had returned from services, Talitha called him into the room.

"Seth," she said, her voice weak.

Good job, Talitha, he thought. *You're a great actress. Maybe you should move to Sepphoris and be in their plays.*

"I'm so sorry," she continued. "I was so mean to you and your friends."

Seth looked at her, believing her apology to be fake. At the very least, Mother had probably made her do it.

"Really," Talitha said and then paused as a coughing fit took over. Finally she spoke again. "I thought I was being funny."

"You ruined my life," Seth told her flatly.

"I really am sorry," she said. Her voice was so quiet, Seth had to strain to hear her. "Until I got sick and couldn't see anyone but family, I didn't realize how important friends are. I thought you were making too much of your friends. But I was wrong, Seth."

He stared at her, not sure what to think. She was apologizing, but she certainly wasn't fixing anything.

"Will you forgive me?" she asked, her eyes pleading with him.

He looked right into those eyes but said nothing. His anger kept guard around his heart, not letting anything in that might make him forgive her.

Without a word, he stood up and left.

CHAPTER 8

"She's dying," the man said as he came out of the dark room.

Seth's mother clapped a hand over her mouth.

"You'd better send for her father," the man added.

Seth stared. This man was part of Talitha's game, right? Sure, he was the doctor, but he had to be playing along. Talitha only wanted sympathy. She wanted to get out of doing chores. She wanted Seth to continue to be the laughingstock of all the other kids.

Any minute, he thought, the doctor would laugh and tell them it was all a joke.

Seth waited. Nothing happened.

"Seth," his mother said, her voice choked with fear. "You heard the man. Go get your father."

Seth wanted to say, *But wait, it's only a joke.* He ran into the room and knelt down to look closely at Talitha. Her face was white and shiny with sweat. He touched her forehead, and it felt hot—like clay baking in the sun. Each breath sounded ragged and slow, like a heavy stone dragging through the dirt.

His throat tightened as he realized it was no joke.

He heard his mother's frantic voice behind him. *"Go!"* she shouted.

He turned and ran.

Seth ran blindly, not seeing anything except as obstacles. He dodged the obstacles—sometimes people, sometimes animals, sometimes a pot, sometimes a building. "Seth!" an old woman called. "Slow down! You'll hurt someone!"

I have already hurt someone, he thought. *I've hurt my sister.*

He ran on, taking the shortcut to the synagogue. But people clogged the streets, slowing him down. *Why are they here?* he thought. *What's going on?* He pushed through the people, ignoring their shouts.

I hurt someone. If she dies, it's my fault. He thought of the three times he'd poured her broth into the dirt. Did the broth have some sort of healing medicine? Had he kept her from the medicine she needed?

He stopped. *Was it the lizard stew?* He felt sick. He started moving ahead. He ducked low and tried to move through the gathering crowd. The people seemed to draw closer and closer together. *I wished her dead. I wished my own sister dead.*

Guilt strangled him as he began to shove his fist into people's sides. Their surprise gave him the inches he needed to move ahead. Finally he burst through the last clutch of people and out the other side.

He ran up the last hill to the synagogue. "Father!" he called. "Father, come quick!"

His father appeared at the door of the synagogue. "What is it now, Seth? Are you in trouble again?"

Seth shook his head. "Talitha's dying," he said, his voice squeaking.

His father looked down at the ground. "I must find him," his father said.

"Who?" Seth asked.

"Jesus. I must find Jesus." His father's face was etched with worry and a desperation Seth had never seen.

He's not making sense, Seth thought, shaking his head. "Father, we must get home right away! Didn't you hear me? Talitha is dying!"

"First we find Jesus. He can help us." His father's face twisted in grief. Tears formed in his eyes and then began to roll down his cheeks. Seth had never seen his father cry. Never.

And it's all my fault, Seth thought, feeling sick to his stomach.

He stared at his father's back as the man moved briskly down the hill.

"Father!" Seth shouted, running after him. "Father, you must go home! What can a rabbi teach you now?"

When he reached his father, he held on to the man's sleeve. "Come on, Father. You must come this way."

His father shook him off.

Talitha is almost dead, Seth wanted to shout. But the words wouldn't come out. *I saw her. I know what dead looks like.*

He remembered the bird. He remembered the lizard. Dead things. Limp, with something missing. Talitha was almost there. Why hadn't he realized it before? Why had he thought she was playing?

His father strode toward the crowd Seth had moved through earlier. He, too, tried to break through. But many had gathered to follow Rabbi Jesus and hear what he had to say.

"Teacher!" someone called out. "Do we tithe a tenth of everything, including the broth we make, or only of our first fruits and animals?"

Seth didn't hear whether the rabbi answered. He clung to his father's tunic, the handful of fabric absorbing the sweat of panic that had formed on his palms. He tucked his head down and let his father guide him.

"Rabbi!" he heard his father call.

There was no answer. So many calls of "Rabbi!" and "Teacher!" filled the air. Jesus wouldn't hear one cry above the others. And what about Jesus' disciples? They were known to be rough men. Would they let them get anywhere near the rabbi?

"Rabbi!" his father called again.

Seth felt crushed by the people, all pushing to see Jesus. The earthy smell of warmth and bodies and garlic and olive oil was suffocating.

"Rabbi," his father said, falling at the feet of Jesus.

Seth, still standing, stared at his father. He had never seen his father so humbled before anyone. His father was an important man. He would never bow before anyone but . . .

Seth's eyes grew wider. *Anyone but God.*

His father cried out, his words tumbling fast. "My little daughter is dying. Please come and put your hands on her so that she will be healed and live."

Seth looked up into the rabbi's face. From what people had said about Rabbi Jesus, Seth had expected him to be extra tall, handsome, and powerful-looking. Yet this man looked like any other man from Galilee. Except for his eyes. There was something in his eyes. Seth wished he could say what it was. There was a strength, a kindness, a peace.

Without hesitation, Jesus agreed to come with them.

Seth hung back. He didn't want Jesus to see him. *What if this rabbi can tell what I've done?* he thought.

Seth couldn't hear any more of his father's words to the rabbi, nor the rabbi's words in return. People pressed in around them, calling to Jesus, wanting his attention.

Who is my father that this rabbi would pay attention to him, while he doesn't seem to hear the voices of others? Seth wondered.

Suddenly Jesus stopped. "Who touched My clothes?" he asked.

Seth looked around him. He could barely move with the crush of people. What did Jesus mean? Weren't lots of people touching his clothes?

One of the men who must have been a follower of Jesus said, "You see the people crowding around you."

Rabbi Jesus acted as though he hadn't heard. He kept looking around him to see who had touched him. Then everyone else in the crowd took up looking.

Seth wanted to shout at the rabbi, *My sister is dying! And you wonder who touched you?* He wanted to whisper to his father that this rabbi was going to be of no help at all if he was going to stop every time someone bumped him. *Father!* he wanted to shout. *We need to go,* now!

A woman nearby fell at Jesus' feet. "I touched you," she said quietly. "I wanted to be healed."

The unclean woman, Mariah? Seth shook his head, disgusted. *She should know better.* Because she was unclean, she'd lived outside Capernaum since the day Talitha was born. Seth's mother often took food to leave outside her home. Doctors traveling through were asked to examine her and see if they could help. But no one could.

Seth frowned. Since she had touched the rabbi's clothes, would he have to be unclean too? Seth put his head in his hands. The rabbi was never going to get to Talitha.

Seth lifted his head just in time to see Jesus look straight into the woman's eyes. "Daughter, your faith has healed you."

Seth raised his eyebrows. She was healed? Just like that? Without medicine? Without a doctor?

"Go in peace and be freed from your suffering," Jesus said to her.

Hope jumped in Seth's chest. Jesus had healed Mariah? Everyone had talked about Mariah for as long as he could remember. The way she stood up straight and walked through the crowd, Seth knew she had to be healed. Maybe Jesus *could* heal Talitha!

"Coming through!" Seth heard someone say. "Coming through. We must get to Jairus. We must get to the synagogue ruler."

The crowd parted until Seth's neighbors stood before his father. "Jairus," they said, "we bring you bad news. Your daughter, Talitha, is dead."

Seth's hope crashed. His stomach seemed to turn over, and it felt like someone had just slugged him in the head. Everything seemed wobbly, blurry.

His father's knees buckled, sending him to a kneeling position. But still the man looked up at Jesus as if asking for help.

Father, Seth thought, *dead is dead. Maybe Rabbi Jesus can heal people who are alive, but no one can reverse death. No one.*

One of the neighbors put his hand on the arm of Seth's father. "Why bother the teacher anymore?"

In the same way that Jesus had looked into the eyes of the woman, he looked into the eyes of Seth's father. "Don't be afraid; just believe."

Seth numbly watched his father nod at Jesus, his face full of hope and trust. Seth wanted so badly to trust as his father did. But he couldn't. *How can I trust this Jesus? He's only a rabbi. He's only a man.*

Seth looked up at the deep blue of the sky, as if he might find an answer. The sun was so strong, it seemed to bake the top of his head. He touched his hair, and it felt hot. In this heat, bodies would begin to smell very quickly. The thought made him sick.

How could I have wished this on my own sister?

He stood there, letting the crowd flow around him, as people began to follow Jesus and his father toward Seth's home.

Home? What would home be like without Talitha? His mother would cry a lot, Seth guessed. Otherwise, it would be so quiet. He would have a room all to himself. None of the kids he knew had that.

Talitha, he thought, almost as if he could talk to her. *I don't want my own room. Not like this.*

He walked toward home, his steps slow. Soon he noticed that the crowd was breaking up, the people shuffling off in several directions. Seth ran up to a small man and tugged on his tunic. "Excuse me," he said, "where is everyone going?"

"The teacher said no one could go with him. He will only let the father and three of his men go." The man shook his head and grumbled. "I don't know why he won't allow anyone else to come."

Seth felt more alone than ever. *I can't even go to my own house,* he thought.

He stood in the middle of the street, not knowing what to do.

"Hey, Seth," a voice behind him said.

Seth turned to see David standing there. David looked down his nose at him. "Do you think it was your sister's sin or the sin of your family that caused your sister to die?"

Seth glared at him. "It was *our* sin, David. *Our* sin."

David tipped his chin into the air and stomped off.

A hand rested on Seth's shoulder. "Do you think sometimes death just happens?" Joshua said into his ear. "Maybe it wasn't anybody's fault. A fisherman sees death all the time. And it just seems to be a part of living."

Seth knew Joshua was trying to be kind, but he couldn't stand to hear any more. Breaking through the crowd, Seth ran as fast as he could. He ran through the streets. He could hear the sounds of the mourners, already beginning their loud cries and wailing.

Not knowing where else to go, he ran toward the synagogue. He ran until his side ached and forced him to slow to a walk.

He stood under the portico, panting. Something inside him had changed. He could feel it.

It was as if a wall had fallen from around his heart. A wall of anger had protected his heart from feeling anything about losing Talitha. But now the wall was gone, as completely as the wall had fallen from around Jericho. But when his wall fell, there seemed to be nothing inside.

It's like I died too. I died inside. It felt strange that his body kept moving. It felt hollow. His eyes saw things, but it was as if they didn't really see.

I hated Talitha enough that she died. And I died too.

He wandered away from the synagogue. Then, walking along the path, he left the village. He walked up the hill, not turning around to look at the lake or to walk backward.

Hadn't he dreamed of this day for a long time? Hadn't he dreamed of his sister being gone forever, relished what it would be like without her telling him what to do?

But his mother was right. She'd said his sister would be missed, and he missed her already. He would never see her again. He climbed a rock, sitting on it, hugging his knees to his chin.

He could hear the wailing of the people below, the ones surrounding his house. The eerie sound crawled up the hill and under his skin. The women wailed, their moans and calls clouding the air, hanging thickly, covering all other sounds. It gave him chills, prickly sensations.

He put his hands over his ears and tried to keep out the sound. "It's my fault!" he screamed.

No one heard him, he knew.

He looked down at the village. He knew he should be there, but he couldn't go. He couldn't face his mother and father, knowing he was responsible for Talitha's death. Hadn't his anger killed her? Hadn't his wish made her die?

He wondered why he couldn't cry. It was as if all the tears had turned to stone inside. They were there; he could feel them. But they wouldn't come out.

He dropped from the rock. He threw himself on the ground, his nose almost to the dirt. A memory came—of when he and Talitha were very little. She had helped him when he'd fallen. She'd gently washed his bloody knee and elbow. She'd sung him a sweet little song and then sent him on his way.

A tear fell, making a dark spot in the dirt.

He remembered how so many times they had talked and laughed and giggled and told stories. They wouldn't stop until his parents had to come to the door of their room and remind them to be quiet and go to sleep.

Another tear fell, and another.

"A new boy is in our village, Seth," she had told him once when he was small. "He looks a lot like you. Come with me. I'll introduce you." She had taken his hand and taught him how to wind around the houses to find the right one. Then she had said, "Hi, David. Here's my brother, Seth. You two will be in synagogue school together."

The tears came faster. His nose began to drip.

He remembered how she'd left him alone with David so that the two could become friends. They would have met in synagogue school in a few days, but she'd been kind enough to introduce them sooner. They had a chance to become friends first, so their first day of synagogue school wouldn't be quite so scary.

He let the tears fall into the dirt, not stopping them. *I've been so wrong. She loved me. She was a pest, but she loved me.*

He'd done something terrible. He wanted to be forgiven. But there was no way he could get forgiveness from God. He was only a boy, and a boy couldn't offer a sacrifice. What would happen to him now? He deserved whatever punishment God decided on.

God, please forgive me, his heart screamed. But he couldn't pray it aloud. He was afraid to. Without a sacrifice, what right did he have to ask God to forgive? Without the shedding of the blood of a perfect animal, there would be no forgiveness.

Seth had never felt so hopeless in his life.

He thought his heart would break open. Then he thought it had. "Rabbi Jesus," he whispered to the air, "can you really heal? Can you make my sister alive again? If you can, will you? Please?"

He blushed, realizing he'd been fingering his prayer tassel. Had he been *praying* to a *rabbi?* Fear raced through him. *Blasphemy.* He looked around and then up to the sky. God could punish him as He'd punished others in the old days who had done horrible things.

But the ground didn't open up and swallow him. No fire from heaven fell to burn him up.

Instead of fear, he felt peace.

That was when he noticed something strange. The mourners had stopped. Mourners were paid to show how upset the family was that a loved one had died. How could they stop?

He jumped up, as if by standing he could hear better. *Not a sound of a single mourner.* They couldn't stop. Didn't they know how sorry he was? They *must* cry—long and loud.

He ran down the hill, slipping, stumbling. He kept running, his chest hurting from breathing so hard.

His feet pounded the streets as he ran to his house. He turned a corner, and then he saw the mourners.

They were *laughing!* He shook his head. How could they laugh?

Getting closer, he listened. Finally he realized they were mocking someone. They were mocking the rabbi! He swallowed. Rabbi Jesus hadn't healed his sister? Is that why they were mocking him?

"Excuse me," he said to one of the mourners. "Why have you stopped crying?"

The woman threw up her arms and laughed to the sky. "The rabbi told us to stop! He told us the little girl wasn't dead, but asleep! As if we don't know what dead looks like! We've all seen her, and she is *dead.* I guess the rabbi hasn't seen death before." She cackled again.

Seth didn't know what to think. He wanted to hope that Talitha really *had* been asleep, that maybe he'd get another chance to be a brother to her—the kind of brother he knew he should have been. But mourners knew what death looked like, didn't they?

He ducked through the crowd of mourners. He felt the rough edges of cloth rub his face—and smooth linen when he passed those who were more wealthy. Most of them mumbled quietly, complaining about the rabbi.

When Seth reached the courtyard gate, a large man stopped him. "You can't go in there. Jesus has told everyone to stay outside."

"But that's my sister in there," Seth argued.

"I'm His disciple," the man replied, "and I'm not even allowed in. Sometimes the Teacher prefers to do His work without people watching. He's not a show."

"Can he do it?" asked Seth.

The man smiled. "He is a man of surprises and power. We can only wait and see."

Moments later the door opened. Seth's father came out first, looking dazed. His mother was next. She ran to Seth and whispered, "Go find some food and bring it back. Hurry. Soup, broth, anything. Perhaps Rebekah has something. She often begins cooking early."

"What happened?" Seth asked, his heart pounding.

"Just go. You'll see when you return. Hurry!" Her eyes sparkled, and she seemed to be trying to hold back a smile.

As Seth plowed through the crowd and into the street, he heard his father telling the mourners, "You may all . . . go home. We don't need your services."

We don't need your services?

Could this be? Could it be that they didn't need the mourners because there was nothing to mourn?

Seth ran past three houses, then turned toward the lake and passed five more. "Rebekah," he called breathlessly as he reached the small house. "Rebekah. Do you have any soup? My mother needs some right away."

Without asking questions, the neighbor ladled some of her soup into a small clay vase so it wouldn't spill. She handed it to him. Seth half walked, half ran back to his house.

In the courtyard, Jesus was speaking with his parents. There was Eli too—standing apart, his face anxious, straining to hear what was being said. Mother looked at Seth and pointed toward his room.

He dashed inside. As his eyes adjusted to the darkness, he saw something that didn't seem real. There sat Talitha.

"I'm starved," she said. "Is that soup?"

Seth couldn't speak. He stared at her. He knelt by her pallet and handed her the soup. He watched as she took the vase and peered inside. "Any lizards?"

Seth shook his head.

"Any dirt? Or dead bugs?"

He shook his head again.

She put the vase to her lips and tipped it up. A few moments later she smacked her lips. "Mmm! Mother didn't make this, did she?"

Seth still couldn't find his voice. He shook his head. Was he dreaming this? Would he wake up in a minute to the sounds of the mourners wailing? Would he wake to find he really did have a room with no sister?

"It's good, but not as good as Mother's," Talitha said, looking at him. "I'm so hungry. I feel like I haven't eaten in . . . forever. How long have I been asleep?"

Seth shrugged his shoulders.

"What are you staring at?" Talitha asked between sips.

Seth kept staring. His heart thumped. It jumped. It felt like maybe it was dancing. Now his insides were alive, but his outsides seemed dead.

"Do you want some? Is that why you're staring?" she said.

Seth shook his head. A smile started slowly and then grew bigger. His voice finally woke up. "Are you feeling better?"

Talitha lowered the vase and closed her eyes. A smile like he'd never seen took over her face. "I feel so perfect," she said, her voice soft. "A man was in here. He spoke to me, and it was like he reached into some sort of darkness and called to me. His hand sent a . . . a kind of power through me."

She opened her eyes and looked at her brother. "Seth, I don't know what happened. I remember being so, so sick. I felt so awful, so weak, and so hot. And then I couldn't keep my eyes open anymore. I couldn't breathe. I thought I stopped breathing. I thought everything just stopped."

"Then what?" Seth asked.

She frowned. "I don't remember anything else."

She took Seth's hand. This time he didn't yank it away. He let her hold it. He wanted her to hold it.

"I feel good, Seth. I feel different. I'm all better."

"I'm glad," he whispered.

Now it was Talitha's turn to stare. "What's wrong with you? I think you really mean that." She tilted her head. "Did Mother make you say that?"

Seth gulped. "No." He looked down at the floor. "I do mean it," he said, his voice barely audible.

She drank a little more soup, watching him closely.

"I'm sorry," he said, his voice squeaking.

"What?"

"I'm sorry. I've been so mean to you."

Talitha dabbed at her mouth with the back of her long tunic sleeve, still watching him.

"I shouldn't have made you sick with the lizard soup and embarrassed you," he said.

She nodded, listening intently.

"I still don't like that you always bother me and my friends." He swallowed. "But maybe it wouldn't have been so bad to let you listen." He said it, but he didn't know if he meant it.

"Seth," Talitha said. "You are such a pesky little brother."

Seth couldn't believe it. His sister thought *he* was a pest?

"But I still like you anyway," Talitha said and then tipped the vase to get the last of the soup. "Let's go outside. I think I hear Eli's voice."

"Now *there's* a pest," Seth mumbled, feeling like his whole self was returning to normal.

"What do you mean?" Talitha asked, defensive.

Seth grinned. "He's been here every day asking about you. He's been very worried."

Talitha stood. To Seth's surprise, she didn't even wobble.

"Do you need help?" Seth asked.

She shook her head. "No. It's so odd. I've never been so sick and gotten better so completely and so fast."

"Maybe it's not so odd," Seth said as they walked through the door. "Rabbi Jesus touched you."

Talitha looked at him, questions in her eyes. "That was Jesus?" Her eyes scanned the courtyard. "Where is he?"

Seth looked around but didn't see him.

"Talitha!" Eli said, approaching quickly. "Are you sure you're well? Should you be walking about?"

"Why does everyone treat me like I just came back from the dead?" Talitha said.

Seth watched the adults exchange glances.

"You were . . . very sick," her mother answered.

Seth wondered why they didn't tell her. She had been dead. The wonder of it swept through him again. Then, without warning, he said, "I missed you while you were sick."

"No you didn't," Talitha said.

"So did I," Eli told her.

"Of course you did," Talitha said and then shyly looked away at the ground.

"Where did Jesus go?" Seth asked.

His father looked out the courtyard gates, his voice far away. "I don't know."

"He told us to speak of this to no one," his mother added, looking directly at Seth.

"Why?" Seth asked, confused.

"He didn't say," his father answered. "But it's clear we must obey."

Seth nodded. He remembered what the disciple said: "He's not a show."

"Can we talk about it to each other?" Seth asked.

His parents looked at each other. "I think so," his father answered.

Eli pulled his robes around him. "If people knew what happened, there would be masses following him, tugging on him, wanting his attention. He would have no peace."

"Did he . . ." Seth began, looking at Talitha.

The adults nodded.

"Did he what?" Talitha demanded.

Mother moved to Talitha's side and put her arm around her. "Sweetie . . . you were dead."

Talitha's knees gave way, and Mother held her up. "No . . . but . . . no!" the girl's voice came out in a whisper.

"You were dead," Father said. "But Jesus touched you, called to you, and you came back to life."

"But how?" Talitha asked.

Father knelt in front of her. "Jesus loved you. I could see it in his eyes. I could feel it in his voice." Tears began to trickle down his face, and he didn't even try to wipe them away. "I thought I couldn't go on if you were dead." He reached over, grabbed Seth's hand, and looked him in the eye. "If either of you was dead. I love you that much. But this Jesus—his love is even stronger somehow."

"I thought I was in the presence of God Himself," Mother said. She clapped her hand over her mouth and looked to the sky. Then she took her hand away. "Please, God. I mean no blasphemy. This rabbi Jesus is from You. He must be."

Eli nodded, his voice barely audible. "Perhaps . . . Jesus is the Messiah."

At that moment, before anyone could speak, two faces peered around the wall. "Can we come in?" Joshua asked.

"Of course," Seth's father said, standing and quickly wiping the tears from his eyes. "Come on, Joshua."

"We wanted to—" When Joshua saw Talitha, his mouth stayed open. His eyes grew wide and he stopped so fast that David ran into him.

David scowled at Joshua. "What's your prob—" When he saw Talitha, his mouth also stayed open and his eyes grew wide.

"But you . . . you . . ." David said, pointing at Talitha. He turned to Seth. "What kind of joke is this? You lied to us to make us feel bad, didn't you?" he accused.

Seth shook his head. "I didn't tell you anything," he reminded him. "Anything you know, you heard from somebody else."

David looked from Seth to Talitha and back. He looked terribly confused.

Joshua's look of astonishment changed to realization. His grin grew wide. "Jesus" was all he said.

David's eyes narrowed. "Jesus keeps touching unclean things. My father won't be happy to hear about this." He turned and walked out the gate.

"This is . . ." Joshua started and then hesitated. "This is so great! My father is going to love this! Was Peter the fisherman here?"

Seth's father spoke. "I think so."

Talitha wrinkled her nose. "I thought I smelled fish."

"I don't want to be rude," Joshua said. "But I really think I should go talk to my father. He thinks Jesus is someone special. Maybe even the Messiah. Would it be okay if I leave?"

"Go ahead," Seth's father said.

"I'm glad you aren't sick anymore, Talitha," Joshua called. "Really I am." Waving, he ran out the gate.

"I'm sure we'll have more visitors," Seth's mother said. "I'd better go prepare a feast."

"You may have one of my lambs," Eli offered. "I'll go prepare it now."

"I'll help," Seth's father said, and the two men strode away quickly.

Talitha turned to Seth. "You know what?"

Seth shook his head. He still couldn't believe any of this was real.

"I'm glad you're my brother. And I'll miss you when I get married."

"You'll only be on the other side of town," Seth said. "We can still get together."

"I'll have you over for stew," she teased.

"I'll practice Torah with you."

Her eyes lit up. "Would you really? Eli has said he isn't opposed to me learning all I wish. So you and I can learn together." She paused. "If you want."

"Maybe not all the time," Seth said. "I mean, I'm glad you're my sister, but I still don't want you bugging me every day."

"Do you think your friends would come back if I talked to them and promised to leave you alone?" Talitha asked. "I mean it. I won't bother you."

"I don't think one of them wants me for a friend." He frowned. "I think the other one might not care as long as you weren't always around."

Talitha threw her arms around Seth, giving him a quick hug. "Oh," Seth said, "and not too much of that stuff either."

Talitha laughed. She reached over and ruffled his curls. "Let's go tell Mother we're not going to fight anymore."

"Well, not most of the time," Seth said, and smiled.

LETTERS FROM OUR READERS

Is this story true? If so, where did you find it? (Curious George, Watertown, New York)

The basis for this story is found in the New Testament of the Bible: Matthew 9:18-26, Mark 5:21-43, and Luke 8:40-56. If you read these passages, you won't find any story about Seth, only about Jairus (Seth's father) and his daughter (Seth's sister, Talitha). We took the real Bible story and asked, "What if?" What if this girl was a pest, and she had a younger brother who finally couldn't stand her anymore? We took what we knew about the real Bible story and what we knew about people and wrote a story so that you, the reader, could see that people in the Bible were just like us (only without all the extra "stuff" like computers, televisions, and telephones). The most important part of the story is the real part—about Jesus' love and power over death.

Why is there so much gross stuff in this story—a dead bird, maggots, lizard soup . . . ? (Misty B., Colorado Springs, Colorado)

Sorry if we grossed you out! But a lot of kids are fascinated by things like that. We figured some kids in Bible times were the same way, and we wanted the boys to seem real, not fake.

Okay, but did Talitha have to throw up? (M.A.B., Danbury, Connecticut)

Uh, well, we guess not . . .

I'm confused. I thought a synagogue was like a church. (Trevor, San Rafael, California)

The synagogue was a place where the Jewish people held services on the Sabbath. Scriptures were read, and men taught the people about them. During the week, people used the building for many other events—school, town meetings, whatever it was needed for. Jairus, the father of Talitha and Seth in the story, was the synagogue ruler, or the *hazzan*. His job was to keep the synagogue in running order. People went to him for permission to use the synagogue. Sometimes the synagogue was even used for travelers who had no other place to stay.

People usually sat on the flagstone floor in the synagogue. Some sources say women sat separately from the men. Others say they sat together. One thing is for certain: The raised stone benches around the walls of the synagogue were for the important men of the village or the male visitors.

Were women really not supposed to learn? (Stacie M., Milwaukee, Wisconsin)

Israelite women were more respected than the women of some other Middle Eastern cultures. They were allowed to learn and were supposed to learn the basics of Torah (God's Law) in order to teach their children. They needed to understand the holy days and festivals, because they had to know what to cook and why they were cooking the foods a particular way.

Since their responsibilities were many, girls didn't have time to go to school, nor were they invited to go to school. Their classroom was the home, where they learned cooking, weaving, raising children, and so on.

Why did Talitha and Seth share a room? Was their family poor? I wouldn't want to share a room with my stinky, smelly, yucky sister. (Matthew W., Antioch, California)

Actually, their family was better off than most—so they had more rooms to their home. Most families had a home with one large room. A corner of it was the kitchen or cooking and storage area. Then they had another area where they rolled out their pallets and slept. Most kept the animals in the house with them at night. The animals had their own dirt area, which was lower than the living space for people.

As for sisters, they actually can be rather nice to be around. As Seth learned, family is important. God wants us to honor our family members, even when they get on our nerves.

ABOUT THE AUTHOR

LISSA HALLS JOHNSON is a freelance writer and story editor, author of novels for teens, tweens, and young adults. Included among her twenty published books are the most recent: *Rich in Love* with Irene Garcia, and *Still Growing* by Kirk Cameron. She has edited over fifty books for publishers, including Howard Books, WaterBrook, Thomas Nelson, and NavPress.

Dangerous Dreams
by Jim Ware

For Chris and Vicky

CHAPTER
1

Livy stirred and opened her eyes. A copper pot fell from her lap and rolled clanging across the stone-paved floor. It was hot in the palace kitchen, terribly hot. She pushed her sweat-soaked, auburn-red hair out of her face and gulped the dry Palestinian air.

A dream! How long have I been asleep?

She shook herself, then drew a long, slow breath. *Write it down!* she told herself. *Quick! Before it slips away!*

Pulling out the stylus and scrap of parchment that she always kept tucked inside her wide, sashlike belt, Livy began to write:

I dreamed again—about Father and Mother and my home back in Gaul. There were snowy mountains and the blue sea and green pines and hillsides covered with wildflowers. Just the way it was almost seven years ago . . . when I was only five. I saw the faces of the people of my village, and . . .

"You there—redhead!" It was the voice of Melanus, Pilate's bald, sharp-nosed Syrian steward. "What do you think you're doing?"

Livy quickly shoved her writing materials back into her belt as Melanus dashed into the kitchen, his arm drawn back to strike her.

"Ow!" she yelled as Melanus cuffed her behind the ear. A noise like the clattering of the pot on the stones rang in her head. A sharp pain shot up her arm and into her shoulder as he seized her by the elbow and dragged her to her feet.

"So! Sleeping at your work again! Scribbling words again! Get up, you stubborn, young she-donkey! Do you think Master keeps slaves just so they can lie around dozing and doodling all day? Get back to scrubbing those pots before I take the whip to you!"

"Yes, sir," muttered Livy, wincing at the pain in her arm. She retrieved the pot and sat down heavily on the bench.

"I don't know what possessed Mistress Procula to teach you your letters," said Melanus, glowering down his nose at her. "It was ridiculous—and dangerous! Slaves don't need to know how to read and write. It puts unsafe ideas into their heads. I'm going to be keeping an eye on you!"

Livy said nothing. Instead, she picked up her pumice scrubbing stone and went back to work, making a rude face at Melanus's retreating back as he left the room.

Old Cook came in as the steward went out, followed by young Quintus, the eleven-year-old Greek who was Livy's closest friend among the slaves.

"In trouble *again?*" scolded Cook, wagging her double chin at the pouting girl. "I might have known."

Looking up, Livy saw Quintus shake his bushy head. He shuffled his sandaled feet, crossing and recrossing his bare, birdlike legs as if to show the embarrassment and confusion he felt for his friend. Cook frowned disapprovingly. But when Livy's eyes met hers, the bulky woman's scowl melted into an indulgent smile.

"Oh, what's the use?" said Cook, relaxing her wrinkled forehead and dropping her hands to her sides. "You're just not cut out to be a slave, are you, child?" She sighed. "What happened *this* time?"

"Fell asleep, I guess," the girl answered with a frown. "I was up all night again—talking with Mistress about her dreams. And what's wrong with that? Isn't that why I'm here? I'm supposed to be her personal servant. I'm supposed to take care of her *personal* needs. *That's* why Pilate bought me—not to be a kitchen maid!" She scrunched up her nose in disgust. Her freckled face reddened to match her hair.

"Melanus doesn't see it that way," warned Cook, stepping over to the kitchen fire to stir the kettle. "He says *all* the servants have to take their turns in the kitchen. And he *can* tell you what to do, Missie. So you'd better pay attention. Cross Melanus one too many times, and you'll regret it! You mark my words!"

"Melanus!" spat Livy. "I think he was born to make my life miserable!"

"Hush!" said Cook with a frown.

Livy scowled again, scooped a handful of sand into the pot, gripped the pumice stone, and returned to her scrubbing. Cook shook her head, muttered something to herself, and noisily slooshed a basket of red beans into the boiling water. Then she stepped out into the pantry. Quintus came and sat beside Livy on the bench.

"She's right," he whispered, smoothing down his short and very rumpled tunic. "You're *not* cut out to be a slave. You're always dreaming of bigger things."

Livy glared at him. "No kidding! No Gaul is cut out to be a slave! I have the blood of Celtic chieftains flowing in my veins! Do you know what that means, Quintus?"

Quintus sighed and nodded his scruffy head. "Uh-huh. You told me already. About a hundred times."

Livy dropped the stone and turned to face him. "Listen! I just had another dream about home. There were pine trees and mountains and wildflowers. And people I used to know when I was very little, all walking around in a place filled with color and light. It was beautiful—almost too beautiful to be real. I don't know if it was Gaul or the Otherworld . . . That's where my people believe you go after you die."

"Uh-huh," said Quintus, blandly scratching his ear.

"My parents were there too—which *could* mean that they didn't survive the Roman attack. I wish I knew!" She frowned and bit her lip. "Quintus," she said, looking straight into his eyes. "It's time we got serious!"

Quintus blinked. "About what?"

"About escaping!"

"Come on, Livy." Quintus frowned. "Do you know what the Romans do to runaway slaves?"

"Do *you* know what they did to my village?" she cried. "To my people? Burned down the houses! Put some to the sword, took the rest away and sold us as slaves! That was almost seven years ago! I still don't know for sure what happened to my parents!" Angry tears filled her eyes.

She was about to say more, but a glance at Quintus's face made it clear that he was no longer listening. His wide, round eyes were fixed on the doorway. His jaw had fallen slack. His face was as white as a sheet of papyrus. His lips were moving wordlessly. She followed his gaze to where a large spotted hound, one of Governor Pilate's household dogs, was trotting over the threshold and across the stone floor toward the steaming stew pot.

Livy's angry tears stopped as suddenly as they'd started. The corners of her mouth crept upward in a knowing smile. Quintus's fear of dogs was legendary in the household. Cook's too. *This could be fun,* Livy thought.

As she watched, Quintus squeezed his eyes tightly shut and let out a piercing yell. "A dog!" he screamed. "A really *big* one! Aaaah!" He jumped up from the bench and burst through the opposite door to the courtyard beyond the kitchen. Just then, Cook stumbled in from the pantry to see what all the ruckus was about.

"Hoi!" she screeched, dropping her basket as she caught sight of the drooling animal. Red beans skittered across the floor. "Who let that mangy thing in here? *Chaneni, Adonai!*" Then she fled too, slipping and sliding through the mess of spilled beans in her haste to find the door.

Livy sat back and laughed—a long, luxurious laugh. It felt good. But as she sat there wiping the tears from her eyes, she caught sight of another figure in the doorway—a tall, stately woman in a Roman robe, or *stola*.

"Domina!" Livy exclaimed, jumping to her feet. "What are *you* doing here?"

Procula, the slim and graceful wife of Governor Pontius Pilate, descended the three steps into the kitchen and silently crossed the floor. A warm feeling of affection welled up inside Livy as she looked up at the lady. Even though Livy used the respectful title domina—mistress of the house—Procula had been more like a mother than a mistress since the day Pilate had brought Livy home from the auction block in Rome. Livy genuinely loved her mistress. And because she loved her, she couldn't help being troubled by the expression she now saw on her face.

The ringlets of Procula's sandy-brown hair, curled in the Roman fashion, couldn't hide the deep creases in her forehead. There was an odd, distracted look in her brown eyes. Her gracefully arched eyebrows were knit closely together. The shadows under her high cheekbones were darker than usual.

"I've had another dream. Early this morning," she said. "I want to tell you about it. Come."

Taking Livy by the hand, Procula led her out across the courtyard and into the shaded colonnade beyond the palace fountain. There she stopped and made the girl sit beside her on a marble bench.

"What was it this time?" asked Livy, watching her mistress's face with a sense of discomfort. The dark cloud in the lady's eyes made her feel as if the warm April morning had turned suddenly cold. She couldn't remember when she had last seen Procula looking so upset.

The lady turned and faced her. "I'm not exactly sure *what* I saw," she said quietly. "In the beginning, I think it was . . . baskets."

Procula often had troubling dreams. It seemed to Livy that she had been having them even more frequently over the past several weeks. She never told these dreams to anyone but Livy. Procula had recognized Livy's special talent for interpreting dreams from the very beginning. It was part of the girl's Celtic heritage. The Celtic nations—the Gauls, the Britons, the Galatians, the Cymrians, the Milesians—were famous for their emotional temperaments, their mystical leanings, their wild imaginations, and their interest in the unseen world. It was also one of several qualities that had earned her a special place in her mistress's affections—and the keen resentment of Melanus, the steward.

"Baskets," Livy repeated, almost as if she were speaking to herself.

"Yes," said Procula. "Baskets full of fire."

Livy pulled back her long hair, pursed her lips, and half closed her eyes. She drew her feet up under her and sat cross-legged on the bench, trying to picture the thing in her mind.

"And there was a man," the lady continued. "A man with piercing eyes—eyes that seemed to look straight into my soul. He was standing in front of the Jewish temple. And a lamb."

"A lamb. With the baskets?"

"No. The temple and the lamb came *after* the baskets. At least I think so. What do you think it all means?"

Livy was silent. She hated to admit it, but she was stumped. "Well," she said at last, letting out a slow breath, "maybe it doesn't really mean anything. Not every dream does. Maybe you're just anxious about being in Jerusalem. Master *did* say that he's expecting trouble this year."

Procula sighed. "Yes," she said thoughtfully. "And that *might* explain the part about the temple . . . and the lamb. The Jews *do* sacrifice a lamb at Passover. But what about the rest of it? The man with the piercing eyes? The baskets of fire?"

"I'm not sure," said Livy, shivering involuntarily.

Procula frowned. After a pause she said, "Those eyes keep coming back to me. I can't get them out of my mind! That's why I want you to come with me."

The girl shot her a questioning glance.

"To the temple," Procula explained. "To look for clues. Maybe we'll see something there that will help you understand the dream. I simply must know what it means! If you can tell me, I . . . well, I'd even be willing to reward you."

"What kind of reward?" Livy asked.

"What kind of reward would you like?"

Livy didn't hesitate. "I want to be set free!"

"Oh, child!" laughed Procula. "For interpreting *one* dream? I don't think so."

Livy's heart sank. Her face fell. Her mistress saw it and hastened to comfort her.

"Of course, I've always thought about setting you free when you've come of age," Procula said. "If you behave yourself. I suppose that's one of the reasons I taught you to read and write."

When I come of age, Livy thought bitterly. *Right! By then I'll probably be too old to care!* Nobody, not even Procula, knew what this meant to Livy. *Nobody,* she thought, *could possibly understand why freedom is so important to me.* Yes, she had a kind, wonderful mistress and a comfortable home. Yes, she was surrounded by good friends like Quintus and Cook. But *freedom* was part of her Celtic heritage too.

All the Celts were fiercely independent. They loved liberty! Her father and mother had been slaves to no one! The thought of her parents reminded her how terribly she ached to see them again—even though she knew that wasn't likely to happen after all this time. Still, she'd search the world over for them if only she were free . . .

She glanced up to see her mistress giving her a probing look. "So," said Procula, "will you help me?"

Livy looked into the deep brown eyes of the woman who had been almost like a mother to her for nearly seven years. "Sure," she said quietly. "I'll do what I can."

Procula's face relaxed into a warm smile. "Good. Then you'll accompany me to the temple tomorrow. I'll call for you early—sometime after the morning meal." She rose, took Livy's hand, and squeezed it. Then she turned and walked away.

That was when Livy caught sight of Quintus. He was edging his way carefully down the portico, keeping to the shadows, flitting stealthily from column to column.

"Hey!" he whispered when he caught sight of her. "Is that dog still around?"

Livy laughed. "No, you big coward! But listen!" She ran over to him and gripped him by his bony shoulders. "Tomorrow Mistress is taking me with her to the Jewish temple. And I want *you* to come along!"

"Me? What for?"

"Don't you know anything?" she said. "It's Passover week! The place will be simply crawling with hordes of people!"

"So what?"

"So what?" Livy pressed her nose to his and lowered her voice. "It will be the perfect time and place to make our escape. *That's* what!"

"Livy! Look!"

Livy was plotting out possible escape routes when Quintus's voice broke in on her thoughts. They were standing with the lady Procula at the top of a wide ramp, beneath a lofty, pillared archway. Inside lay the first of the temple's outer courts, the Court of the Gentiles. It was a large, paved plaza teeming with men, women, and children from every part of the known world. Quintus touched Livy's arm and let out a low whistle.

The people in the court were as different as the countries from which they'd come. There were dark-eyed Jews from Egypt; fat, oily merchants from Parthia; exotic black Ethiopians; olive-skinned Greeks and Syrians; a few fair-haired Galatians (who made Livy feel at home); toga-clad Roman officials; soldiers in bright armor; and lots of native Jerusalemites. Most of the Jewish men had covered their heads with the traditional blue-and-white prayer shawl. Around their forearms and heads were bound long, snaky leather straps to which were attached tiny scripture boxes, or *phylacteries*. The courtyard echoed with the bleating of sheep and goats, the calls of the money changers, and the hum of voices. The fragrance of roasting meat filled the air—the result of the almost continual animal sacrifices.

Livy sighed as she looked out over this multicolored sea of people. Would she see anything here that might help her grasp the meaning of her mistress's dream? And what if she *did* interpret it correctly? Procula's promise to free her when she "came of age" meant at least eight or nine more years of slavery. *Eight or nine years!* She made a face and shook her head. *It might as well be forever!*

How much easier, she thought, *to get lost in the crowd and make a quick break for it!*

A trumpet sounded in the distance—the ritual *shofar,* or ram's horn. At the noise everyone turned toward the sanctuary, the house of the Jewish God. The massive structure of square blocks and towers overshadowed the entire temple area.

"This way!" said Procula, motioning to them to follow her. Carefully they threaded their way through the multitude of worshippers and visitors.

Livy craned her neck and stared. The sight of the temple itself nearly took her breath away. To her it looked like a fairy palace, all shining and golden in the morning sun. She recalled a snatch of verse she'd once heard Cook recite:

Far off appearing like a Mount of alabaster,
Topped with golden spires . . .

Soon they stood before a low wall of marble decorated with carvings of grapevines and pomegranates. Beyond it stood the entrance to the first of the temple's *inner* courts—the Court of the Women. Upon this wall was a stone tablet, and on the tablet was inscribed a message in Latin and Greek:

NO FOREIGNER MAY PASS THIS BARRIER.
ANYONE CAUGHT DOING
SO WILL BE RESPONSIBLE
FOR HIS OWN DEATH THAT FOLLOWS.

"Does that mean *us?*" asked Livy, scrunching up her freckled nose.

"Yes," said Procula, unveiling her face just long enough to give the girl a warning look.

"You mean they'd actually *kill* us? Just for going past this little wall?"

"They would," the lady replied.

"I don't believe it!"

Quintus rolled his eyes. "Believe it, Livy," he said.

Hmph! thought Livy. *How am I supposed to find any clues if I can't even get inside?*

Suddenly she had an inspiration. Elbowing Quintus in the ribs, she whispered, "You stay here. And keep watching for a good chance to get away. I'm going to see what I can find out about Domina's dream."

Quintus blinked and stared. "Okay," he said.

Eluding her mistress's watchful eye, Livy ran straight up to the guard who kept the entrance to the Court of the Women. He was a large, thick-lipped, burly man, who wore the brass helmet, white turban, and blue tunic of the temple guards. In his right hand he held a long, iron-tipped spear; in his left, a polished, round shield. Livy stood in front of him and uncovered her head.

"Excuse me, sir," she said in a loud, official-sounding voice. "I represent the governor's wife."

A dark man in a gray, hooded cloak who stood nearby gave a short laugh. "That's a good one!" he observed, stroking the head of a big black dog that sat patiently at his feet.

Livy ignored the dark man's comment and kept her attention fixed upon the guard. He lowered his brassy shield and stared straight into her eyes. It was clear that he had never seen anyone quite like the tall, blue-eyed, freckle-faced, copper-haired girl.

"What *are* you?" he said at last, curling his lip and raising his bushy eyebrows.

"Not *what*," she said. "*Who*. And I told you. Servant to Procula, wife of Pontius Pilate." She jerked a thumb in the lady's direction. "My mistress would like to have a look around inside."

The man in the gray cloak raised his dark eyebrows. Livy glared at him.

The guard's face turned very red. "Gentiles," he said, "are forbidden to enter."

Livy wasn't about to give up. "Don't you get it? I'm not talking about just *any* Gentile. This is the wife of *Caesar's representative* in Jerusalem!"

"Huh!" grunted the guard. "Caesar *himself* would not be permitted to pass!" He straddled the opening in the barrier, holding his spear diagonally across the space. "Now go away!"

Livy scowled. *Regroup. Rethink.* She bent her head, wrinkled up her nose, and pressed the palm of her left hand against her forehead.

"Oh no!" she said after a moment's silence, looking up suddenly as if distracted by a noise. She pointed urgently to the shaded portico across the courtyard where the tables of the money changers had been set up. "Over there! Is that a robbery? I'm almost *sure* it's a robbery!"

The guard bent down and sneered in her face. "Sorry," he said. "Your tricks won't work here. Now go!"

Maybe if I make him really *mad* . . . Livy thought. "All right," she said, edging away. "I'll go. But I'm going to tell Governor Pilate about you."

"Ha!" laughed the man. "And just what are you going to tell him?"

"That you've got a nose like a *pig*—that's what!" She flattened her own nose with the tip of her thumb and stuck out her tongue. Then she turned and ran. The dark man in the gray cloak burst out laughing.

"Why, you little—!" sputtered the guard, gripping his spear with white-knuckled hands. "When I catch you, I'll . . . I'll . . ." He took off after her with fire in his eyes.

Livy darted between a lanky, bearded worshipper in a prayer shawl and a gray-headed woman carrying two pigeons in a small wooden cage. The guard, in hot pursuit, tripped over the woman, knocking her cage to the ground and freeing the birds. They soared into the sky along with the guard's curses.

Livy chuckled and dodged back toward the entrance to the Court of the Women. Then, covering her red hair with her cloak, she dashed past the forbidden barrier, across a paved walkway, and up the steps to the magnificent Nicanor Gate. She stopped, panting and breathless. *Did anyone see me?*

Glancing nervously to one side, then the other, she couldn't help thinking of the words inscribed on the tablet: *Anyone caught doing so will be responsible for his own death that follows.*

Deciding the coast was clear, Livy turned her attention to the Court of the Israelites, then to the Court of the Priests and the sanctuary itself. Was there something—anything—that might help her understand the meaning of Procula's dream?

Finally she found it.

Near the door of the sanctuary, atop a massive stone pedestal mounted by a wide ramp, rose a high, four-horned altar of rough-hewn stones. Beside the altar stood a bearded priest dressed in white. A large knife glittered in his right hand. His left hand rested on the head of a lamb that lay stretched upon the altar. As the priest raised the knife, the lamb turned its head and looked directly at Livy. It was strange, but even at that distance she could see the animal's face clearly—a sad, silent, suffering face. Suddenly she let out a gasp.

"Oh!" she said. "The eyes!"

How could it be? The lamb's eyes looked . . . human. The eyes of a man. Deep, piercing eyes. Eyes that seemed to look straight into her soul.

Lifting her hand to her mouth, Livy gave a stifled cry. The knife fell. She turned and ran.

She burst into the Court of the Gentiles, only to find the whole place in an uproar. People were rushing in every direction, knocking one another down, tripping over each other, shoving each other aside. From the portico of the money changers came the voices of men raised in angry protest. Livy heard shouts, the crunch of shattering wood, and several loud cracking sounds.

Then she saw a man—a tall, strong man in a peasant's tunic—swinging a whip made of leather thongs. He tipped over the tables of the merchants and brokers, freeing the sacrificial animals that were for sale. Doves and pigeons went fluttering into the faces of befuddled onlookers. Young lambs skittered through the crowd; goats ran this way and that. Children laughed and cried as men yelled at the tops of their voices.

All at once it hit her. *This is it! The perfect chance to make a run for it!*

But first she'd have to find Quintus. Frantically she searched the chaos for some sign of the skinny boy with the wild hair. At last she saw him within shouting distance, emerging from behind a man with a pair of goats on a tether.

"Come on!" she called. "Let's go! It's now or never!"

But Quintus wasn't listening. Once again his face had gone pale, his brown eyes wide with terror. He was staring past her.

What is it this time? she thought.

In the next instant a streak of black fur bounded past her, closely followed by the dark man in the gray hood and cloak. The dog leaped up at poor Quintus, knocking him to the ground and licking his face.

The man in the gray cloak charged up and pulled the animal off the boy. Then, without a word of apology or explanation, he hurried off through the crowd with his dog. When he'd gone, Livy dashed over to Quintus and helped him to his feet.

She felt a hand on her arm. She turned to see Procula standing beside her.

"It's all right, Domina," said the girl, her heart sinking at the thought of the lost opportunity. "He's shaken, but I don't think he's hurt."

But a glance told her that Procula wasn't thinking about Quintus or the dog at all. Instead, she was pointing urgently at the scene in the colonnade.

"That man!" she said breathlessly. "The one with the whip! I think it's *him!* The one I saw in my dream!"

CHAPTER 3

"Drove them all out," said old Hatshup, grinning and bobbing his grizzled head. "Sent them packing, he did! Every last one of them. They say you could hear those money changers howling and whining all the way across the Hinnom Valley!"

Livy looked up from the flat, round loaf of bread she'd been half-heartedly nibbling. Somehow she didn't seem to have much appetite this morning. She'd missed the perfect chance to escape—all because of Quintus and his fear of dogs! She chewed the dry bread and swallowed hard.

"He's an amazing man, this Jesus of Nazareth," Hatshup was observing. "I don't care what the priests say about him."

From her place in the corner near the charcoal brazier, Livy stared across the smoky kitchen at the gray-haired Egyptian gardener. He was squatting on the stone floor beside the big clay oven, slurping hot broth from a wooden spoon. Slowly she realized what the old man was talking about. The scene in the temple. The man with the whip of thongs—the one Procula said she'd seen in her dream. Livy listened with greater interest.

"He's a good deal more than amazing if you ask me!" said Cook, turning from the big kettle and shaking her ladle at the old man. Her sleeves were rolled up for work, and her flabby upper arms jiggled as she gave her head a vigorous nod. "Some think he might be the Messiah!"

Livy laid her bread aside. "What's the Messiah?" she asked.

No one responded. Instead, bald Melanus put down his bowl, wiped his chin, and rose from the table. "*Some?*" he scoffed. "Like the rabble that followed him into the city on Sunday, for instance? Ignorant peasants!

Waving their palm branches and singing songs about the 'Son of David.' Honestly!" He gave Cook a condescending smile. "My dear woman, do we really need any more messiahs? What's the count so far this year?"

"Well, there's the one who caused all that trouble up in Galilee last fall," volunteered Hatshup. "Leader of the zealots. What do they call him?"

"Bar Abbas," said Cook with a snort. "Fine messiah he'd make!"

"What are *zealots*?" asked Livy.

"Freedom fighters," said Hatshup. Tipping up his bowl, he gulped down the last of his broth. "The kind who'd like to see Master Pilate and the rest of the Romans on the end of a skewer!" He smiled and nodded, then rose shakily to his feet and handed his bowl to Cook for a second helping.

Freedom fighters! thought Livy. She pulled the piece of parchment from her belt and made herself a note:

Bar Abbas. Freedom fighters. Find out more.

Looking up, she noticed Quintus, who sat beside her munching his own loaf of bread. He watched her intently with narrowed eyes. "What are you writing?" he asked.

Livy made a face at him and said nothing.

"Yes, indeed!" laughed Melanus as he started toward the door. "I'd say old Bar Abbas has more muscle in his arm than this fellow from Nazareth. Perhaps *he's* your messiah after all!"

Cook stopped stirring. Dropping the ladle into its rest and wiping her hands on her apron, she turned a withering glance on the retreating steward. "You mark my words, Melanus," she said, shaking a finger at him. "The real Messiah—when he comes—won't be a thing like that Bar Abbas!"

Livy was becoming exasperated. "What are you talking about? What's a *messiah*, anyway?"

Cook turned and looked at her. "The Deliverer," she said with an earnestness in her voice that nearly took the girl's breath away. "The Liberator. The true King. The One who will set us *all* free."

"And long may he reign!" said Melanus with a smirk. "But just re-member: Anyone who goes around talking about a king other than Cae-sar will be severely dealt with. And I do mean *anyone*," he continued, glancing around the room.

"The same is true of anyone whose quest for freedom leads him *or her* to challenge the authorities," he added. "Rebels must not be tolerated. That's Master's view, and I share it." He stepped out into the passage. "Now! To work, all of you. The day's wasting!" He strolled off, the back of his bald head reflecting the dim light as he went. Old Hatshup tottered after him, grinning and muttering.

Livy pursed her lips, bowed her head, and wrote again: *Messiah. Lib-erator. King.*

What if it's true? she thought, biting the end of the stylus. *Would he set me free?*

"Now, then . . . no dawdling, you two!"

The voice of Cook startled Livy, who shoved the parchment and sty-lus into her sash. Cook was standing over her, waving a thick finger in her face and pulling Quintus up from the bench by the collar of his tunic. "I've put on a stew for the midday meal," Cook continued, "but I need more water and firewood. Hurry up, now, or I'll send old Melanus after you with a big stick!"

Quintus got up and grabbed a water jar. "I'm going!" he said.

"You too, Missy," said Cook, taking Livy by the arm and hauling her up from her seat. The piece of parchment fell to the floor beside the bra-zier as the big woman shoved her toward the courtyard door. "Out to the fuel bin with you. And keep that door shut . . . The courtyard gate too. I've seen one of those street dogs nosing around out there—a big black one—and I don't want him anywhere near my stew!"

"A big, black dog?" said Quintus, turning pale. He clutched the water jar to his chest and hurried out toward the fountain.

Livy stood at the door, chuckling as she watched him go. Suddenly an idea struck her. *Perfect!* she thought.

She walked into the courtyard and glanced around. No one. Even the guard had stepped away from his post for a moment. Livy ran to the gate. Sure enough, there was the dog—a big, snuffling, woolly black thing—a lot like the dog that had jumped all over Quintus at the temple.

Slowly and soundlessly she unlatched the gate and pushed it open. Then she hurried to the fuel bin, grabbed an armload of grape wood, and carried it into the kitchen, making sure to leave the door just slightly ajar.

"Here's the fuel, Cook," she said, trying hard not to smile.

"Over there," said Cook, waving a bouncing arm at the opposite wall. "Now you just keep stirring this," she added, handing the ladle to Livy, "while I—"

The door flew open. A black blur exploded into the kitchen. Cook screamed. Picking up the skirts of her tunic, she hurried out the door.

The big black dog knocked over a table, scattered a bowl of shelled lentils across the floor, and bounded over to the pot. Laughing, Livy dipped a ladleful of broth into a bowl for the hungry animal. "Good boy!" she said. "You were *great*! Right on time too!"

The dog barked happily, wagged his tail, and began lapping up the broth. Livy leaned against the wall, watching him eat and smiling. *Who would've thought a woman that size could run so fast?* she thought. *I wish it had been Melanus!*

She stroked the dog's head and filled the bowl a second time. "But Quintus is the one I *really* wanted you to meet. I wonder what's taking him so long?"

She reached for the door and yanked it open. "Quintus!" she called. "Where—"

Staring, she caught her breath.

There in the doorway stood the dark man in the gray, hooded cloak. It was the same man she remembered seeing at the temple the day before.

He smiled at her from behind a thick black beard. "Good morning," he said. "I believe you have my dog."

CHAPTER 4

"Who are you?" demanded Livy, backing into the kitchen as the man pushed his way inside. "What are you doing here?"

"I came to talk to *you*," he said. Firmly but noiselessly he shut the door behind him. Then he threw back his hood, revealing short hair and a muscular neck. His eyes were as black as his beard. A ragged scar stretched from the middle of his forehead to his left temple. The top half of his left ear was missing.

"Me?" Livy eyed him carefully. "Why do you want to talk to *me*?" He looked dangerous, yet she didn't feel afraid of him—only curious. The scar, the wounded ear—they were the marks of a fighter. What did he fight *for*?

The visitor, apparently unsurprised by her boldness, moved slowly into the room. As he did so, the dog trotted over to him, wagging its tail and licking his hand.

"Good dog, Kalb," said the man, gently stroking the animal's head. "I sent him to follow you," he explained, looking up at Livy. "I've come to make you an offer—an offer I believe you will find most interesting."

She shook the hair out of her face. "Really?" she said with a laugh. "You don't even know me!"

It was fun to swagger and put on a brave front, she thought. And she found this intruder fascinating. She hadn't met anyone like him since the day the Romans captured her and took her away from her home in Gaul six years ago. He was completely unlike the grown-up Romans she'd been living with—except for her mistress, who wasn't as predictable and proper and boring as the others.

This man seemed wild, free, with an air of adventure and mystery. He was obviously a Jew, but there were qualities about him she'd never seen in a Jewish man: a fierce passion, an intense fire in the eyes. He reminded her of her father—the bold, defiant Celtic warrior-chief, a man who carried the scars of many battles and bowed his knee to no one.

"You're right," the man said with a cool stare. "I *don't* know you—yet. But I know something *about* you. You're a slave, a personal servant to the governor's wife. You said so yourself yesterday, in the Court of the Gentiles. I saw what you did there. Very resourceful. 'The girl has spirit,' I said to myself. That's why I sent Kalb after you. That's why I looked you up."

He paused and squinted at her. "You don't like being a slave, do you?"

Livy scowled. "Would *you?*"

His smile suddenly faded. "No. I *don't!* And I *won't* go on being a slave to the Romans—not without a fight. For years I've dreamed of throwing off their rule—of being free! That's why I'm here. I need your help."

"*My* help?"

"I know I'm taking a big risk. But after seeing you in action yesterday, I'm convinced it's worth it. I'm fighting to free my people from slavery to Rome. And I believe you can help me."

Freedom fighters, she thought. *Zealots. So that's it! He's one of them.*

So he was fighting for freedom! It was clear that he wanted it badly enough to die for it, and that he wanted it *now*—not eight or ten years from now. He looked like the kind of man who could fight and win, the kind of man she and Quintus needed on their side in their own quest for freedom.

"But how can *I* help *you?*" she asked. "What do you want from me?"

His eyes narrowed. His voice was low and intense. "I need someone inside the governor's household—someone with ears to hear and eyes to

see. I need to know how much the Romans know . . . what they're thinking, what they're planning."

"A *spy*, you mean?"

Waiting for his answer, she noticed he was no longer looking at her
face but at her feet. No, not her feet—something on the floor *next* to her
feet. Then she saw it.

The parchment! There it lay, faceup on the paving stones, the words
on its surface plain for anyone to see.

Before she could think or make a move, the man in the dark cloak
lunged forward. He seized the parchment, came up with it in his hand,
and stood reading it, a slow smile spreading over his face.

"Well!" he said warmly. "What have we here? *Bar Abbas . . . Freedom
fighters . . . Messiah . . . Liberator . . . King . . . Find out more.* Looks like
somebody's a step ahead of me! Did *you* write this?"

Livy's palms began to sweat. Her heart was pounding so hard she
thought the man must be able to hear it. She scrunched up her nose.
"What if I did?"

"Well, for one thing, it could be very uncomfortable for you if this
were to fall into the wrong hands. *Very* uncomfortable."

"Like *your* hands, for instance?" she shot back.

His thick eyebrows lifted. "What do *you* think?"

"How do I know what to think? I can't trust you."

He smiled. "Looks like you haven't any choice . . . now that I've got
this," he said, holding up the parchment. "But there's an even better reason. I think you share my dream—the dream of freedom. It's a dangerous
dream. But you believe the danger's worth it. Am I right?"

Livy said nothing. But pictures she'd seen in her dream of home—her
mother's face, her father's flashing sword, the sea, the pink and purple
and yellow flowers—raced through her imagination. She wanted it all so
badly she could taste it.

"Think of it!" the man in the kitchen was saying. "If my friends and I
succeed, you'll be free to go anywhere you want to go!"

There were footsteps outside. *Oh no!* Livy thought. *Cook's coming back!*

The man threw himself against the door and held it shut. Someone on the other side began to knock.

Livy felt her stomach knotting. What would happen if she were caught talking to a freedom fighter? If he handed over her parchment? If she were discovered plotting revolution, planning escape?

"C'mon, Livy!" called a small voice from the other side of the door. "No more jokes, okay?"

She breathed a sigh of relief. *Quintus!*

The stranger searched her face. "Hold the door," he whispered, "while I find a place to hide!" He held up the parchment. "And don't forget, I've still got *this*!"

Livy laughed. "It's just Quintus." She cast a glance at Kalb and smiled to herself. "Go ahead and open the door."

The stranger studied her closely.

"Go on," she said. "It's all right."

Without a word, he eased the door open a crack. Quintus shoved his way inside, water jar first. "Took you long enough!" he said.

As the door closed behind him, the boy stopped and stared. Resisting an urge to laugh, Livy followed his eyes to the dark, furry shape in the corner.

"The dog!" Quintus cried. "Aauugghh!"

Quintus's eyeballs rolled up into his head as the huge animal, its tail wagging happily, sprang on him. The dog planted its paws on the boy's shoulders and began licking his face. Quintus tottered, swayed, and fell. The water jar crashed to the floor, spilling its contents across the paving stones.

The man in the gray cloak, his eyebrows raised, glanced over at Livy.

"Don't worry," she said, smiling. "He's on *our* side."

On Wednesday morning, Livy's mistress woke her when the sky outside the window was just beginning to tremble with a pinkish glow. The girl rubbed her eyes, brushed the red hair out of her face, and stared sleepily as the lady explained her reasons for coming so early.

Procula had dreamed again—the same disturbing dream. She was determined to see the man called Jesus once more. She wanted to speak to him if possible, to listen to his words. She'd heard he was teaching in the temple every day. So Livy and Quintus would accompany her to the Court of the Gentiles that very afternoon.

Perfect, Livy thought. It would be a perfect chance to talk with the man in the gray cloak. Parting yesterday, they'd agreed to communicate whenever they could.

Kalb showed up in the street that morning, according to plan. It was understood that the dog signaled his master's presence in the neighborhood. Slipping out of the courtyard, Livy found the zealot under a shadowed archway just outside the gate, and quickly arranged to meet him at the temple that afternoon.

The zealot. That was what she called him. She didn't know his real name. When she asked him for it, he merely smiled, winked, and said, "I am the son of my father. What else do you need to know about me?"

By the time Procula, Livy, and Quintus reached the temple grounds, the sun was angling down over the Hinnom Valley to the west. The air was still very hot. Except for the absence of the whip and the money changers' shouts, the scene was almost as hectic as it had been on Monday. If anything, the number of visitors and worshippers in the plaza had increased.

The festival atmosphere was even more pronounced. The bleating of goats and sheep and the fluttering and cooing of doves and pigeons could be heard everywhere. The blue smoke of burning sacrifices hung in the air above the enclosure.

"Over there!" said Livy suddenly, tugging at her mistress's sleeve and pointing to a shady spot under the portico. Livy was proud of herself for having spotted Jesus. He sat in the middle of a large crowd of people, speaking to them in a clear, strong voice.

"Come," said Procula, pulling the edge of her short cloak, or *pallium*, up over her head and taking Livy by the hand. Together they moved toward the knot of people for a closer look. Quintus followed at a safe distance.

As they neared the edge of the audience, it was difficult to see the speaker's face. Livy stood on her toes and ducked this way and that in an attempt to gain a clearer view. Quintus, she noticed, was doing the same. Catching his attention, she mouthed the words, "Keep an eye out for *you know who*." Quintus nodded and went back to the work of seeking a glimpse of Jesus' face.

"Anyone who sins becomes a slave of sin," the voice of Jesus was saying. "So stop sinning! Let the Son set you free. That's the way to be *really free!*"

Slave. Free. Really free! Could it be that Cook was right about this man? Livy wondered. Had he really come to free the slaves? She had to admit his stunt with the whip was pretty daring. She decided to listen more closely.

"What's he talking about?" mumbled a portly man in a blue-and-white prayer shawl who was standing at her elbow. "Just who is this 'son,' anyway?"

"I think he means himself," responded a slight, plain-faced young woman beside him—apparently his daughter.

Livy, still holding Procula's arm, felt her mistress tremble. She looked up and saw that the lady's eyes were fixed on the speaker. An indescribable light seemed to glow in her face. Livy saw it and shivered.

"*Himself!* Well, no wonder then!" scoffed the man in the prayer shawl, puffing out his cheeks and blowing.

"No wonder what?" asked Lady Procula, turning suddenly.

"No wonder the priests and the Pharisees are so anxious to see him locked up—that's what!" he answered. "They aren't a bit pleased with *him*, I can tell you!"

Livy raised an eyebrow. What kind of man could inspire that kind of fear in the hearts of the rulers? *Deliverer. Liberator. The true King. Messiah.* Somehow she had to get a better look at this Jesus.

Leaning heavily on Procula's shoulder, she raised herself to the tips of her toes. Then she craned her neck and strained to see over the heads of the people in front of her.

The first thing she noticed was his eyes. Livy held her breath. Was it possible? They were like the eyes she'd seen in the face of the lamb on the altar. Incredibly deep, full of more feelings than she could name. There was sorrow and pain but also quietness and a strange kind of joy. Now she understood why those eyes had so haunted her mistress, and why Procula was so driven to seek out this man.

As for the face in which those eyes were set . . . Well, it was rather disappointing. Unimpressive. Normal. Definitely not the face of a fighter or a king.

"Come to Me," the voice was saying, "if you're tired, worn out, and weighed down. I will give you rest. I will give you peace. Follow My example. I am gentle and humble."

Gentle. Yes! *Humble.* That was the whole problem in a nutshell, Livy thought. She couldn't imagine any chieftain back in Gaul talking about being gentle or humble. She couldn't picture any Celtic warrior with a face like this man's face. It showed no trace of the pride she remembered seeing the last time her father rode out to do battle with the Roman legions. It was a gentle, humble face, all right—the face of a common peasant.

How could a man with such a face set anybody free? Livy scrunched up her nose and dropped back down on her heels. She'd seen enough.

Suddenly there was a tug at her sleeve.

"Livy!" Quintus whispered. "Look! Over there! It's him!"

She turned. Quintus was pointing to a dark corner behind two huge pillars about fifty paces from the edge of the crowd. Sure enough, it was the zealot. His bearded face was half hidden in the shadow of his gray hood, his great black dog panting patiently at his side.

Livy glanced up at Procula. It was obvious that the lady was aware of nothing but the teacher's voice. *Looks like the coast is clear*, the girl thought.

Livy grasped Quintus by the shoulders and shoved him in the direction of the dark man. "Let's go," she whispered. "We've got an appointment to keep!"

Quintus, whose eyes were riveted on the black shape hunched at the man's side, shook his head until his hair stood out like a ball of freshly washed lamb's wool. He raised a skinny arm and waved her on. "You go ahead," he said.

"Come *on*! He won't bite."

"Which one? The dog or the man?"

Livy glared at him. "Neither one. But *I* will if you don't follow me right *now*!"

Finally Quintus budged—slowly. *He makes a terrible spy*, she told herself as they crossed the pavement. After all, they actually had something to tell the man in the dark cloak. Quintus had overheard an important bit of information while serving at Pilate's table during the midday meal. This business of spying might be dangerous, but it could be fun too.

The zealot flashed his teeth at them from behind black whiskers as they approached. He beckoned to Livy with his hand. "What have you heard?"

"Tell him, Quintus!" she said.

But Quintus hung back. "If you'll promise to hold on to that dog," he said, frowning.

The zealot smiled again. "Don't worry, my young friend," he said. "I've got him firmly in hand. He won't hurt you."

Quintus slipped into the shaded corner and wiped his nose with his sleeve. "Well . . ." he mumbled, "Master Pilate got a message from Herod Antipas last night."

The zealot tightened his lips and squeezed his eyebrows together in a dark knot. "The ruler of Galilee? What did he say?"

"Antipas told Pilate to be on the lookout for two men." Quintus pointed in the direction of Jesus. "One was this Galilean teacher. The other was somebody else named Bar Abbas. He's expected to show up in Jerusalem soon. Maybe this week."

"Do you know him?" Livy asked the zealot. "Is he a friend of yours?"

"Possibly." The man lowered his eyes, shadowed by his hood. "And what's Pilate thinking? What's his strategy?"

Quintus glanced nervously at the dog. "Um . . . when I was serving at the table, I heard him say he wants more soldiers in Jerusalem."

"Sounds like he's expecting trouble," Livy said.

"More soldiers," repeated the zealot, fingering the handle of a sword that he wore concealed beneath his cloak. "That's bad. Very bad. We may lose our chance if we wait any longer."

"Lose our chance?" asked Livy.

"Yes. Perhaps the time for action has arrived." He stood straighter, taller. "Thank you, my young friends. I'm grateful for your help. And I *will* make it up to you." Looking at Livy, he reached into his cloak and pulled out the parchment. "Provided, of course, that we maintain the terms of our agreement."

Livy looked away, feeling a flash of anger.

"Stay true to me, and I won't betray you. And be ready for anything. If nothing changes, look for Kalb outside your gate about this time tomorrow. When you see *him*, you'll know *I'm* not far away. Until then, see what else you can find out. *Shalom!*"

He held up his hand in a gesture of farewell. The next moment he and the dog disappeared into the crowd.

CHAPTER

6

"A silver drachma for your thoughts, Domina," said Livy that night as she poured water from a glossy black Greek urn into an ornate porcelain basin.

Procula was kneeling before the basin on an embroidered Persian cushion. The room around her was richly appointed with every comfort and luxury. There were thick, patterned rugs from Arabia, tapestries and wall hangings from India, shiny Parthian brass lamps spouting bright tongues of yellow flame, a couch spread with the finest Egyptian linen. The scent of perfumed lamp oil filled the air. Through the lacelike gratings over the windows, a strange, restless sound drifted up from the streets of Jerusalem.

The lady loosened the flowing sleeves of her robe, leaned her head back, and waited for Livy to tie up her sandy-brown curls. The tension in her face relaxed into a smile. "You don't have a silver drachma," she laughed.

"Well, if I did, I'd give it to know what's on your mind," said Livy. "You've been awfully quiet since we got back from the temple this afternoon."

Procula sighed. "You're right, of course. But then it's not every day that you hear such words. Or look into the eyes of a man and come away feeling that . . . well, that you've been changed somehow."

Livy scrunched up her nose. "Are you talking about Jesus?"

The lady turned to face her. "What did you think of him?"

"Me?" Livy replied. "I thought that he had a nice voice, I guess. I didn't really understand what he was talking about, though. How can you be humble and gentle and still set slaves free? Besides, he wasn't exactly what I pictured when I heard Cook talking about a messiah and deliverer and king."

Not much of a king at all, she added to herself as she held the soft mass of her mistress's hair between her hands. As her fingers touched the brown curls, a picture of the man in the gray cloak appeared in her mind. The muscular neck, the scarred face . . .

Now that's *a man who could beat the Romans if he tried*, she thought. She saw him standing in the shadows, his hand fingering the hilt of his sword. And she thought about the plot into which she had entered with him . . . and of what might happen to Pilate and Procula if it succeeded. Tenderly she secured the fragrant hair with a gilded ivory comb.

"But you *will* admit," said the lady, turning her head again, "that there is something remarkable about him." She paused a moment and then said, "Did you notice his eyes?"

Wait! thought Livy. *Yes! The eyes! The dream! The lamb on the altar!* She *knew* she had been trying to remember something! Why hadn't she realized it before?

She knelt on the cushion beside Procula and peered intently into her face. "Domina—I never told you what I saw on Monday . . . in the temple."

Procula returned her look. "No, you didn't. And *I* never told you the rest of my dream. We both had too much on our minds, I suppose."

"There was *more* to your dream?"

"Yes. And I'm beginning to believe more firmly than ever that it all has something to do with *God*. And with my desire to know more about Him. It's got something to do with Jesus too. He *is* the man I saw in the dream—the man with the piercing eyes! There is so much that I don't understand . . ." Her voice trailed off.

"Go on," pressed Livy. "What else did you see in the dream? Tell me."

"Well," the lady continued, "I don't think I mentioned that the baskets I saw—the baskets filled with fire—were absolutely *huge*. As big as houses. Or that someone was walking among the flames . . ." She faltered, staring at her own reflection in the bowl of water.

Suddenly Livy clutched her mistress's arm. "Just a minute!" she said. "Huge baskets? On fire? With someone inside?" *It can't be!* she thought. It was too horrible to think about . . . and yet the picture was familiar. It was something out of her childhood in Gaul. "I know what it is!"

Procula turned to her. "Then tell me!" she said. "Somehow I feel that it is *extremely* important!"

Livy swallowed. "It's a sacrifice!"

"A *sacrifice*?"

"Yes! It's the way they make sacrifices to their gods back home in Gaul." Livy shivered just thinking about it. "Those weren't baskets you saw, Domina," she continued in a moment. "They were *cages*—big cages made of wattle, or wickerwork. The Gauls put people inside those cages and set them on fire!"

"People?" gasped Procula. "I've heard of such things, but I didn't dare believe it!"

"Sometimes—not always—the victims go willingly. For the good of the tribe. You know, to save failing crops or get rid of a plague or something like that. And the Gauls believe that when they *do* go willingly, they pass into the Otherworld after death. That's a place of light and beauty and endless summer where no one ever dies again. I remember it all now!"

Procula searched the girl's face. "But there's more," she said in a moment. "And it seems even more important in light of what you've just told me. You remember that I spoke of a lamb? A lamb is the *sacrifice* the Jews offer to *their* God at this Passover season! And I saw the lamb again near the end of my dream. Only this time the piercing eyes were in the face of the lamb. *The lamb had human eyes.*"

Livy gasped. She squeezed the lady's arm tightly. "But that's exactly what *I* saw!" she exclaimed. "That's what I was going to tell you! In the temple! On the altar . . . under the priest's knife . . . before the door of the inner sanctuary! There was a lamb—and it had human eyes!"

"The door to the inner sanctuary? But how did you—?"

"I'm sorry, Domina! I know I wasn't supposed to look inside, but I just *had* to! In the middle of all that excitement, while everyone was so upset about Jesus turning over the tables of the money changers, that's when I—"

A knock at the door interrupted her. Melanus, the steward, entered in great haste, a pink flush glowing on the top of his shiny head, a grim look on his narrow face. Behind him the sound of great turmoil could be heard in the street outside.

"My lady," he said, folding his long-fingered hands and bowing his bald head, "Master has asked me to escort you to the Tower of Antonia . . . for safety's sake. It appears that fighting has broken out in the streets."

CHAPTER 7

Livy quickly packed a few things in a bundle and followed Melanus and her mistress out of the room. Five soldiers led them, and a number of other servants and household members, out of the palace. They turned north and left the Upper City by way of a series of narrow streets and dark alleys. Their path followed the wall closely until it reached the city gate that led to the Skull Place—the Roman place of execution.

From there the group turned east and took a winding course across Jerusalem to the Tower of Antonia. The battlements of the tall gray fortress frowned down on the temple enclosure from the northeast corner of the city.

It seemed the entire household was making this sudden move. Quintus was in the company. Cook too. Even old Hatshup, bent as he was with arthritis and gout, was doing his best to keep up with the stiff pace set by the military men. At the head of the group Livy saw her master, Pontius Pilate, governor of Judea, conferring earnestly with the five Roman warriors. She wondered what *his* feelings were about this emergency.

As they hurried along, Livy heard the sounds of a desperate struggle behind them—angry shouts, hopeless screams, the clash of iron weapons. When she turned around she could see the flicker of flames lighting the walls of the buildings and wisps of white smoke floating in the moonlit air. The houses seemed to huddle together in fear along the sides of the crooked, winding street.

Livy's heart pounded in her chest. This had to be it. The revolution had come. The fight for freedom!

She imagined the voice of the zealot speaking to her once again. *"The time for action has arrived."* She pictured him in the thick of the fight, sword unsheathed, cloak thrown back, head uncovered, teeth bared in a fierce expression of the joy he found in battling his enemies.

That was how she remembered her father. He'd looked exactly like that the very last time she saw him. And now at last, perhaps, she'd have a chance of seeing him again—when she was free. A wave of pride and self-satisfaction swept over her. With her help the zealot had made his decisive move! It wouldn't be long now!

Livy marched through the strange, silvery night, following Procula, Melanus, and the soldiers. But in her mind she stood once again in the kitchen facing the gray-cloaked man. *"If my friends and I succeed,"* she remembered him saying, *"you'll be free to go anywhere you want to go!"* She wished she could be with him now, fighting the Romans at his side. She hoped he'd know where to look for her when the fighting was over.

As they passed the city gate, Livy glanced into the darkness beyond the wall and caught a glimpse of Golgotha, the Skull Place. It looked eerie and lonely in the moonlight—a patch of bare rock streaked with the shadows of several posts fixed in the ground, like the gaunt trunks of dead, bare, branchless trees. She wondered what it would be like to be a condemned criminal—or a runaway slave—heading to that awful place to be crucified. *Not me!* she thought. *And not the zealot either!* For reasons she couldn't explain, Livy had complete confidence in the man. Perhaps it was because of his own confidence. She never doubted that his rebellion would succeed.

At last they reached the Tower of Antonia. Livy nudged Quintus and stared up at the massive stone walls that loomed above her head. Looking tired and cold, Quintus frowned, bent his bushy head, and hugged himself.

A guard on the tower shouted a challenge. One of the soldiers replied with a password. This was followed by the creaking and grating of the heavy iron gates as they swung open to let the governor's party inside.

Quintus cast a relieved glance behind him and shuffled forward into the safety and security of the fortress. Livy looked back toward the palace and the Upper City and wondered how the battle was going.

"Don't worry, my lady," said a smart-looking, square-jawed centurion, saluting Lady Procula as she and her servant girl stepped into the fort. "We've already beaten them. But it's best you stay here for the time being. There's no telling what they might try next."

Beaten! Livy stopped and stared at the man. With that one word, her hopes and dreams of freedom crumbled into a heap of dust and ash. *The zealot and his friends? Beaten?* She felt as if a cold knife blade had suddenly pierced her lungs. Sucking in her breath, she shot a quick and silent glance at Quintus. Her co-conspirator answered with a shrug and a confused grin.

"There weren't as many rebels as we had feared," continued the centurion. "Our men quickly gained control of the situation. Some of the zealots escaped. A few were arrested—those who survived the fight."

The governor himself, wrapping his toga about his shoulders against the chill of the April night, approached the centurion. "What about the leader?" he asked, his balding head and eagle's-beak nose shining in the flickering light of the torches. "I've forgotten his name."

"He was taken, Excellency," answered the soldier. "In fact, he's here in the fortress. He's awaiting trial before your tribunal in the morning. As for his true name, no one has been able to discover it. He calls himself Bar Abbas."

Bar Abbas! Livy gasped and searched the centurion's face.

"Bar Abbas . . . hmm, yes, that was it," mused Pilate, stroking his smooth-shaven jaw. "What kind of name *is* that?"

"Aramaic," replied the centurion. "It means 'Son of his father.' Not really a name at all. We think it's a ruse—a scheme to protect his family and friends. Either that or a code name of some kind. But we'll crack it."

"And the other one," continued Pilate, cocking an eyebrow. "What was his name? Jesus, the Nazarene. Did you arrest him as well?"

"No, Excellency," said the centurion. "Apparently he wasn't involved."

There was a flurry of excited talk as the governor and his group followed the soldiers down a long, echoing hallway toward the commandant's quarters and the rooms in which they would stay. Livy walked beside her mistress.

A brisk breeze wafted through the mosaic-tiled corridor that opened to a broad, flagstoned courtyard. It seemed to Livy that the spring air had grown unusually chilly during their walk from the palace to the fortress. She felt cold inside too. *Another chance lost!* she thought. *But the zealot won't give up! He and his friends will try again! I know they will. They don't need this Bar Abbas!*

They rounded a corner. A connecting passageway rang with the tread of heavy footsteps. Torchlight flared. Toward them strode two more Roman guards with a chained and hooded prisoner between them.

"Well, well!" said the centurion, smiling at Pilate. "Speak of the Devil! Here's your chance to ask him about it yourself, Excellency!" The soldier's smile turned to a frown as he turned toward the prisoner. "Uncover your face before the governor and his wife, dog!"

With a proud toss of his head, the prisoner threw back his hood and faced them boldly. Livy choked back a gasp.

The bearded jaw, the close-cropped head. The long, snaking scar. The half-missing ear. There was no mistaking him.

She looked at him and he looked at her. Then he smiled—a bright, white smile behind thick black whiskers. Putting one chained hand inside his cloak, he lightly patted his belt. That was all.

"Get moving, Bar Abbas!" said one of the guards, giving him a rough shove. "Your chamber's waiting! You'll have your chance to talk to the governor in the morning!"

L ivy sat on a stone step before the entrance to the Tower of Antonia's prison, her chin in her hands. *What a night!* she thought.

Looking up, she shielded her eyes against the glare of the late-morning sun. A figure was coming toward her across the flagstones of the courtyard. Its back was to the light, its face in shadow, and an explosion of wiry hair was flaming around its head like a halo. *Just like one of the angels Cook is always talking about*, she thought.

But it wasn't an angel. It was Quintus.

"Morning," said Quintus, rubbing his nose as he shuffled to a stop in front of her. "How are you?"

Just like he hasn't got a care in the world. Tired as she was, Livy felt like getting up and punching him. "How am I?" she snarled. "How do you *think* I am?"

"I dunno. How am I supposed to know? Did you get any sleep?"

She scrunched up her nose and shook her red head at him. "This is no time to sleep! It's a time to be thinking, planning, doing! No, for your information, I didn't get any sleep! I've been up all night trying to figure out what we should do next. We've had a setback, but we're not beaten yet! We need to put our heads together and get busy if we still want to win our freedom. Don't you understand that?"

The boy crossed his legs and scratched his left ear. "Sure I do. But things could be worse. At least there aren't any dogs around here."

She picked up a handful of gravel and threw it at him. "You're impossible!" she said.

Quintus ducked and retreated before the shower of small stones, his face buried in the crook of his elbow. "Stop it!" he cried. "I only came to tell you something!"

She glowered at him. "What?"

"Something I thought you'd want to know about. Mistress too—especially her."

"Go on," Livy muttered.

"Well, I was serving at Master's table early this morning when some men from the Jewish priests came in to see him."

"And?"

"And they were talking about Jesus of Nazareth, the one we heard teaching in the temple yesterday."

"I know who he is," Livy said impatiently. "What about him?"

"They want Master to send soldiers to arrest him. They think he's dangerous. They're afraid—especially after last night—that he might, you know, pick up where Bar Abbas left off . . . get the people all riled up to fight the Romans or something."

Livy laughed. "*Him*? I don't think so!"

"Well, *they* do," Quintus said. "They know where to catch him too . . . after dark and away from the crowd."

Interesting, thought Livy. "So is Master gonna do it?"

"He said he'd loan them some troops from the fortress. Tonight, after dark. I thought you should tell Mistress."

Livy squinted up at him. "You're right. She won't like it. She thinks an awful lot of this Jesus. Personally, I prefer a messiah like Bar Abbas. I think our chances were better with him." She paused and rubbed her chin thoughtfully. "Maybe they still are."

Quintus looked doubtful. "Whaddaya mean? He's in jail! He's no good to us now."

"Maybe. Maybe not. Besides, he's holding evidence he could use against me. Which makes me think I'd better stick with him as long as I can."

"But Livy! He's a goner! By this time tomorrow he'll probably be—

you know—*chkkk!*" With his finger he made a slicing motion across his throat. "Why don't you just forget the whole thing?"

Livy raised an eyebrow. "You give up too easily, Quintus." Cupping one hand around her mouth, she looked from side to side to make sure no one was listening. Then she whispered, "Bar Abbas may still have a few tricks up his sleeve. I've been talking to him about it."

"Talking to him! When?"

"This morning."

"You mean in *there?*" Quintus turned pale. His finger shook as he pointed down the dark stairway into the dungeon.

"Sure. Why not?"

"But . . . I didn't think the guards let anyone down there!"

"I have my ways," Livy said with a sly smile. "Want to see?"

"N-not really," said Quintus. But before he could utter another word, she'd taken him by the arm and was leading him under the frowning archway and down toward the cells beneath the fortress.

At the first landing a rather sleepy-looking soldier stumbled to his feet and barred their entrance with his spear. But in the next moment, a look of recognition crossed his face, and his features relaxed into a lopsided smile. "You again?" he said. "So what do you want now? And who's your friend?"

"Marius, this is Quintus," said Livy, bowing smartly as she presented the boy to the guard. "Quintus, Marius. Quintus is one of Governor Pilate's *personal* servants. In fact, he's just come from the governor's *personal* presence. To accompany me on an inspection tour of the prison facility."

Marius eyed Quintus with a skeptical grin. "Is that so?" he said.

"Livy!" whined Quintus, trying to free his arm from her iron grasp.

"Mm-hmm," said Livy. "What do you say?"

Marius shook his head and mumbled something to himself, smiling all the while. He yawned and let out a loud burp. "I say anything's possible," he said with a wink. "*If* you can get me some more of that wine and cheese."

"There's plenty more where that came from." Livy smiled. "I'll be right back."

Shifting nervously from one foot to the other, Quintus waited with the soldier while Livy dashed off on her errand. Soon she returned with a bulging wineskin and a small goatskin bag filled with curdled white *leben*. She and Quintus left the guard happily eating, drinking, and humming to himself. Then they stepped down the stairway to the lowest level of the prison.

"Where did you get that stuff?" whispered Quintus as they wound their way into the darkness.

"I told Cook that Mistress is waiting for her breakfast," Livy explained with an innocent look. "Which, of course, is true."

At the bottom of the stairs was a dank and murky spot lit only by the flame of a clay hand lamp that burned weakly in a shallow niche in the wall. Livy squeezed Quintus's arm and stopped in front of a thick wooden door bound with heavy iron straps.

"This is it," she hissed. She slid back a strip of iron that covered a narrow slot in the door and whispered through the opening: "Bar Abbas! It's me! I brought Quintus with me this time!"

Scraping, scuffling sounds reached their ears from the other side of the door. In a moment a single black eye, overarched by a bushy black eyebrow, appeared in the slot. A voice, harsh and gravelly but still recognizable, said, "Good. I've been working out a plan. And I have an assignment for you."

"An assignment," moaned Quintus. "Oh no!"

The voice continued. "We've still got one chance left. Now listen carefully. You remember the agreement your master made with the Jews a few years ago? About releasing a prisoner of their choosing during the Passover festival each year?"

Livy thought for a moment. "Uh, right. He was trying to buy friends."

"Exactly," said Bar Abbas. "Well, I intend to *be* that prisoner this year."

A slow smile spread across her face. Down in that small space just beneath her heart Livy felt the dying embers of her dream—the dream of freedom—being fanned back into life. *"How?"* she asked.

"I have friends who can make it happen," Bar Abbas said. "They know the right people. They have contacts in every corner of the city, allies in almost every workshop and merchant's booth. I want you to go to them and tell them what I'm thinking. They'll have the word all over Jerusalem in less than an hour."

"You really think it will work?" Livy said.

"There's a good chance," he replied. "Anyway, we've got to try."

Livy glanced over at Quintus. He had dropped to the floor and was sitting with his head in his hands. "So where do we find these friends of yours?" she asked.

"Make your way back to the governor's palace and follow the street that goes past its main gate. Five houses beyond the palace of Caiaphas the High Priest, you'll come to a house built of reddish stone. There's a mosaic in the pavement in front of the door—a picture of fishermen on the sea. You can't miss it. The house has an upper room that the owners rent out to visiting pilgrims. You'll find my friends on the lower level."

"And then what?"

Bar Abbas pulled a ring from his finger and passed it to her through the narrow slot in the door. "Give them this. Tell them what I told you. They'll know what to do. But you'd better go quickly. They may come and drag me before Pilate anytime. Once he passes sentence on me, he won't wait long to carry it out."

Livy tucked the ring into her belt and grabbed Quintus's hand. "Got it!" she said. "Come on, Quintus. Let's go!"

Quintus just shook his head and moaned.

It wasn't as easy to carry out Bar Abbas's assignment as Livy had hoped. She wasn't sure how she and Quintus would get beyond the fortress gate, but figured they could manage if given a chance. Unfortunately, Cook kept them busy the rest of the day with kitchen chores.

To make matters worse, they just couldn't seem to get away from Melanus. During six years in Pilate's household, Livy had never seen anything like it. Most days Melanus joined the other servants in the kitchen for breakfast, handed out orders, and then slipped off somewhere by himself to work on accounts. But today he seemed to be everywhere, watching, checking, threatening. Livy was sweating twice as much as usual before the day was half over, more from worry than work.

Not until the evening meal was finished and the last cooking pot had been scoured and stored did Livy see a chance to slip out. Cook and Melanus were in another room, discussing the state of household provisions. The sun was setting, and most of the inhabitants of the fortress seemed to have gone indoors for the night. Outside, the city was unusually quiet; this was the night on which many of the Jews celebrated the Passover meal with their families.

"Quintus!" Livy whispered as the boy came in with an empty water jar. "Get a cloak and meet me at the side entrance. You know, the small gate where they bring in supplies."

Quintus looked like he was about to protest, but she shoved him out the door. Then she ran to get the cloak she'd left in the suite of rooms that had been reserved for Procula.

Maybe, she thought as she ran through a deserted stone passageway, *just maybe we won't ever have to come back! Maybe I can deliver Bar Abbas's message and then stay with his zealot friends! Then, once they convince Master to release him, he'll come and smuggle me out of the city, and I'll be on my way back to Gaul!*

She smiled to herself as she ducked inside the lady's chamber. Her cloak was there, draped across the ivory stool where Procula sat whenever Livy combed out her hair. She picked it up, threw it over her shoulder, and hurried to the door.

"Livia!"

Livy turned to see her mistress coming in from another room. "I'm so glad you're here! I was just about to go looking for you. Come—sit beside me."

Livy's cheeks began to burn. "Domina," she said. "I was just . . . well, I—"

"Not now, child, please! I *must* talk to you! I have never felt so . . . so disturbed, so worried . . ."

Looking up at her mistress, Livy could see it was true. Never had she seen Procula looking so worn and weary. The skin of her face was extremely pale, almost transparent. Every bit of color had drained from her lips and cheeks. "What is it, Domina?" Livy asked, going up and laying a hand on her arm.

Procula dropped into an armchair of carved ebony. She motioned to Livy to sit on a scarlet cushion that lay on the floor beside it. Then, passing a hand over her eyes and sighing, she said, "After last night's trouble and our trek from the palace to the Antonia, I . . . well, I found it impossible to sleep. I paced this floor until well after sunup. Then, when my legs could no longer support me, I collapsed across my bed and fell asleep.

"I dreamed again, Livia! I saw the man with the piercing eyes. It was Jesus, I'm sure of it! He was carrying the lamb, and he had a circlet of gold on his head. And this time he and the lamb went into the cage of fire!

They were consumed by the flames! I wept and shouted, but I couldn't stop it from happening. What do you think it means?"

"I'm not sure," Livy said after a pause, her eyes fixed on the lady's face. "Back in Gaul, kings and chieftains wear golden circlets on their heads. The dream seems to be saying that the man with piercing eyes—Jesus—is a king. And a sacrifice too."

"A king *and* a sacrifice?" It was clear that Procula was struggling to take it all in.

"Yes," said Livy slowly. "Whatever that means."

That was when it came back to her—the news Quintus had brought that morning outside the prison. The news he'd wanted her to deliver to Procula. How could she have forgotten?

"Domina!" she said, jumping to her feet. "I just remembered something I was supposed to tell you! They're going to arrest him!"

"Arrest *Jesus?*" said Procula, taking the girl's two hands in her own. "Who's going to arrest him?"

"Master! And the Jewish priests! They're sending soldiers—tonight! Quintus heard them say so!"

Procula got up and crossed the room. She stopped in front of a small writing table. Taking up a stylus, she scratched a few words on a piece of parchment. She folded the parchment, sealed it with a spot of sealing wax, and pressed the insignia of her ring into the seal. Then she walked over and handed the parchment to Livy.

"You must follow the soldiers!" she said. "This letter will secure your passage out of the fortress. Take Quintus with you. Make sure the soldiers don't notice you. When all is done, come back and tell me what you've seen. Now go!"

"Yes, Domina!" said Livy, taking the parchment from the lady's hand. Then she pulled her cloak up over her head and hurried out the door.

By the time Livy found Quintus, she'd realized she was facing a nearly impossible task. She'd accepted two difficult assignments: Follow the soldiers on Procula's behalf *and* deliver Bar Abbas's message to his friends. And she had to complete both of them in a single evening. Already her palms were sweating and her heart was beating as if it would jump out of her body.

Darkness was gathering as she and Quintus approached the soldier who stood on guard at the fortress gate. The man eyed them doubtfully as Livy pulled Procula's note from her pouchlike belt.

"*Seems* to be in order," he mumbled, studying the words on the parchment and chewing his lip thoughtfully. "Though I can't imagine why Lady Procula would send a pair like *you* two into the streets after dark. What's this all about?"

"Shhhh!" said Livy, pointing her freckled nose straight at the man's square chin and laying a finger to her lips. "It's top secret!"

The soldier frowned. Livy smiled back and gave him a wink. He cocked an eyebrow and glanced over at Quintus. Quintus just grinned and nodded.

Once outside the gate, Livy began to breathe a little more easily. *That part wasn't so hard,* she thought. She tugged at Quintus's sleeve and pulled her own cloak up around her shoulders. "Let's get going!" she said.

Her companion scratched his bushy head with nervous fingers. "What for?" he whined. "*I'm* in no rush to land myself in a big heap of trouble!"

Instead of answering, Livy took him firmly by the arm and dragged him after her over the uneven paving stones. She knew there wasn't a moment to lose.

Following Bar Abbas's instructions to the letter, they hurried west to the gate that stood opposite the Skull Place and then south along the wall to the old Upper City. It wasn't long before they were passing the gates to the grand old Herodian palace, the governor's usual residence in Jerusalem. Its massive stonework towered above them like a cliff. Except for a few sentries posted at the entrance, the place was deserted—dark, empty, silent.

As she rushed past, Livy couldn't help wondering whether she'd ever return to the palace. She hoped not. If only Bar Abbas's plan worked! There was still a chance that her days as a slave were nearly over.

A few blocks south of the palace and on the opposite side of the street stood the elegant, Greek-columned structure that served as home to the high priest, Caiaphas. It doubled as an occasional meeting place for the Sanhedrin, the Jewish supreme court. Livy recognized it at once.

"Five houses beyond . . ." She repeated the words of Bar Abbas to herself as she and Quintus rushed ahead. "One . . . two . . . three," she counted, ". . . four. I think this is it, Quintus! Reddish stone . . . mosaic in the pavement . . . upper story . . . Yes, this has to be it!"

For a few moments they hesitated, staring first at the fishing scene pictured in the tiles at their feet and then at the low-arched door before them. Then came a sound from above their heads. They looked up.

The door to the upper room had opened, and a group of plainly dressed, dark-bearded Jewish men were coming down the stairway. At the head of the line was a tall man with a familiar face—a face Livy had seen before. A face with dark brown eyes that seemed to pierce her very soul.

It was Jesus of Nazareth.

Slowly Jesus and his men descended the stairs. When he reached the bottom, he paused and turned to look at Livy. It was a sad look, she thought. Without intending to, she gripped Quintus's arm more tightly and backed away. Something caught in her throat. In that small space beneath her heart she felt something fluttering like a dry leaf in the wind. Why was he here? What would she say to him if he spoke to her? What would he think if he knew what she was doing? *Did* he know? How could he?

But the Galilean didn't speak. Instead, he turned and led his followers up the street. Dumbstruck, Livy and Quintus watched them go. In a few moments the men had rounded a corner and were heading up a road that led to the eastern portion of the city.

Livy let out her breath with a small sigh as the last of them disappeared. "Let's go!" she said. "It's getting late. I can feel it."

"What do you mean 'late'?" asked Quintus.

But Livy didn't answer. She was already at the door of the red-stone house, pounding on it loudly with her fist. She waited and then knocked again. The door began to open slowly, very slowly, just a crack. Around its rough wooden edge appeared the dirty fingers of a hardened hand. From the darkness within, two shining eyes peered out. A low voice spoke: "Who's there?"

By way of answer, Livy reached into her belt and drew out Bar Abbas's ring. Its gold surface glinted in the night. She thrust it into the crack between the door and the frame. The callused hand seized the ring eagerly and drew it inside. Then the door closed.

Livy turned and looked at Quintus. Quintus frowned. "Is that it?" he said. "Can we leave now?"

"Leave?" she cried. "We haven't even delivered the message yet!"

She was about to knock again when the door reopened, and the hand beckoned them inside. Quintus turned on his heel, but Livy grabbed him by the tail of his cloak and pulled him in after her.

Once inside, she found herself looking up at the owner of the two bright, beady eyes she'd seen through the crack in the door. They were burning under bushy eyebrows, set deep within a large-nosed, shockingly scarred, gray-bearded face. The face leered at her in the light of a handheld lamp. She swallowed.

"Where did you get this?" said the man, holding up Bar Abbas's ring.

It glittered in the yellow lamplight. There was a musty smell in the house, like the stench of something rotten. Livy thought she heard drunken shouts coming from an inner room. She let go of Quintus, planted her feet firmly beneath her, and tried to sound braver than she felt.

"It's from Bar Abbas!" she blurted in a voice that seemed too high and thin to be her own. The tiny inward trembling had grown so strong it was shaking her entire body. "He gave it to me . . . in the Antonia prison."

"Then he lives!" breathed the man, nodding his head and examining the ring closely in the lamplight. He turned his face toward her. "What's his message?"

Livy smoothed down her cloak and tunic and cleared her throat, searching for her voice. When she thought she'd found it, she answered, "He says the governor will release a prisoner for the Passover. He wants to be that prisoner. He said you'd know what to do."

The man regarded her with a strange, toothless smile. "Of course we do," he said. "When's his trial?"

"He's already been tried! And condemned!"

"Then we'll have to work fast," the scarred man muttered. He held the lamp above his head and kicked the door open. "Now you'd better make yourselves scarce—fast!" With that, he thrust the two children out into the street. Quintus collapsed on the pavement with a sigh of relief. Livy stumbled over him.

"Wait!" she called. "Bar Abbas and I made a deal! He said that when he's released, he'll—"

The door slammed shut. Livy and Quintus were alone in the cave-dark street. She shook herself, picked herself up, pushed her hair out of her eyes, and turned to give Quintus a hand.

"Well," she said shakily, "I guess that's that. Come on—we'd better get back to the fortress as fast as we can! I just hope those soldiers haven't left yet!"

CHAPTER 11

"There's no point in going back inside," she whispered to Quintus when they found themselves standing once again in the black shadow of the Antonia tower. "I don't want to have to convince that guard Mistress Procula is sending me out on *another* top-secret errand!"

Quintus nodded. "I don't even want to *go* on any more top-secret errands," he said.

Livy ignored the comment. "We'll just stay right here," she said, leading him close to the wall. "Keep to the shadows—until we see the soldiers of the cohort. I just hope we're not too late."

They didn't have long to wait. Soon the sound of voices reached them from somewhere within the darkened archway. This was followed by the scraping and grating of the heavy iron gates swinging open and the thudding of the soldiers' feet as they marched out of the fortress. Livy and Quintus flattened themselves against the wall to avoid the light of the torches. It was hard to be sure in the darkness, but Livy guessed there were at least two hundred of them.

"A whole army to arrest one man?" she wondered aloud as they passed. "I don't believe this!"

Once beyond the gate, the soldiers turned left and began moving in the direction of the temple. Livy and Quintus followed cautiously at a distance.

"What're they going in *there* for?" whispered Quintus as the troops made another left turn into the temple grounds.

Livy didn't answer. Instead, she grabbed his hand and followed the soldiers.

"What's this?" she said when they emerged inside the Court of the Gentiles. "*More* soldiers?"

It was true. Across the open square marched a smaller band of temple guards in their brass helmets, white turbans, and blue tunics. Some were armed with clubs and spears. Others carried torches and lanterns. Search dogs paced restlessly back and forth.

"*Big* dogs!" said Quintus when he saw them, turning pale and ducking behind Livy. "Livy, you don't expect me to face all those dogs, do you? I couldn't do that for *anything*! Not for Mistress Procula or freedom or Bar Abbas or—"

"Quiet!" she whispered. "They're all on leashes. Besides, they're after Jesus, not us!"

As Quintus settled into a soft whimper, Livy stared narrowly at the man who walked at the head of the troop of temple guards. She was almost certain she'd seen him before . . . maybe one of the men with Jesus at the temple. One of his friends!

What does it mean? she wondered. *Has he come to beg the soldiers to leave his teacher alone?* But there was no time to ask. Already the combined Roman and Jewish forces, their armor and weapons glittering in the torchlight, were leaving Jerusalem by way of the Golden Gate and marching down into the Kidron Valley.

"Come on, Quintus!" she said. "We've got to keep up with them!"

It was easier said than done. Quintus wasn't the only one who had trouble matching the soldiers' pace. Livy, too, teetered on the edge of exhaustion. She'd had little sleep over the past two days, and too much constant stress.

To make things worse, the path became much harder from this point. The importance of remaining unseen forced them to hang back, beyond the range of the torches and lanterns. In the thick darkness it was nearly impossible to pick their way down the valley's steep and rocky side.

They stumbled, tripped, and fell several times before reaching the brook. Their attempts to get across the water left them soaked and muddy. By the time they were on the other side, they'd lost sight of the soldiers altogether.

Livy's heart sank. What would she tell her mistress?

Stumbling up the other side of the valley, Livy felt her determination beginning to break apart. *Why are we even doing this?* she thought.

Was it for Procula? For Bar Abbas? For those piercing, sad eyes turned upon her at the bottom of the stairs?

What did it all mean? A lamb under the priest's knife, a basket of fire, and a man with a circlet of gold on his head—what was the point? What did she care about this man Jesus, anyway?

What could Bar Abbas do for her now that he was in prison facing execution? She didn't want to think about either of them. All she wanted was her freedom!

So tired was Livy that Quintus actually moved ahead of her as they continued their climb up the slope beyond the brook. Vaguely, through the darkness, she saw the boy approaching a line of dark brush—almost like a hedge—at the top of the rise. A sudden thought struck her. She stopped and called out to him, "Quintus! Wait! I've got a better idea!"

Quintus turned and stood squinting down at her as she ran to catch up with him. By the time she reached his side, she was fighting to get her breath.

"*What* better idea?" Quintus asked.

"Don't you see?" she said when she was able to speak at last. "We're outside the city! Outside the walls! This is what we've been waiting for!"

Quintus scratched his head. "It is?"

"Take a look around!" she said. "There's nobody out here! It's dark! This is our chance to make a break for it! We don't need anybody else's help. We can be free! We *are* free!"

Quintus was backing away, staring at her as if he couldn't comprehend what she was saying. "But what about the soldiers? And Mistress Procula? And Jesus of Nazareth? And Bar Abbas?"

"Forget about them!" said Livy. "Let's just go for it!"

At that moment, from somewhere in the surrounding darkness, a chorus of loud barking broke into their discussion. Quintus turned white. His bottom lip began to tremble.

"I knew it!" he moaned. "It's those dogs, Livy! They're here! They're gonna get me!" He turned to run but tripped over a tree root and went crashing through the tangled hedge in front of them.

"No!" cried Livy. "Don't do this to me *now*!" She plunged after him into the bushes.

To her great surprise, she emerged in the midst of what looked like a neatly kept garden. Even in the moonlight she could see the white roses, yellow chrysanthemums, and pink coriander blooming in well-watered beds. Ferns lined stone-paved paths that went winding away into the night. Twisted olive trees gently bent their limbs over the scene.

Quintus was lying on his back beside her, a dazed look on his face. All at once the place was blazing with light. Torches were flaring. Dogs were barking. Angry voices were shouting.

Suddenly Livy realized that the soldiers and temple guards they'd been following were in the garden too. But to her great relief she also concluded that none of them had seen her. Their eyes were directed elsewhere, at someone who was standing on the other side of the garden. In a glare of light and a confused hubbub of noise, they pressed toward that person—weapons drawn, shields at the ready.

"That's the one!" someone was shouting. "The one Iscariot just kissed on the cheek! Seize him!"

"Betrayed with a kiss!" laughed another harsh voice. "That's a good one!"

Fear caught at Livy's throat. *Betrayed?* Who were they talking about? She looked wildly from side to side but was unable to see anything clearly.

Suddenly there came a lull in the noise and the confusion. A gap opened in the crowd. Livy looked up and saw him—Jesus of Nazareth—

standing in the midst of the guards and soldiers with a calm, unworried expression on his face.

"Who is it you want?" she heard him call as several armed temple guards approached him.

"Jesus of Nazareth," they responded.

"I am He," answered Jesus, fixing them with his piercing eyes.

Those eyes, Livy thought. As she watched, those deep, clear eyes seemed almost to glow with an unearthly light. They shone—or so it looked to her—like pale stars in the heaven of Jesus' plain, humble face. It was the strangest, most wonderful thing she had ever seen.

Livy rubbed her own eyes and stared. Could it be true? For just a second, when he spoke those three simple words, "I am He," had the night air around Jesus' head really shimmered like the air above hot desert sands? Had his beard actually flashed from brown to snowy white? Had a tongue of flame really shot across the space between him and the guards?

Livy didn't know what to think, or what to believe.

But whatever she'd seen, the soldiers appeared to have seen it too. Their faces went colorless with terror. The muscles in their arms and legs went slack. Some cried out, some whimpered, some moved their lips soundlessly. Dropping their weapons, they all stumbled backward and fell to the ground beneath the Nazarene's gaze. Jesus stood looking down at them—waiting, it seemed.

"Wow!" said Quintus, sitting up and gaping. "Did you see that?"

"I . . . I think so," said Livy. *Maybe I was wrong about this man.* Who could look and speak like that? Only . . . the gods?

The men, looking stunned and embarrassed, rose to their feet and brushed themselves off. Jesus put his question to them a second time: "Whom are you seeking?"

The soldiers timidly picked up their weapons and retreated a step or two. An officer who seemed to be in charge cleared his throat and said again, "Jesus of Nazareth."

"I told you that I am He," said the Nazarene. His voice was quiet, but inside Livy's head it sounded like thunder. Jesus pointed toward a handful of his followers. "If you are looking for Me, then let these men go."

At this the barking and shouting broke out afresh. The soldiers rushed forward, seized Jesus with rough hands, and bound him with a rope. A moment later his voice and face were swallowed up in the crowd.

Livy grabbed Quintus and pulled him back into the safety of the bushes as several men—followers of Jesus—went running this way and that. The soldiers, dogs darting around their legs, led Jesus out of the garden and down the hill.

The light of their lanterns faded into the quiet distance. Livy and Quintus found themselves alone.

"Now what?" said Quintus, rubbing his head. "Are you serious about trying to escape? I'd hate to have those dogs on *my* trail!"

Livy frowned into the darkness and watched the glow of the torches as they retreated into the valley. Her mind was a blank. What had she just seen? She couldn't be sure until she'd gone home and had a good night's sleep. Yes, that was it. She was overtired—completely worn out. First she'd rest. Then she'd have to think the whole thing over for a while.

Of one thing she was certain: She'd misjudged this man Jesus. He didn't look like much on the outside, but it was obvious that he had some kind of terrible power within. She had to know more about him. She couldn't run away, not yet. Not without finding answers.

She bit her lip and chewed the inside of her cheek. Then she brushed the red hair out of her eyes and turned to face Quintus.

"No," she said. "I've changed my mind. We're going back."

CHAPTER
12

Livy woke with a start in the predawn darkness. Her eyes popped open at the sound of a rooster crowing in the black emptiness outside the window.

Something in the bird's voice chilled her. So raw and shrill in the early morning air. Shivering, she sat up and pulled her linen tunic on over her head.

At once the events of the previous night flooded back into her mind. The soldiers with their torches and lanterns . . . the hike across the Kidron Valley and up the Mount of Olives . . . the arrest . . .

She shook her head. Jesus had been arrested? A man who could knock down a troop of soldiers with a mere glance? Surely that picture would remain etched in her memory for a long, long time.

Never had she seen any man, in Gaul, Rome, or Palestine, who had that kind of power. Maybe Cook was right. Maybe this Jesus *was* the Jews' long-awaited Messiah after all—the Liberator, the Deliverer . . . the One who would set everyone free. But if so, why had he let the temple guards bind him and lead him away?

She couldn't take the time to figure it out now. Not when her mission was still unfulfilled. She hadn't given her mistress a report on last night's events! She had to find Procula at once and let her know what had happened in the garden on the hill outside the city. Getting up, Livy threw her cloak around her shoulders and ran down to the kitchen.

Cook was there, wrapped in a blue-and-white shawl, brooding silently over a steaming pot. A fire blazed on the great stone hearth. There was a comforting, yeasty smell of barley broth and baking loaves in the air.

The big woman looked up slowly as Livy came running in. Her eyes said it all. *She knows*, Livy thought.

"Where have they taken him?" Livy blurted. "Do you know? Can you tell me?"

Cook's eyes grew round with surprise. She obviously hadn't expected the slave girl to be so concerned about the Nazarene's arrest. "Caiaphas's house, so far as I can tell," she said, shaking her head sadly. "Leastwise I haven't heard anything about them bringing him *here*. Master's up, but he's still at his breakfast. I'm not sure what he's got planned for today."

"Livy!" said Quintus, shuffling in behind her. "There you are! I've been looking all over for you. I've got news I thought you'd want to hear."

"What is it?" she asked. "Something about Jesus?"

Like Cook, Quintus seemed taken aback at the urgency in Livy's voice. "Well, yes . . . as a matter of fact."

"What? Tell me!" she demanded, grabbing him by the sleeve.

"Leggo of me, wouldja?" said Quintus. He backed away and smoothed the wrinkles out of his tunic. "He's going to stand trial before the master. Right away. I heard it while serving at table this morning. Messengers from the chief priests were just here."

"Here?" said Livy. "They're bringing him *here*?" Even she was a bit startled at her tone. Why was her stomach churning? Why this feeling that something *had* to be done?

"Isn't that what I just said?" Quintus cried, throwing up his hands.

"It was bound to happen this way," observed Cook, still shaking her head. "And I have a feeling it'll lead to no good. You mark my words."

A trial before Master Pilate! thought Livy. *Maybe there's something Mistress Procula can do to help!*

"Cook!" she said. "Have you seen Lady Procula this morning?"

"Not yet, child," said Cook, turning back to her pot. "Probably still in bed. She's hardly ever up this early. Can't blame her, either. Doesn't sleep well with all those dreams and such."

Livy didn't wait to hear any more. She was out the door at once, crossing the flagstones, heading toward the stairs that led to Procula's apartment on the second level of the fortress. But as she crossed the courtyard, she saw something that made her stop for a closer look. A crowd of Jewish priests and officials was gathering in front of the open space before the governor's quarters. It was the judgment place known as *Gabbatha*, sometimes called the Stone Pavement.

They're here—already! Livy thought. *And Jesus must be with them! Master will be coming out to speak with them any minute!* Her mistress would want to know about this development at once.

Again she ran, passing beneath an archway, through a series of columns, and around a dark corner. The stairs lay straight ahead. But when she reached the bottom step, she stopped and stared. There on the first landing stood a tall, dark figure, awaiting her approach and blocking her path.

It was Melanus.

"Well, well," smiled the bald steward in his most soothing, melodious voice, "if it isn't the very person I've been looking for!"

"M-me?" stammered Livy. "What for?"

"It's actually rather interesting," he responded, calmly folding his long-fingered hands. "The captain of the dungeon guards came looking for me last night. In my role as overseer of the household slaves, you understand. He asked about you specifically. Apparently there's a prisoner down below—a condemned man—who wants to see you."

Bar Abbas! thought Livy. In the midst of all the excitement about Jesus' arrest, she'd forgotten about him. He, too, was expecting a report!

Melanus unclasped his hands and took a step toward her. "Is it possible that Lady Procula's *personal servant* actually knows rebels and criminals of that sort?" His thin-lipped smile looked forced. "It's hard to imagine! Definitely not the kind of information one wants to get around. You'd have been wiser to keep the thing hushed up. Perhaps it's time you and I had a little talk." He reached the bottom of the steps and stretched a hand toward her.

Livy swerved, dodged, and started running back the way she'd come. Tearing across the courtyard, she again passed the place of judgment. The governor was addressing the small crowd that had gathered before his tribunal bench. Quintus was standing behind him and off to one side. Apparently he'd been assigned to attend to his master during the course of the trial.

"What charges are you bringing against this man?" she heard Pilate say as she hurried toward the entrance to the prison.

"If he were not a criminal," someone answered, "we would not have handed him over to you . . ."

No chance of seeing Mistress Procula now, thought Livy. *Not until Melanus is out of the way.* She looked up and saw the dark stone archway that led to the dungeon on her left. *This may be my only chance to talk to Bar Abbas,* she thought, ducking into its shadow. *But I'd better make it quick!*

She hesitated only a moment. Then she hurtled down the steps, past the dozing guard, all the way to the lowest level of the prison. There she stopped, breathing heavily, and leaned for a moment against the cool stone wall of the passageway. Sliding the strip of iron away from the peephole, she pounded heavily on Bar Abbas's door. "It's me!" she said.

The dark eye quickly appeared at the opening. Livy thought she detected a glint of fear in its expression. "Finally!" said the voice from within. "What took so long?"

"No time to explain," she answered breathlessly. "I can't stay. Melanus is after me! But I delivered your message, just the way you told me. Any news here?"

"Yes," was Bar Abbas's somber reply. "They brought me before Pilate yesterday afternoon. The long and short of it is I'm scheduled to die today.

Crucifixion. Along with another poor wretch they took on the night of the uprising." She couldn't mistake the note of despair in his voice.

There was a pause. "I'm sorry," Livy said at length. *I wonder what he's done with my parchment,* she thought. *I wonder if they searched him when they brought him to trial.*

She tried to ignore the sinking feeling in the pit of her stomach. "But . . . well, you just can't give up hope!" she went on. "Not now! Your friends are spreading the word this very minute! I-I'm sure they'll fix everything so that you're the one released for the festival. And then . . . and then . . ."

She stopped. *And then what?* Livy had to admit she didn't know. What about Jesus? What about Procula's dream? Was she *really* hoping for Bar Abbas's release? Should the zealot go free while someone else, maybe someone innocent, was punished?

"I-I've got to go now," she said with a sigh. "Melanus is sure to find me here if I stay another second! There's another trial going on. I'll keep you posted if I can."

"Another trial?" she heard him say as she jumped back up the stairs. But she didn't dare stay to answer. She still had to see her mistress, and there wasn't a moment to lose.

For the third time Livy crossed the courtyard. As she passed the tribunal, she saw Jesus standing before Pilate. Despite her fear of being caught, she felt she had to stop and listen.

"*Are* you the king of the Jews?" she heard her master say, his voice echoing over the paving stones and off the fortress walls.

"Is this your own idea," Jesus replied, "or did others talk to you about Me?"

King of the Jews. It reminded Livy of Lady Procula's dream—the man with the piercing eyes, crowned with a circlet of gold. Could it be that Jesus really *was* a king? Was the governor simply mocking him? Or did he really want to know?

From across the open plaza came a familiar sight—the reflection of the rising sun off the top of a shiny, bald head. Melanus had seen her and was striding in her direction. She turned and ran.

Between the columns, around the corner, and up the staircase she flew. She reached the door of her mistress's chamber and beat upon it loudly.

"Who's there?" came the lady's weary voice from behind the door.

"It's Livia!" She could hear the steward's sandals scraping on the stairs. "Please, Domina! Let me in!"

The door flew open, and Livy slipped inside. She fell into her mistress's arms and clung to her. "Lock it!" she pleaded. "Quickly!"

The lady did so, giving her servant girl a worried look. The sound of footsteps passed and faded in the passage outside. Livy breathed a sigh of relief.

"What is it?" said Procula, sounding alarmed.

"They've taken him!" Livy said. "Arrested him—Jesus! He's on trial this very minute . . . before Master's tribunal! I don't know what they might do to him, but Cook says it won't be good!"

Procula said nothing. Her mouth hardened into a firm, straight line. The creases in her forehead, only half hidden by her curls, bunched together. The fear and anxiety melted away and were replaced by a look of determination.

She stepped to her writing table, took up a stylus, scribbled a note, and sealed it. When she was finished, she crossed the room again and handed the parchment to Livy.

"Deliver this message to Pilate," the lady said. "Immediately."

Livy's face brightened. Perhaps the lady's note would save the Galilean's life! "Yes, Domina!" she said. Shoving the door open, Livy burst into the passage.

Down the stairs she raced, and across the fort's broad middle courtyard. She didn't stop until she'd climbed the ten steps to the tribunal.

Quintus glanced at her as she crossed the platform. He frowned and mouthed the words, "What are *you* doing here?" In reply Livy merely put a finger to her lips and held up the parchment. Then she stepped straight up to the governor.

The eyes of Jesus gripped her as she drew near. Mesmerized, she stopped and stared. She heard him speak, apparently in answer to another one of Pilate's questions. "My kingdom is not of this world," he said. "If it were, My servants would fight to prevent My arrest by the Jews. But now My kingdom is from another place."

"You *are* a king, then!" said Pilate, stroking his jaw. He smiled—a doubtful smile. Then, as if coming out of a daydream, he suddenly turned and saw Livy standing at his side.

"What is this?" he said with a scowl. "Who authorized this interruption?"

"Begging your pardon, Excellency," said Livy in the sweetest and most timid voice she could manage. "But my lady, your wife, Mistress Procula, has sent me to you with a message." She held the parchment out to him.

Pilate's eyebrows arched upward. "From my wife?" He frowned. "Very well, then. Give it to me."

Hoping her master wouldn't notice, Livy sidled up next to him and peered over his toga-clad arm as he unfolded and read the note. It said:

Don't have anything to do with that innocent man, for I have suffered a great deal today in a dream because of him.

"A dream," sighed Pilate. "Yes, and what else is new?" Then he turned to the servant girl and said, "Tell your mistress that her message has been delivered. That will be all."

"Yes, *Domine*," said Livy.

With that she hurried away from the pavement. She still wasn't sure why she was so concerned about this Galilean teacher. Perhaps it was what she'd seen in the garden the night before. Whatever the reason, she returned to her mistress's chamber feeling she'd done everything in her power to help him.

CHAPTER 13

Livy spent most of the rest of the morning in her mistress's room, trying to sort out her feelings about the events of the past two days. Now that the excitement was over and the waiting had begun, she couldn't help feeling as if a dark cloud were hanging over her head. There was a kind of numbness in that small space just beneath her heart, as if she were just too tired to care about anything anymore.

She sat on the little ivory stool with her chin in her hands. Procula noticed her silence.

"You, too, are troubled," said the lady, glancing over at her servant girl with a look of deep concern.

Livy looked up and tried to smile. "I'm just thinking," she said.

Procula was anything but silent, however. Livy had never seen her mistress so jumpy. The lady worried aloud about the outcome of the Nazarene's trial. She paced the room, talking nervously, referring constantly to her dream and the strange pictures it contained. She couldn't stop thinking, she said, about Livy's explanation of those symbols. There were so many unanswered questions. How could Jesus be *both* a king *and* an innocent victim? She didn't understand it, though she was convinced it must somehow be true. Nor could she bear to think that her own husband might be the cause of his innocent suffering. She hoped Pilate would heed her message and let the prisoner go.

Likewise, Livy couldn't stand to think that the teacher from Nazareth might become the victim of Roman abuse. She didn't want to think about suffering. Hadn't there been enough of it already? She wanted to get *away* from suffering. She wanted to go back home to Gaul. Not the real Gaul, but the Gaul of the Otherworld. The land she'd seen in her dreams. That place where sunlight gleamed on the blue sea waves and flowers bloomed all year, where there was no slavery, pain, or death, but only brightness and unending joy.

What good can suffering—and dying—possibly do anyway? she thought. *How can that set anybody free?* She thought back to the first time she'd seen Jesus, a whip in his hand, a righteous fire in his eyes. Why didn't he rise up and drive Pilate and the priests away as he had the merchants and money changers in the temple? Maybe he wasn't so special after all. Who needed a suffering Messiah?

Perhaps she should have changed her mistress's note to read: *Pilate, you must release the prisoner Bar Abbas at all costs. Signed, Procula.*

Livy squeezed her eyes shut, shook her head, and sighed. *What a crazy idea!* she thought. It wouldn't have worked anyway. There was no solution here, no hope.

She frowned. Why had she allowed this thing to weigh her down so heavily? True, most of the Celts she knew tended to see the worst in any situation. But she wasn't used to feeling depressed. She had to get out of this stuffy room and find something to do—anything at all—to help her forget about Jesus and Bar Abbas and slavery and freedom and . . . everything. She stood up and walked to the door.

"Livia! Where are you going?" said her mistress as Livy laid her hand on the latch.

"I'm sorry, Domina. May I have your permission to get out for a while? Maybe . . . I can find out what's happening and let you know. I'll be back soon."

Procula studied the girl's face for a long moment. "Very well," she said softly. "Bring me good news, Livia."

In the corridor Livy found a back stairway that didn't lead to the open courtyard. She darted down the steps, taking them two at a time. From there she reached the northwest corner of the fortress, away from the center of the action. Then came the gate that led through the city wall and toward the hills north of Jerusalem.

The portal opened onto a drawbridge that crossed a narrow rectangle of water known as the Struthion Pool. The bridge could be pulled up during a siege but was usually left down. There were iron gates at both ends of the wooden span. The outer gate was locked and guarded by a sentry; the inner one was kept open except when invaders threatened.

This is perfect, thought Livy. Bending down, she picked up a handful of loose gravel from the base of the fortress wall and stepped onto the bridge. There she sat, dangling her feet over the dark water, and began dropping pebbles into the pool. She glanced toward the sun. As near as she could figure, it was already past noon—the sixth hour of the day.

She took a deep breath, held it, then slowly let it out. The fresh air was sweet. She just needed to forget the past week, that was all.

Choosing a small rock, she reached back and heaved it toward the outer gate. It struck the iron bars with a tiny *clang*.

The soldier on guard peered through the grating and scowled at her. Livy snickered, shrugged her shoulders innocently, and gave her dangling feet a little kick.

But what was this? As Livy watched, another shape appeared beside the soldier outside the gate. It reminded her of Kalb, the big black dog. In a few moments she realized it *was* Kalb, the big black dog.

Kalb's big feathery tail began to wag back and forth. He whined and gave a short, friendly bark.

Livy got to her feet. *What in the world?* she thought.

The sentry prodded the dog with the butt of his spear. "Off with you, mutt!" he growled.

Kalb refused to move. Livy had the feeling he wasn't looking at her but at something beyond her, at the other end of the bridge. His tongue was hanging out, and his tail lashed happily from side to side.

Just then a voice came from behind her.

"Livy!" called Quintus. "I've been looking all over for you!"

What's he doing here? she wondered. *Isn't he supposed to be waiting on Master at the trial?* She turned and saw the boy approaching, then had an idea.

Turning, she called to the soldier at the gate. "Oh, thank you, sir! I'm so glad you've found him!" she called.

The man looked confused. "Found who?" he said.

"My dog!" Livy answered, running up to the gate and reaching through the bars to stroke Kalb's black head. "I thought he was lost for good!"

"*Your* dog?" the guard said.

"Actually, he belongs to my mistress—the Lady Procula," replied Livy.

The guard looked skeptical.

"Could you please open the gate and let him in?" Livy asked. "Oh, she'll be *so* happy to see him!"

The guard frowned. "Well, I suppose I'll have to if he really belongs to the governor's wife."

No sooner was the gate unlocked and opened than Kalb bounded inside with a joyous bark—just as Quintus set foot on the other end of the bridge. With a happy yelp the big animal shot past Livy and lunged at the boy, catching him off guard.

Livy saw the look of surprise in Quintus's eyes. But then it was her turn to be surprised as the boy continued his approach. Waving his arms over his bushy head, he shouted, "Livy, I've got something to tell you! Something important!"

Before he could say another word, though, the dog was upon him. The two of them tumbled over the edge of the bridge and splashed into the Struthion Pool.

Looking down into the water, Livy saw Quintus's head come bobbing to the surface. She watched as he coughed and spluttered. She started to laugh, but stopped when the boy opened his eyes. Whatever his message was, it had possessed him entirely, and he was bursting to deliver it. He opened his mouth and let it out.

"Livy!" he shouted. "They let Bar Abbas go! They're going to crucify Jesus!"

CHAPTER 14

Let Bar Abbas go?

That was Livy's first thought. It tumbled quickly through her mind as Quintus struggled to keep his head above water. *Bar Abbas free? So his plan really worked! And that means . . .*

"Couldja help me out of here, Livy?" sputtered Quintus, flailing an arm in her direction.

It means I've got to find him somehow!

"Livy!" Quintus cried.

Her second thought was more disturbing. *Crucify Jesus? The gentle, humble teacher? The man with the piercing eyes? It can't be!* There was a sudden, empty ache in the space beneath her heart.

"Please, Livy! I can't swim!" The desperation in Quintus's voice finally caught her attention.

She knelt and gave Quintus her hand. "Crucify?" she said, pulling him to a sitting position on the edge of the bridge. "But *why*? What did he do? Bar Abbas tried to lead an armed revolt! He killed people! Jesus didn't do anything like that!"

Quintus sat there shivering and pushing his dripping locks out of his eyes. Kalb scrambled out of the water beside him and shook his black body from head to tail, soaking both children with a shower of spray.

"As far as I could tell," said the boy, reaching up to scratch the top of his head, "the only thing they had against him was that he's some kind of king. King of the Jews. I didn't know it was a crime to be a king."

A king! Livy remembered the words she'd heard Jesus speak as he stood before Pilate at the place of judgment: "My kingdom is not of this world . . ." *Of what world, then? Could he be King of the Otherworld? Wouldn't that make him some kind of god?* Of course! That would explain what she'd seen in the garden!

"I don't understand it," Quintus was saying. "I mean, nobody punishes me for being a slave. Master's the governor, and that's all right for him. If Jesus is a king, then let him be king. What's wrong with that?"

But Livy wasn't listening. Her thoughts were on a scene she'd passed a few times during the last few years but wanted to forget: upright wooden posts in the rocky ground, gaunt, still, black, and silent in the moonlight outside the city gate. *The Skull Place! That must be where they've gone,* she thought.

Suddenly it struck her: She'd helped Bar Abbas's friends obtain his release. And because Bar Abbas had gone free, Jesus, the King of the Otherworld, was going to the Skull Place to die! She felt sick to her stomach.

"Come on, Quintus!" she said, grabbing him by the sleeve of his soggy tunic. "We've got to follow them! We've got to stop them somehow—or at least try!"

With a single yank she hauled her bewildered companion to his feet and pulled him along after her. Then the two of them, followed by the great black dog, tore across the bridge, through the inner gate, down the echoing corridors of the fortress, and out the main entrance. When the guard challenged her, Livy simply flashed him the note her mistress had given her the night before. It was enough to keep him from asking any more questions.

From the fortress they followed the winding city streets that led across Jerusalem to Golgotha, the Place of the Skull—the Romans' place of execution. They could see that a large crowd had recently passed that way; bits of broken pottery, a head scarf, a leather pouch, lay scattered across the ground. They must have been dropped by onlookers, Livy thought—people following prisoners who carried their own crosses.

She saw spots of blood on the uneven paving stones—probably blood from the backs of the condemned, who would have been beaten with whips before being led to the place of crucifixion. A few stragglers were hanging behind, talking in hushed tones about the executions Pilate had ordered for the eve of Passover Sabbath. Convinced she was on the right track, Livy pushed on.

She followed the trail over the cobbled, narrow streets, beneath dark arches, through the shadows of the crowding houses. The sky had grown dark—strangely dark, she thought—darker than she'd ever seen it in the middle of the day. Kalb and Quintus stepped closely at her heels as she turned left and right and left again, the three of them panting with the effort, until the wall and the Western Gate appeared before them.

Through the gate Livy could see the gathered crowd. In spite of the darkness, dull light glinted from the helmets of soldiers assigned to the execution detail. She heard the chatter of the casual observers, the rough laughter of the rabble, the harsh shouts of the officers. Here and there arose the cry of a child or a woman's muffled groan.

Above the crowd, atop a rise of rocky ground, she saw three upright posts. To the posts had been attached three heavy wooden crossbeams. Hanging from the crossbeams were the unmoving forms of three dying men.

Livy sucked in her breath and put her hand to her mouth. At this distance it was impossible to see the faces clearly, but somehow she knew. The one in the middle was Jesus of Nazareth.

She turned to Quintus, who stood beside her, pale and dripping with sweat. "We can't stop here," she said. "Let's see if we can get any closer."

"Why is it so dark?" said Quintus as they passed beneath the arched gate and began to climb the rocky hill of Golgotha. Through the dusky air Livy could see the terror in his eyes. "Cook said no good would come of this! What do you think is happening?"

"I don't know," she answered softly. She tried to remember the old stories her mother used to tell her back in Gaul. Could the King of the Other-world—a god himself—possibly die? And if he did, would everything else die with him? Was that the reason for the darkness? Was the whole world coming to an end?

"We shouldn't have come, Livy," Quintus was moaning. "What're we gonna do *now*?"

"I think I might be able to suggest something," said a deep voice at their side. Startled, Livy turned to face the speaker.

In the half-light Livy saw a row of white teeth in the midst of a black beard. A closely cropped head took shape against the sky. Kalb let out a happy bark and leaped toward the dark, stocky figure. A thrill of hope, mixed with fear and doubt, seemed to jump within Livy.

"Bar Abbas!" she said.

The zealot reached into his belt, pulled something from it, and held it out to her. "I believe this belongs to you," he said. "I no longer need it."

"The parchment!" she gasped. She snatched it from his hand and quickly shoved it into her belt. "Th-then it's true!" she stammered. "You've been set free!"

"Yes. And I've come to free you too!" he said.

"But where are you going?" asked Livy.

"Oh, I don't know," he said, waving his hand carelessly. "Far away from here for the time being—to Damascus, maybe. With my friends. Long enough for things to settle down. We'll take you along if you like. From Damascus you can get passage to Asia Minor, and then to Greece, Macedonia, and Gaul. What do you say?"

Slowly Livy drew the piece of parchment out of her belt and peered at it through the gloom. The words scrawled on its surface struck her now as harsh, mocking questions—*Bar Abbas? Freedom fighters? Messiah? Liberator? King?* She still hadn't found any good answers.

A chill came over her. This was the moment she'd been waiting for, wasn't it? *Freedom.* It lay within her grasp at last! So why didn't she feel happy? Why wasn't she excited? Why this anxious feeling in the pit of her stomach?

"I don't know, Bar Abbas," she said, looking up at him. "I—"

She stopped. There was a hand on her shoulder. A hand with a firm, pinching grip. A narrow, long-fingered hand.

"So!" said a calm, smug voice behind her. "Still consorting with criminals, I see. Is the Lady Procula aware of your choice of friends?"

"Let go of me, Melanus!" said Livy, wrenching herself from his grasp.

Bar Abbas stepped forward and planted a finger on the steward's chest. "Correction," he said with a sneer. "A *pardoned* criminal."

Melanus looked up with a sour smile and pushed the zealot's hand away with the back of his wrist. "Apparently so," he said with a tone of distaste. "But *your* good fortune has little bearing upon *my* responsibility as head steward of the governor's household. And at the moment my responsibility is to return these two *escaped slaves* to their master. *If* you will excuse me."

Bar Abbas looked at Livy. Livy looked at Quintus. Quintus closed his eyes. Kalb bared his teeth and growled.

Suddenly a loud volley of thunder set both earth and sky trembling. The ground began to shake violently. A cry of dismay went up from the crowd. Some of the people turned and started running back to the city.

Quintus groaned. "We're all gonna die!" he said.

Then came a rumble like the sound of stampeding elephants as, without warning, a deep crack opened in the earth at their feet. Melanus leaped backward with a shriek, narrowly avoiding a fatal tumble into the widening trench. "The day is accursed!" he shouted. Then he took to his heels as more large cracks opened in the ground around them. Rocks and boulders came rolling down the hillside, scattering the frightened spectators in every direction.

Quintus stared, wide-eyed. Kalb barked, then howled. Livy put a hand to her forehead and swallowed hard.

"Let's go!" shouted Bar Abbas, taking Livy by the hand. "I don't know what's happening, but we'll never get another chance like this!"

But Livy pulled away. She set her jaw and looked him in the eye. "No!" she shouted.

Bar Abbas's forehead wrinkled. "What do you mean, *no?*" he said. "We're going! Leaving! Escaping! You're on your way to freedom! Isn't that what you want?"

Slowly the quaking of the earth weakened and stopped. A chilling rain began to fall. Livy sat down on a rock and put her head in her hands. She felt hot tears welling up in her eyes. "I *did* want it," she said, glancing up at the zealot. "But now I'm not so sure."

"Not sure?" said Bar Abbas, his face turning red. "Why not? What are you talking about?"

Livy stared straight into his eyes. "It's all wrong!" she said. "I *can't* leave now. Not until I know what's going to happen to *him.*" Through the rain and the scattering crowd, she pointed to the top of the rocky hill, where the Nazarene and two other men hung dying on Roman crosses.

"Him?" said the exasperated Bar Abbas. "I can tell you what's going to happen to *him*! He's going to die . . . If he's not dead already! Now, are you coming or not?"

"No," Livy said in a trembling voice. "Don't you see? It's because of *me* he's hanging there! It's because I helped *you* gain your release instead of him! And I was wrong! It should never have happened this way! But now that it has, I . . . have to know whether he's really . . ." She buried her face in her arms.

Sighing, Bar Abbas pulled his gray hood over his head. "Have it your way, then," he said. He whistled to his dog. Kalb whined and licked Quintus's hand.

"I won't forget what you've done for me," added Bar Abbas. Then, without another word, he turned on his heel and strode into the pouring rain.

It was a long time before Livy realized the rain had stopped—hours, maybe. She felt empty, eerily quiet inside—like the night sky after a violent storm has passed. When she looked up at last, she saw that Quintus was sitting on the ground beside her. He shrugged but said nothing.

Livy turned her eyes toward the top of the hill. Everyone had gone home. The crosses were empty. Ragged clouds were drifting off to the east. The late-afternoon sun was sinking toward the sea.

"We'd better get back, Quintus," she said, getting to her feet. "Domina will be wondering what's become of us."

CHAPTER 15

No one knew what to make of Melanus's disappearance. Though Pilate's men searched the city for two days and asked questions in the surrounding villages, no trace of the steward was ever found.

The servants, of course, had their pet theories. Livy's was that he had fallen into one of the huge cracks that opened in the earth during the quake on the afternoon of the crucifixion. Quintus thought sheer terror must have driven him crazy and caused him to run away. Cook believed heaven had struck him because of his proud and disrespectful statements about the Messiah.

But on the third day—the first day of the week—there was something else to talk about.

It all began at breakfast. The threat of further rebellion being past, the governor's household had moved back to the old Herodian palace, and the servants had gathered in the kitchen for a share of Cook's broth and bread. Hatshup, the Egyptian gardener, was squatting in his accustomed spot near the oven, hunched over a bowl of broth, chewing his bread with gusto and enthusiastically nodding his old gray head.

"I'd gone down there very early to dig up a few lilies and anemones," he was saying. "Master Joseph's gardener had promised me some—for that bed out near the fountain. It needs a bit of brightening up. The crocuses were a disappointment this year, and—"

"We don't care about your crocuses!" Cook cut in, turning fiercely from her pot. Her upper arm jiggled as she shook her ladle in his face. "We want to know exactly what you saw!"

"Yes, Hatshup," said Livy. "Please tell us." She drew her stylus and parchment from her belt, ready to catch anything that might be worth jotting down.

Hatshup's bony frame shook with silent laughter. "I wish you could have seen the looks on those guards' faces!" he said with a grin. "Like they'd seen a ghost! Maybe they were *expecting* to see one—or something even more terrible—at any minute. I don't know. But I *do* know that the stone had been rolled away. I saw that much myself! And they had no idea how it happened! Doesn't take much to put one over on *them*, I guess!"

"Wait a minute!" said Livy, looking up from her parchment. "You're saying that the big stone had been rolled away from the entrance to the tomb? Why? Did somebody try to steal the body?"

"Don't know," said Hatshup, and swallowed the last of his bread. "Couldn't stay to find out. Had to get those lilies transplanted before they started to wilt."

Quintus whistled. "But it would take at least ten men to budge a stone that size!"

Hatshup raised his eyebrows, nodded, and then slurped his broth noisily from a wooden spoon.

Livy bent over her parchment, pushed her red hair away from her face, and wrote: *Sunday morning. The tomb of Jesus. Stone rolled away. Don't know why.*

She couldn't wait to tell her mistress. Once her own breakfast was finished, she quickly prepared Procula's and hurried with it up to the lady's room. But no sooner had she stepped inside the door than Procula began pouring forth some exciting news of her own.

"I've had another dream, Livia! Please come in—set the tray down. Another dream! But so different this time! I don't know when I've slept so well or so deeply. And in the deepest part of my sleep I saw myself on a hillside covered with flowers. The colors were brighter, more intense, more *real* than anything I've ever known! Not dreamlike at all. It was as if the world had been created all over again.

"Jesus of Nazareth was there, coming down the slope toward me. He was dressed all in white, with the golden circlet on his head. And behind him came a great crowd of people from every nation on earth—like the crowd we saw that day in the Court of the Gentiles! He came to me and took my hand. Then I joined the others, and together we walked toward the sunrise." She paused, her eyebrows compressed in thought. "Since Jesus of Nazareth is dead, what can it mean?"

"I'm not sure," said Livy, setting the tray of food on a carved and polished table of acacia wood beside the lady's bed. "But I've got something to tell you too! Old Hatshup was in that garden early this morning—the garden near the tomb where they laid his body—and . . ."

There was a knock at the door, and Quintus came bursting in. "Livy! Mistress Procula!" he said. "I thought you'd want to know! I was serving at Master's table when some soldiers came to see him. They looked really worried. They said that the garden tomb wasn't just open. It was *empty*!"

Livy and Procula looked at each other. "And what do they take it to mean, Quintus?" the lady asked.

"They don't know," said Quintus, hitching up his tunic. "But I heard that some of his followers—Jesus' followers, I mean—are already saying that he's alive again! Risen from the dead! One of them says she saw him walking around in the garden!"

Procula turned to Livy, a hopeful light shining from her eyes. "What do you think?" she said.

Livy chewed her lip. "I think," she answered slowly, "that if the King of the Otherworld *could* die, he would only do it if he knew it would help the rest of us somehow. And I think that, when it was all over, he'd *have* to come back . . . like the morning sun and the flowers in spring.

"My mother told me a story like that once, when I was very little. It was about a king who went on a journey to the land of the dead, suffered many things for his people, and then returned to them again. I also think," Livy continued, "that if he *could* defeat death and if he *did* come back, then maybe he'd—well, find a way for us to live forever too!"

Procula said nothing but simply watched the girl with a curious look of anticipation on her face.

"Most of all," Livy added, "I think we'd better go and find out if all this is true."

"My feelings exactly," agreed her mistress, reaching for her cloak and throwing it over her shoulders. Then she glanced from Livy to Quintus and frowned. "But how?"

"We could try to find some of his followers and ask *them*," suggested Quintus.

"Good idea," Procula said. "But do you know where to look?"

"Yes!" said Livy, a tingle of excitement running down her spine. "I *do* know! The house down the street! The red-stone house with the fishing mosaic in front. The one with the upper room! Maybe they're still staying there!"

"All right, then," said Procula. "Let's not waste another minute."

"I'll lead the way!" said Quintus, almost tripping over his own feet in his haste to get out the door.

Livy was about to follow him over the threshold when Procula laid a hand on her arm.

"Just a moment, Livia," she said. Then she bent her head and took off the fine gold chain she always wore around her neck. "I want you to have this."

"Me?" Livy looked up into the lady's eyes, a warm but confused feeling growing in that small space beneath her heart. "But why, Domina?"

"As a token of my gratitude. For helping me find what I believe will be the path to a new life," said Procula. She smiled and then added, "And as a symbol of your newfound freedom."

Livy blinked. "My . . . *freedom*?"

"Yes."

Livy shook herself. "You mean when I come of age, right?"

"No. I mean today. Right now. As of this very minute. And if you're willing—if you freely choose it—I'd also like to make you my daughter. I will ask Pilate to help me arrange the adoption as soon as we return. What do you say to that?"

For a moment Livy didn't know what to say. It seemed her heart had jumped into her throat. Procula saw her hesitating and laid a hand on her shoulder. "I understand if you'd rather not give me your answer right away," she said. "I know how you've always hoped to find your real parents again someday. If you'd rather think it over and . . ."

"No," said Livy, looking up into her face. "It's not like that. There's a place in my heart where I've always felt that . . . that I'd never see them again until we all get to the Otherworld. That maybe they didn't survive the raid and the battle after all. I don't know. What I *do* know is that you've been like a mother to me all these years, and . . . well, I don't think they'd blame me for loving *you* too. Do you think they would?"

There were tears in Procula's eyes. "Of course not," she said. "And what's to stop us from searching for them together?"

"Nothing!" said Livy with a sudden burst of joyous energy. She hugged her mistress and buried her face in the folds of her long white *stola*. At last she blurted, "In that case, I don't need to think it over. My answer is *yes!*"

Then, hand in hand, they went out together—the slender, graceful woman and the tall, red-haired girl. For Livy, it was the end and the beginning. The end of a life of slavery. The beginning of the freedom she'd fought so hard to gain.

There were still a lot of questions, but at least now she knew where to look for answers. They'd start by finding out where Jesus was now, and what it might mean to follow . . . Him.

But I never thought it would happen this way, Livy thought as they stepped into the bright April day. *Not even in my wildest dreams!*

LETTERS FROM OUR READERS

Who was Bar Abbas, anyway? (Brendan J., St. Paul, Minnesota)

The Bible doesn't say a lot about Bar Abbas, also known as Barabbas. We just know he was a zealot who was involved in a plot to overthrow the government, and that he was the prisoner chosen for release during the Passover. Bar Abbas is mentioned in Matthew 27:15-26, Mark 15:6-15, Luke 23:18-19, and John 18:40.

Wasn't it dangerous for Livy to trust and help a man like Bar Abbas? (Holly M., Newark, New Jersey)

Yes! Your parents have no doubt warned you about trusting strangers. Bar Abbas was a stranger *and* a criminal. But sometimes people do unwise things. Livy had been kidnapped and taken away from her home and her people at a very young age. Her longing to see her family overcame her natural fear of this man.

Livy didn't know the whole story about Bar Abbas, either. She saw him as a man who was willing to fight for freedom—someone who could help her escape. She didn't know he was a murderer. Once she recognized the consequences of helping Bar Abbas—that she'd unwittingly played a part in Jesus' crucifixion—she realized how mistaken she'd been in helping him.

Did Pilate's wife really dream about Jesus? (Annie Britt P., Oshkosh, Wisconsin)

Yes, she did. In Matthew 27:19, the Bible tells us that Pilate's wife asked her husband to release Jesus because of a dream she'd had. God has often used dreams to give special messages to people, both believers and non-believers. Check out these examples: Jacob (Genesis 28:10-17); Pharaoh (Genesis 37:1-11; Genesis 40–41); King Nebuchadnezzar (Daniel 4); Joseph, husband of Mary (Matthew 1:20; 2:13).

However, we must not assume that our dreams will come true or that they're special messages from God.

Who were the Celts? How could their weird religious beliefs possibly help Livy understand who Jesus was? (Tristan F., Waukegan, Illinois)

The Celts, called "Gauls" by the Romans, were a group of people who in ancient times inhabited parts of France, Spain, Britain, Ireland, and Asia Minor. They were the ancestors of today's Irish, Welsh, Bretons, and Scots. The Celts believed in many false gods and practiced many strange religious rites—including human sacrifice.

The Bible tells us that all the world's people—even unbelievers who've never heard of Jesus—have an empty space in their hearts that only the true God can fill. They may not realize it, but everyone is searching for Him (see Ecclesiastes 3:11; Acts 17:24-31; Romans 2:14-15). Their desire to know God sometimes shows up in the religious beliefs they invent for themselves.

For example, the Celts believed in the need for human sacrifice. That concept was, in a way, a little like the Christian concept of a sacrificial Savior. But the Celtic method of finding favor with their gods—killing innocent people—was wrong. Only God could provide a sacrifice for our sins. But because Livy was familiar with the idea of an innocent person as sacrifice, she recognized Jesus as the Savior and the sacrifice her people had been looking for all along—without even knowing it!

ABOUT THE AUTHOR

JIM WARE is a graduate of Fuller Theological Seminary and the author of *God of the Fairy Tale* and *The Stone of Destiny*. He and his wife, Joni, have six kids—Alison, Megan, Bridget, Ian, Brittany, and Callum. Just for fun, Jim plays the guitar and the hammered dulcimer.

Escape
Underground

by Clint Kelly

To my daughter Amy,
for including everyone in the fun.

Mara made the worst face she could think of. It was unladylike, but so what? She couldn't be a lady twenty-four hours a day. It was too exhausting, especially when you were eleven years old.

This meeting of the Way was going nowhere fast. People were arguing and calling each other crazy. They sounded like bees in a hive all buzzing at once. There was nothing of interest to kids here, so why did they have to sit in this stuffy, dreary room?

"You're full of hot desert wind! The world's not going to end!" snapped one man.

"You dreamer! Jesus warned of Judgment Day, and it sounded pretty close to me!" said another man, pointing an accusing finger.

"That's because you're deaf in both ears and afraid of your own shadow!" the first man shot back.

Mara yawned. She dreamed of being in the market by the western temple wall. Admiring the fabrics. Sampling the perfumes. Listening to the clash of languages. Soaking up the crowds and the colors and the excitement. Certainly not sitting here listening to the same old men go on and on about the same old things.

It was time to do something about it!

She arched her eyebrow—a signal to her skinny, ten-year-old brother, Nathan. He wrinkled his nose at Obadiah. Obadiah tugged his ear at Sarah. Sarah rubbed both eyes. Mara felt a flush of excitement. The members of the New Israel Club were ready. The game was on.

Mara always went first. She stared at a perspiring, thin-necked man with grape-stained fingers. He looked an awful lot like a camel.

She turned to the others and pointed at the man. She twisted her mouth into a rubbery, pouty-lipped muzzle. Teeth bared, she began to chew imaginary cud.

The other kids giggled while the men argued on without noticing.

It was Nathan's turn. He studied the potter's tight, woolly curls and thick, stubby neck. Nathan turned his head, forced a cough, and stuck out his tongue, mimicking the silent bleating of a stupid sheep.

Mara couldn't help it. Laughter burst out of her mouth with all the grace of a busted vase.

Unfortunately, the adults chose that exact moment to catch their breath. The sound of Mara's hoarse snort filled the room.

Her mother glared at her. Mara's cheeks burned. She was going to get the "lady lecture" later, for sure. *I wonder if the governor's wife ever scratches or burps?* Mara thought. *I bet she does.*

The arguments resumed, and after sitting still for a few minutes, Mara slipped carefully and quietly to the back of the room. The other New Israel kids faded back too. She gave them a nod, and they made their escape.

Outside, the members of the New Israel Club poked and wrestled each other, glad to be free.

"If Jesus had been that boring," Sarah said, dancing away from the boys, "nobody would have listened!"

"But He wasn't," Mara said in a superior tone. "He told great stories and let kids sit on His lap. I wish He was still here."

The others nodded. Jesus had shaken everybody up, sometimes with miracles but mostly just with words. People couldn't stop talking about Him.

As soon as they were out of earshot of the adults, Mara gave the signal. Obadiah placed his index fingers against the gaps in his teeth and blew a piercing whistle. Immediately, the others left their horseplay and fell in behind Mara, who led them in the club theme song.

> We are New Israel, kids of strength and might;
> Messiah has favored us, given us new light!
> Do not get in our way or we will stand and fight.
> We stand the test, 'cause we're the best.
> We know that we are right!

"Obadiah sang it wrong again, Mara," complained Nathan, checking to see that his orange-and-brown-striped cloak hadn't gotten smudged. His mother had woven the wool on her loom and colored it with special dye. Nathan was very careful about his clothes.

"Did not!" objected Obadiah, his considerable roundness covered by a red-and-blue cloak.

"Oh yes, you did," corrected Nathan. "You ended with 'tight' instead of 'right,' like you always do."

"Look, Mr. Perfection," Obadiah said, "what difference does it make? We're right *and* tight, so what's the big deal?"

Nathan pulled his matching turban more firmly into place over his mop of black hair. "The big deal is that I wrote the song, and it's 'might,' 'light,' 'fight,' and 'right,' not 'tight.' Got it?"

"Bright," said Mara.

"Huh?" Nathan threw a confused look her way.

"Bright," said Mara again. "I think 'bright' is better. It's got 'right' in it, but it says more." She walked carefully, staying in the lead. She was tall for her age, and considered herself practically a woman. *Wise too,* she thought smugly.

"I like Mara's idea," said Obadiah. "We can use 'tight' in the first line."

"'Kids of strength and *tight'?*" Nathan said with a sneer. "You think about as well as you sing."

Obadiah growled. "My parents think I sing just fine."

"That's because your father's a bullfrog and your mother's a screech owl," Nathan declared. "I wrote the song, and I ought to know the right word. And in this case the right word is 'right.'"

Mara had had enough. "Stop it! It's a stupid argument, and you know it!"

"We're not arguing," said Nathan with a sniff. "We're—" One look at Mara's face, and he realized he'd better not finish the sentence.

Mara began walking again, trying to imagine herself away from there. She strode the dark, narrow streets of the Old City as if she owned them. Sometimes she imagined that she owned the whole city—every merchant's stall, every official's marbled home, every fine steed in the Roman stables.

Her bearing was tall, her chin strong. Her dark eyes flashed with the fire of leadership. And she was beautiful. Her father said so. Sarah's aunt thought she must have a royal branch in her family tree. Mara liked Sarah. Sarah didn't say much.

One day Mara would have the respect of the whole city. For now she was the leader of New Israel. She was proud of their club for *true* Hebrew Christian kids. The Jewish kids from Greece and Cyprus and other foreign places who had moved to Jerusalem would just have to form their own club. They didn't even speak Aramaic. They chattered away about their strange beliefs in Greek! Mara had to admit that one of the reasons she didn't like those kids was because the foreigners were the cause of half the arguments in the church.

She adjusted the fine white cloth of her meeting dress and patted her pale-pink head veil. It flowed over raven-black hair that reached halfway down her back.

She straightened and felt that she must look regal. Maybe she would be queen of an entire country one day.

"Must you walk like an ostrich?" Nathan asked. Six inches shorter than Mara, he still acted like he owned the rule book. He spent his school days with the teachers of the Law called rabbis. Most of the time he came home sounding like them.

"Go away, baby rabbi," Mara said. "I'm thinking."

Nathan didn't go away. "You need to respect the males of your family. We can teach you many things."

Mara patted him on the turban. "You barely wash behind your ears. You ought to listen more and speak less."

Nathan looked at her with indignant brown eyes. She knew what was coming. "In synagogue school, we're taught that female children should master the skills of the home and proper ways of cooking. They should not make fun of teachings they know nothing about."

"Speaking of cooking, did you finish off the cinnamon flat bread I baked for Father?" Mara accused, suddenly suspicious.

"Someone had to." Nathan shrugged, but his face broke into a sly grin. "I couldn't allow Father to be poisoned."

Mara looked at him and frowned. "I liked you better when you were the size of a squirrel and had the vocabulary of a centipede."

"Centipedes can't talk," Nathan retorted.

"Exactly," she said.

They arrived shortly at the cool, sheltering walls of the Pool of Siloam. The sweet waters of the Gihon Spring flowed through the tunnel that good King Hezekiah had dug into Jerusalem beneath the city wall. The shaded pool made a perfect meeting place for their club.

The New Israelites knelt by the pool and drank the refreshing water from cupped hands.

Mara was about to call the meeting to order when she noticed someone slouched in the dark recesses of the tunnel's mouth. A shiver slithered down her regal spine.

It's Karis the river rat. What's she doing here? she thought in annoyance.

"Eeewwww! What's that smell? I think it's coming from something in that moldy old tunnel." Sarah pointed at the figure in the shadows.

"Yeah, it stinks like old garlic and rotten olives," said Obadiah. He held his nose and stomach and lurched about as if he would lose his breakfast.

Karis emerged cautiously from the tunnel. Her hands were behind her, hiding something.

The New Israel kids shrieked in mock terror.

"It's the girl from the ground!" one cried.

"The brat from below!" said another.

Karis's shoulders slumped. She was plain and small for her age. Barefoot, clothed in a shapeless, frayed cloak of drab brown, the girl from Caesarea by the Sea had been in Jerusalem less than a year. Mara felt sorry for her in a way. She knew Karis just wanted to be friends with the New Israelites. She wanted to feel close to the Hebrews who'd seen Jesus and heard Him speak.

On the other hand, Karis was always boasting about what an explorer she was. How back home in Caesarea, she knew every square inch of the vast underground sewer system built by Herod the Great. She was as proud of poking around in the dark, smelly old tunnels as the Egyptians were of building their pyramids. It was embarrassing! Plus she tied her dull black hair on top of her head in a sorry little knot resembling a dead animal.

Still, Mara felt a moment's guilt. What if she were in Karis's place and unaccepted by others—a foreigner? Karis's family was penniless, supported only by what the church could spare.

Well, it's their own fault, Mara thought impatiently. No one had forced them to leave Caesarea and move to Jerusalem, where unemployment was high—especially for believers of the Way. Surely they had relatives they could go back to. Mara had to look after her own. She was the head of New Israel, after all. She was born in Jerusalem. Her father was a respected architect, a leader in the church, and her family had money. God must have wanted it that way.

"What are you hiding behind your back?" Mara demanded, speaking the Greek all the educated Hebrew children were taught along with their native Aramaic. "Show us."

Karis, less schooled and unable to speak Aramaic, was outnumbered but wiry and quick. Mara watched her closely. If she'd discovered something valuable while traveling the tunnels, it wouldn't do to frighten her, or they'd never get to see it.

"I don't think you want to know what's in here," Karis said, bringing a rough woven sack into view.

"You'll never be allowed to join New Israel if you don't learn to cooperate," said Mara. But she was thinking, *It'd be easier for you to stuff a camel through the eye of a needle than to get into this club.*

Mara shuddered. The thought of Karis climbing around underground through dangerous, scary places gave her the creeps. But she wasn't about to let Karis get away with saying no to the leader of New Israel.

"Okay, don't say you weren't warned." Karis stepped forward, and the curious members of the club crowded around. Mara leaned over for a better look. Karis held her arms straight out and opened the top of the sack.

A severed calf's head lay in the bottom of the bag, and its unseeing right eye caught the light so that it seemed to wink at them. Blue flies crawled over the dead face. A reeking aroma flooded the kids' noses and made their eyes water.

"That's awful!" Mara shouted and jumped back.

Karis laughed. "Not as awful as a person who sticks her head in a sack before she knows what's in it—*that's* just *stupid*!"

"She makes a pretty good point," said Nathan.

"Be quiet!" Mara snapped. She took two steps forward and wagged a finger under Karis's nose. "Don't call me stupid!" she yelled. "I'm not the one walking around with my brains in a bag!"

"It's *not* brains!" Karis replied.

"Is too! What do you think that calf's got between its ears, sister?"

"The same thing you do—nothing! And don't call me 'sister'!"

"You're taking that home so your mother can make boiled calf's brains for supper," Mara taunted. "That's what poor people eat!"

Mara was sorry the second she said it, but there was no way to take it back. *A real queen would never speak to her subjects that way—even the strange ones,* she thought.

Karis looked at the ground. Mara felt a moment's regret. These were hard times for followers of Messiah. Timon, Karis's father, was one of the seven men appointed by the church to help the widows and others who struggled. But it was only a volunteer position. Maybe a calf's head for supper was all Karis's family could afford.

Mara's embarrassing words hung in the air until she suggested that the club members get going. "We'll have the meeting at my house, okay?" The others mumbled in response and started to leave.

"Wait!" Karis called to them. "I'm sorry. That was mean. I should have told you what was in the bag first. Do you want to see my new twin goat kids? They suck on your fingers and have the cutest little white circles around their eyes!"

The New Israelites stopped and looked at Mara. Their faces said they wanted to see the baby goats. She hesitated, unsure of how she felt about this smudged girl who smelled of damp and dirty places. But she was sure of how she felt about baby animals. She loved them. One day she would own a royal game park and raise all the babies by hand.

"I guess so," Mara said. "Just keep that sack away from me."

Karis brightened. "Great! This way." She started toward the tunnel entrance.

Mara and the others halted. "Not in there," Mara said.

"But the goats are grazed outside the city walls by a friend of ours," said Karis. "Come on. I'll show you."

"Let's go out through the city gate," Mara insisted.

"You're not scared, are you?" Karis challenged. "I can find my way through these tunnels blindfolded."

"We're not scared," said Mara, giving Nathan a look guaranteed to keep him quiet. "We're wearing our nice meeting clothes, and we don't want to come out smelling of dead fish."

That was true enough, but Mara knew that Karis knew the whole truth: The New Israel kids were frightened to go underground. The dark, winding passages were tight and smelly. It was too easy to get lost in them. The kids had all heard horrible tales of terrifying creatures and of children who wandered into the tunnels never to be seen again. Mara suspected the stories were made up to protect the kids from accidents. If so, the stories worked.

Karis sighed, shouldered her sack, and reentered Hezekiah's tunnel. "Suit yourself," she said, "but I came this way, and I'm going back this way." The words sounded deep and hollow, as if they came from the bottom of a barrel. The dark tunnel swallowed Karis first, followed by the rough brown sack with the calf's head inside.

Mara shuddered. Karis could just forget about her goats. Who wanted to hang out with a girl who liked dark places and carried dead things on her back?

CHAPTER 2

"Let's run!" Nathan yelled to Obadiah. "We'll meet you girls at the nut merchant's stall by the western temple wall. Last one there's a rotten pomegranate!"

Off they raced. Mara shook her head and watched them take the first corner in perfect stride . . . right into an angry tide of people rushing toward them. Shouting and cursing, the mob was pulling a familiar-looking man down the street by a rope that bound his wrists together.

Mara caught up to the boys and snatched Nathan out of the crowd by the belt of his robe.

"He mocks the temple!" cried one sweating accuser, so upset that blood dribbled from his lips. Apparently he had chewed them in fury.

Others shouted, "The Sanhedrin rulers know what to do with this mocker!"

Mara trembled and could feel Nathan trembling too. Sarah looked ready to faint. She could talk pretty bravely, but she was thin and sick a lot of the time. Now even her freckles were pale. Mara put an arm around her shoulders.

New Israel never wanted to fall into the hands of the Sanhedrin. They were stern men with beards longer than anyone else's. They judged disagreements among the Jews, and their word was final. People who scorned the temple died.

As the mob passed, Mara looked closely at the kind, bearded face in the middle of the stampede. The man's wrists were swollen from the rope.

Stephen! It's Stephen! But he's famous in the church. Why's he being yanked along like an animal?

This wasn't the first time something like this had happened. Jesus had also been shoved through town on His way to the cross.

"Stone him! Stone him!" The terrible cry came from every direction. Mara covered her ears. *"Crucify Him! Crucify Him!"* That's what they'd said. *I was a little girl then. His face was kind like Stephen's. He smiled at me. I know He did.*

Nathan glanced anxiously at his sister. Obadiah yanked nervously at his cloak. Sarah looked as if she'd swallowed a big cup of sour milk. Mara could see that the rest of New Israel didn't want to be there either.

Suddenly, there was Karis across the way, standing back among the camels and mules laden for market. *What's she doing here?* Mara watched the girl's mouth try to form words, but they seemed frozen on her lips. The sack slipped from her fingers and fell into the street.

A bull camel with sad, droopy eyes and an even sadder, droopier hump did not like the shouting and commotion. It reared away from the angry scramble. What looked like four hundred pounds of market goods tied to its back swayed precariously from side to side. The creature and its load nearly backed into Karis, spilling a crate of grapes in the process.

The camel stamped and kicked and sent grapes flying in every direction.

Karis stumbled sideways. The beast's wide, dirty foot landed on the sack. The camel's weight smashed the calf's head inside.

Mara dodged the procession and rushed over to Karis. She started to scold, but then she said, a little more kindly than she felt, "Are you okay?"

Karis nodded, but her face was pale. "That's Stephen. What are they doing to him?" she asked in Greek.

Mara ignored the question. She didn't want to hear the answer herself. Instead, she fished in the pocket of her gown and said, "It looks like your dinner is ruined. I have a few coins. You can have boiled mustard greens for supper."

From the look on Karis's face, Mara guessed that Karis hated boiled mustard greens. So did Mara. *But more than boiled calf's brains?* she wondered. *No way!* She shrugged and left the coins in her pocket.

The noisy crowd had passed up the street. A thick cloud of dust followed them. Each time Stephen slowed to speak to someone who dared ask what was going on, he was jerked forward by the rope. "Why are they so mad at him?" Karis asked.

"They don't like what he says," answered a tall boy who appeared at Karis's elbow. He spoke Greek and was one of the other foreign kids who had attended the meeting of the Way. Mara figured they must have gotten sick of the meeting too. Three more stood with him. "I heard he bad-mouthed Moses. God too!"

Nathan, Obadiah, and the other New Israelites joined Mara.

"That's crazy," Obadiah said. Eyes hard with suspicion, he stared at the tall boy. "Stephen just helps little old ladies. I heard that what makes him really different is he does miracles!"

The tall boy shrugged. "Naw, he thinks Jesus changed everything, even the Law. He's right. Nothing around here's been the same since Jesus came."

The New Israelites gasped. "Hey, what do you mean?" Obadiah demanded. "The Law has been around forever."

"Yes!" said Nathan, getting red in the face. "It came from Moses. Moses wrote the Torah. Torah teaches us how to live." He shook his finger in the boy's face. "You take it back, or I'll report *you* to the Sanhedrin!"

"Stop it!" said Mara. She didn't like this talk one bit. She switched to Aramaic so the foreign kids couldn't understand what she was saying to New Israel. "We are the true Jews. We knew Jesus. Don't let these outsiders ruin things for us!"

The New Israel club members nodded. Then they glared at the nonmembers.

"Stop talking in your secret code," Karis said. She put her hands on her hips and glared at Mara. "If you're so smart, you should speak Greek and not talk behind our backs!"

"If you were smart," Obadiah shouted back in Greek, "you could speak *two* languages, like we can. But instead, you wear garlic perfume and stink like camel dung!"

"Oh, that was helpful, Obadiah," said Mara, wrinkling her nose.

"Yeah, helpful as a broken leg!" added the tall boy.

Mara thought his name was Akbar. He was dark and from somewhere along the Nile River in Egypt. He could be nice. Sometimes. Right now he was clenching his fists and looking ready to punch someone.

"At least I don't *look* like a pile of camel dung!" Karis finally said, although she looked more like she wanted to cry than to name-call.

"Good one, Karis!" Akbar's encouragement made her smile a little.

Nathan stepped between the two groups, hands folded, face serious, looking for all the world like a miniature Pharisee. Mara groaned. She could guess what was coming.

Nathan cleared his throat. "In synagogue school, Torah teaches that we must learn to live with our neighbors. Because you foreigners have moved to Jerusalem to live, you must learn to live with us. We're your new neighbors. The Law is good. The Law is life."

The other New Israelites clapped and cheered the speech as Mara rolled her eyes. The foreigners stuck their tongues out at them.

"Thank you, Nathan, that was just what we needed," said Mara sarcastically.

"I try," Nathan replied, trying to look as wise as possible and missing her sarcasm.

"Put a sandal in it, little brother!" Mara grabbed Nathan, shoved him to the back, and took his place.

"I feel dizzy," said Sarah, sitting down on a packing crate. Mara fanned her own face and tried to ignore the camel that was standing nearby, coughing and showing his yellow teeth.

"If you're *our* neighbors, then who are *yours*?" Akbar demanded.

The camel looked sour and ready to spit.

"What are you saying?" Obadiah asked.

"I'm saying, who do *you* have to learn to live with?" Akbar replied. "Or does your Law go only one way?"

"The Law *is* the way," Obadiah said with a sneer. "Why don't you go back to Egypt or Caesarea or wherever you came from? The sun has baked your heads until nothing's left inside!" The New Israelites thumped him on the back and stuck their tongues out at the foreigners.

Karis trembled and looked angry. "I wish I *could* go back. It's no fun to live in a city with kids like you. You are tiny Jews with faith as small as grains of dirt. I have more faith between my toes!"

She turned and started home. Akbar and the others marched off beside her.

Obadiah had heard enough. He bent down and scooped up three bunches of fat grapes from the ground. He threw one at Karis's back. It landed between her shoulder blades with a satisfying splat.

"Outsider!" Obadiah growled.

Karis spun, snatched up a grape, and let it fly. Obadiah ducked and it missed. When he straightened, Akbar's grapes caught him in the arm and smeared juice and pulp from elbow to wrist.

Grapes filled the air. So did name-calling.

"Mule!"

"Maggot!"

"Cockroach!"

"Sewer beetle!"

"Lawbreaker!" Nathan looked pleased with the sound of that one.

Akbar slipped on some grape skins and fell knees-first into donkey droppings. *Fresh ammunition*, Mara thought.

But just then a boy ran up to the war zone and shouted, "They're taking Stephen outside the city walls. Come on!"

The war ended as quickly as it had begun. The whole group, Mara and her friends and Karis and hers, ran after the boy.

They arrived together, breathless and splattered and quite unprepared for the awful sight they saw.

CHAPTER
3

Stephen's crumpled body lay at the bottom of the rock quarry. He had been pushed from the edge thirty feet above. This was to show "mercy," since the condemned man would already be half dead from the fall before the stones came raining down on his body.

Several men were reaching for stones. Others had large chunks raised above their heads, ready to strike.

Mara felt cold and sick.

"We'd better go," suggested Sarah, but no one moved.

The stones fell, Stephen moaned, and Mara covered her eyes.

A young man stood apart from the others, tall and stern. He studied the executioners and watched the stoning closely. Once in a while he nodded approval.

"It's Saul of Tarsus," whispered Obadiah, out of breath. "Stephen's not the first Christian he's killed."

"I thought only the Roman governor could execute a person," Karis protested. "We've got to tell somebody!" Tears ran down her face, mingling with the grape stains.

"Shhh, quiet," said Akbar. "Do you want them to hear you? It wouldn't take much of a rock to shut you up!"

"He's right," Mara said, hugging herself to keep from shaking. "There's nothing we can do."

"Poor Stephen," Karis whimpered. "He helped my dad care for the poor, and he brought us food. He gave me sweet figs to eat. He and my father talked about Jesus for hours."

The dull thud of rock striking flesh made them cringe. The condemned man groaned. The kids groaned. The crowd hushed. Mara wondered if any of them were sorry they were getting what they had asked for.

"You children should not be here!"

Mara jumped. A short, squatty man glared at her. "Run away!" he scolded, shooing her off with a pudgy hand. "There's going to be trouble. This won't be the end of it, you'll see!"

He almost spat at her. Mara backed away and motioned the others to higher ground.

From a little hill of rubble, they watched the sweating men bending down for more rocks, their faces full of heat and hate.

Mara prayed for a miracle. *God, don't let Stephen die!* She reached for Nathan. He wasn't there.

"Nathan! Where's Nathan?" Panic gripped Mara.

"He was here a minute ago," said Obadiah, breathing hard.

"Nathan!" called Mara. "Nathan!"

"Here. Here, Mara!" Nathan scrambled up the rocky mound. Dirt streaked his sweaty face.

"You mud ball!" she scolded. But she couldn't hide the relief in her voice. "Where were you?"

"I wanted to get nearer to Saul of Tarsus, but he was swearing and threatening every member of the Way. I think he wants to kill us all!"

Mara shivered and pulled her brother close.

"Look!" Karis cried. "He's getting up!"

They all watched as Stephen, horribly bloodied, staggered to his feet. His lips moved, and a hush fell over the crowd.

He looked toward heaven. His expression was one of pain mixed with peace. Loudly he cried, "Lord Jesus, receive my spirit!"

He stumbled and dropped to his knees. He cried out again, "Lord, do not hold this sin against them!" Then he collapsed and was still.

Mara looked at Saul, who was watching the body for signs of life. There weren't any.

He forgave his murderers! Mara couldn't believe it. Jesus had done the same thing on the cross.

"How could he forgive those people?" Obadiah asked, an angry look on his face. "They killed him." He shook his head. "I couldn't forgive them."

"Me either," said Sarah, tears streaming down her face.

"Come on," Mara said, an ache in her throat. "We need to go back." They left the quarry, their heads hanging, tears streaking paths through the dirt on their faces.

Nobody talked much on the way home, until Nathan finally said quietly, "In synagogue school, the rabbis teach that it's right for you to forgive someone up to three times."

"Some of those men threw a lot more than three rocks," Obadiah said angrily.

"Jesus said to forgive seventy times seven, if you have to," Akbar said. He sounded anything but ready to do that.

"He meant we shouldn't keep track," Mara said shakily. "We should just forgive whenever someone says he's sorry."

"But none of Stephen's murderers said they were sorry." Obadiah practically spat the words. Then he sniffled and lowered his head to hide his tears. "He asked the Lord to forgive them anyway. I don't think I could have done that," he finished quietly.

"He was different. We're supposed to be different too. We're the Way, followers of Messiah," Karis said in a dull voice. Her face was gray as ash.

Gloom settled over them. They walked slowly. Mara was afraid to think what she was thinking. For the first time since her family had put their trust in the Way of Jesus, she wondered if it was such a good idea.

Then Nathan spoke her thoughts aloud. "I don't feel safe anymore." He looked as if he might cry.

"What do you mean?" his sister asked, afraid of what he would say.

"I mean, who's next?" he said. "What if Saul decides to hunt down the rest of us? Where could we hide?"

Mara had no answer. *Where* could *we hide?* she wondered.

They all looked scared. Really scared.

Mara tried to forget what they'd just seen. To make her back straight again, like a queen's. To walk her royal walk. The truth was, though, she felt about as royal as a flattened grape.

She knew that the memory of that awful stoning would never leave their heads. Stephen's words repeated again and again in her mind: *"Lord, do not hold this sin against them."*

Mara tried instead to think of the New Israel theme song. But she couldn't remember a single word. Even if she had been able to recall the words, there was no way she could possibly sing it.

The next day, Mara's father, Joshua, called an emergency meeting of the Way. Joshua was a leader in the new church.

Mara loved to watch him. He was tall, strong, and handsome. He looked like royalty. When he spoke, people stopped their chatter and listened closely. His voice, deep and clear, commanded attention. Today it made heads shake, lips tremble, and mothers clutch their babies tighter. As Mara listened, she felt proud and petrified at the same time.

"Believers in Jesus, listen! Stephen's death will not be the last! In the night Saul's thugs broke into John's and Justin's homes, taking them and their sons captive. Six more, friends. Six *more*!" A shudder passed through the crowd in the main room of Mara's house.

As soon as the emergency meeting of the Way had been called, Mara had called another for New Israel. Karis and a bunch of her friends had come with their parents and wanted to sit with New Israel. Mara was annoyed. *Can't they form their own club?*

Most of the kids, whether in or out of New Israel, had a younger brother or sister to watch. Sarah had two little sisters. The children stood bunched together in the hot room, made hotter each time one more person squeezed into the back.

People filled the room. Fear filled the air. The babies felt it and fussed. Mara felt it, and her knees shook.

"I knew it!" It was the short, squat man who'd frightened the children at the quarry. "I knew we shouldn't start separating ourselves and calling ourselves 'believers.' People think we're different. It makes us look suspicious!"

"We *are* different!" cried a bent old man with a long white beard. Many others nodded. "We know Jesus is the Messiah. He was sent by God to help us, and men like Saul killed Him to shut Him up. Now they've killed Stephen too. It's not going to end there!" People raised their voices in fear, and chaos threatened to erupt.

"Keep your voices down!" Joshua said in a fierce whisper.

Mara was worried. Her father, who usually looked calm and collected, now looked awfully scared. For the first time in her life, Mara didn't know if even he could keep their family safe.

"Where'd they take the brothers?" Timon, Karis's father, inquired.

"To prison!" another man answered from the crowd.

"On what charge?"

"That they encouraged others to quit the old ways and to begin anew."

That started another argument. Faces flushed in anger. Fingers pointed.

"Please, my friends, no fighting," Joshua urged, trying to bring peace. He spoke in Greek so that all would understand. "This is not about who's right and who's wrong. Our lives are in danger. We've got to have a plan!"

Mara tensed. Sometimes she thought her father spent too much time trying to include the Greeks in everything. Let them look after themselves. In fact, let them get their own church. They could worship in their own odd way, eat their own funny food, and jabber away in their own language. Leave the Hebrew believers to worship, eat, and speak according to the ways and laws handed down from long ago. *For hundreds and hundreds of years,* she thought, *we true Jews have kept our ways of thinking and worshipping. It's what makes us special. Jesus is our Messiah!*

"Whatever the plan," her father continued, "we've got to be prepared to go to jail. Don't think being a law-abiding citizen will save you. Saul doesn't need an excuse. He isn't concerned about the truth. He thought Jesus was a troublemaker, and he thinks we're just as bad."

"Since when is believing in God's Son a crime?" the white-bearded old gentleman asked.

"Punishable by stoning to death?" piped up the short, squat man.

"It's because we call sin what it is," cried another. "That makes us dangerous."

When Joshua had them quieted once again, he said, "What makes us really dangerous is that we don't put our trust in priests or governors. We trust in Jesus, the One who died for our sins! But for that, friends, we will suffer."

Her father's words upset Mara more. She hated feeling angry and scared and confused all at once. She wished she could forget the nightmare in her mind of poor Stephen bloody and dying. She didn't want her family or friends to suffer. What if that had been her father being stoned?

Mara dug her fingernails deep into the palms of her hands. It was too horrible to imagine. And too unfair. If Saul wanted to throw somebody in jail who was really different, why didn't he pick on Karis the tunnel girl? Now *there* was a weird person.

She felt a jab in the ribs. It was Karis's elbow. Mara glared at the other girl. Karis glared right back. "Why'd you poke me?" Mara demanded.

"Because you deserve to be poked—and worse!" Karis said. "Haven't you been listening to your father? Of course not. You think you're too good for most people. You give the Way a bad name. You and your slave of a brother!"

Now Karis had two people glaring at her.

"You take that back, you overgrown water bug!" growled Nathan, making a fist. "I'll show you who's a slave!"

Karis was as jumpy as the rest, but it didn't hide her disgust. "Saul could come here and take us any minute, but you still want to pick fights. Baby rabbis don't go around slugging people, unless of course they're looking for work with the Sanhedrin!" She turned away.

Nathan sputtered but relaxed his fist. "Good thing for you that Torah doesn't let me punch a girl," he muttered at her back.

"Does it let you punch a boy?" Suddenly Akbar practically stood on Nathan's toes, and the look on his face said it wasn't a friendly visit.

Mara grabbed Nathan. Sarah grabbed Mara. Obadiah bumped into Akbar, belly first, ready to defend Nathan. No member of New Israel looked happy. No nonmember of New Israel looked happy. No one else in the room looked happy either.

Mara hadn't been paying attention to what was going on in the room, so she was surprised when a chunk of stale bread suddenly sailed from somewhere over the heads of the crowd. The bread nearly landed in a clay pot that was filled with lamp oil and was sitting on a bench near the fireplace at the center of the room. Two young men at the front of the room stood chin to chin, ready to tear each other's beards out.

Forgetting his own warning to keep it down, Joshua bellowed, "Stop it! Animals behave better than this!"

Startled, the men released each other's clothing and took a step back. Some people looked embarrassed. All looked uneasy. They turned to Joshua.

"Would Jesus be pleased with us?" he asked, arms spread to include everyone.

The people shrank back, murmuring to themselves. Mara, Karis, and the others stared at the floor.

Suddenly the door burst open with a crash. Mara stood frozen to the spot as five men she'd never seen before stormed the meeting, swinging clubs and lunging for anyone they could grab. Screams and shouts and the shrieking of children turned the room into a madhouse.

The bench toppled to the floor, dumping lamp oil with a splash. The oil caught fire, but a man quickly stamped it out. Mara watched her pretty, hand-woven fruit basket fall beneath stampeding feet. Two huge clay water pitchers fell from the shelf and broke against the floor in a thousand pieces. *Mother will be sick. Where is she?* Mara wondered. She tried to see through the crowd, but all was confusion.

People shoved and crawled for the doorway. The cows and chickens at the front of the house bawled and squawked in terror.

Mara searched frantically for her father. He was wrestling one of the attackers, trying to yank the thick wooden club out of his hand. What could she do?

A shriek from Obadiah's little sister made up Mara's mind. She would save the kids and pray that her father and mother could get away.

Separated from their parents by the intruders in the confusion, the children looked dazed. Mara pushed and herded four of the youngest out the door to the street. Sarah had one in each hand and a third on her back. The older boys followed with the rest.

"Quick!" Mara ordered. "To the roof! Hurry!"

She carried and pulled four children up the stone stairs beside the house. After she'd shoved them onto the roof, she reached back for the others running up the stairs behind her and pushed them forward. Karis joined them and with the older boys made everyone lie flat against the roof.

Mara peered over the edge and watched the men and women, her parents included, being herded down the street like cattle. Other people stopped to watch the spectacle and point at the prisoners.

"Where'd those kids go?" one of the attackers shouted from the street.

"We'll come for them later," shouted the one in the lead. "They can't hide forever."

The last thing Mara saw before they turned the corner was her father looking back toward the roof. No doubt he knew she would hide up there. It was where she'd loved to go as a little girl. She'd take her pet lamb and watch it graze in the grass that grew in the mud and clay roof. *Jesus, Messiah, don't let them hurt Mother and Father.* Without thinking, she started to raise a hand to wave, but Nathan yanked it down.

"Saul's men!" Nathan warned. "They've taken our parents, Mara. They've taken *all* our parents!"

The little ones looked wide-eyed and stunned. Mara put her finger to her lips, and Nathan grew quiet.

"I think we should pray," Mara said. She looked at Nathan.

"I can't," Nathan said in a small voice and then started to cry.

Mara felt the cold of the empty house below come right up through the roof into her heart. "They'll be back for us," she said. "We'd *better* pray!"

We have to get away from here, Mara thought. *Saul's men will come back. And when they do, they won't think twice about hurting us.*

Though it was a hot day, she felt chilled all over. Her pretty royal dreams were gone. The memory of sharp rocks raining down on Stephen's head and body tormented her. Would the same thing happen to her parents and the others? How long would it take for rocks to finish off her mother and father?

Mara tried to think of what to do. The kids of New Israel crowded around. Their little sisters and brothers cried. The harder she tried to quiet them, the louder they bawled.

She looked into her brother's tear-streaked face. He rubbed his eyes with his fists and tried to pretend he hadn't been crying. "I want Mom and Dad."

"I know, Nathan, I know!" she murmured, putting a comforting arm around his shoulders. "I'm trying to think of something . . ."

She looked at Karis at the other end of the roof trying to comfort the others. Their cries were getting steadily louder as the children began to realize what had happened. Soon they would be heard from the street. It was hopeless.

Karis came over and frowned at Mara. "We aren't safe here," she said, stating the obvious.

"I know that!" Mara snapped.

"So what's the plan?" Karis hissed. "You got us up here!"

"And I'll get us down!" Mara insisted forcefully, though she didn't feel forceful. Getting down was the easy part. What then?

She closed her eyes. *What do I do now? The neighbors don't believe in Jesus. They've never liked us holding meetings in our house. They must know we're up here. They might turn us in.*

"Well?" Karis demanded.

"We can climb that giant olive tree in the Garden of Gethsemane and hide out in the branches."

"Right," said Karis sarcastically. "And we can make like olives. They'll never guess we're really kids!"

"Yeah," Akbar joined in. "If we painted Obie a dark green-black, he could pass for the world's biggest olive!"

"You take that back or I'll give you an 'olive' right between the eyes!" Obadiah pulled a wicked-looking slingshot from his cloak and scanned the roof for suitable ammunition.

"Would you two knock it off?" Mara yelled, forgetting to be quiet. "Obie, put that thing away. Can't you see the kids are scared enough as it is?"

"You don't have a clue what we should do, do you?" Karis put in. "I thought the leader of New Israel knew everything!"

"She's trying, Karis," Sarah said, arms tight around her sniffling little sisters. "Please give her a chance."

Mara smiled gratefully at Sarah and ignored Karis. "I've got it! We'll go to the Dead Sea and hide out in the caves. Nobody'll find us there!"

"Including our parents," Akbar snorted. "You can get lost in those caves."

"It's a bad idea," Karis agreed. "They'll be watching the city gates. Besides, it's fifteen miles to the Dead Sea. How far do you think we'll get with those?" She pointed to the short, chubby legs of Obadiah's four-year-old sister.

"About half a mile," sniffled Nathan.

Mara gave her brother a "Whose side are you on?" look. "Do you have a better idea?" she asked Karis.

"As a matter of fact, I do," she said. "Follow me."

The New Israelites looked at Mara for guidance. She hesitated a moment. She didn't know what to do, and Karis seemed to have a plan. Surrendering her pride, she nodded.

The children streamed down from the roof, Karis in the lead. She darted from doorway to doorway, and they darted after her in twos and threes like hesitant shadows.

A woman yelled from a window, "Where are you going? Come back here!"

The children ran as if wild dogs snapped at their heels. They grabbed and pulled one another along, the older carrying the younger. When some stumbled, others picked them up. All ignored scraped knees and torn clothing.

When Sarah started to fall behind with her little sisters, Obadiah and Akbar carried the little girls. If they saw a commotion or a group of men in the main street, the children squirted away down a side alley. At one turn they panicked when a ragged man pointed a bony finger their way and shouted, "Runaways! Somebody stop them!" But they were gone in an instant. If an alley looked too dark or dangerous, they stuck to the main street, trying to act like children at play, as if nothing was wrong.

But plenty was wrong, Mara knew. There was tension in the city. People hurried along and looked at each other with suspicion. There wasn't the usual market-day laughter and excitement. Even the noisy beggars were silent. She half expected to see a wanted poster painted on the side of the fish market: "Reward for Believers in Jesus—Dead or Alive!" Even the stiff fish in the baskets they passed seemed to look at her with accusing eyes.

It was only then that she noticed Karis was cupping a three-inch clay lamp in one hand. A tiny flame flickered at its tip.

"Hey, where'd you get that?" Mara demanded. "That's one of my mother's olive oil lamps. You stole it from my house!"

Karis shrugged. "We'll need light where we're going. Mine ran out of oil. Besides, it was a little hard to ask your permission in the middle of a war!"

Suddenly Karis slipped down a narrow passage where sunlight never penetrated. "Come on!" She motioned them to follow between the buildings. "It's this way."

When they caught up with her, Karis was lifting two paving stones from the side of the passage. Before Mara could say a word, Karis's bottom half disappeared into the gap between the stones. "It's all right," she said. "I'll help you down. Mara comes first, then the little ones, then you bigger boys. It's wet down there, and you'll have to crawl a ways on your knees, but soon you'll be able to stand. Hand me the lamp once I'm down." She dropped from sight.

The kids hung back, even the ones banned from New Israel. The non-members liked Karis, but they did not like going underground.

"Come on, you guys," encouraged Mara shakily, determined not to quit. "She knows what she's doing. We've got to trust her. We're out of choices."

With that, Mara followed Karis into the hole and dropped with a splash onto her hands and knees in six inches of water. The slow-moving water swished past her, smelling like the damp dirt of an open grave. She fought back a scream and wound her soggy veil around her neck to keep it up. Her pretty gown soaked up water like a sponge. She pulled it above her knees.

"Thanks for trusting me." Karis's voice echoed in the tunnel. She set the lamp on a small ledge in the rock.

Mara glared at her. "You'd better know what you're doing."

Karis pointed in the direction of the moving water. "You'll want to go that way. The main tunnel's not far. You can stand up there, and it's not as dark. Here, take the lamp." She handed Mara the light and reached up for Nathan, who insisted on not letting Mara out of his sight. He splashed down beside her. "Follow Mara," Karis instructed. "I'll send along the others."

One by one, the other children dropped into the tunnel with a splash, many of them whimpering and shivering from fright and the shock of the cold water. But when Karis said crawl, they crawled.

Mara sloshed forward into the darkness on one hand, her other hand holding the lamp safely above the water. The damp, musty smell of the cool air grew steadily stronger. She soon emerged into a taller and wider chamber where she could stand. The others popped from the side tunnel until they all stood in a tight circle around the comfort of the tiny, flickering flame.

"I'll take that," Karis said as she joined the group. Mara hesitated and then handed her the lamp.

"That tunnel leads to the north cistern," Karis explained, pointing back the way they'd come. "We're in the main tunnel now." Pointing downstream, she added, "That way leads to the center of the business district out through the Pool of Siloam, where we met yesterday." Finally she pointed upstream. "That goes under the city wall and out of Jerusalem. We'll go that way. There's a place where everyone can get out of the water and dry out. Then we can decide what to do next.

"And one more thing." Her words bounced off the walls like startled bats. "As long as you're in my world, we talk in Greek, okay? I don't want any secrets down here." She looked right at Mara.

No one said anything, but someone coughed, and they all jumped.

The place gave Mara the creeps. She should never have let this foreigner lead New Israel to a watery grave. Her imagination began to conjure up images of the group wandering aimlessly through the tunnels for days, starving and forgotten. What had she been thinking?

"Well?" Karis's one word echoed through the darkness with a dozen *l*'s at the end.

Mara began to vigorously wring the water out of her gown to hide her nervousness. She squeezed the soggy end of her pretty cream-colored veil until it looked like a big wad of muck. Were the tunnels what really bothered her, or was it that Karis was in control?

"Okay," Mara said after a moment, "but you'd better be able to get us out of here." Something wet plopped onto her shoulder from the ceiling, and she jumped back, frantically trying to shake it off.

"Look, I know my way around down here," Karis said, flicking off the clump of mud that had fallen on Mara's shoulder. "You've got to trust me." The hand holding the lamp shook and made the reflection on the tunnel wall jerk around. "I'm worried about my parents too, you know. We've got to work together if we want to help them. While you've been playing queen for a day, I've been making up a map here of all the tunnels," she said as she tapped her forehead. "The perfect escape. Keep the little kids quiet, and let's get going!"

"Hey!" Obadiah piped up in a shaky voice. "Who put you in charge?"

Karis shrugged. "You were too chicken to ever come down here before. And most of you didn't want me for a friend. But now what? Now you're in trouble, and I'm all you've got. Let's be grateful one of us knows these tunnels."

The little ones had stopped sniffling. They were too frightened now to cry.

"Akbar, you take the lamp and the little kids and take the lead," Karis commanded. "You older kids stay in the back with me. I want you where I can see you."

"You don't trust us?" Obadiah asked.

"I don't trust you not to get lost," Karis said. "It looks like I'm responsible for keeping you alive, so would you please do as I ask?"

They went forward, but nobody talked except Karis, who gave Akbar directions. The floor began to slant slightly upward. The water rushed against their feet and ankles, and the footing was slippery. The walls of the passage narrowed until it was barely the width of an adult. Husky

Obadiah had to shuffle along sideways. Sarah, just ahead of Mara, started breathing hard. Mara reached out a hand and gave Sarah's elbow a comforting squeeze. She knew Sarah didn't like small spaces. Who did?

The lamp disappeared around a bend in the passage ahead, and those at the rear of the line were almost in total darkness. Mara's heart began beating faster and faster. The dark was where the monsters lived.

She rubbed against the slimy walls. It seemed like tons of rock were pressing in on her. The farther they went, the sorrier she became that she'd let Karis bring them all here. In the inky darkness, she could barely breathe.

"Karis," Akbar called back from the front of the line. The line stopped moving.

"What?" Karis replied.

"There's something here you should see."

"It can wait. We're almost there. The big chamber is only a little ways more. The tunnel widens out soon," Karis said.

"I-I think you'd better come look," Akbar called out shakily.

"What is it?"

"Come see."

Karis sighed and squeezed past Mara and the others. Now Mara was the last in line. In the pitch dark. *Dead last,* she thought.

She wished Karis hadn't left. There was comfort in knowing the other girl was behind her.

Suddenly, something cold and clammy clamped itself around her neck from behind. Mara screamed.

CHAPTER 6

"Shhh!" Nathan's shaky voice sounded in her ear.

"Why did you sneak up on me like that?" Mara yelped, finding her brother's ear and giving it a yank. "I thought you were ahead of me."

"Ow!" Nathan cried. "Let go of my ear! Can't you take a joke?"

"A joke? I'll tell you a joke. *You're* a joke!" Mara was furious. The water that swirled around her ankles wasn't going to cool her down either.

"Calm down, Sis. The rabbis teach that a cool head and a sense of humor go together. You'll need that when you're queen."

Mara snorted.

"Queens don't snort," said Nathan. "They hire servants to snort for them."

She yanked his other ear.

"Ow! Cut it out! Do you want me to go around with elephant ears because you couldn't control your yanking?"

Mara giggled nervously. *That* she couldn't control.

"What do you think they've found up there?" Nathan asked. He didn't have to wait long for the answer.

"Is everything okay back there?" Karis called out.

"Fine," answered Mara. "It's just my stinky brother acting like his usual stinky self."

"Well, screams aren't a good idea right now," Karis called out in a shaky voice. She hesitated and then added, "We don't seem to be the only ones down here."

Mara's heart hammered. With Nathan shadowing her every step, she made her way to the head of the line.

They had reached the big chamber as Karis had promised. At one end was the tunnel through which they'd just entered. At the other end, the passage left the big chamber and immediately branched into three separate tunnels. The place where they joined formed a wide floor slanted on the sides like the bottom of a bowl. Two of the tunnels produced slow streams of water. A small torrent rushed downhill toward them from the third, but the slanted sides rose above the water and formed a low shelf. As long as they stood on the shelf, they remained dry.

Karis was bending over something on the dry part of the floor. Then she stood up and stepped back. The others looked. It was a long arrow, hand-drawn in white chalk, pointing to the right-hand chamber.

"It isn't yours, is it?" Mara questioned, her voice dry and barely more than a whisper. "You didn't draw it, did you?"

Karis shook her head but didn't say anything. Nathan peered around Mara and gulped. His face went pale as if he were staring at a poisonous snake set to strike. "They're hunting for us!"

"They're not hunting for us," Karis tried to reassure him. "But if they find us, we're in big trouble, no matter why they're down here."

"Look there," Akbar said as he pointed. A set of nearly dry footprints along the shelf disappeared into the darkness of the tunnel to the right from which water rushed.

"Don't tell us that's the way we have to go," Sarah whispered.

Karis nodded and held a finger to her lips in warning.

"Looks like you've gotten us trapped underground with the enemy!" Mara whispered furiously.

Karis held the lamp high and looked Mara in the eye. "We don't even know it's them," she said quietly. "But if it *is* Saul and his men, they don't know these tunnels like *I* know these tunnels. That's why they had to mark the main branch so they wouldn't get lost. The other two tunnels dead-end at pools for collecting rainwater. Would you rather still be on that roof scared as rabbits waiting to be grabbed?"

"No, I'd much rather be stuck in a dark, smelly underground tunnel scared as rabbits waiting to be grabbed!" Mara shivered with fear and cold.

"Have a little faith and follow me," ordered Karis as she started back a short distance along the way they'd come. She dropped flat on her belly. There was a low opening at the bottom of the wall easily missed in the dim light. Only a very little water leaked from it. She wriggled through.

For a minute the others heard nothing. Mara was about to turn around and go back when the lamp showed at the opening. A hand slid out from under the wall and motioned for them to follow.

Feeling as if she were going down, down, down to the center of the earth, Mara hesitated. Now that they were in the tunnels, they needed Karis to get them out. And they needed someplace where they could hide without Saul's men stumbling over them. If they ever saw the sun again, Mara would tell the girl from Caesarea just what she thought of her getting them all buried alive. But for now, she knew she had no choice.

Fuming, Mara helped the young ones crawl after Karis. She tried to make a quiet game of it so they wouldn't be so afraid. She murmured, "Little fish, little fish, swimming up the stream; slippery rocks, slippery rocks, we are all one team . . ." Like minnows, the youngest kids flopped and wiggled one by one into the opening and vanished from sight.

"I should have finished that grape fight while I had the chance!" Obadiah grunted as he made his tight way through the hole.

"Shhh!" Mara hissed—but quickly stopped when the echo in the tunnel sounded louder than the original shush. It took some shoving from the others, but Obadiah finally made it with a groan and a relieved "Oof!"

Sarah followed and then Akbar. When it was Nathan's turn, he put his mouth close to Mara's ear. "Queen Mara, promise me that in your kingdom you'll have wide doors and high ceilings!"

Mara, the last through, crawled a short distance and then was helped into a large, square room with sides that looked sixty feet high. The walls were slimy and crumbling but thick enough that the kids could talk quietly without fear of attracting outside attention. A dim light filtered down from somewhere at the top of the walls. Karis walked over to four oil-soaked torches hung from the walls and lit them with the flame from the lamp. Then she blew out the little lamp to conserve oil.

The smoky light from the torches was welcome, though it showed just how bare their hideout was.

Nathan looked around and made a shivery sound. He pulled on Mara's arm. "This place isn't much better than a tomb!"

Karis frowned at them. "This would not be a good time to complain about the hideout. You have to admit, we're out of sight. It's a forgotten rain storage well that's been sealed over at the top. If we keep our voices down, nobody will know we're in here."

Mara gave Karis her best "What now?" look.

Karis turned her back. "Let's catch our breath. Give me time to think." She plopped herself down against the wall, released her hair from the pins that had kept it in the pitiful little bun that Mara disliked, and closed her eyes. Absentmindedly, she chewed on a strand of hair.

Mara found a partially dry spot and sat down, her back against the wall. Her gown was ruined. She thought of the hours her mother had put into the stitching. Her heart ached for home and her parents. She tried not to imagine what might be happening to them.

She heard a stirring of wings high above and thought she saw a shadow cross in front of a weak beam of light.

"Pigeons?" she asked hopefully.

"Bats," Karis replied, not opening her eyes.

Nathan clamped a hand tight over his sister's mouth.

After what seemed like hours, the little ones started crying quietly.

"I'm hungry."

"I'm cold."

"I feel sick."

"Can you take me to my mama now?"

"We're lost. When are we going to get out of here?"

The grumbling continued. Mara watched Karis for signs of life, but the girl sat apart from the others in stony silence, eyes closed. Was she thinking or sleeping?

Mara forced a cough. And another. And a third. But Karis, if she was conscious, didn't budge an eyelash.

"Maybe she's turned to salt," Nathan whispered.

"Maybe your brain has turned to mush," Mara said.

"My cloak sure has. Mother spent hours making this, and it only took minutes to ruin. Look at that." Nathan fingered the ragged edges of a large tear. "A hole you could drive a chariot through. Even if we make it out of here in one piece, I'm doomed."

"With a capital *D*," Mara agreed.

Her brother frowned. "We've got to do something."

"What would you suggest, O Wise One?"

Nathan huffed. "All I know is that if you ever get to be the queen, you're going to have to lead better than this."

The warning on Mara's face brought the conversation to a halt.

Some children whimpered for their mothers. Others slept. One of Sarah's little sisters pretended to hold a doll and sing to it. The silence lasted barely five minutes.

"Mara?"

"What, Nathan?"

"If you tell me the tooter rhyme, I'll tell you a joke."

Mara sighed. "I thought you learned serious, important things at synagogue school."

"Jokes are what I learn going *to* and *from* synagogue school," Nathan announced. "Please? I'm bored stiff. Two flute tooters tooted on a teeter-tooter . . ."

Mara stopped him. "Don't. You'll only mess it up like you always do. It goes like this: A tooter who tooted a flute tried to tutor two tutors to toot. Said the two to the tooter, 'Is it harder to toot or to tutor two tutors to toot?'"

Nathan laughed, stifling his snickers with both hands. No matter how many times he heard the rhyme, it always made him smile. Mara felt pleased to take his mind off their situation, even if just for a moment. "Your turn," she said warily.

He wore the silly grin he always did when telling dumb jokes.

Mara sighed. She was trapped.

"What belongs to you, but other people use it more than you do?"

"I give up."

"Your name."

"That's not a joke. It's a riddle."

"Okay, okay. Here's one. Why do bees hum?"

"I give up. Why?"

"Because they don't remember the words."

The little kids moved closer. Nathan had an audience.

"You give up too quickly," he told his sister. "This time you have to think about it."

"I thought you said you'd tell me a joke, as in *one* joke."

"It would have been just one if you'd answered it right. Are you listening?"

Mara sighed again, as only one who was waiting to be queen could. "One more," she said, "then you're done."

"Okay. A turtle, a lion, a camel, a bear, a pig, a frog, two mice, and a snake all got under one tent. How many got wet?"

Mara pretended to think about her answer a long time before saying, "Nine."

Nathan rolled his eyes. "Wrong."

"How many, then?"

"None. It wasn't raining."

"That wasn't funny."

"*They* thought it was." Nathan pointed to the three children about them who were giggling.

"Their combined ages add up to eight. What do you expect?"

"Okay, I'll keep telling jokes until you find one you think is funny," Nathan said.

"Sorry, little brother, people don't live that long. But *I* will leave you with something funny just so you'll know what a real joke sounds like. Ready?"

"Go ahead."

"Knock, knock."

"Who's there?"

"Amana."

"Amana who?"

"Amana bad mood, so no more stupid jokes!"

As Mara got up to talk with Karis, she saw Nathan point to her and heard him whisper to the little kids loud enough for her to hear, "When she's queen, she'll have to pay people to laugh at her lame jokes. But when I'm rabbi, people will write down everything I say!"

At first, Mara just slid down beside Karis and said nothing. The minutes dragged on. Nathan soon ran out of jokes, and the complaining started again.

"My leg hurts."

"My scarf is torn and I'll get in trouble."

"You *are* in trouble!"

"I'm *really* hungry now!"

"Why are we just sitting here doing nothing?"

"I want to look for my parents."

"No, we should stay put and let our parents find us."

"They sure won't look for us here."

"What's that in the corner? Is it a rat?"

The children whined for someone to do something. Akbar grabbed

Obadiah's slingshot, loaded it with a hard bit of the crumbling wall, and started cautiously toward a small, dark shape in the far corner. Ten feet away, he suddenly leaped forward and landed on the shape, stomping on it twice for good measure. He reached down, picked it up, and waved it in the air. "One of Obadiah's sandals," he said disgustedly.

"Obie!" Mara scolded. "Why didn't you say so?"

Obadiah shrugged and grinned. "I was going to, but we had to see how Fearless Akbar the Hunter would save us from my sandal."

Akbar shot him a dirty look. Obadiah stuck out his hand for the slingshot. Akbar tossed it to him. "Let's get out of the city and hide in one of the villages," he said angrily. "I'm tired of this."

Sarah objected. "As long as we're right here, they don't know where we are."

Mara nodded. "I agree. It's probably still too dangerous to go out yet."

"But how will we know when it's safe to go out?" Sarah asked.

The whole time, Karis had kept her eyes closed and hadn't budged. But now she jumped to her feet and surprised Mara with a big smile. "I know how we'll find out."

"How?" asked Mara.

"We'll *spy!*"

"What do you mean, 'we'?" Mara said. She wished for a small fire to dry her gown. She did *not* wish to go outside and spy.

"Suit yourself," said Karis with a shrug. "You're probably right. It would be better for you to stay here and babysit the little kids."

Mara ignored the remark. "And just what will *you* be doing?"

"I'll look for our parents and the other adults," she said. "I'll listen for the news in the market and bring back some food."

Obadiah shook his head. "You'll get caught, and we'll be stuck underground wondering what happened to you."

Nathan cleared his throat and stood, hands folded in front of his chest. "The rabbis teach that when the Lord is with us, He will fight our battles. I say we let the Lord pound Saul good before we poke our heads out."

"Yeah, he's right for a change," Akbar said. "We should stick together until they give up looking for us."

Several of the others booed and said they'd rather be anywhere than where they were.

Sarah, who was usually quiet, said, "I don't know why we let Karis drag us down here." That drew several "yeahs" of agreement from the others, New Israel or not.

Mara was torn. Should she let Karis leave them in the strange, wet world under the city? Could she be trusted to come back for them after the way New Israel had treated her? She might even turn them in! No, that was silly. Their best chance was not sitting around getting on each other's nerves. They had to take action.

But the strongest thought Mara had was also the most unexpected. *What if Karis is caught spying, and they hurt her?*

"I can't let you go alone," Mara said to everyone's surprise. "I'll go with you."

Karis stared at her. "Really? It'd be safer to work together, that's for sure." She paused. "Thanks," she said at last.

They spent the next few minutes collecting coins from the kids for food. As usual, Karis had no coins to contribute.

"You never have any money," Mara said. "Can't your dad juggle or sing or do anything for spare change? He should stop sponging off the church, you know. I've seen monkeys at the market that earn more than he does!"

Mara bit the inside of her cheek. She was irritated that she cared if Karis got caught, so she let the hateful words tumble out. But she did manage to stop the other mean words she had in mind.

Instantly, the friendliness in Karis's eyes disappeared, and Mara felt horrible. She didn't like that feeling, so she turned her attention to the others and tried reassuring them that this was the best plan. "Just two of us looking will draw a lot less attention than all of us running around," said Mara.

The others grumbled, and Mara started to sing, "We are New Israel . . ." With little enthusiasm, the other club members halfheartedly finished the rest.

Karis frowned. "We've got to come up with some new words for that song. Something for everyone, and definitely more praise and less brag." She smiled a little. Reluctantly Mara smiled too.

The girls said their good-byes, left Obadiah and Akbar in charge, and dropped to the ground to wiggle out of the room the way they'd wiggled in. Nathan dropped down beside his sister.

"What do you think you're doing?" Mara questioned.

"Going with you," Nathan said. "The rabbis teach that a cord of three strands is not quickly broken. I make three, and that's stronger than two." He waited until Karis was through to the other side before speaking low in Mara's ear. "Can we trust her? You need me. The queen always needs a bodyguard."

Mara looked at her brother's skinny body. It would be another ten years before he sprouted any muscles. Still, she figured it would be nice to have him around. "Okay," she said. "But no more jokes. I mean it!"

"Yes, your royal bossiness!" he said, bowing.

Out of the room they crawled, with only the faithful little lamp—now relit—for light. After the bright torches, the tunnel seemed pitch-black again, despite the tiny spot of lamplight.

Karis stood nose to nose with Nathan, the unexpected third party. Her face was half shadowed, half lit, eye sockets dark and empty like a skull's. But way back in there, a small spark in each eye said he'd better not cause any problems. "Stay close," she said before starting back at a trot along the passage the way they'd come.

It took the trio far less time to wind back to the paving-stone entrance than it had to herd all the children to the abandoned water well. Mara saw that Karis must have arranged the paving stones back in place to cover their escape. Now Karis listened for sounds of someone moving above. Apparently hearing none, she shoved the stones away, took a fast look around, and then motioned for Mara and Nathan to follow.

Quickly they darted back to the central business district, their clothes drying in the warm late-afternoon air. Then they melted into the crowd of people who were shopping for plums and cloth and live chickens. Vendors called to the shoppers, each trying to make a sale.

"Fresh, nice fish pulled from the Sea of Galilee!"

"Beautiful fabrics, the color of the sky!"

"Fine white wool of the highest quality!"

A donkey caravan clanked up the street of metalworkers. Hammered brass utensils glinted in the sun.

Coming close to the wine vendor's stall, the three kids overheard a heated exchange of news.

"Another dozen believers in the Way were arrested just an hour ago!" said a large, red-faced man with a wheeze. "Add them to those taken in this morning's raid at the ringleader Joshua's house, and we'll be paying taxes for a new jail to hold them all. Of course, they shouted that they have hurt no one, but we all know the strange ideas they spread. The Way, indeed! The way to ruin, I say!"

"That's nothing!" said a thick barrel of a man, tugging down the sleeves of a dirty gray cloak that was much too small for him. "Saul broke into the nut vendor's cellar and found twenty or more of them praying beneath the floorboards! If they have nothing to hide, how come that's where you usually find them?"

"Jail them all!" sputtered the owner of the wine stall. "They buy little from me. Instead, they raise much of their own food and share it with one another. Why? Isn't our meat and drink good enough for them?"

The donkey caravan clattered by, the little animals looking hot and tired and in need of a cool drink.

From across the street came the angry shouts and threats of a terrible argument. A throng of people spilled into the street, yelling and pointing. The donkeys stopped in their tracks, and the kids dropped to their knees in the dusty street, using the animals to shield them from view.

They peered between the bony legs of the beasts at the realization of their worst fears. Saul, grim-faced and determined, was crossing the street flanked by armed police. He was coming straight toward them.

Just then, a beautiful woman in silky yellow grabbed Saul by the arm and tried to stop him. Roughly he shoved her away. She stumbled and fell to her knees but was instantly up, pulling on Saul's arm and beating against him with her fists. Others swarmed noisily about them like irritated hornets and in turn were hit and pushed by the men at Saul's side.

"My husband!" the woman screamed in Aramaic. "Where is my husband? Where have you taken him?"

"What's she saying?" Karis asked. Mara told her.

Two big men with sweat-smeared faces grabbed the woman's arms and pulled her back. Saul threw her a chilling look of disgust and moved on.

"Your husband trusts in this Jesus Messiah, and he must pay for the false beliefs he teaches to others!" another woman shouted. "They will track down as many 'believers' as they can get their hands on!"

"Murderer!" the woman in yellow screamed at Saul's back.

Mara peeked around the hind legs of a sleepy-eyed donkey with enormous ears, hoping for a better view. She saw the awful hatred in Saul's reddened eyes. It was the look of evil.

And suddenly those evil eyes seemed to look right at her.

"Hyah! Move, you miserable creatures! Hyah!" The donkey driver whacked the rear donkey across the rump with a switch, and the caravan lurched forward.

The kids scrambled to their feet. Crouching over so as not to be seen from the other side, they kept in step with the caravan until they could hide behind a pile of fruit sacks.

"Phew!" Karis exclaimed. "That was close!"

"Did you see his eyes?" Mara said shakily. "Maybe Saul's the monster everybody says lives in the tunnels!"

They both looked at Nathan, who was as pale as parchment. Without taking his eyes off Saul and his thugs, he muttered, "Did you see what I saw?"

"Of course we did," said Mara. "We were right there with you."

"No, no, you were too busy watching the argument," Nathan said. "Didn't you see what Saul and his men had on them?"

The girls gave him a quizzical look. "What?" they said in unison.

"B-blood," Nathan stammered.

The three gulped as one.

"Let's go," Karis ordered.

"Yes," said Nathan. "Suddenly those tunnels don't seem so bad."

"Not the tunnels," said Karis. "This way." She set off in the direction Saul and his men had gone.

Mara stopped her. "What do you think you're doing?"

"Yeah," agreed Nathan. "What do you think you're doing?"

Karis rolled her eyes. "Is there an echo out here? We've got to follow them and find out what they're up to. The last time we saw our parents, Saul had them!"

"Good point," Mara said.

"This is stupid," Nathan said. "Why don't we just have Saul over to the house for supper? After dessert, we'll ask him if he would please take us to our parents."

"Your brother's got a mouth," Karis said.

"You should hear him when he's in a bad mood," Mara replied.

The girls smiled at each other. Nathan shook his head. "Queen, you make a bodyguard's job very difficult."

Mara patted him on the head. "I meant to thank you for guarding me from the big, bad donkeys."

Nathan started to stick out his tongue but must have thought better of it.

The trio crept after the men. Saul led his band into the stall of Porteous the potter. In front of the stall, beautiful horses the color of fine black tea were tied to iron rings set in a horizontal post. Two of the men checked on the horses before following Saul and the others beneath a shady awning.

"Thank you, Porteous, for watching the horses while we checked the area for fugitives," said one of the men. "Those 'believers' would hide in a camel's nose if they could find a way in."

His friends laughed with him. All except Saul, whose face was like a dark thundercloud. They sat on upturned water pots and began to discuss the coming evening's activities. Porteous, in a white turban and an expensive green cloak, looked nervous at having them there. They were rough and dirty men and looked like they wrestled lions in their spare time. And Mara noticed that their garments were streaked with blood.

"How are we going to get close enough to hear what they're saying?" asked Mara uneasily.

Karis looked around. "There. He'll help us."

"He" was the water vendor, working his way along the street with two large goatskins on his belt and an impossibly large water urn balanced on his head. "Ho, you thirsty ones, come and drink!" he cried. An occasional customer would stop the man and pay him for a cup of fresh springwater.

The men ignored the water man. But just as he came even with the stall of Porteous, the children ran up and paid for drinks with a few of the coins they had collected from the others underground. The man stood in the shade cast by the huge, carefully balanced water urn and cheerfully filled three metal cups. He waited for the children to finish.

They took their time. A very long time. And while their mouths sipped the cool water, their ears strained to catch every word of the men loudly talking a few feet behind them.

"We've got to wipe these 'believers' out," said one. "There are too many of them. They're upsetting our religious leaders."

Mara snuck a peek at the men.

"And when the religious leaders become upset, we all become upset," said a particularly burly man with a jagged scar from one ear to the point of his chin.

"Few will miss them," a third man offered. "It's not like they hold important offices or contribute much to the economy. Many of them are old, and some are women."

Mara shivered despite the midday sun. *If women and old people aren't important to these guys*, she thought, *then children must not be very valuable either. Why doesn't Saul say something?*

"I told you we shouldn't have let those people go this morning," accused the man with the scar. "You can frighten them, but it only seems to make them stronger and more determined. We should have killed them while we could!"

Nathan choked on his water, and Mara and Karis both pounded his back. "Our parents," he squeaked. "They might be free! Maybe we can go home!"

Mara and Karis laughed loudly to cover Nathan's words. Mara peeked under her arm again. Saul sat still as stone, his eyes burning with a fanatical light.

"Here's what we do," came the voice of the first man, looking annoyed at the noisy children in front of the potter's stall. "We must rid Jerusalem of these unwelcome people and stop this foolish faith in that crucified Jesus before it has a chance to grow by even one more person."

"When?"

"Tonight. My friends tell me the church of the Way plans a meeting at the same house we were at this morning. The fools think we won't raid the same place twice. There they'll be, giving thanks that we didn't keep them in prison after all. We take one hundred armed men, and we storm that meeting. This time we finish the job."

Nathan choked again. The girls pounded him again.

"Are you done, children?" cried the water vendor impatiently. "I have other customers waiting. Do you wish more water? No? Then your cups, please. Give me your cups."

The man with the scar startled them. "What's the matter here? Vendor, do you not see we're trying to have a discussion? Move along and take these—"

He stopped and peered at Karis, nearest him, who was pulling her hair across her face. "Hey, weren't you at that meeting of the Way this morning?"

Mara and Nathan edged away, averting their faces.

The water man repositioned his huge water urn and hastily moved off. Mara and Nathan stayed ahead of him in the shadow cast by nine feet of man and jar. He shooed them off.

Karis stayed right where she was, the shoulder of her threadbare gown tight in the grip of the scar-faced man. "Yes, you were there!" he shouted eagerly. "You and those other kids slipped out before we could catch you!"

Safely away from Saul's company, Mara and Nathan looked back.

Nathan laughed dryly. "She doesn't look so sure of herself now that she's about to get what's coming to her!"

Mara stopped and just about lifted Nathan out of his sandals. "No!" she snapped, giving him a good shake. "Do you remember what our father said at the meeting this morning when everyone was ready to fight each other? He said, 'Would Jesus be pleased with us?' Would He, Nathan? Would Jesus want us to let those men hurt Karis?"

Mara surprised herself. Was she changing her mind about Karis? She couldn't stop thinking about the rocks raining down on poor Stephen. She wouldn't want the same thing to happen to Karis.

Nathan's eyes dropped, and he shook his head. "Naw," he said, shame-faced. "He wouldn't want that."

"Then you'd better ask God to make you invisible," she told him, "because we're going back there!"

Nathan tried to give her a look as if she'd lost her mind, but she was already twelve steps ahead of him.

They hurried back the way they'd come, hidden behind a large cart piled high with baskets of every size and shape. When the cart drew abreast of the potter's stall, Mara and Nathan dropped to a crouch so they couldn't be seen. Large, decorative clay pots blocked them from the view of the men who were still shouting at Karis and paying no attention to the street.

"Where are the other children? Tell us!"

"You're not from Jerusalem, are you? Where are you from?"

"You'd better loosen your little Greek tongue. Or we'll loosen it for you."

"Take a good look at the setting sun, girl, because you won't be seeing it again for a very long time!"

Mara and Nathan scurried quietly between the horses that were tied to the post, then turned and faced the tall animals. Mara reached up and untied the reins of the horses nearest her, and Nathan followed suit with those nearest him.

At first the animals only shuffled their feet and bobbed their heads, uncertain of what was happening. Mara looked at Nathan, and he nodded. On the silent count of three, they jerked upright, flapped their arms, and screeched like crazed owls.

With a wild whinnying, the horses stampeded. Ears flattened, snorting madly, they whirled and bucked and kicked away down the street in opposite directions, nearly taking Porteous's awning with them.

The stunned men chased after their horses, forgetting Karis, who had twisted out of the big man's grasp. They ran, yelling terrible curses and threats at anything that moved. Saul's rage was the worst. He swore to put an end to the Way. He wouldn't rest until he had killed them all.

Mara, Karis, and Nathan ran for their lives. Back to the tunnel entrance they flew. Suddenly the terrifying underground passage looked like one of the safest places on earth.

CHAPTER 8

"Did you see the look on that big horse when I jumped up in his face?" Nathan was bent over, partly from lack of breath, partly from laughing so hard.

"Just like nearsighted Aunt Isabel looked the time she asked for the hairbrush, and you handed her a donkey's jawbone," Mara gasped, trying to regain her own wind.

"Yeah," Karis said, "but it was no worse than the look on my face when I saw you two sneaking away with the water vendor. I actually thought you were going to leave me with those goons!"

Nathan stopped laughing. He couldn't look either girl in the eye. Mara took a sudden interest in her fingernails.

"Oh, great!" Karis huffed. "You *were* going to leave me there!"

"Not Mara, just me," Nathan mumbled. "And I . . . well, I wasn't thinking very clearly." His face reddened with shame. "Sorry."

"*You're* sorry? So am I!" Karis yelled. "Here I risk my neck to help New Israel to safety, and the minute you have the chance, you feed me to the hyenas. Is that what Torah teaches?"

"No." Nathan looked miserable. "Go ahead. I deserve it. You won't tell the rabbis, will you?"

Karis looked ready to blast him with a few more choice complaints, but she clamped her mouth shut instead. She shook her head and started off at a trot. "It's getting late. We've got to hurry."

They headed for the tunnels and the secret hideout where the others waited.

Mara hurried to catch up with Karis's flying feet. She felt all funny inside, like she'd swallowed a pound of squirming caterpillars, and they weren't planning to stay down. Karis had every right to be mad. They hadn't treated her well at all. Once they were safe again, Mara would have to think of some way to make it up to her. Good queens made sure of things like that.

After several twists, turns, and shortcuts through the city, they were once again in the alley with the removable paving stones. Mara stopped, realizing she'd been panting to keep up. As she leaned forward with her palms on her knees, the faces of her parents flashed through her mind. Were they running, too? Or were they . . .

She sent up another prayer.

Then she stood up straight—and couldn't believe what she saw. Karis was pulling at the paving stones and singing the New Israel song. At least it was the club tune. But as Mara drew close, it was obvious they weren't the club words:

> We are New Israel, kids who fuss and fight;
> People avoid us 'cause we kick and bite!
> About your bad kids, we hurt feelings left and right.
> We think we're good, but we're just rude
> And offend everyone in sight!

Mara helped Karis push the stones aside. "You've got too many syllables in the last line," she said. "And 'good' and 'rude' don't rhyme so well."

Karis rolled her eyes. Mara smiled weakly.

At last Karis smiled too. "Songwriting is hard work," she said. "It takes a long time to write something worth singing."

Mara let it go.

Once they'd wiggled their way back into the secret hideout, Mara, Nathan, and Karis were pelted with questions from the other kids.

"What took you so long?"

"Are our parents okay?"

"Can we go now?"

"What did you bring us back to eat?"

The last question was perhaps the most difficult to answer. Everyone talked at the same time, and it was hard to get the story out.

Mara tried. "We spent some of the food money on water."

"Water! But we're hungry!"

"It was too dangerous to buy food once they recognized us," she explained. "Besides, we didn't have time. We had to scare the horses."

"Horses? What horses?"

"Did she say she bought us horses to eat?"

"Not to eat!" Mara corrected. "We spooked the horses to run from the owners who were holding Karis . . ."

"My tummy's howling," Obadiah's little sister cried.

Obadiah gave her a hug. "No, Rebecca, you mean your stomach is growling."

She patted her round belly. "No, 'diah," she insisted. "Listen. It's howling!"

Akbar took off a sandal and stared at it. "This is starting to look tastier by the minute."

"We can eat later. Right now we've got to do something and do it fast," Mara said, taking charge. "It'll be dark soon, and our parents will be worried sick about us. Their lives are in danger. We've got to go back home and tell them to get out of Jerusalem as fast as they can. If Saul and his men find them gathered at my house tonight, there's no telling what they'll do." *If they haven't already*, she thought.

And she could imagine exactly what they'd do. But she wasn't about to tell the little ones. The worry in the eyes of the older kids told her they also knew what Saul the executioner would do to their families.

By the time they got it all sorted out, everyone was grumpier and hungrier than ever. But they had a plan.

The group slowly wormed its way out through the well entrance and froze. Far down the passageway, in the direction the chalk arrow pointed, the flickering of flames reflected off the tunnel walls. Voices. Distant shouts. The trampling of feet on stone. Saul's men were coming!

"Quickly!" Karis whispered. "Hold hands and walk swiftly. We can move faster than they can."

Single file, hands tightly holding hands, the children made their way back to the spot where they'd entered the wet world beneath Jerusalem.

Obadiah and Akbar got on their hands and knees to form a step up. Mara helped the children onto the big boys' backs, and Karis reached down a hand and pulled them up and out onto the street.

Halfway through this operation, Karis called down. "Wait! Someone's coming. Not a sound!"

She plugged the hole haphazardly with the paving stones and sat down on them with two children on her lap. Her legs blocked the place in the pavement from which several children had just emerged.

Mara gulped as the way of escape was shut off. Faint echoes from behind grew louder. Then they stopped.

"Here!" The word was clear and angry.

"Hurry! Stop them now!" This was followed by sounds of splashing. Saul's men were closing in!

". . . and the goat and the rooster decided to travel to Judea all by themselves." Mara could hear Karis talking loudly, as if telling the others a story. "So the goat says to the rooster, 'Do you think that if I crowed to the rising sun every morning, I would grow beautiful red feathers just like yours?' 'Well,' said the rooster, ruffling his shiny coat of fine red feathers, 'I suppose that will happen just as soon as I'm able to grow horns by butting the farmer every time he bends over . . .' "

Mara felt caught between two jaws of a trap about to slam shut. She couldn't go back, and she couldn't go forward. She prayed, *God, please save us!*

Sudden dim light. Hands reaching down. Pulling. The danger above had passed, and Karis was pulling them out of the tunnel. They were free!

When all were finally out, Akbar and Obadiah included, the bigger kids forced the stones back into place.

"Nobody . . . will . . . be . . . any . . . the . . . wiser," puffed Obadiah, giving each of the stones a couple of last, mighty shoves. The first one fit snug as could be, but the second stone was slightly smaller than the opening. With the large boy's encouragement, it went right on through and fell into the stream at the bottom of the tunnel with a disheartening splash-thud.

"Oops!" Obadiah said. The others stared at him in disgust and fear.

"Obie, you're a real menace to society sometimes," said Akbar.

"Listen!" Karis commanded. "Voices from below! They're here!"

The children ran as if their feet had sprouted wings.

"Split up!" Mara yelled when they reached the business district. "That'll make it harder for them to chase us. Obie, you and Akbar each take a group. Karis, you and Sarah take another. The rest of you, come with me and Nathan. We'll meet at my house. Quick now, go!"

They went, darting under carts, dodging through crowds, leaping over beggars, and racing to warn the believers as if the devil were at their backs. Mara believed he was—and Saul was his name.

All the kids reached Mara's house at about the same time and were set to burst in on the gathering, except for one thing. A three-hundred-pound man blocked the door.

"Whoa! Why are you kids in such a big hurry? The meeting's already begun," said the man with a shake of his hairy head. "You don't get inside unless you've got a note from Caesar himself!"

"Benjamin!" cried Mara, throwing her arms partway around the man's tree-trunk-sized waist. "Are we ever glad to see you!"

Benjamin's eyes widened in surprise. "Miss Mara! Nathan! You're all here! I didn't recognize you, all soggy and dirty like that. We've been worried sick about you. Your parents are inside . . ."

"Not for long," replied Mara grimly. "Saul is on his way. Quick, let us in!"

Benjamin practically took the door from its hinges. The kids tumbled into the room amid cries of disbelief and joy from the adults who crowded inside. Mara's father, who'd been on his knees leading the church in prayer, leaped to his feet and hugged Mara until she thought her bones would crack.

"Friends! Believers! Rejoice!" Joshua shouted to be heard. "Our prayers are answered! Let's sing a hymn of thanks to God for the safe return—"

"No, Father!" Mara cried. Before people could recover from their shock at her behavior, Mara climbed onto the eating table that had been shoved to one side of the room. That produced another gasp from the crowd. But there she stood, back straight, knees rattling like dried beans in a bowl. "Forgive me, but we don't have time to sing. Saul and his men are close by. They're coming to destroy our meeting. They're coming to destroy *us*. We've got to escape!"

Fear froze everyone as still as statues. From outside, shouts and footsteps grew steadily louder.

Benjamin opened the door a crack to peer out and then slammed it shut. He turned, planted huge feet against the floor, and braced his broad back against the oncoming attack. "They have swords and knives," he announced. "There are fifty or sixty or more."

"This way to the courtyard," shouted Joshua, indicating the back of the house. "We must go out the gate or scramble over the wall and scatter in every direction. It's our only hope. Find the best way out of the city that you can. If God wills, we will meet again one day. If not on earth, then in heaven. Hurry now! Don't look back!"

The mob reached the door and, with bloodcurdling yells and curses, threw their weight against it. Benjamin strained to shove them back, his great shaggy head a sweaty tangle. With a startling bang, something heavy and solid bashed against the door, wood on wood.

"Battering ram!" grunted Benjamin. "Can't hold them much longer!"

But when Joshua moved to help him, Benjamin growled, "No, friend, no! Take your wife and young ones and run! Old Benjamin will see what our neighbors have in mind. *Run!*"

They ran, Joshua with an arm around his wife, and Mara and Nathan right on their heels. Other New Israel kids and their parents, and some of Karis's friends and their families, fled with them. Past the shrubs and flowers that were the pride and joy of Mara's mother. Past the pretty little olive tree that Mara had planted and watered day after day. Past the small brick well that Nathan and Joshua had proudly built together, brick by brick.

Night was falling, a large harvest moon lighting their way.

"Where can we go?" moaned Mara's mother. "Our whole lives are here."

"Hurry!" urged Joshua, motioning them out the gate. "We have money. We can buy passage somewhere."

Loud, angry voices sounded from inside the house. Benjamin bellowed like a wild bull. Something tipped over and landed with a crash.

Behind them, Karis's mother stumbled and fell, catching the dangling ties of her cloak in the gate. Timon, her husband, yanked frantically to free her, but the more he pulled, the tighter the cords became entangled.

"Take it off!" gasped Timon. "Hurry!"

Terrible screams sounded from the house. Karis's eyes darted from the house to her parents struggling to get the cloak off and then to Mara up ahead. "Help us!" her eyes pleaded. "Don't leave our family here to die!"

Mara reached toward her. "Karis, give me your hand. We can't wait for anything. Run!"

But Karis shrank back, not sure what to do.

"Karis, go with Mara," Timon shouted. "We'll catch up!"

More bloodcurdling screams. Karis covered her ears, eyes squeezed shut, and didn't move. She was frozen to the spot with fear.

"Mara!" her father shouted, holding the gate open for his daughter. "Come on! There's nothing else we can do here!"

Mara started after him. *If it weren't for Karis, New Israel would be in the Jerusalem jail.* Mara stopped. *She stuck her neck out and kept you safe even after you treated her like sewer slop.* The thoughts were like daggers stabbing at her brain.

"Father!" Mara called. "My friend and her parents need help. Can we take them, please?"

"Bring them!" Joshua ordered. "This way! Hurry!"

Mara ran back and helped Timon pull the cloak away and untangle his wife. Mara grabbed Karis's hand and pulled. "Come! Now!"

The two families ran for their lives. Whenever someone dropped back from fatigue, the others pulled and carried the tired one along. Saul had sworn to kill every believer. If they hesitated, Jerusalem would be their grave.

Mara and Karis led the group down the less-traveled side streets with which they were becoming increasingly familiar. After ten minutes of this, they were within sight of the western gate of the city.

It was swarming with soldiers and citizens armed with clubs. Torch flames danced like orange demons, turning the shadows of the men into Goliaths against the high stone walls. The fugitives couldn't tell exactly what was being said, but the tone of the voices left no doubt that all of Jerusalem was on the alert for runaway believers.

It didn't appear that they had been followed. The families crouched inside the toolshed of a wheelwright who was a believer. But he was no-where around, and the shop was eerily silent. The walls flickered with distant torchlight. Both sets of parents discussed their predicament for a while but were unable to find a solution.

Then Joshua turned and spoke in a low whisper to the children. There was no mistaking the concern in his voice. "This means all routes out of the city are blocked," he said.

"Not all," said Karis.

"Don't be silly, girl," said Joshua. "Anyone can see we're trapped."

"Anyone but God," Mara said, smiling at Karis. "He's given our underground sister here a special talent."

Karis's mom looked questioningly at Karis's dad.

Joshua looked sharply at his daughter. Her mother frowned. "Mara, this is no time for make-believe."

Nathan adjusted his turban and placed his hands together like a priest. "Better listen to her, Dad. Torah speaks of gaining wisdom. Um, recent experience has taught me that it may be possible for even a female to do so." He looked embarrassed. "Mara knows a lot for a girl," he finished in a mumble.

Nathan's mother looked at him in amazement. "Are you feeling all right?"

Mara looked at him with suspicion. "Think. At any time were you kicked in the head by a horse today?"

Karis put her arm around Mara. "Nathan was just stating a fact. Mara does know a lot." She grinned. "Now, if you'll all just please follow us . . ."

"Whoa, there," Nathan interrupted. "What about those muscle men of Saul's that nearly grabbed our tails before we got out of the tunnels? They may still be down there, ready to toss our turbans the minute we come down."

Karis shook her head. "That's what you think. Aren't you taught many ways to tunnel into Torah? There are also many ways to enter and leave the underground tunnels of Hezekiah. I know one way it would take the brains of a thousand kings to figure out. Follow me!"

"One minute," Joshua said. "We need more light."

He walked toward a group vigorously arguing over which way to go in search of Jesus' followers. "A torch, my good man?" he said loudly to a young fellow with two. "A person needs all the light he can gather to spot something so slippery and low to the ground as a 'believer'!" The young man laughed and tossed Joshua a torch before settling on a direction in which to continue the hunt.

Joshua waited for the rest of the mob to follow the young man and then hurried back to the shed, much to the relief of the others.

They wound down a dozen different streets and alleys, sometimes waiting long, anxious minutes in hiding for a noisy crowd or troop of soldiers to pass before continuing. In those moments of waiting, many prayers were whispered and the children received reassuring hugs from their parents. When danger passed, they hurried again after Karis, guided by the moon, their torch, and their strong faith.

An hour later they turned the corner of a low stone fence and entered a deserted courtyard close by the city wall. In the middle stood a decaying stone well. Karis stopped at the well, leaned over, and started untying the frayed rope that ended in a bucket made of animal skins.

"Good," said Nathan wearily. "Now that you've taken us by the scenic route, I could use a drink."

"Wait until we're down," Karis replied, freeing the bucket and giving the thick rope several tugs. After a few seconds, the wheel that raised and lowered the bucket turned easily.

"D-d-down?" Nathan faltered. "What do you mean 'down'? What do you mean 'we'?"

"I mean," said Karis, "that at the bottom of this dry rain well is a break in the wall eventually leading to the main water system where we were this afternoon. Saul doesn't have enough men to guard every tunnel and entrance. They'll be looking for us where they heard us last, not way back here in a bunch of passages nobody uses anymore. Ladies first?"

Mara and her family looked dubiously at the flimsy bucket of sewn camel hide.

Karis's father saw their hesitation and spoke. "I know my daughter. If she says it's safe, we can trust that it's safe."

Karis's mother pulled her daughter close and nodded. "My husband is right," she said. "And the longer we stand here in the moonlight, torch blazing, the greater the chance someone will come to investigate."

Realizing the truth of that statement, both families lined up for the ride down the well. The men first lowered the mothers, then the daughters, and then Nathan by way of the rope and bucket. Joshua insisted on being last and lowered Karis's father next.

It was about twenty feet to the bottom, where Karis had long ago spread a large quantity of sour hay that a stabler had discarded behind his stalls. She had thrown it down the well and then come in by a different entrance to spread it out on the floor below. Several layers later, she had herself a semisoft landing.

Joshua, the last, tied the bucket as low as possible and then climbed down and hung from it, subtracting a good eight feet from his fall. He focused on the light of the torch below, said a prayer, and let go.

The landing was not a graceful one, but with no bones broken, they all thanked God and scrambled through a low, narrow opening into a passage where they could stand. Mara missed the friendly moonlight the minute it was gone.

Karis looked in one direction and then the other. But she was taking too long. Mara could see Karis hesitate. She was unsure.

The weight of the world above pressed down upon them. Fury, hatred, swords, knives . . .

"This way!" Karis finally declared. "Quickly!"

For what seemed like hours, they wound through narrow places. The underground chill crept into their bones and left them shivering. Sometimes the stone floor was slick and the footing difficult. Mara worried about someone turning an ankle that would slow them down and make it easier for Saul to find them. She worried about her skinny brother, especially when he stumbled into her and she could feel his body shaking with cold and fright.

If anything were to happen to Karis, Mara wondered how they would ever find their way to the surface.

But at least here in these caverns the water didn't flow. The dry season had lessened the amount of water coming in from the springs in the valley of Kidron, and this lessening seemed to keep the water channeled into the main tunnel.

Mara worried about why they hadn't yet reached the main tunnel. She forced her mind away from the one word that made her eyes well with tears: *lost.*

Karis stopped. Mara and the others stopped too, their rapid breathing the only sound in the barren passageway.

"Wait here." Karis ran ahead with the torch, plunging the others into utter darkness. Mara could hear the girl's footsteps scraping against the hard rock floor ahead, her breathing growing more ragged with each step.

Something was wrong.

"Cave-in," Karis called out. The word sent a stab of cold right through Mara's heart. They'd have to go back. But they couldn't climb up the sheer sides of the well. Was there another way out?

As if in answer, angry voices sounded from another direction. Saul's men! Coming closer. *That must be the way to the main chamber, but we can't use it now! They're coming. We've got to get away!*

Karis reappeared, her face grim in the torchlight. She wouldn't look at Mara—or anyone else. "I was sure that was the way past the main channel, but it's completely blocked," she said faintly. "I thought there was a way around it, but . . . but I can't find it. We'll have to go back to the well. Th-there might be enough loose stones for us to make a pile to stand on so that our dads can grab the bucket. Hurry up! At least maybe we can hide."

She turned abruptly and started along a passage Mara didn't remember at all.

"Wait. That's not the way we came." Mara felt panicky and was about to use the word she knew they were all thinking. *Lost. Admit it. L-O-S-T. We should never have—*

The floor beneath their feet began to shake and roll. From deep within the earth came a low rumble. Karis jumped back and knocked into Mara and Nathan. All fell in a heap just as the ceiling ahead let go with a deafening roar. Tons of earth and rubble filled the passage where Karis had been, as well as the one Mara thought was the right one.

Earthquake!

The torch rolled away into a patch of water and sputtered out. They lay on their backs against the cold stone floor, stunned by the collapse. Clouds of dust swirled into their eyes and lungs and left them choking for air.

Mara felt confused. *The torch went out. How come we can still see?*

Shouts again, closer this time. The sound of running feet. Saul coming. Mara prayed, *God, don't let us die like this! Open the earth and pull us out!*

"Look!" Karis cried, pointing upward. The dust was clearing, and a shaft of light—bright, silvery moonlight—streamed down through a hole in the ground above made by the fresh cave-in.

"Swiftly!" ordered Joshua. "Children, you first. Climb toward that light with everything you've got. Go!"

Joshua didn't need to say another word. Saul's men did it for him. "This way!" came the clear shouts, now fearfully close.

Karis, Mara, and Nathan clawed and pulled their way upward. Dirt and rock showered down on their parents below, but it didn't stop the adults from scrambling up after them. Sweet, warm air met them at the top, along with a wonderful surprise. They were outside the city walls!

"Messiah has saved us!" Joshua declared.

"Amen!" Nathan yelped.

Timon threw his arms wide to the sky. "Praise God!" he cried.

The seven fugitives grabbed each other's hands and ran like the wind in the direction of Caesarea. They ran until they looked back and saw no sign of any torches. Nothing but darkness and the bright moon.

Mara's panting slowed, and she gave her brother a giant hug. Then came the same for each of her parents. Head down, she went to Karis. "What I said earlier about your father and earning money, it . . . it was a stupid thing to say. I've said a lot of stupid things. I'm sorry for making you feel bad about little stuff that isn't important at all. I believe in Jesus and so do you. And back there when we escaped the house? I was just as scared as you were!"

Karis gave her a big smile. "Does this mean I'm good enough to be in New Israel?"

Mara looked at Nathan, who nodded and then frowned. "Except compared to the way we acted, she might be too good for the club!" he said.

Mara smiled. "No, we're done with that. Besides, wherever we end up, we'll have to start another club. Let's call it *Brand-New* Israel!"

Nathan groaned.

Karis rolled her eyes.

CHAPTER 10

"Please pass the goat cheese," Nathan said, wiping his mouth on the sleeve of a rough cotton cloak that easily had room inside for another boy and a half. But it was warm, clean, and dry. Nathan hungrily helped himself to a hunk of cheese as thick as a man's hand.

"We may have escaped with little more than the clothes on our backs," Joshua was saying, "but here we have found a king's treasure in brotherly love and concern. Christ be with this house!"

The seven who had escaped underground from Jerusalem had traveled three more days to reach Judea's major seaport of Caesarea. At first they attempted to stay off the roads as much as possible, but on the second day, Joshua paid for a ride the rest of the way in the smelly wagon of a cheerful fish merchant returning with his catch from the Mediterranean Sea.

The fisherman said nothing about the troubles in Jerusalem. If he suspected that his four adult and three child passengers were running away from something, he didn't say so. In fact, he spent most of the journey whistling lively tunes that Mara figured could easily charm fish into the man's boat. Who needed a net? Before they reached Caesarea, the kind whistler had offered both Timon and Joshua jobs mending nets and drying fish.

The footsore travelers had arrived at the home of Azariah Bar-jona, Timon's brother. Azariah owned a clothing stall that sold beautiful woolen fabrics woven by his wife, Ruth, and two neighbor women who worked for her. There was a new baby in the house and three other small children.

Now all thirteen people were gathered around a table that the Bar-jona brothers had quickly built of wooden planking from an old rowboat falling to pieces behind the house.

Mara smiled at Karis, who smiled back. "I think what I've been missing all along is a sister," said Mara.

"Me too," said Karis, giving Mara's hand a squeeze.

"Hey!" protested Nathan around a mouthful of cheese. "I thought I was all the sibling you ever needed!"

Mara winked at Karis. "No, brother, you'll be much too busy polishing my crown and scepter. The queen needs a sister."

"For what?" Nathan bit into a thick slice of fresh-baked bread and butter.

"Lots of things," Mara replied with a sniff. "To go shopping with. To do each other's hair." She looked at the straight black hair on Karis's head and vowed to fix it. At least the tangled knot was gone. After a nice hot bath, they all looked and smelled better. "And to order you around when I'm too busy feeding the peacocks and bathing in milk," Mara finished. She shared a grin with Karis.

"Yuck!" Nathan's face twisted as if his mouth were full of something sour. "I'd rather be sprinkled with maggot spit and buried in eel slime!"

"Such a gentleman," Mara said with a laugh. "My hero!" She leaned over and kissed him.

"Knock it off!" he yelped, rubbing frantically at his cheek. "Torah does not encourage public displays of affection. You really must learn proper manners . . ."

"Thank you, Rabbi Maggot Spit. I'll try to remember that."

Mara's mother shook her head and frowned, but everyone else laughed. Karis leaned across Nathan and whispered in Mara's ear. "There's another thing a sister's good for."

"What?" Mara whispered back.

"Exploring. Caesarea has tons of marble and lots of hiding places around the harbor. And best of all, there's a six-mile-long tunnel cut through Mount Carmel to bring water into the city from underground springs. I'll show it to you!"

Mara rolled her eyes. "No way! At least not right now. Give it a rest for a few days, and we'll see."

The two girls giggled, and Nathan showed them the ugly wad of goat cheese in his mouth.

But soon all were giving thanks for each other and for how God had brought the three families together as friends.

Joshua asked, "Is Jesus pleased when we argue over whether we worship the heavenly Father in Greek ways or Hebrew ways?"

"No!" the others answered in unison. Even the littlest ones, though their "nos" were late, joined in the fun. Only the wide-eyed baby kept silent.

"Does Jesus say Hebrew customs are better than Greek customs?"

"No!"

"Does Jesus love both those who speak Greek and those who speak Aramaic?"

Several of the smaller children, sure of the right answer this time, answered with a loud "No!" as the adults were answering with a resounding "Yes!" Mara laughed at the sheepish looks on their faces.

"Are all of us who follow the Way of Christ really brothers and sisters in Christ?"

"Yes! Yes! Yes!"

Timon reached for his wife's hand. She reached for Joshua's hand just as his hand took hold of Mara's. Mara grabbed Nathan's hand before it could get away, and he shyly placed his other hand in Karis's. When the circle of hands was complete, Azariah prayed:

"Merciful Father, thank You for forgiving our foolishness and protecting us from evil. Thank You for bringing the ones we love and the ones we have come to love safe from the dangers of Jerusalem. Bless the believers still there and keep them from harm. But should they die for their faith, Father, please give them a place in heaven with You and Stephen. Make the church grow, Lord, and may it spread across the Roman Empire and beyond. In the strong name of Jesus the Messiah, we pray."

Mara asked if she could add a prayer. Nathan started to say, "The rabbis do not permit a woman to lead prayer in pub—" but Azariah cut him off.

"Of course you may pray, Mara," Azariah said. "Jesus would stop no one from talking to the Father."

Mara bowed her head and tried not to cry. "Father God, please watch over Sarah and Obadiah and Akbar and the other kids and their families. Please let us see them again someday. Thank You for Stephen and his faith in You. And I ask You to change Saul's heart. Help him to trust in Jesus. And thank You for changing my heart so—so—I mean, forgive me for the way I treated Karis. Bless her family for giving us a place to stay. Help me to be a nicer person. In the name of Jesus."

"Amen!" Nathan said with too much enthusiasm. Mara poked him with her elbow.

"Lord," said Karis, so softly that she could barely be heard. "Please forgive me for thinking every kid in New Israel has dirt for brains."

"A-double-men!" Nathan said, earning himself another elbow.

The three friends waded along the shore, enjoying the fresh sea breeze and the rush of water on their bare feet. Gulls circled and kept an eye out for fish, skimming so close to the water that one good wave might have given them a soaking.

Mara lost herself in her favorite daydream. There she sat in royal white in a palace designed by her father. People fussed over her. Buffing her nails. Fanning her face. Fixing her hair. Arranging her jewels. *Cake for breakfast. Camel races at noon. Dancing beneath the stars with a handsome prince dressed in gold.*

"Hey, dream queen, you're hunching again," said Nathan, giving her his favorite "You're my weird sister" look. Mara straightened her back. She hated to hunch. She'd never look good on a throne all hunched over.

But after all that had happened, maybe she would look after the horses in the royal stables instead. Or work with leather and fashion the fancy saddles that made an ordinary rider sit proudly. She really didn't want to push people around. Jesus didn't do that, and He was the King of Kings!

She could do as her mother did and visit the sick. Or help clean the houses of the old widows. Something, anything, to bring glory to God and make people smile and be glad she was around.

Mara started to hum, and Nathan quickly joined in. It was the New Israel club song. Karis looked doubtful.

"Don't worry," said Mara. "You're going to like these words."

> We are New Israel, kids of strength and might;
> Messiah has loved us, shown us a new light!
> We are strong in His name, brave kids who know what's right.
> We stand the test, 'cause Christ's the best.
> He's given us new sight!

And in an exaggerated voice, Nathan added, "Greek and Hebrew . . . are . . . all . . . right!"

"Too many lines," said Karis. "Too many syllables."

"Who made you choir director?" Nathan joked.

"Not choir director," Mara said, putting an arm around Karis and looking her way. "You're looking at the club's new vice president."

"Only until the next election," Karis said with a sly smile. "Then I'm running for *your* job!"

"Hey!" Nathan protested. "How come *I* don't get to be vice president?"

Mara sniffed and held her head high in the queenly way. "You are officially our rabbi-in-training. *Nobody* can do that job like you."

"You really think so?" Nathan asked, tugging his borrowed turban more securely into place. It was two sizes too big. They could barely see his eyes.

"Oh yes," Mara said, winking at Karis, "I'm absolutely positive."

LETTERS FROM OUR READERS

Was stoning really a way to execute people in Bible times? (Elisa B., San Antonio, Texas)

It was a common form of punishment called for in the law of Moses for crimes deserving death (Leviticus 20:2). An important part of stoning was that all members of the community were to carry out the punishment (Joshua 7:25). Moses and Jesus were both threatened with stoning by angry mobs (Exodus 17:4; John 8:59; 10:31). Saul, who held people's coats while they stoned Stephen to death, himself became a follower of Jesus and was once stoned and left for dead (Acts 14:8-20). He recovered, however, and went on to tell many others about Jesus Christ.

Why did they kill Stephen? Was he doing something wrong? (Carey R., Omaha, Nebraska)

The Jewish religious rulers didn't believe that Jesus was the Messiah, so when Stephen claimed that He was, they believed Stephen was committing blasphemy against God. (Blasphemy is showing irreverence for God or claiming to be just like Him.) They also thought Stephen was saying Jesus came to get rid of the temple and tradition. That really upset them because they were very religious, and their traditions were important to them.

Some people believe that Stephen was illegally executed because Roman law said that the Jews had no authority to carry out executions without the permission of the Roman government. You can read about Stephen and the Hellenist believers in Acts 6–7.

Who were the Hellenists? Why didn't they get along with the other Jewish believers? (Jessica L., Rochester, New York)

The word *Hellenism* refers to the Greek culture. Hellenists were Jews who spoke Greek and followed Greek customs. Although they were usually from other places, some were natives of Palestine.

The Hebrews, on the other hand, were Jews who spoke Aramaic and were from Palestine, although they were sometimes from other places too. The main problem between the two groups seems to have been that the Hebrews followed the law of Moses and Jewish cultural practices more strictly than did the Hellenists. Some of them looked down on the Hellenists, whom they saw as less righteous or holy. Naturally, that caused a lot of arguments between the two groups.

Did people actually eat calf brains? (Brianna M., Springfield, Illinois)

Yes, and not always just poor people. Headcheese—considered by some today to be a delicacy—is made from parts of animal heads, feet, and sometimes hearts and tongues. These parts are cut up fine, boiled, and pressed together into a solid food that can be sliced and served. Seconds, anyone?

What were the underground tunnels used for? (Justin C., Great Falls, Montana)

The underground tunnels that Karis's and Mara's families escaped through kept the city supplied with water. Jerusalem doesn't get much rain, and it's far away from both the Mediterranean Sea and the Jordan River. Several hundred years before Christ's time, King Hezekiah wanted to be sure that Jerusalem wouldn't run out of water if it was attacked and surrounded by the Assyrians, so he built a tunnel from a place called Gihon Spring (2 Chronicles 32:30). It emptied into the Pool of Siloam. Later, the people of Jerusalem built more tunnels and aqueducts to bring water from the surrounding springs into the city. All of the water had to come from higher elevations because it flowed into the city with the help of gravity.

The tunnels in Caesarea—where Karis was from—were the city's sewage system. They were built in such a way that they would be cleaned out by the sea tides. So, anybody want to go for a swim?

ABOUT THE AUTHOR

CLINT KELLY loves telling action stories spiced with adventure and suspense. His ten novels cover wide territory, from Armenia to the Congo rain forest. As a forest ranger and wilderness expedition leader, he has explored and paddled by canoe as far north as Great Slave Lake in the Northwest Territories. Closer to home, he is a communications specialist for Seattle Pacific University, father of four, and lucky husband to Cheryl, his best friend.

FOR PARENTS AND TEACHERS

CRAZY JACOB
▶ *Background*

When Jesus came to earth, interactions in His part of the world were complicated. As you read *Crazy Jacob*, notice the groups of people who come into conflict for various reasons.

- The *Jewish people* still took pride in their centuries of tradition and religious rites, but it had been about a thousand years since the glory days of David and Solomon. In time their love for God had turned cold and they'd started worshiping other gods. When they stubbornly refused to repent, God had eventually allowed enemies to conquer them—including Babylonians, Assyrians, and Greeks. When Jesus came, the Roman Empire was in control.

- Then there were the *Gentiles*—a term describing anyone who isn't Jewish. Jesus came as a fulfillment of everything God had promised the Jews, but He was also "a light for revelation to the Gentiles" (Luke 2:32). God sent His only Son because He loved the *whole* world (John 3:16). The Jews generally maintained a higher level of moral and spiritual standards than much of the rest of the world, and they tended to look down on the Gentiles.

- One thing Jews and Gentiles in the Middle East had in common was resentment toward the *Romans*. Roman citizenship carried with it privileges that Jews and non-Roman Gentiles didn't have. For example, a Roman soldier could walk up to you and demand that you carry his backpack (which could weigh one hundred pounds or more) for a mile.

Throughout *Crazy Jacob* you'll find examples of tension between Jews, Gentiles, and Romans. But other conflicts were taking place in first-century Israel as well. The story also reveals *spiritual* conflicts, and how people were affected.

The Jewish people posed little threat to the mighty Roman Empire, so the Romans allowed them to worship as they wished. The Jews had Scripture that informed them of the one true God, and some followed the Law so strictly that they became arrogant, legalistic, and intolerant of others. Some, like Jacob and Andrew in the story, had become confused by the many different beliefs of the surrounding culture. The Romans had dozens of gods and goddesses, and in that part of the world the influence of Greek and Egyptian deities could also be felt.

Jesus came not only to speak the truth of God's kingdom, but also to model it. He pointed out that a blatant disregard for God's kingdom would lead to problems. But surprisingly, it could be just as bad to allow blind obedience to Jewish law to prevent an authentic relationship with God. He made it clear that His Father also wants to be *our* Father—a loving, caring, and forgiving "Daddy" to those who believe in Him (Romans 8:15-17).

Spiritual conflicts arose as they do now—whenever people allow other gods and spiritual forces to distract them from the truth of the one true God. Paul would later warn us, "Our struggle is not against flesh and blood, but against the rulers, against the authorities, against the powers of this dark world and against the spiritual forces of evil in the heavenly realms" (Ephesians 6:12).

Yes, it can sound scary to consider that all Christians are in an ongoing spiritual battle, though it rarely gets to the point at which Jacob was in this story. The good news, as the story shows, is that Jesus is far more powerful than any and all other powers—including people, "gods," and dark spiritual forces. As long as we maintain a loving and growing relationship with Him, we have little to fear from anyone or anything else (see Romans 8:35-39).

CRAZY JACOB
▶ *Learning Activities*

If *Crazy Jacob* got you to thinking and you'd like to know a little more, here are some projects to consider:

- Study the biblical account of this story in Mark 4:35–5:20 or Luke 8:22-39. Write a "first-person" account from several people's perspectives (the man with the unclean spirit [Jacob], one of Jesus' disciples, a passerby from that part of the country, one of the pig farmers, etc.).

- Read the following accounts of other confrontations between Jesus and evil spirits that affirm His power over them:
  Matthew 9:32-33
  Matthew 12:22-23
  Mark 9:17-29
  Luke 4:33-35

- Make a list of questions you have about what Jewish people believe. Then arrange to interview a Jewish rabbi or someone from a nearby synagogue.

- Do some research on the Roman Empire, particularly during the first century in the Middle East.

CRAZY JACOB
▶ *Discussion Questions*

1. Has anyone ever made fun of your faith? If so, how did you handle it? If not, what do you think you would do if someone began to use your beliefs as a way to put you down every time he or she saw you?

2. Have you ever been embarrassed by any of your friends or family members because of their behavior or a physical or

mental disability? What can you do to help these people feel better about themselves rather than making the matter worse? Who can you talk with to help you work through your feelings?

3. If you could meet Jesus face-to-face, what would you ask Him? (For a favor? For an answer to a hard question?)

4. In the story, why do you think Jesus didn't let Jacob go with Him? Do you think it would be more challenging to be a disciple around strangers or among people who know you well? Why?

THE WORST WISH
▶ *Background*

It may be hard for us to relate to the world of Seth and Talitha. Most people today have easy access to Bibles, classes, and other resources to help us understand who Jesus was and how important He was in the history of the world. Yet that information often isn't as personal as we might like it to be.

So put yourself in the sandals of someone experiencing firsthand the ministry and teachings of Jesus. He taught the same things that had been in the Old Testament Scriptures for thousands of years, but somehow that old information started sounding fresh and relevant. Clearly something was special about Jesus, but what was it? No one had yet written any creeds or theology books to explain that He was the Son of God, was part of the Holy Trinity, had existed forever, and had left His home in heaven to come to earth to save humans from their sin. People just knew that this mysterious Jewish teacher was a skilled storyteller and often exhibited great power that no one but God could possess.

And nowhere was Jesus' power more evident than in His ability to raise people from the dead. As this story of Talitha shows, He wanted to keep the miracle private. It makes sense, doesn't it? Once word began to spread that the new rabbi in town could bring the dead back to life, everyone with a friend or relative who'd recently died would want that loved one back (which could get more than a little creepy). But later in Jesus' ministry, shortly before His crucifixion, He restored Lazarus to life after His friend had been dead for four days (John 11). This time the resurrection was in public, before both friends and critics. No one was able to deny what had happened, and it was a turning point when many people started to believe in Jesus (John 11:45).

Yet even the ability to raise the dead wasn't enough to convince others to put their faith in Jesus. They couldn't fit Him into their preconceived notions about who God was. And that division has continued throughout the centuries. Jesus still brings new life to those who believe in Him. Those who don't are still missing out on wonderful new opportunities.

THE WORST WISH
▶ Learning Activities

The Worst Wish may have left you with a few questions. Consider the following projects you might want to undertake to get a better understanding of the setting and characters in the story:

- Read the following gospel accounts of how Jesus brought Talitha back to life. (She won't be mentioned by name. "Talitha" is an Aramaic word for "little girl." And no mention will be made of a brother.) Suppose you had witnessed the event. How would you have responded?

    Matthew 9:18-26

    Mark 5:21-43

    Luke 8:40-56

- The Bible records only two other instances of Jesus resurrecting a dead person. Read Luke 7:11-15 and John 11. Why do you think Jesus took action in each of those situations, and in Talitha's case, when He didn't make a regular practice of resurrecting the dead?
- Spend some time getting more familiar with Jewish customs and culture. To begin with, see what you can find out about the following:

> the Torah
> rabbis
> the synagogue
> the *tzitzit* (fringe) on the *tallit* (prayer shawl)

THE WORST WISH
▶ *Discussion Questions*

1. Have you ever told someone, "I wish you were dead!"? If so, did you regret it afterward? After reading this story, do you think you'll ever say that again?

2. Do you and your friends ever have disagreements over Jesus, church, or other spiritual issues? If so, what are some of them? Do you respect one another's opinions? Do the discussions sometimes get heated?

3. In the story of Talitha, why do you think Jesus didn't want anyone to know what He had done for her? If something like that were to happen today in the Internet age, how long do you think it would remain a secret?

4. Have you ever plotted revenge on anyone? What did the person do to provoke you? Did you carry out your plans, and if so, what did you learn from the experience?

5. Are you anxious about anything in your life right now? Did you notice in this story the difficulty of waiting for Jesus, especially when you're worried about something? Seth and his father had to wait until Jesus could work His way through the crowds and then heal the other woman before He got to Talitha. At one point the author tells us, "Seth had never felt so hopeless in his life." But it was at that point that he prayed and, surprisingly, found peace. Have you ever had a similar experience? What do you do when you get really worried about a difficult situation?

Dangerous Dreams
▶ *Background*

In this story, Livy worked in the home of Pontius Pilate, an actual historical figure who was governor (prefect) of Judea from AD 26 until AD 36. By most accounts, he was not a very nice man. The Bible mentions one instance in which Pilate apparently had some people killed while they were offering sacrifices to God (Luke 13:1). Other historians give additional examples of Pilate's violent nature and harsh temper.

Yet Pilate's interactions with Jesus were more complicated. When he discovered that Jesus wasn't interested in leading a revolt or immediately starting an earthly kingdom, Pilate appeared genuinely fascinated with Jesus and wanted to set Him free (John 19:6-12). In his position as governor, Pilate had the authority to make that happen. Take a look at some of the things he did to either sway the crowd of onlookers or acknowledge Jesus' innocence:

- He tried to avoid being the judge altogether, but the Jewish leaders were seeking the death penalty and only Pilate could pronounce it (John 18:31).

- He gave Jesus a chance to reply to the accusations against Him, and was amazed when Jesus calmly remained silent (Matthew 27:13).
- He pressured the crowd to state exactly what Jesus had done wrong, to no avail (Matthew 27:23).
- He said he found no basis to prosecute Jesus (Luke 23:4).
- He tried to get another venue for the trial by sending Jesus to Herod, the ruler of the territory of Galilee (Luke 23:6-7). Herod mocked Jesus, but passed no judgment and sent Him back to Pilate.
- He suggested three times that he could punish Jesus, but then release Him (Luke 23:16-22).
- When the crowd would not be swayed and began to get unruly, Pilate publicly washed his hands and declared himself innocent of Jesus' death (Matthew 27:24).
- Finally, he had a sign posted on Jesus' cross with a message in three languages: "Jesus of Nazareth, the King of the Jews." The Jewish leaders complained that the sign should declare that Jesus only *said* He was King of the Jews, but Pilate refused to change it (John 19:19-22).

It's not clear exactly why the usually heartless Pilate became so intrigued with Jesus. He had previously had no problem making life difficult for the Jews. Certainly he must have been impressed by Jesus. And perhaps his wife's note (Matthew 27:19) also had something to do with his level of concern.

In spite of Pilate's appeals for mercy, he gave in to the crowd and sentenced Jesus to be crucified. Crucifixion was an agonizing punishment the Romans used to impose a maximum level of pain, brutality, and humiliation. You've probably seen pictures of T-shaped crosses, but crosses could also be shaped like an I, an X, or a Y. Condemned people were sometimes forced to carry the crossbar, which was then attached to the upright post at the execution site. We know Jesus needed help carrying His cross (Luke 23:26). He had been beaten and flogged (Matthew 27:26-31), a ruthless punishment that sometimes killed the person before he could be crucified.

In spite of this ferocious and demeaning death, Jesus rose again in three days and still lives.

DANGEROUS DREAMS
▶ *Learning Activities*

If you'd like to know more about the historical events during which *Dangerous Dreams* is set, here are some projects you might want to undertake:

- Read the following gospel accounts of Jesus' trial and crucifixion and look for the events mentioned by the authors: Jesus' betrayal (by Judas), the darkness, the earthquake, the crowing of the rooster, His resurrection, etc.

    Matthew 26:31–28:20

    Mark 14:10–16:8

    Luke 22:1–24:53

    John 18:1–20:31

- Jesus was crucified on a Friday, but the previous Sunday He'd ridden into Jerusalem, receiving great praise from the people. Read Matthew 21:1-11. How do you think a crowd that was so enthusiastic could, within a week, turn into a group shouting "Crucify him!"?

- Look up "Pharisees" and see what you can discover about this group of Jewish leaders. Certain members of the Pharisees strongly opposed Jesus and convinced Pilate to convict Him (Matthew 12:9-14; 26:3-4, 62-66). Why do you think they refused to acknowledge Jesus' authority, in spite of all His teachings and miracles?

- Like Livy, we might not always respect our leaders. Yet the Bible instructs us to obey and submit to them (Hebrews 13:17). In some cases they may oppose our best interests, but even then Jesus challenges us to learn to pray for our enemies (Matthew 5:43-48). Spend a few minutes praying for your parents, teachers, and all those who have authority over you—even those you may not like very much.

DANGEROUS DREAMS
▶ *Discussion Questions*

1. Why do you think this story is titled *Dangerous Dreams*?
2. Have you ever been in a situation where you were desperate to escape? What were the circumstances, and how did you handle your feelings?
3. If you had been Bar Abbas in this story, how do you think you would have responded when you received unexpected freedom and a new life?
4. Suppose Livy were your friend. What do you know about Jesus that might encourage her? Who are some other friends of yours who might be helped by knowing more about Jesus?

ESCAPE UNDERGROUND
▶ *Background*

This story takes place during an exciting, yet frightening, time for God's people. In our society it might be hard to understand why there was such a fuss over where people went to church and with whom they worshiped. But in the first century there were a lot of details to be worked out.

For thousands of years the Jewish people had lived and worshiped according to the Law that God had given Moses. But during the series of kings that followed David and Solomon, they'd drifted away from obedience. They ignored God's instructions about how to live and they worshiped other gods.

Consequently, they were defeated by their enemies; many Israelites were removed from their home country of Israel and carried off as captives. Some eventually returned home, but others stayed where they were. As a result, small groups of Jewish people were scattered throughout the known world.

In the 300s BC, when the Greek Empire was the world superpower, Alexander the Great wanted to unify all his subjects. He immersed them in Greek culture and language. The Jewish people resisted conforming to Greek religion, but the language spread. (That's why Karis and Mara in *Escape Underground* could speak Greek. Mara and her friends also spoke Aramaic, which was a more local language—most likely what Jesus spoke most of the time. Some people in Syria, Iraq, Turkey, and Iran still speak a form of Aramaic.)

Jesus had come to earth, ministered in Galilee, and been crucified in Jerusalem. His death came during the Jewish Passover, a time when great crowds traveled to Jerusalem to worship and offer sacrifices at the temple. Naturally, there was much discussion about who He was and whether, indeed, He was the Son of God. And it was natural that the church arose in Jerusalem as believers began to meet together and take care of one another. In fact, one of the first "emergencies" of the early church arose because the Hebrew and Aramaic-speaking people were getting better care than the Greek-speaking ones. To remedy the problem, the twelve apostles appointed seven other leaders to oversee those daily needs. Two of those seven were Stephen and Timon (Karis's father in the story). See Acts 6:1-7 for more details.

But the problems within the church were small compared to those arising outside it. Jesus had faced much opposition from some of the established Jewish leaders (the Pharisees) throughout His ministry. They thought their problems were over with His crucifixion. But then the resurrected Jesus appeared to the disciples and told them to wait in Jerusalem for the Holy Spirit (Acts 1:4-5). The day the Holy Spirit arrived, three thousand new people became believers and the first Christian church began to take shape (Acts 2:41). No big church buildings existed at the time, so believers met in homes (and it's no wonder their leaders needed more help taking care of such a crowd).

It didn't take long for Jesus' critics to become harsh opponents of the new church, which they saw as a threat to the religion God had given their Jewish ancestors. The rapid growth of "the Way" must have been especially worrisome for them. One of the most aggressive opponents was a young man named Saul, who appears throughout the story. But God had other plans for Saul, and the church that sprang to life during that time has spread throughout the world today, and continues to grow.

Escape Underground
▶ Learning Activities

If you'd like to continue learning about the background of *Escape Underground*, here are some projects you can do to follow up:

- See what happened to Saul shortly after this story concluded. Read the account in Acts 9:1-22 (a story repeated in Acts 22:1-21 and Acts 26:9-23). How would you have felt if the same thing happened to you? How would you have responded?

- After his conversion, Saul took on the more Greek-sounding name of Paul as he began his Christian ministry. Read the opening sentence of all the books of the New Testament. Write down the books that mention Paul's name (which identifies him as the author). How much of the New Testament did he write after Jesus got him on the right track?

- *Escape Underground* mentions the Sanhedrin. See what you can find out about this group. (Some of these high-ranking Jewish leaders were not very nice men in their dealings with Jesus. But read John 3:1-21 and 19:38-42 to see that there were exceptions.)
- Suppose you wanted to start a club for young believers like yourself. Write a theme song to express what you believe and stand for.
- Believers in some countries still face persecution as Mara and Karis did. Do some research and try to find ways to write letters of encouragement to young believers in other parts of the world, or take up a collection to help those who face ongoing persecution.

ESCAPE UNDERGROUND
▶ *Discussion Questions*

1. Think about your friends. Do you have a nonrelative who's as close as a sister or brother to you? Do you have any friends you're close to now, but whom you didn't like much when you first met? If so, what caused the change?
2. What are some things adults do at your church that you don't really understand? Who might explain those things to you?
3. If you knew you were in danger every time you wanted to get with friends to worship God, do you think your faith would get stronger or weaker? Why?
4. Can you think of a time during the past week when you had an opportunity to help someone, but didn't? Why didn't you? What might have happened if you'd acted? What might you do differently the next time a similar opportunity arises?

Start an adventure!
with Focus on the Family

Whether you're looking for new ways to teach young children about God's Word, entertain active imaginations with exciting adventures or help teenagers understand and defend their faith, we can help. For trusted resources to help your kids thrive, visit our online Family Store at:

FocusOnTheFamily.com/resources